Soaring in Faith

Wings of Faith Book 2: An Inspirational Love Story

BARBARA JANE OLIVER

SYNERGISTIC CONNECTIONS, LLC

Paperback ISBN: 978-1-968938-03-1

E-Book ISBN: 978-1-968938-02-4

Beta Reader: Kate Marie at Beta Reader Bookings, LLC

Proofreading: Brandy Patton at WordWiser Ink Editing Lab

Book Cover: Miblart Book Cover Design

First Edition 2026

Visit the **Author's Website** at https://barbarajaneoliver.com/

Published by Synergistic Connections, LLC

Also By Barbara Jane Oliver

ALTHOUGH THESE NOVELS ARE part of a series featuring interconnected characters, the main romance centers on a unique storyline with its own arc and resolution. Each book can be enjoyed as a standalone novel, making it a pleasurable independent reading experience.

WINGS OF FAITH SERIES

- Before the Blessing: A Bristol Heights Novella (Colton & Nicole): Download FREE When You Subscribe to My Newsletter

- Renewing His Hope Book 1: Daniel & Samantha: Available Now

- Soaring in Faith Book 2: Aaron & Meghan: Available Now

- Running with Grace Book 3: Brandon & Grace: Available 25 May 2026

BRISTOL HEIGHTS SANCTUARY SERIES

- Sanctuary in His Arms Book 1: Joshua & Simone: TBA

- Sanctuary of Truth Book 2: TBA

Dedication

I dedicate this book to my Lord and Savior, Jesus Christ. Thank You for giving me life, breath, and your everlasting love. You are always with me, walking beside me and guiding me through all the pathways of my life. I am eternally grateful. It's all for Your Glory! Amen!

Inspirational Scripture for Wings of Faith Series of Books

Isaiah 40:31: But those who hope in the Lord will renew their strength. They will soar on wings like eagles; they will run and not grow weary, they will walk and not be faint.

Acknowledgements

I WOULD LIKE TO express my heartfelt gratitude to my husband, Ronald. I appreciate your unwavering support, strength, and love. Thank you for consistently being present in my life. I hold you in the highest regard. Furthermore, I extend my appreciation to my daughter, Erica, for enlightening me on the existence of living miracles. You genuinely fill me with cheer! Additionally, I wish to thank my parents, Mom and Dad, as well as my brother, Willie Jr. There are no greater cheerleaders in this world than you. I cherish each of you deeply!

To Page and Michele, my Mastermind sisters! Thank you for showing up faithfully every Monday on Zoom, for cheering me on, and for sharing your wisdom so generously. Your encouragement, honesty, and support have been such a gift on this author journey. I'm deeply grateful to walk this path with you both.

I extend my sincerest gratitude to Beta Reader Bookings, LLC for your insightful and thoughtful feedback on this narrative. Additionally, I express my appreciation to WordWiser Ink Copy Editing Lab for your meticulous attention and dedication to clarity. Both of you have offered candid reflections, and your diligence in detail has significantly enhanced the quality of this book.

To my friends and family, the members of my church, my ARC readers and reviewers, and every person who shared a note, a call, or a message of encouragement... THANK YOU! Your support, prayers, and kindness carried me through this journey more than you know. This book exists because of you.

Contents

Soaring in Faith

Wings of Faith Book 2: An Inspirational Love Story

Barbara Jane Oliver

Synergistic Connections, LLC

Chapter 1

Aaron Grant gripped the steering wheel of his white pickup truck, knuckles tight as he pulled into a parking space at Greater Pines High School. The August sun beat down mercilessly through the windshield, forcing him to squint despite his dark sunglasses. The air conditioning labored against the Georgia heat, barely taking the edge off the suffocating warmth that had followed them from Bristol Heights.

He cut the engine and took a moment to collect himself. Drawing a long breath, he sent up a half-formed prayer, the kind he had grown reluctant to offer since his mother's diagnosis.

Lord, give me strength for this. The silence that followed felt as vast as the parking lot stretching before them.

"We're here, Naomi."

No response. His fourteen-year-old niece sat beside him, headphones covering her ears, eyes locked on something in the middle distance. Her face, so much like his mother's, gave nothing away.

Same cheekbones, same stubborn chin. Aaron tapped her shoulder, swallowing the frustration that seemed to live in his chest these days.

"Hey? It's time to head in."

She pulled the headphones down around her neck with obvious reluctance, eyes never meeting his. "Whatever."

Aaron bit back his first response. These past three months tested every boundary he thought he had. Three months since the funeral. Three months since guardianship papers transformed him from a sporadic uncle who showed up on holidays into the man responsible for raising a teenager drowning in grief. Three months navigating a wilderness neither of them had chosen to enter.

"Principal Watkins is waiting for us." Aaron checked his watch. "We've got about thirty minutes before registration closes."

Naomi grabbed her backpack, climbed out of the truck, and slammed the door harder than necessary. The sharp sound made Aaron flinch. He let it go. Dr. Harrison had warned him about moments like this.

Pick your battles, Mr. Grant. Kids in grief fight for control wherever they can find it.

The school building loomed before them, red brick and glass gleaming in the late summer light. Students and parents streamed through the entrance, voices echoing across the parking lot in a chorus of greetings, laughter, and animated conversations. Aaron reached to touch her shoulder, but she pulled away.

"I can walk by myself," she mumbled, striding ahead.

Aaron followed, his work boots thudding on the pavement. Construction had been his life for nearly twenty years. He understood overseeing crews, interpreting blueprints, and calculating load-bearing requirements. The predictable nature of properly poured foundations and accurately measured beams were certainties he could grasp. But this? Two decades of building structures hadn't equipped him for the delicate work of rebuilding a traumatized teenage heart.

And nothing had prepared him for the silence that followed his prayers. Not after what happened with his mother. Not when every plea had gone unanswered.

Inside, the main office buzzed with back-to-school energy. A woman behind the front desk looked up, her silver-rimmed glasses resting low on her nose. Her voice carried the warmth of someone who had lived her whole life in Georgia.

"Can I help you?"

"Aaron Grant. We have an appointment with Principal Watkins." His words emerged clipped and efficient, the same tone he used with new subcontractors to establish authority and minimize small talk.

"Yes, Mr. Grant. I'm Mrs. Richardson. We've been expecting you and Naomi." She turned toward his niece with a warm smile. "Welcome to Greater Pines, sweetheart. We're glad to have you."

Naomi offered a barely perceptible nod, but said nothing.

"Principal Watkins will be right with you." Mrs. Richardson directed them to chairs near the principal's office. "Can I get either of you something cold to drink? It's blazing hot out there today."

"We're fine, but thank you." Aaron settled into a chair that protested beneath his six-foot-three frame.

Naomi took out her phone and started scrolling through social media feeds. Aaron studied her profile, noting the shadows under her eyes that revealed sleepless nights. With the weight of guardianship, he found himself hyperaware of everything about her. He monitored her eating habits, sleep patterns, and how she withdrew further into herself each week.

"Are you nervous?" Aaron asked, attempting conversation.

She didn't look up. "About what?"

"New school, new town. It's a lot of change."

"It wasn't like I had a choice." Her voice remained flat, offering nothing beyond the words themselves.

Aaron stifled a sigh. Every conversation forced him to tread carefully. One wrong step, and she would withdraw even deeper into the shell she had built around herself.

"I know this isn't perfect." He lowered his voice. "For either of us. But we'll find a way to make it work."

She glanced up, skepticism written across her features. "How exactly? You work all day. I'll be at school. Then what? We just hang out in the same apartment and pretend we're a family?"

Her words stung. Before Aaron could formulate a response that didn't sound like an empty platitude, the office door opened, and a tall man with warm brown skin and a neatly trimmed beard stepped out, hand extended.

"Mr. Grant? I'm Jeremy Watkins. Welcome to Greater Pines High."

Aaron stood, accepting the handshake with the firm grip his father taught him was the mark of a man worth his word. "Thanks for meeting with us on such short notice."

"Not at all." Principal Watkins smiled at Naomi, his expression warm and welcoming rather than the usual condescension adults often showed teens. "And you must be Naomi. We're pleased to have you in our ninth-grade class."

Naomi offered another slight nod, but nothing more.

"Please come into my office. We have your transfer records, but I'd like to go over your class options before we finalize your schedule."

Aaron guided Naomi forward with a light touch between her shoulder blades, following Principal Watkins through the doorway. A blur of motion caught his attention as someone rushed past with arms full of papers.

The collision happened too suddenly to avoid. Aaron pivoted and struck another person with considerable force. Papers erupted into the air, falling like rectangular snowflakes. A surprised gasp echoed amid the chaos.

"Oh my goodness! I'm so sorry!" A rich, melodic voice spoke from somewhere beneath the shower of falling lesson plans.

Aaron crouched automatically, gathering scattered sheets. "That was on me. I wasn't watching where—"

The words died in his throat as he looked up.

The woman knelt across from him, hands moving quickly to collect the papers. Her dark, naturally curly hair was pinned in a loose bun, with a few tendrils slipping free at the sides. Almond-shaped, dark brown eyes met his with a mixture of em-barrassment and amusement. Her warm brown skin glowed with health. Aaron noticed her full lips curve into a polite smile, revealing dimples that transformed her entire face.

"You must be Mr. Grant. I'm Ms. Townsend. Meghan Townsend. I teach ninth-grade history." She gathered the last few sheets, straightening gracefully.

Aaron rose, nearly bumping heads with her as they stood. Her presence filled the space around them. It wasn't her size, but an indefinable quality that captured his attention. She was about five feet seven, with a slender yet curvaceous figure, dressed in a deep blue wrap dress that complemented her complexion.

"Aaron Grant," he replied, extending his hand. "I'm register-ing my niece, Naomi."

When Meghan's hand met his, he noted the contrast. His palm was rough and calloused from years of construction work, while hers was smooth but strong. The brief contact sent an unexpected current up his arm.

"I heard we'd have a new student today." Meghan turned toward Naomi with genuine interest. "I'm looking forward to having you in class."

For the first time since entering the building, Naomi looked directly at an adult. "Thank you."

"Ms. Townsend also coordinates our culinary arts program," Principal Watkins interjected, rejoining the conversation. "It's quite popular with our students."

"Cooking?" Naomi's voice carried the first hint of curiosity Aaron had heard all morning.

Meghan's smile widened. "We explore cultural history through food traditions. Last month, we studied the Great Depression by making recipes that families used in order to stretch ingredients. Next week, we're starting a unit on immigration patterns through Ellis Island, featuring dishes from different countries."

Aaron watched his niece's posture shift, the rigid defensive stance softening by degrees. This woman had accomplished more in thirty seconds than he had managed in three months.

"That sounds..." Naomi paused, as if afraid to show too much interest. "Different."

"I hope you'll consider joining us. We meet on Thursdays after school." Meghan's tone remained warm but not pushy. "And family members are always welcome to participate."

Aaron felt her gaze settle on him briefly, and something in her expression suggested the invitation wasn't merely polite protocol.

"We should probably finish up with registration," Principal Watkins said gently. "Ms. Townsend, thanks for helping with the paperwork rescue."

"My pleasure." She gathered her remaining papers, then looked back at Naomi. "I'll be seeing you. I'm in room 112."

As she walked away, Aaron found himself watching until she disappeared around the corner. When he turned back, he caught Principal Watkins regarding him with barely concealed amusement.

"Ms. Townsend is one of our finest teachers," the principal said as they entered his office. "She's very dedicated to her students."

The next thirty minutes passed in a blur of forms, schedules, and policy explanations. Aaron signed documents while keeping one eye on Naomi, who had retreated into silence. When they finally left the office, she walked ahead of him again, schedule clutched in her hand.

"That wasn't so bad," Aaron ventured as they headed toward the parking lot.

"I guess." She paused beside a bulletin board covered with college brochures and club announcements. "Uncle Aaron?"

The sound of his name in her voice, tentative and almost vulnerable, stopped him short. She hadn't called him anything but *"Aaron"* since the funeral.

"Yeah?"

"Do you think..." She looked down at her schedule again. "Do you think Grandma would have liked this place?"

The question hit him hard. His mother had agonized over every educational decision, researching programs and visiting schools even when money was tight. She had wanted the best for Naomi... always.

Aaron answered carefully. "I think your grandma would have loved seeing you in that cooking program. She always said you had her gift for making people feel at home with good food."

Naomi's eyes filled, but she blinked quickly. "I miss her cooking."

"Me too, kiddo. Me too."

They stood there for a moment, surrounded by the noise and bustle of other families navigating their own first days. Then Naomi straightened her shoulders, a gesture so reminiscent of his mother that Aaron's chest tightened.

"We should probably go," she said. "You have that meeting with Mr. Donovan at four."

Aaron checked his watch, surprised she remembered his schedule. "Right. Let's head home."

They walked toward the truck, and this time Naomi matched his pace instead of racing ahead. It was a small change, barely noticeable, but the shift hit him with the warmth of sunlight edging through a break in the clouds.

In the truck, she buckled her seatbelt and pulled out her phone. But instead of immediately putting her headphones back on, she turned toward him.

"The cooking teacher," she said. "Ms. Townsend. She seemed nice."

Aaron started the engine, considering his response. "She did. And that program sounds like something you might enjoy."

"Maybe." Naomi was quiet for a moment. "She looked at you funny."

Heat crept up Aaron's neck. "What do you mean?"

"I don't know. Just... different. Like she was really seeing you, not just being polite because you're a parent."

Out of the mouths of babes. Aaron pulled out of the parking space, uncertain how to respond to his niece's unexpected perceptiveness.

"Sometimes adults connect over shared concerns," he said finally. "We both want what's best for you."

"Mmm-hmm." Naomi's tone indicated her skepticism toward his explanation, yet she refrained from probing further.

As they drove toward home, Aaron's thoughts drifted back to those few moments in the hallway. Meghan Townsend had looked at him with genuine interest, not pity or obligation. For just an instant, he felt like more than an overwhelmed guardian struggling to keep his head above water.

The light turned green, and they continued toward their new life, carrying between them the fragile hope that this beginning might lead somewhere better than where they had been.

Chapter 2

THE SUN HAD BARELY crested the horizon when Meghan Townsend unlocked her classroom door at Greater Pines High School. These quiet morning hours before the building filled with colleagues and students were sacred to her, when time transformed sterile walls into a space where history lived and breathed.

She stepped back from the display case at the center of the room, tilting her head to examine her work. At its heart lay a replica of Frederick Douglass's letter to his former master, surrounded by black-and-white photographs from the Civil Rights Movement. Some showed young protesters braving fire hoses in Birmingham. Others captured marchers crossing the Edmund Pettus Bridge, and there was even a rare image of Fannie Lou Hamer, her expression fierce and fearless.

Her fingers traced the glass over Hamer's determined expression. "Let them see you," Meghan whispered to the photograph. "Let them see what real courage looks like."

Creating these displays was more than decorating. It was honoring those ancestors on whose shoulders she stood, whose stories deserved to be remembered beyond sanitized textbook paragraphs. Her father, a culinary instructor at Brookside College before the highway accident claimed his life, had instilled this reverence for historical truth.

His words still echoed in her memory. *History isn't just what has already happened. It's who we become because of it.*

It had been over twenty-four years since his passing, and still, these moments caught her unaware. When she lost him, she was barely finding her footing as an adult, forced to navigate the world without his guidance.

Pushing aside the melancholy, she moved to her desk. The Harlem Renaissance unit needed finishing touches before Monday's first classes. She had prepared recordings of Duke Ellington and Louis Armstrong to play as students entered, as well as Langston Hughes' poetry to analyze, and reproductions of Aaron Douglas' paintings to spark discussion.

A knock interrupted her reverie. Principal Watkins stood in the doorway, coffee mug in hand.

"Your classroom makes the district office jealous every year," he said, admiring the displays. "You always raise the bar."

Her face brightened. "I'm just trying to make these historical figures real to the students. It's hard to care about people if they're just names in a textbook."

He nodded, sipping his coffee before speaking again. "I wanted to check in about our new student, Naomi Grant." His voice lowered. "Her records came in from Bristol Heights. She was an excellent student until about eight months ago. That's when her grandmother's health started declining. Her grades tanked during the last semester."

"That lines up with what I noticed." Meghan leaned against her desk. "She showed some interest in the Civil Rights display yesterday and mentioned her grandmother used to tell her stories from that era."

"Her uncle seems..." Principal Watkins paused, searching for the right word.

"Overwhelmed?" Meghan suggested.

"That's a generous way to put it. I'd say he's in way over his head." He shook his head. "He's a construction foreman who's suddenly responsible for a grieving teenager. The social worker said their apartment was barely furnished when she did their home assessment."

This troubled her. "How long has he been Naomi's guardian?"

"About three months. Her grandmother's funeral was in May." He checked his watch. "By the way, we're having a faculty meeting in fifteen minutes. I wanted to give you a heads-up since Naomi will be in your homeroom."

After he left, Meghan added materials to Naomi's welcome folder. She knew the terrain of grief all too well. The girl's situation stirred memories of her own disorientation after losing her father. The world hadn't stopped, but it had no longer seemed to make sense.

Starting the cooking program helped her reclaim some of that grounding. Each Thursday afternoon, students gathered in the renovated home economics room to prepare dishes tied to historical and cultural traditions. For some, it was a fun elective. For others, it offered a safe space. For Meghan, it was a way to carry her father's legacy forward by passing on his belief that food could tell stories that words sometimes couldn't.

By lunchtime, Meghan had welcome packets ready for all her incoming students. She grabbed her lunch bag and headed to the faculty lounge.

Daniel Forrester waved her over, his wedding band glinting as he motioned to an empty chair. Marriage suited him. The shadows that clung to him after his late wife's death had lifted. These days, he looked happier and content.

"First day back and you already look like you're solving a world crisis," he teased as she sat across from him.

She unwrapped her sandwich. "Just thinking about a new student. Naomi Grant. She lost her grandmother recently and moved here with her uncle. Principal Watkins filled me in on some of their background this morning."

"The construction guy? I met him at the community center project last month." Daniel's face took on a serious expression. "That man looks like he's under immense pressure. He doesn't talk much, but when he does, everyone listens."

"What's his story?" The description intrigued her, as it was so different from the overwhelmed man she had encountered.

Daniel shrugged. "Not much to tell. Frank Donovan brought him in from Bristol Heights to run the Brookside expansion of his construction company. Rumor has it that he only moved here because his mother was being treated at Brookside General. After she died, he ended up with guardianship of his niece."

"When I saw Naomi in the hallway yesterday..." She paused, stabbing at a cucumber with her fork. "I recognized that look. It was the same one I had after my dad's accident. Like the world kept spinning, but yours just... stopped."

Daniel studied her. "And you're already figuring out how to help," he said, not a question but an observation.

"Is it that obvious?"

"Only to someone who's watched you adopt every stray student who's ever needed some help." His tone was gentle, without judgment. "It's why you're such a great teacher."

"I was thinking the cooking program might help. It could give her structure." A thought occurred to her. "Maybe she could invite her uncle. He looks like someone who's been surviving on takeout."

Daniel raised an eyebrow. "The uncle, too?"

"I'm just being practical," Meghan said quickly. "Research shows adolescents do better when their caregivers are involved in school activities."

"Mmm-hmm." Daniel's knowing expression suggested he wasn't entirely convinced by her academic justification.

"So, how's Sam?" she asked, deliberately changing the subject.

Daniel's face transformed, radiating joy. "She's doing great. Cutting back on her ER hours gave her time to help with our church outreach. She's even thinking about mentoring."

Warmth filled Meghan's expression. Daniel met Samantha after he lost his late wife Teresa to a sudden aneurysm, and she changed his life forever.

Their relationship had developed quickly, from chance meetings to dating and then to an engagement. It all culminated in a beautiful spring wedding this past March. Daniel's transformation had been remarkable to witness. He went from a man struggling with his faith after a devastating loss to someone who had found joy again.

They spent the rest of lunch swapping updates about the school calendar and the upcoming fall festival. By the time lunch ended, Meghan had almost convinced herself that her interest in Naomi and her uncle was just part of her job.

That illusion held until evening, when she was in Grocery Haven's produce section, mentally listing ingredients for tomorrow's dinner. A movement at the edge of her vision caught her attention. A tall figure stood before the vegetable display.

Aaron Grant held a shopping list in one hand, his expression suggesting he was deciphering ancient hieroglyphics rather than grocery items. He wore faded jeans and a gray T-shirt, revealing strong forearms dusted with what looked like sawdust or drywall powder. Without his niece beside him, some of yesterday's guardedness faded, replaced by simple bewilderment at the array of produce.

Before she could second-guess herself, Meghan walked over. "Need some help decoding the vegetable jungle?"

He turned, surprise flickering across his features before recognition dawned. "Ms. Townsend."

"Meghan," she corrected with a smile. "We're off the clock."

"Meghan," he repeated, as if testing the name. "I'm looking for..." He consulted his list. "Fresh basil? Naomi wants pasta tonight."

"You're in the wrong section for that. The herbs are over by the lettuce." She gestured toward the far wall. "I'm headed that way if you want to follow."

Relief crossed his face, there and gone so quickly she nearly missed it. "Thanks. Blueprints, I get. Grocery stores? Not so much."

As they walked, Meghan noticed his shopping basket contained jarred sauce, spaghetti, and a baguette.

"Are you making pasta from scratch?" she asked.

A low chuckle escaped him. A surprisingly warm sound from someone who appeared so guarded. "Not even close. Just trying to do better than takeout for the third night in a row."

"Third night? What about the first two?"

"Monday was burgers, and Tuesday was cereal." His admission came with a self-deprecating shrug. "I'm not winning any guardian-of-the-year awards."

They reached the herb section, and Meghan selected a package of fresh basil, handing it to him. "Here. And don't be so hard on yourself. Adjusting to a new role takes time."

He accepted the herbs, studying them with the focus some-one might give a complex mathematical equation. "Thanks. Do I just toss this in? Or should I sprinkle it on top?"

"You could, but if you want to upgrade that jarred sauce without much effort..." Meghan reached for a bulb of garlic from a nearby display. "Mince two cloves of this, sauté in some butter, then tear in some basil leaves right at the end. It takes three extra minutes, but it'll be worth it."

Aaron's brow furrowed as he added garlic to his basket. "But-ter, garlic, basil. Got it."

"You seem like a quick study."

"Construction's all about details and following instruc-tions," he replied. "Though I'll admit, feeding a teenager is way harder than building a three-story apartment complex."

The admission revealed his dry sense of humor. This wasn't the same guarded man from yesterday's school meeting.

"Speaking of feeding teenagers, my after-school cooking pro-gram starts Thursday. Nothing complex... just basic skills, cul-tural dishes... stuff like that. Naomi's welcome, and so are you, if you'd like to come."

His expression changed. "I appreciate the invitation, but—"

"Before you say no, it's not just for students," Meghan in-terjected. "We've had parents, grandparents, and even Principal Watkins occasionally joins in. No experience necessary."

Aaron shifted his stance, torn. "My schedule is a mess. Con-struction deadlines don't always care about school hours."

"Well, the invitation stands, whenever you can make it." Meghan recognized his instinct to retreat. "Sometimes, having a routine helps when you're trying to find your footing in a new situation."

As their eyes met, Meghan caught a fleeting glimpse of the man beneath the armor he wore. But just like that, he blinked, and the moment slipped away.

"I should let you finish your shopping," he said, the connection broken as quickly as it had formed. "Thanks for the help."

"Anytime." Meghan hesitated. "If Naomi ever needs a quiet place after school, my classroom's open most days until four."

Aaron nodded, a muscle working in his jaw. "I'll keep that in mind. Good night, Meghan."

He lifted his basket in farewell.

"Good night, Aaron."

She watched him walk away, noticing how his shoulders straightened, as if consciously resuming the weight of his responsibilities. That simple act, the deliberate squaring of shoulders before facing the world, stayed with her long after he was gone.

Later that evening, as she prepared a stir-fry in her modest kitchen, she thought about Aaron's struggle to provide normalcy for his niece. He hadn't chosen the role, but he hadn't walked away from it either. He was trying, one small step at a time.

The cooking program might be exactly what both of them needed. Naomi for the structure, Aaron for the support. And if she was honest with herself, it might be something she needed too.

She made a mental note to prepare extra welcome materials in case they decided to attend.

After all, everyone deserved a place where they belonged.

20

Chapter 3

MORNING SUNLIGHT STREAMED THROUGH the skeletal framework of Brookside's future community center, casting geometric shadows across the freshly poured concrete foundation. Aaron crouched at the edge of the slab, running his calloused hand over the surface. The smooth texture confirmed what his eyes told him. His crew had done quality work.

He stood with a quiet groan, his lower back reminding him that he wasn't twenty anymore. At forty-two, the physical demands of his work reminded him daily of the passing years.

Aaron took a moment to admire the progress. Steel beams reached skyward, outlining what would become a two-story atrium. The completed structure would house meeting rooms, a recreational area, and a state-of-the-art kitchen, providing a space for the community to gather.

Unrolling the blueprints across a makeshift table of plywood on sawhorses, Aaron traced the planned electrical routes with his finger. This project was more than just another contract for his company. It was a way of planting roots in Brookside, whether he intended to stay or not.

"Earth to Aaron," a voice called, breaking his concentration.

Aaron looked up. Darius Washington approached with his hard hat tilted over his close-cropped hair. As foreman, Darius managed the day-to-day operations that Aaron couldn't oversee personally, especially now with Naomi's needs demanding more of his attention.

"Checking the foundation pour," Aaron replied, rolling up the blueprints. "Looks good so far."

Darius crossed his arms, his expression skeptical. "You've been staring at that same section for ten minutes. The concrete's fine. You, on the other hand..." He gestured toward Aaron with one hand.

Aaron secured the blueprints with a rubber band. "I'm good."

"Right." Darius leaned against the makeshift table. "That's why you've checked the same measurements three times and snapped at Campbell when he asked about the delivery schedule."

Aaron sighed, removing his hard hat to wipe sweat from his brow. The August heat pressed down, oppressive in the early morning hours. "Yeah... sorry about that. I'll talk to him."

"I already handled it." Darius studied him with frank assessment, preferring straight talk to polite evasion. "Look, everyone knows you've got a lot on your plate right now with your niece and managing this expansion. But your head's been somewhere else all week."

He could have brushed it off or offered a half-answer. But Darius deserved his honesty. "Naomi's old school sent her records. There was stuff I didn't know about."

"What kind of stuff?"

Aaron glanced around to ensure their conversation remained private. The rhythm of hammering and the whine of circular saws provided adequate cover.

"She was skipping classes and blowing off her assignments. And it looks like she got into some fights. It all started about eight months ago when my mom's health went downhill." Aaron rubbed the back of his neck. "The counselor flagged her records, saying she thought Naomi was showing signs of depression. But Naomi wouldn't talk to them."

Darius nodded. "Man, that's tough. How's she doing now?"

"She started school at Greater Pines. But she talks to me about as much as this concrete does. She stays in her room with her headphones on and keeps her door closed. I feel like I'm living with a stranger."

Darius nodded in agreement. "Teenagers are a mystery on a good day. Add grief to the mix and—"

A buzz from Aaron's pocket interrupted them. He pulled out his phone to find a text from Greater Pines High School, confirming Naomi's enrollment in ninth-grade history with Ms. Townsend.

Meghan Townsend. His thumb hovered over the screen longer than necessary. They had crossed paths twice, once at the school and again at the grocery store. Both times, her presence shattered his preserved emotional distance. Those keen eyes seemed to see past his facade, recognizing the uncertainty he worked so hard to conceal.

Darius eyed him. "There's that look again."

Aaron pocketed his phone. "What look?"

"Like you're trying to solve quantum physics while standing in quicksand."

A reluctant chuckle escaped Aaron's lips. "That's... weirdly accurate for how I feel trying to raise a teenager."

Darius laughed, rich and full. "Brother, I've got three daughters, so trust me, I know the feeling." He clapped Aaron on the shoulder. "Listen, the foundation will cure without you hovering. Why don't you take off early? The crew's got this handled."

Aaron's instinct was to refuse. Work had been his refuge, the one area of life where problems had clear solutions and effort yielded predictable results. But the text reminded him he had responsibilities more important than concrete and steel.

"You sure?"

"Positive. Family comes first." Darius gestured toward the site. "Besides, Donovan's not scheduled to inspect until next week. And we're ahead of schedule."

Aaron hesitated, then nodded. "Thanks. I'll wrap the calls with the supplier first, then head out."

Two hours later, Aaron parked outside their apartment. The complex was spotless and modern, though utterly lacking in personality. Each unit mirrored the next, right down to the identical balconies. When he signed the lease, the sterile neutrality fit the numbness he had been living with. Now, the place echoed with emptiness.

Their third-floor unit offered a view of Providence Park in the distance, green space interrupting the urban landscape. Inside, the apartment looked lived in, though only in the most technical sense. A handful of family photographs lined a bookshelf, a colorful throw blanket lay draped over the sofa, and potted plants sat on the balcony. He tried to stitch together something resembling a home, but the air held only an expectant hush rather than genuine warmth.

Aaron dropped his keys on the kitchen counter and checked the time. It was five o'clock.

Naomi would be in her room. He opened the refrigerator. There wasn't much to work with. Tuesday's pasta had been a step up, thanks to Meghan's basil-and-garlic tip, but beyond that, his culinary skills were limited.

He pulled out chicken breasts and vegetables he purchased during that fateful grocery store encounter. Following a recipe from an online search, Aaron assembled a sheet pan dinner, sliding it into the oven with more hope than confidence. *Please don't let me burn this.*

While the food was cooking, he knocked on Naomi's bedroom door. "Dinner will be ready in twenty minutes," he called.

No response came, but he could hear the movement of bedsprings creaking and the soft thud of socked feet on the floor.

Dinner unfolded the way it did most nights. Aaron attempted conversation, and Naomi responded with little more than monosyllabic answers while she pushed her food around the plate.

"How was school today?" Aaron asked, breaking the silence.

"Fine."

"Do you have homework?"

"A little."

"Did you get your schedule?"

"Yeah."

Aaron took a breath, forcing patience into his voice. "Want to show it to me?"

Naomi shrugged, but after a pause, she reached into her backpack and slid a folded paper across the table.

Aaron scanned it. She had Ms. Townsend for history and Mr. Forrester for English. The school placed Naomi in honors courses despite her recent academic struggles. Someone at the school saw potential in her.

"These look like good classes," he observed. "Principal Watkins must think you can handle it."

Naomi hesitated, her fork halfway to her mouth. She briefly looked up, giving him a fleeting view. Uncertainty? Surprise? Then she looked down again, letting her braids fall like a curtain.

"I guess," she murmured.

"Do you need supplies before Monday? Like notebooks or pencils?"

"No. I have everything."

Aaron watched her nudge a lone piece of broccoli to the edge of her plate. She had eaten three bites of chicken and nothing else.

A familiar surge rose in him. He was frustrated with the silence, frustrated with himself, and frustrated with the widening gap he still couldn't bridge. His mother would have known what to say. She always read people with ease and knew what they needed without asking a single question. Aaron lived in the world of measurements and tools. Emotions had no clear markers, no tidy scale to read.

He glanced out the window at the deepening twilight. "I was thinking about taking a walk in Providence Park before it gets dark. Want to come?"

The suggestion was spontaneous, born of desperation rather than planning. He half expected immediate rejection, another shrug, or perhaps hostility.

Instead, Naomi looked up, surprise in her expression. "You're going to the park?"

"It's not far. Might be nice to check out the neighborhood."

She studied him, as if searching for ulterior motives. "I guess," she said. "There's nothing else to do anyway."

Relief washed through him at this small victory. "Great. Let's clean up these dishes, and we can head out."

Chapter 4

Providence Park spread across twenty acres at the heart of Brookside, featuring walking trails, a small lake, and gardens maintained by local volunteers. As Aaron and Naomi stepped through ornate iron gates, the golden hour bathed the landscape in soft light, warming the area with amber tones.

Naomi walked ahead, arms swinging loosely at her sides, shoulders less rigid than usual. She stopped occasionally to examine flowering plants and watch the ducks glide across the lake's surface. These moments of unguarded curiosity gave Aaron glimpses of the child she must have been before grief changed everything.

They followed the winding path that looped around the water, passing parents with strollers and couples on evening walks. Aaron maintained a slight distance, unwilling to break this fragile peace by forcing a conversation.

Near a wooden footbridge, Naomi crouched to examine purple flowers growing along the path's edge.

"Grandma had these in her garden," she said softly. The words were clearly not intended for Aaron but spoken aloud, nonetheless.

"Coneflowers." He was grateful for the knowledge gleaned from countless visits to nurseries with his mother. "She planted them every spring. She said they attracted butterflies."

Naomi glanced up at him. "You remember her garden?"

"Sure. I helped her sometimes when I came to visit." Aaron knelt beside his niece, balancing on the balls of his feet. "She taught me the names of everything. I was never as good with plants as she was."

The corner of Naomi's mouth lifted slightly. "She said you killed her tomatoes one year."

He chuckled, the memory bittersweet. "I did. I over-watered them. She never let me live it down."

This shared recollection hung between them, delicate as spider silk. Aaron wanted to seize the moment and build on this tentative connection, but he resisted the urge to push. How much pressure would send Naomi retreating again?

The decision was made for him when movement on the jogging path caught his attention. A familiar figure approached, her rhythmic strides slowing as she drew near.

Meghan Townsend wore fitted black leggings and a loose blue tank top. Her hair was pulled in a ponytail, revealing the graceful curve of her neck. Even with minimal makeup and dampened by perspiration, she radiated natural beauty.

"Well, hello there," she called, altering her course to approach them. "Fancy meeting you two here."

Naomi straightened, her momentary openness vanishing behind the familiar mask of teenage indifference.

Aaron nodded in greeting, hoping his voice sounded more composed than he felt. "Out for an evening run?"

"Yes. I'm trying to maintain some routine before the chaos of the school year begins." Her smile created those captivating dimples. "Providence Park has some of the best trails in town."

She turned to Naomi. "I see you've discovered our coneflower patch. They're beautiful, aren't they?"

Naomi shrugged noncommittally, but her eyes remained on the flowers.

"The local garden club maintains these beds," Meghan continued, seemingly unfazed by the tepid response. "They've created themed gardens throughout the park. The butterfly garden around that bend is my favorite."

"My grandma had coneflowers," Naomi said suddenly. "And zinnias. And these tall purple ones..."

"Liatris?" Meghan suggested. "Little star-shaped blooms on long spikes?"

Naomi nodded, animation entering her expression. "Yeah, those. She said they were prairie blazing stars."

"That's right. That's another name for them." Meghan's voice carried genuine interest rather than the condescending encouragement many adults used with teenagers. "Was her garden in Bristol Heights?"

"Behind her house. My grandpa built the raised beds before he died." Naomi glanced at the park's flowerbeds. "These look like hers. They even have the same layout."

Meghan wiped her brow with the small towel draped around her neck. "The butterfly garden has similar raised beds. If you're up for a short walk, I'd be happy to show you."

Aaron expected Naomi to decline or retreat into sullen silence. To his astonishment, she nodded.

"Is that okay?" she asked, looking at Aaron for permission. It was the first time she had sought his approval for anything.

"Sure," he said smoothly, recovering quickly. "Lead the way."

They followed her along winding paths until reaching a secluded corner of the park. Here, raised wooden beds overflowed with colorful blooms, attracting butterflies and bees that danced from flower to flower in the evening light.

Naomi knelt beside one bed, watching a monarch butterfly land on a cluster of bright orange blossoms. "These are beautiful. Grandma would have loved this."

"Gardens connect us to the people we miss," Meghan said quietly. "My dad taught me to cook. Every time I make one of his recipes, I feel like he's right there beside me."

Aaron watched them, struck by how naturally Meghan drew out responses from Naomi, something he struggled to achieve for months. There was no pretense in her method, no visible technique in play. She was the first adult who managed to get more than one-word answers from his niece since they left Bristol Heights.

"Do you garden?" Meghan asked Aaron.

He shook his head. "Not really. Construction is more my specialty. It's less delicate than handling plants."

"Not necessarily. Both require understanding materials, planning for growth, and patience throughout the process."

Aaron blinked. He hadn't considered that comparison before, but it made sense. "I hadn't thought of it that way."

"Containers," Naomi said suddenly.

Both adults turned toward her. "What's that?" Aaron asked.

"Grandma said people in apartments should grow things in containers, on their balconies." She glanced between them. "We have a balcony."

The suggestion was an offering so fragile that Aaron feared his response might crush it entirely.

"We could do that," he replied thoughtfully. "Maybe start with something small."

Meghan's encouraging smile bolstered his confidence. "Container gardening is perfect for beginners. You can grow herbs and flowers... low commitment, but high reward."

Naomi looked at him. "Could we, Uncle Aaron? Can we start it this weekend?"

Aaron could hardly believe this shift in their dynamic. "Yeah. We'll visit the garden center Saturday morning."

As twilight deepened toward dusk, they thanked Meghan for her impromptu tour and began walking toward the park entrance. Aaron stole glances at her as she described the cooking program, which was starting on Thursday. Her passion was obvious, and it resonated with his own approach to craftsmanship.

"I should let you both enjoy the rest of your evening," Meghan said as they reached the main path. "It was nice running into you."

"Thank you for showing us the gardens," Aaron replied, meaning it sincerely. "And for the invitation to your program. We'll think about it."

"I hope you do." Her gaze held his just a moment longer before shifting to Naomi. "I'll see you in school. Take care and enjoy the rest of the park."

They watched her jog away, her form disappearing around a bend in the path. Aaron became aware of Naomi studying him with unexpected scrutiny.

"What?" he asked.

She shrugged. "Nothing. Can we go now?"

They walked back to the truck without speaking, the silence softer than usual, as though her walls had shifted rather than hardened. As they reached the parking lot, Naomi stumbled, her backpack sliding from her shoulder.

Aaron reached out to steady her, but she caught herself against a car bumper. The impact knocked her backpack open, spilling its contents across the asphalt.

He crouched to help gather scattered pens, crumpled papers, textbooks, and a slim black notebook with worn edges. Without thinking, he picked up the journal, intending to return it to the backpack.

The notebook fell open in his hands, revealing tight, cramped handwriting that covered the margins. Dark, angry words leaped from the page:

Everything ends. Everyone leaves. First Dad, then Mom, then Grandma. What's the point of caring when people just disappear? Why try when nothing lasts?

Aaron's heart clenched as his eyes fell on the final entry, dated just three days earlier:

Uncle Aaron tries, I guess. But he'll get tired too. No one stays anyway.

The hopelessness of those words sent ice through his veins. He closed the journal quickly. When he looked up, his niece stood frozen, her expression a mixture of horror and betrayal.

"Naomi, I didn't mean—"

She snatched the journal from his hands, shoving it deep into her backpack. "You had no right!" Her voice shook. "That was private!"

"I know. I'm sorry." Aaron rose slowly, hands spread in a placating gesture. "I wasn't trying to read it. It fell open when I picked it up."

Tears welled in her eyes, but she blinked them back. "Whatever. Just forget it."

"Naomi, wait." Aaron struggled to find the right words. "If you're feeling this way, I want to help."

"You can't fix it," she said flatly. "No one can."

Before he could respond, she stalked toward the truck. Aaron followed, helplessness clawing at him. Should he insist on talking about what he had read? Contact the school counselor? Pretend it never happened?

None of these options addressed the core issue revealed by those heartbreaking words. Naomi didn't believe anyone would stay in her life. And why would she? Everyone who was supposed to stay—her parents, her grandmother—were gone, leaving her with an uncle who hardly knew how to relate to her.

As he started the engine, he glanced at Naomi. Her jaw was set, her gaze fixed on the road ahead. The temporary breakthrough at the park had vanished, replaced by walls higher than before.

No one stays anyway.

The phrase haunted him during the drive home. She expected everyone to leave because that's all she had ever experienced. How could he convince her otherwise when neither of them had ever planned for his lasting presence in her life?

As they pulled into their apartment complex, Aaron made a silent vow. To Naomi. To his mother's memory. Whatever it took, however long it required, he would prove those words wrong.

She would not be abandoned. Not again. Not by him.

Some people stayed. And he would be one of them.

Chapter 5

THE SCHOOL HALLWAYS HAD grown quiet hours ago, leaving only the occasional sound of a distant vacuum cleaner or the janitorial staff's muffled conversations. Meghan treasured these peaceful moments after the final bell, when her thoughts could settle, and grading could be done without interruptions.

Red pen in hand, she circled a line from a sophomore's poetry analysis. Teaching involved more than imparting historical facts. It meant cultivating critical thinking and fostering emotional connections to the past. Her students' growing engagement with Langston Hughes' work proved she was making progress, even if the victories came in small increments.

The soft sound of knuckles against her open door broke her concentration.

"Excuse me."

Meghan looked up, her pulse quickening at the familiar voice. Aaron stood in her doorway, one shoulder leaning against the frame. Dust from the construction site clung to his faded jeans and tight gray T-shirt. The afternoon light cast shadows under the strong angles of his jawline, revealing the fatigue etched around his mouth.

"Mr. Grant," she said, setting her pen aside. "This is unexpected."

"Aaron," he corrected, the corner of his mouth lifting slightly. "I'm sure we covered that at the grocery store."

"Right... Aaron," Meghan amended, rising from her desk. "What brings you to Greater Pines after hours?"

His entrance seemed to shrink the classroom. "I was meeting with Principal Watkins about Naomi's schedule and thought..." He paused, rubbing the back of his neck. "Honestly, I'm not sure what I thought. I should let you get back to work."

He turned toward the door.

"Wait." Meghan gestured toward a student desk near her own. "Please, sit. I could use a break from grading."

He hesitated, then nodded and walked over. His large frame folded awkwardly into the too-small chair, knees jutting upward at uncomfortable angles.

"These aren't built for adults," he observed dryly.

"They're not built for comfort at all," Meghan replied with a smile. "It helps me remember how it feels to be young and uncertain about your place in the world."

Aaron's expression grew serious. "Speaking of young and uncertain..." He exhaled slowly. "I found something in Naomi's journal the other night. Not intentionally. It fell open when she dropped her backpack."

Meghan remained silent despite her internal alarm.

"What I read..." He shook his head, his jaw tightening. "It was dark. *'No one stays anyway,'* was how she put it."

An ache bloomed in Meghan's chest. The pain behind those words and the isolation they revealed spoke volumes about what Naomi was experiencing.

"That must have been difficult to read," she said quietly.

"Difficult doesn't cover it." Aaron leaned forward, forearms resting on his thighs. "I build things for a living. When something's broken, I know how to fix it. But this is beyond me. A grieving teenage girl who has lost everyone? I don't have the tools for something like this."

The metaphor struck Meghan as fitting. "What tools do you think you need?"

Aaron looked up at her question. "I don't know. Patience, I suppose... and understanding. I need a way to connect with her that doesn't feel forced." His shoulders dropped. "I can't replace her grandmother."

"No, you can't," Meghan agreed. "And trying to would probably backfire. What she needs isn't a replacement. She needs to know you're not erasing what she's lost, and that you'll stay, even when it gets hard."

"So, what am I supposed to do?" The question held no challenge, only bewilderment.

Meghan thought carefully about what to say. "Build something new, perhaps. A different kind of relationship. One that honors what came before while making space for what you two could become."

His expression grew thoughtful. "What about your cooking program? Naomi seemed interested after we saw those gardens at the park." He hesitated before continuing. "Do you think your program could help her connect to good memories?"

Meghan felt a surge of admiration for his insight. This man was more perceptive than he gave himself credit for.

"The program would be perfect for her," she confirmed. "We focus on family recipes, but it's also about culture and stories. It's a safe environment, and it creates connections naturally."

Hope flickered in Aaron's expression. "What would she need to bring?"

"Nothing but herself. We provide all the supplies." Meghan paused, considering her next words. "And you should come too."

His posture stiffened with resistance. "Me? I don't think—"

"It's not restricted to students. Several parents participate, and some grandparents too. Daniel Forrester from the English department drops by when he can."

Aaron's brow furrowed. "I don't have much cooking skill. I burn toast."

"That's the point of a class." She allowed a hint of teasing into her tone. "Besides, Naomi needs to see you trying something new, too. It levels the playing field when you're both beginners."

"My schedule's a nightmare. The community center project is running on tight deadlines."

"Even one session would make a difference," Meghan pressed. "It's Thursdays from three-thirty to five in the home economics room."

Aaron's gaze met hers. "You think it would help?"

Meghan leaned forward, matching his posture. "I do. When I lost my dad, cooking became something I could hold on to. His voice guides me when I'm adding spices. Cooking his recipes brings order to the chaos in my life, and purpose to my grief."

His gaze softened. "I didn't know... about your father."

"It was a car accident when I was thirteen." The familiar ache accompanied the words, duller now but never entirely absent. "My mom died seven years later from a heart attack, though some said heartbreak played a part."

Aaron nodded slowly. "I'm sorry."

"I'm sorry about your mother, too." Meghan's voice remained steady. "Grief rewires us, whether we want it to or not. Naomi's trying to make sense of a world that doesn't feel safe anymore. Cooking might not be her answer, but it could offer a moment's peace from the storm."

Aaron straightened, resolution settling into his shoulders. "Thursday at three-thirty. We'll be there."

Relief washed through Meghan. "Wonderful. I'll add your names to the roster."

"I should let you get back to your grading." He unfolded from the student chair with visible relief. "Thanks for this."

"For what?"

"For looking past the obvious. With Naomi... and with me. Most people look away when emotions get complicated."

A faint, unwelcome stir rose in Meghan, brushing against thoughts she didn't want to explore. "My dad loved literature. He said the best stories never have simple characters. And neither do the best people."

A smile reshaped Aaron's face, releasing the tight pull at the corners of his mouth. "Wise man, your father."

"He was," Meghan agreed, her throat tightening. "I'll see you Thursday, then."

Aaron nodded, turning toward the door. He paused at the threshold, looking back over his shoulder. "For what it's worth, I think Naomi's lucky to have you as her teacher."

Before she could respond, he was gone, his footsteps echoing down the empty corridor.

Meghan sat motionless, absorbing what had transpired. The calm she usually found in her classroom after difficult conversations didn't return. Something had shifted. She told herself this was all about Naomi. This was a professional concern for a student who needed extra support.

But as she began packing her things to finish grading at home, Meghan couldn't shake the memory of Aaron's smile or the way he looked at her when she mentioned her father.

She paused, her hand resting on a stack of ungraded papers, and wondered if she was about to step into something far more complicated than a cooking class.

Chapter 6

Hearthside Reads Bookstore welcomed Meghan with the comforting scent of paper, leather, and freshly brewed coffee. Oak shelves stretched from floor to ceiling, their dark wood polished to a warm glow. Mr. Finch, the owner, nodded a greeting from behind the counter, wire-rimmed glasses perched on his nose despite the warm September afternoon.

Meghan headed straight for the cookbook section. She needed to finalize the lesson plan for the cooking class. The recipes were important, but the emotional atmosphere of the session was just as crucial. She wasn't only preparing meals with her students, she was creating a space for healing.

Her fingers moved over the spines of books about food and heritage. She searched for something that would speak to the idea of legacy, and how recipes passed down more than flavors, as they carried memories, connections, and hope.

"Well, if it isn't my favorite prayer partner looking suspiciously preoccupied."

Meghan turned to find Olivia Stewart walking toward her. A smile lit her petite features, and her light brown hair fell in waves around her shoulders.

"Olivia," Meghan greeted her, pleasure pushing aside her distraction. "What brings you here?"

"New veterinary journals finally came in," Olivia explained, hefting a small stack of publications. She studied Meghan intently, her gaze revealing the connection that came from sharing countless confidences. "But more importantly, why have you been fixated on that same cookbook for the past five minutes without flipping a page?"

Meghan looked down, realizing she had been holding *Heritage Cooking Passing Down Traditions Through Generations* without actually opening it.

"I'm planning for Thursday's cooking session." She slid the book back into place.

"Mmm-hmm." Olivia's tone dripped with skepticism, clearly indicating her doubts. "This wouldn't have anything to do with that construction worker you talked about after church on Sunday, would it?"

Heat crept up Meghan's neck. "He's Naomi Grant's uncle and guardian. You remember I told you about her. She's a new student, and she lost her grandmother recently."

"And the uncle?" Olivia prompted, amusement in her expression.

"He's..." Meghan hesitated, searching for the right words. "He's doing his best. He suddenly raising a grieving teenager while juggling a full-time job. It's hard for the both of them."

Olivia's demeanor shifted. "And you're stepping in to help. Because that's who you are."

"It's my job to support the students," Meghan pointed out.

"And the hunky uncle? Is supporting him part of your job too?"

The teasing held no judgment, only the honesty of deep friendship. Olivia had been Meghan's companion through more than a few heartbreaks. Reverend Jameson Morrison, pastor of New Hope Baptist Church, introduced them years ago after Meghan's painful breakup with Finn Lockwood.

"He's signing up for the cooking program." Meghan selected another cookbook from the shelf. "For Naomi's sake."

"Right," Olivia agreed, unconvinced. "Strictly for Naomi's sake. I'm sure it has nothing to do with those *soulful eyes* you went on about in detail on Sunday."

Meghan shook her head. "I mentioned his eyes once."

"Three times, but who's counting?" Olivia's smile faded. "Look, I just want you to be careful. You have this gift for finding people in pain and trying to carry their healing on your own shoulders. I don't want to see you hurt again."

Meghan's stomach tightened. Olivia wasn't wrong. It wasn't her teacher's instinct that pulled her toward people in pain. It was personal. Helping others find healing gave her a sense of purpose she couldn't always articulate.

"It's not like that," she insisted, though a hint of uncertainty crept into her voice. "I know where the boundaries lie."

Olivia squeezed her arm. "I know you do. Just keep in mind what you always tell me... being equally yoked isn't optional. Remember what happened with Finn."

The mention of her ex-boyfriend sent a familiar pang through Meghan. She had invested three years in a relationship that collapsed because Finn couldn't grasp why her faith mattered so deeply to her.

"That was different," Meghan said quietly. "And besides, there's nothing romantic happening here. Aaron's trying to help his niece, and I'm in a position to offer resources. That's all."

Even as she spoke the words, Meghan recognized the half-truth in them.

"If you say so." Olivia's tone remained unconvinced.

"Okay, enough about me." Meghan deliberately changed the subject. "How's the adoption process going?"

After years of prayer and consideration, Olivia had finally begun the adoption process three months ago. As a single woman with a deep desire for motherhood, she already faced numerous hurdles, but her determination never wavered.

"The home study is scheduled for next month. I'm obsessively scrubbing baseboards and panicking that they'll find some reason to reject me." She hesitated. "My caseworker called yesterday. They want an additional character reference. They have yours, but they want someone who's known me longer than a few years."

"What about your coworker, Imani?"

"She's dealing with her own custody issues with the divorce. I can't ask her to vouch for my stability when hers is being questioned in court." Olivia's voice carried a strain Meghan hadn't heard before. "I'm starting to wonder if this whole thing is a sign."

"A sign of what?"

"That maybe I'm not meant to be a mother. That maybe wanting this so badly when I don't have a husband is..." She trailed off.

Meghan felt a surge of protectiveness for her friend. "That's not true, and you know it."

"Do I?" Olivia's laugh held no humor. "I'm thirty-five, single, and trying to convince strangers that I can provide what a child needs. Meanwhile, I feel like my own life is falling apart."

The raw vulnerability in Olivia's voice caught Meghan off guard. She had never seen her friend this shaken about the adoption.

"What about Mrs. Solomon from church? She's known you since you started attending."

Olivia shook her head. "She's helping with Imani's situation. I can't ask her to do both." She forced a smile. "Sorry, I didn't mean to dump this on you. I'm just stressed."

"Don't apologize. What can I do to help?"

"Pray. That's about all I can think of right now." Olivia glanced at her watch. "I should go. These journals won't read themselves."

"Wait." Meghan touched her friend's arm. "You're going to be an amazing mother. Don't let the paperwork make you forget that."

Olivia nodded, but the doubt in her eyes remained. "Thanks. I'll call you later."

As Olivia walked away, a knot tightened in Meghan's stomach. Her friend's usual confidence had slipped, revealing an anxiety Meghan hadn't noticed before. How had she missed that Olivia was struggling this much?

After purchasing several cookbooks, Meghan headed home. The late-summer sun washed Brookside in warm light as she turned onto her street, her small bungalow welcoming her with its worn front steps and blooming hydrangeas.

Inside, she changed into comfortable clothes, prepared a simple meal, and settled at her kitchen table with the day's mail. The quiet that usually brought peace, now felt strangely hollow. Her thoughts kept circling back to Aaron, but also to Olivia's strained expression.

After dinner, she retrieved a weathered leather journal from the bookshelf. The binding was cracked, and the pages yellowed at the edges. Her father's handwriting filled the pages with recipes, observations, and occasional scriptural references.

She turned to the *Comfort Foods* section, and read recipes for dishes that sustained her family through difficult times. Southern-style mac and cheese, sweet potato pie, and honey-glazed cornbread. Each recipe carried layers of meaning beyond its culinary purpose.

A passage from Psalm 34:8 was inscribed in the corner of one page: *Taste and see that the Lord is good; blessed is the one who takes refuge in him.*

The verse brought unexpected moisture to her eyes. Her father lived that truth with his whole being. He taught her that food could be ministry, and a meal shared in love could become holy ground.

This was what she hoped to give Naomi. Moments of safety and belonging.

Taking out her lesson planner, Meghan began selecting recipes for Thursday's class. Simple enough for beginners but rich with history. Her father's cornbread made the list first. It was easy to make, easy to share, and always a favorite. She copied the recipe onto index cards and added notes about African American culinary traditions.

As night deepened, Meghan closed the journal and moved toward her bedroom. Her evening prayer routine centered her thoughts after the emotional day.

"Lord," she whispered, kneeling beside her bed. "Help me walk this line with grace. Help me love people without losing sight of who You've called me to be. If this thing with Aaron is empathy, show me. If it's something more, then give me wisdom and patience. And help Olivia through this adoption process. She needs Your peace."

She stood, her body tired but her spirit steadier. As she crawled into bed, Aaron's words from the day before echoed in her mind:

For what it's worth, I think Naomi's lucky to have you as her teacher.

But tonight, Olivia's doubt-filled eyes lingered too. Her friend was struggling, and Meghan wondered how many other people in her life were carrying burdens she hadn't noticed.

Thursday's cooking class would bring its own challenges. She just hoped she was ready for all of them.

Chapter 7

Aaron sat in his idling pickup truck, fingers drumming the steering wheel as he watched students filter through the doors of Greater Pines High School toward after-school activities. It was 3:25 PM, five minutes until Meghan's cooking program began.

He turned toward Naomi. "You ready?"

She hugged her backpack to her chest, her gaze flicking between the building and the dashboard. "I guess."

It wasn't much, but it was more than he usually got. Aaron counted it as progress, one of several small victories since their encounter with Meghan at Providence Park. Their weekend trip to the garden center had been quiet, but she had chosen containers, picked herb seedlings, and even arranged them on the balcony herself. The basil was already reaching for sunlight.

"Remember, I'll pick you up at five," Aaron said, rehearsing the plan they discussed that morning. "Text me if you need me to come sooner."

Naomi nodded and reached for the door, but hesitated—one foot out, one still in the truck.

"You're not coming in?"

Aaron blinked. He hadn't expected that. "I figured you'd want to do this on your own."

She looked away, shoulders tensing. "Ms. Townsend said other adults would be there."

Aaron swallowed, unprepared for this unexpected opening. His first instinct was to decline. The community center project demanded his attention, and his boss, Frank Donovan, was expecting updates. He had emails to return, materials to order, and a full report due by morning.

Yet something in Naomi's voice stopped his automatic refusal.

"Would you like me to stay?" he asked.

Naomi shrugged, her standard response. "Whatever. You probably have work stuff."

Behind the indifference, Aaron detected something else. Was that hope?

"Work can wait." He switched off the engine. "Go ahead. Lead the way."

As they entered the school building, they followed the signs to the home economics classroom. Aaron resisted the urge to place a hand on Naomi's shoulder, respecting her independence while staying nearby for support.

The kitchen classroom hummed with activity. Students arranged ingredients, parents and teachers tied on aprons, and laughter punctuated the cheerful chaos. Gleaming stainless-steel appliances lined one wall, while central islands provided workspace for small groups.

At the center of it all stood Meghan, clipboard in hand, directing participants to their stations. Her ponytail swung as she moved. When she saw them in the doorway, her face lit up.

"You came!" She crossed the room to greet them. Her gaze swept from Naomi to Aaron, pleasure evident in her expression. "Both of you."

"I hope that's still okay." Aaron was suddenly self-conscious about his work clothes. He still wore his faded jeans and a navy button-down with the sleeves rolled to his elbows. He had at least taken time to wash the construction dust from his hands, but he felt out of place among the other adults in casual, but neat attire.

"It's perfect," Meghan assured him, her welcome undiminished. "We have exactly the right number of people for our group stations now." She turned to Naomi. "There's a spot at the blue table with some other ninth graders if you want to join them."

Naomi's eyes darted toward the table. A few teens were arranging vegetables, laughing.

"Or, you and your uncle could team up at the green station. It's entirely up to you."

Aaron held his breath, waiting. To his surprise, Naomi looked up at him, a question in her eyes.

"It's your call," he said quietly. "I'm good either way."

After a beat, Naomi nodded toward the teenagers. "I'll try the blue table."

Pride swelled in Aaron's chest. It wasn't much, but it was brave.

"I'll be right over here if you need me," he assured her.

As Naomi walked away, Meghan handed him an apron. "That was well handled." Her voice was low enough that only he could hear.

"What was?"

"Giving her the choice. Letting her know you're there without pushing." Meghan's perceptive gaze met his. "That's exactly what she needs."

The unexpected praise caught him off guard. "I'm just winging it."

"Then you have good instincts." Meghan gestured toward the green-labeled workstation. "You'll be with Daniel Forrester and a couple of our regular parent participants. Daniel teaches English here. I'll be moving between the groups."

Aaron tied the apron, feeling oddly exposed. He wasn't used to environments without tools and blueprints. Kitchens weren't his terrain.

A tall man with short locs extended his hand. "Aaron, right? I'm Daniel Forrester, from the English department."

Aaron returned the handshake, noting the wedding band on Daniel's finger. "Nice to meet you."

"You're Naomi's uncle," Daniel stated. "I have her in my fourth-period class. She's bright. Quiet, but her writing shows real depth."

Relief flooded Aaron at this positive assessment. "That's good to hear. She doesn't share much at home."

"Give it time," Daniel said, his tone easy. "My wife, Sam, says healing can't be rushed."

"Your wife's a teacher too?"

"She's an ER nurse at Lakeside Community. We met when I was—" Daniel paused, glancing around as if remembering where they were. "Well, when I was going through a rough patch myself. I lost my first wife to an aneurysm."

Aaron tensed, uncomfortable with the personal disclosure from someone he had just met. "I'm sorry."

"Thanks. Point is, I know what it's like to rebuild your life after everything falls apart." Daniel's voice dropped. "Meghan mentioned you took in your niece after losing your mother. I know it doesn't seem like it now, but it will get better."

Before Aaron could respond, Meghan called the room to attention from her position at the demonstration counter.

"Welcome, everyone! Today we're exploring comfort foods and the stories they tell. Each station has recipe cards and ingredients for dishes that connect to different cultural traditions."

Her voice carried through the room without being loud, commanding attention through presence rather than volume.

"Before we begin, I'd like to share something about myself." She lifted a weathered leather journal from the counter. "This belonged to my dad. He passed away when I was thirteen. Inside are recipes he collected and created. Each one connects our family to traditions that span generations."

The room hushed, attention sharpening at the personal disclosure.

"After he died, cooking became my anchor." Meghan's voice was clear yet intimate. "Each time I make one of his recipes, I feel close to him. That's the power of food traditions. They bridge the gap between what we've lost and what remains."

Aaron's throat tightened. His mom's kitchen had been the heart of their home. Since her death, he hadn't touched her recipes. He couldn't. The absence was too loud.

"Now, let's create some connections of our own. We'll be working on southern-style cornbread, a staple that sustained communities through hard times."

She held up a worn recipe card. "This cornbread recipe represents resilience... simple ingredients like cornmeal, buttermilk, and a cast-iron skillet. It was on countless family tables during the Great Migration."

Daniel grinned at Aaron. "I hope you're ready to get your hands dirty. I'm more of a taste-tester."

The next hour passed in a blur of measurements, stirring, and unexpected laughter. Aaron approached the recipe like a methodical and exact blueprint. The textures and aromas began to ease his tension. The scratch of cornmeal, the warmth of the skillet, the smell of browning butter—it all transported him back to his mother's kitchen.

He glanced over at Naomi. She was chopping vegetables, quietly engaged. Once, she even smiled.

Then, just as quickly, she withdrew again, shoulders hunching as she concentrated on her task. Two steps forward, one step back, like always.

"First time participating?" asked a woman working beside him at the green station. Her silver-streaked hair was pulled back, her movements confident as she mixed cornmeal and buttermilk. "You measure like an engineer."

"I'm a construction foreman," he corrected with a half-smile. "Precision matters in my line of work."

"I'm Carol Bennett," she introduced herself. "My daughter graduated from Greater Pines years ago. Now I volunteer because Meghan's too good at what she does to walk away from."

Aaron glanced toward Meghan, who was demonstrating a technique at the red station. "She seems to have a gift."

Carol's gaze turned thoughtful. "More than she knows. Her mother and I were best friends. After her mother died, Meghan poured herself into creating safe spaces for people to heal. This program feeds souls as much as bodies."

The insight reflected what Aaron had noticed in their few interactions. Meghan's teaching went beyond academics. She seemed to understand unspoken needs and address them with grace.

His thoughts were interrupted by a loud crash. A mixing bowl had slipped from Naomi's hands, shattering against the tile floor. Silence fell across the room as all eyes turned toward the disruption.

Aaron tensed, anticipating the withdrawn hostility that typically followed Naomi's mistakes. His niece stood frozen, horror across her features as she stared at the ceramic shards and spilled batter around her feet.

Before Aaron could move, Meghan was already there.

"Perfect timing, Naomi," she said as if the accident had been planned. "I was about to demonstrate what to do when you have a kitchen mishap."

Confusion replaced horror on Naomi's face. "But I broke—"

"A bowl," Meghan finished. "Which gives us all a chance to learn. The first rule of cooking is that accidents happen to everyone." She addressed the entire room. "Hands up if you've never dropped or broken something in the kitchen?"

Not a single hand raised.

"Exactly," Meghan continued, retrieving a broom and dustpan from a closet. "The second rule is that safety always comes first. We clean up to prevent injuries, then continue cooking. Ceramic shards require special care, so never use your hands. Always sweep thoroughly, then wipe with a damp paper towel to catch tiny fragments."

As she demonstrated the proper cleanup method, Meghan kept speaking in that same matter-of-fact tone. "When I was twelve, I dropped my father's favorite mixing bowl while trying to surprise him with birthday pancakes. I cried for an hour, convinced I had ruined everything. But he hugged me and said, *'Meggie-girl, things break. People don't.'*"

Naomi's shoulders relaxed as she helped clean up the mess. When Meghan handed her fresh ingredients to restart her mixture, determination replaced the look of defeat in his niece's expression.

The remainder of the session proceeded without incident. Aaron's group produced cornbread that emerged from the oven golden and fragrant. The rich, nutty scent transported him instantly to his mother's kitchen, where family gathered after church for meals that fed both body and spirit.

Daniel insisted that Aaron take home a portion wrapped in foil.

"First efforts deserve a celebration. My wife says sharing food builds stronger bridges than steel." He pressed the warm package into Aaron's hands.

As the session wrapped, Meghan handed recipe cards to everyone. "These are yours to keep and adapt. Make them part of your own story."

Aaron watched Naomi slide her card into her backpack like it mattered. She didn't look away when she caught him watching, as she might have days earlier.

"Ms. Townsend says we're doing desserts next week." Her voice carried an interest that made his heart swell. "We're supposed to make something with apples."

"That sounds good. We'll have fresh cornbread with dinner tonight to test our results."

As the crowd thinned, Aaron lingered. Meghan moved between stations, her presence drawing people toward her without demanding attention.

When most others had departed, he walked to where she organized materials for storage.

"Thanks for the way you handled the broken bowl."

Meghan looked up, those expressive eyes meeting his. "It was nothing. Everyone deserves grace when things fall apart."

The double meaning wasn't lost on him. "Not everyone offers it so freely."

"My dad was a master at turning mishaps into teaching moments." A shadow of old grief passed across her features, quickly replaced by humor. "Although I think I staged some accidents on purpose to prove the point."

Aaron smiled. "Smart kid."

"Sometimes I still reach for the phone to call my parents when something big happens. All these years later, that reflex hasn't gone away."

The confession surprised him. This confident, composed woman was allowing him a glimpse of her vulnerability. "Does it get easier? The missing them part?"

"Different, but not easier," Meghan replied. "It gets less raw with time. The edges soften, but the space they occupied never fills." She met his gaze. "But God sends people for that part of the journey. When they come, we have to be open to letting them in."

The mention of God created a momentary hitch in Aaron. Once, faith had been the cornerstone of his life. When had he stopped building on that foundation?

"Thank you for inviting us," he said, sidestepping the spiritual reference. He glanced toward Naomi, who was gathering her belongings. "I think it's what she needs. What we both need."

Meghan's smile returned, creating those distinctive dimples. "Same time next Thursday?"

"We'll be here."

The drive home unfolded in comfortable silence. Aaron sensed a shift in their dynamic. Nothing dramatic, but a softening of the rigid boundaries Naomi had maintained since his mother's passing.

After dinner, which featured the cornbread with honey butter, Aaron cleaned the kitchen while Naomi disappeared into her room. Later, passing her door on his way to the laundry closet, he glimpsed something that stopped him.

Naomi sat cross-legged on her bed, a notebook open before her. With care, she copied the recipe card from Meghan's class, adding small notations in the margins. Beside her lay the journal he had accidentally seen that day in the park. The one filled with dark thoughts. But instead of writing bleak reflections, she was transcribing cooking instructions.

Aaron continued down the hallway, not wanting to intrude. His chest tightened with gratitude, hope, and the first tentative stirrings of joy breaking through grief's hard soil.

Much later, as he lay in bed, he thought back to the afternoon. Meghan's joy when she saw them in the doorway. The way she had turned Naomi's mistake into a learning opportunity. Her honest words about loss.

Things break. People don't.

The phrase echoed in his thoughts, carrying wisdom his mother would have appreciated. He wondered what she would think of Meghan Townsend. His mother always valued authenticity above all else. He was sure she would have approved of Meghan's unpretentious strength.

Aaron closed his eyes, and for the first time in months, anticipation stirred within him. Thursday couldn't come soon enough.

Chapter 8

MEGHAN SECURED THE FINAL image to her classroom wall, a vibrant reproduction of *Song of the Towers* by Aaron Douglas. The painting depicted a Black man holding a saxophone, silhouetted against swirling bursts that suggested sound waves and the promise of a new dawn. Early morning sunlight streamed through the windows, illuminating the timeline she built to bring 1920s Harlem to life.

She stepped back, examining her work. The classroom walls now featured a visual timeline of the Harlem Renaissance with photographs of prominent writers engaged in animated conversation at a café, sheet music from Duke Ellington's compositions, and poetry excerpts written in elegant calligraphy on parchment-colored paper.

"If I can help them see it, then they'll understand why it matters," she murmured, adjusting a framed reproduction of *The Creation* by James Weldon Johnson.

The sound of shoes clicking down the hall interrupted her thoughts. Stanley Michaels appeared in her doorway, his tall frame filling the space with a commanding presence. The football coach's dark hair had begun to gray at the temples, giving him a distinguished appearance that belied his playful nature.

"Morning, Meghan." A manila folder was tucked under one arm. "Turning your classroom into a museum again, I see."

She smiled, stepping down from her stepladder. "History should be experienced, not memorized from a textbook. What brings you out before the first bell? Don't you have strategies to plan and players to intimidate?"

Stanley's expression brightened with boyish enthusiasm. "I come bearing news from the teachers' lounge. Daniel's floating around like he won the lottery."

"Good news, I hope?"

"Sam's pregnant." Stanley's grin widened. "He announced it this morning. She's due in late spring or early summer."

"That's wonderful!" Joy bloomed in Meghan as genuine happiness for her friends washed through her. "They've wanted this for so long."

"You should've seen him. He's half terrified, half thrilled. He showed everyone the ultrasound picture at least three times." Stanley chuckled, leaning against the doorframe. "I thought you'd want to know before the rumor mill gets to it."

Meghan laughed, but beneath the happiness, a familiar ache stirred. Not pain, exactly, but the hollow echo of longing. She was thirty-seven years old. The life she once envisioned of marriage, children, and a home filled with laughter seemed to drift further away each year.

"I'll call Sam tonight to congratulate her." She focused on her friends' blessings rather than her own unfulfilled dreams.

Stanley glanced at his watch. "I'd better head back. First period starts in twenty minutes."

After he left, Meghan allowed herself a moment to acknowledge the complexity of her emotions. Gratitude and grief rarely traveled alone. She had made peace with God's timing, but mornings like this reminded her that peace didn't always mean the absence of yearning.

She smoothed her dress and gathered her materials. Her students would arrive soon, and the Harlem Renaissance wouldn't teach itself.

By the third period, Meghan found her rhythm, and the morning's news settled into proper perspective. She stood at the front of her ninth-grade history class, voice animated as she described the Great Migration and how it laid the foundation for the Harlem Renaissance.

"Picture leaving everything familiar behind." She moved between rows of desks, her hands gesturing to emphasize her points. "Hundreds of thousands of African Americans journeyed north, packing hope into suitcases and determination in their hearts. What they found wasn't perfect. Discrimination and segregation existed in New York, too. But something powerful emerged from their struggle... a cultural rebirth of talent, ambition, and shared experience."

She scanned the room. Most students followed along, some more engaged than others. But one stood out. Naomi, who was usually distant, was bent over her notebook with her pencil moving steadily.

Meghan continued without drawing attention to the girl's participation.

"The Harlem Renaissance wasn't art for art's sake. These creators understood that culture shapes perception, and perception influences reality. They reclaimed the narrative of Black life in America through poetry, music, visual arts, and literature."

As she clicked through slides of jazz clubs and art salons, Meghan walked the rows, glancing down at her students' notes. What she saw at Naomi's desk made her pause. There were names, dates, and quotes written with care, and small sketches tucked between lines of text. This wasn't busywork. This was a student connecting with the material.

When the bell rang, she approached Naomi's desk as students gathered their belongings.

"I noticed you took detailed notes today." She kept her tone conversational rather than making a spectacle of this progress. "The sketches help the concepts stick, don't they?"

Naomi looked up, surprise crossing her features before her usual guardedness returned. "The paintings were... interesting." She hesitated before speaking again. "My grandma had a book about Jacob Lawrence. She showed me his *Migration Series* once."

The disclosure, another small milestone, sent hope through Meghan. "Lawrence's work is extraordinary. I have several books about him if you'd ever like to borrow one."

Naomi nodded, not quite making eye contact, but not immediately withdrawing either.

"Maybe. Thanks."

She gathered her backpack and headed toward the door, pausing at the display of Harlem Renaissance photographs before continuing into the hallway.

Meghan watched her go, satisfaction warming her chest. Aaron's participation in the cooking class was making a difference. Small steps, but in the right direction.

The day passed in a steady rhythm of lectures and lesson preparation. After the final bell, Meghan met Audrey Sinclair in the workroom to finalize plans for next week's cooking class collaboration.

Audrey radiated energy. Her black curls were streaked with electric blue, and her silver bangles chimed as she spread watercolor sketches of desserts across the table.

"Food presentation is an art form," she declared, pointing to a detailed drawing of an elaborately plated dessert. "Students need to understand that visual appeal affects taste perception. It's a psychological fact."

Meghan nodded, examining the beautiful sketches. "These are gorgeous, Audrey. Could we incorporate this into next week's apple dessert session?"

"Perfect! We should have stations where students rotate through preparation, baking, and presentation." Audrey's enthusiasm was infectious. "We could work on simple techniques like fan-slicing apples and creating caramel drizzle patterns. We'll make it social media worthy."

As they refined their plan, Meghan mentioned Naomi's participation in both her history class and the cooking program.

"I've noticed changes in her during art class, too." Audrey rearranged papers with paint-stained fingers. "The first two weeks, she barely touched her brushes. But this week, she painted a watercolor landscape with raised beds that had real emotion and depth. Her technical skills need work, but the feeling was there."

Meghan nodded. "Her uncle mentioned they're starting a container garden on their apartment balcony. I think having something to nurture is helping her."

"Speaking of the uncle..." Audrey's expression shifted to impish curiosity. "Daniel mentioned he joined your cooking class. Isn't he tall, strong, and the serious type?"

Heat rose to Meghan's cheeks. "His name is Aaron Grant, and he's doing his best to connect with Naomi while managing his construction business."

"Mmm-hmm." Audrey's knowing smile suggested she caught more than Meghan intended to reveal. "Must be tough, becoming an instant parent through such tragic circumstances."

Meghan was grateful for the redirection. "It is. He's learning to balance when to be the authority figure and when to listen. I think their relationship is improving."

"And your cooking program gives them neutral territory for that relationship to develop. Smart approach." Audrey's artistic perception extended beyond canvases.

"It works for several families." Meghan deliberately focused on educational outcomes rather than her personal interest in one particular guardian. "There's something about creating food together that breaks down barriers."

They gathered their materials as the afternoon slipped toward early evening. Outside, the sun dipped low, casting amber streaks across the campus.

"Daniel mentioned he saw Aaron and Naomi at New Hope Baptist last Sunday," Audrey remarked as they walked toward the parking lot.

Meghan stopped short. "Really?"

"I thought you'd want to know," Audrey replied with a meaningful glance. "Given your... professional involvement."

Meghan caught the pause but chose not to address it. Instead, she bid Audrey goodbye with promises to finalize their collaborative materials via email.

As she drove home, Aaron lingered in her thoughts. Church attendance was positive for both him and Naomi, regardless of what it might mean for anything else developing between them. She prayed that whatever had brought them through those church doors would take root and grow.

Chapter 9

Driving home, Meghan couldn't stop thinking about what Audrey had said about Aaron and Naomi being at New Hope last Sunday. The news stirred an unexpected warmth she hadn't anticipated.

Evening drifted over her modest home as she prepared a simple dinner of grilled chicken with vegetables. The quiet that once soothed her now carried an unexpected emptiness. News of Samantha's pregnancy, paired with watching families interact during Thursday's cooking session, awakened an uncomfortable awareness of her solitary status.

After dinner, she reached for her phone and scrolled to a familiar contact. Carol Bennett had been her mother's closest friend, stepping into a guardian role after her mother passed away. Though not related by blood, Carol had become the closest thing Meghan had to a connection with both parents she had lost too soon.

Carol answered on the third ring. "Meghan, sweetheart! I was thinking about you today."

Meghan smiled, settling into her favorite chair. "Must be good timing. How are you feeling? Is the new medication helping your arthritis?"

"I'm much better this week. I even managed some gardening yesterday." Carol's voice carried that gentle resilience that sustained Meghan through her darkest days. "But I doubt you're calling to discuss my joints. What's on your heart, child?"

The question opened floodgates Meghan hadn't realized needed releasing. She shared Daniel and Samantha's news, her observations of Naomi's progress, and the unexpected information about Aaron's church attendance.

Carol listened without interruption, their decades of relationship allowing Meghan to speak freely without fear of judgment.

"I'm genuinely happy for Daniel and Sam." Meghan struggled to articulate her conflicted emotions. "They deserve this blessing. But it reminds me that at thirty-seven, my own dreams seem..." She trailed off.

"Further away?" Carol supplied gently. "And I'm sure this construction worker with his niece has stirred something in you. Something beyond your usual concern for a struggling student."

"I've only known them a few weeks." Meghan's protest sounded weak even to herself. "Besides, I'm Naomi's teacher. Boundaries exist for good reasons."

"Mmm-hmm." Carol's skepticism traveled clearly through the phone. "Is that why you've mentioned him in our last three conversations?"

Heat rose to Meghan's cheeks despite being alone in her living room. "I mentioned him because he's relevant to explaining Naomi's progress."

"Of course." Carol's knowing patience was evident. "Just as relevant as his eye color, which you also felt compelled to share last Sunday."

"Carol!"

Soft laughter drifted through the connection. "Meghan Elise, you forget who helped raise you. I recognize the signs."

Meghan surrendered to her surrogate mother's perception. "Even if there were... interest, the timing and circumstances are completely wrong. I'm Naomi's teacher, and Aaron's her guardian."

"True," Carol acknowledged. "I'm not suggesting you abandon professional ethics. But I'm reminding you that God doesn't always work on our timelines or follow our scripts. Remember how your mother pined after your father? They worked in the same department for two years before he finally asked her to coffee."

"That was different."

"Was it? Honey, there's rarely a perfect moment for the heart to recognize something real." Carol's voice softened. "What matters is what you do when it happens."

Meghan sighed. "I'm not even sure what's happening here. I want to be wise about this."

"Then stay prayerful," Carol advised. "Let God unfold it in His time. Meanwhile, don't slam the door on something He might be opening."

They talked for another hour, moving to lighter topics of Bible study highlights, neighborhood news, and a hilarious story about a bake-sale fiasco involving salt mistakenly labeled as sugar. When they said goodnight, a gentle ease settled over Meghan. Not because she found answers, but because she remembered where to carry her questions.

Later, after her evening devotional, she prepared for bed. While tidying the kitchen, she spotted Aaron's business card near the fruit bowl. He gave it to her after the cooking class in case anything came up with Naomi's schedule.

She picked it up, studying the simple text: *Aaron Grant, Construction Foreman, Donovan Building Contractors.*

Meghan traced the card's edge with her thumb. For a moment, she was tempted to call. What would she even say? *I heard you went to church...?*

She shook her head, set the card down, and walked to her bedroom. From the nightstand, she retrieved her leather-bound prayer journal. Opening to a fresh page, she wrote the date at the top, then began her nightly reflection.

Lord, help me celebrate others' blessings while continuing to trust in You. If my connection with the Grants is purely professional, give me clarity. But if there's something deeper unfolding, show me Your will, not mine. I'm listening.

After listing other prayer concerns, Meghan closed the journal and placed it beside her Bible. She turned off the lamp, casting her bedroom into darkness softened only by moonlight filtering through sheer curtains.

Your will, not mine.

As she settled into sleep, Meghan couldn't know that across town, Aaron stood on his apartment balcony among newly planted herb containers, his own thoughts drawn to the history teacher who had somehow begun breaking through the emotional barriers around his heart.

Neither could foresee that their individual evening reflections were part of larger intertwining paths on an unexpected journey, guided by the same loving hand that carried each of them through loss, and was now nurturing seeds of connection between them.

Seeds that, with proper care and divine timing, might bloom into something beautiful neither dared to imagine.

Chapter 10

MORNING SUN BEAT DOWN on the community center construction site, casting harsh shadows across exposed beams and half-finished walls. Aaron adjusted his hard hat, sweat already trickling down his temples. He knelt to check the cured foundation. It was solid, clean, level, and ready in preparation for the next stage.

"Looking good, boss," Darius called, clipboard tucked under one arm as he approached. His skin glistened with perspiration under the Georgia heat. "Inspector signed off on the electrical. We're cleared for the next phase."

Aaron allowed himself a moment of satisfaction. "Right on schedule."

His phone buzzed. He pulled it out, expecting a supplier update. But the screen displayed *Greater Pines High School.* His stomach dropped.

"Hello, Mr. Grant? This is Principal Watkins."

"Yes, sir, what can I do for you?" Aaron straightened, turning away from the construction noise.

"There's been an incident with Naomi. She was involved in an altercation with another student. I need you to come to the school as soon as possible."

Aaron gripped his phone tighter. "Is she hurt?"

"Physically, she's fine. But we need to talk through what happened."

"I'm on my way."

He ended the call, his mind racing through possibilities. Things had been looking up. Naomi was participating in class, and the cooking program had sparked her interest. But now this.

"Everything okay?" Darius asked, noting Aaron's expression.

"That was the principal. There was an issue at school involving Naomi. I need to go."

Darius clapped him on the shoulder. "We've got this covered. Family comes first."

Twenty minutes later, Aaron strode through the entrance of the high school, dust still clinging to his work boots. The hallways stood empty, classes in session behind closed doors. His footsteps echoed against polished floors as he made his way to the administrative wing.

Rounding the corner, he spotted Naomi seated on a bench outside Principal Watkins' office. Her shoulders were hunched, her gaze fixed on the floor. Beside her sat Meghan, speaking in low tones. Seeing them together filled him with relief and gratitude, though he couldn't quite understand why Meghan's presence mattered so much to him.

"Naomi," he called, quickening his pace.

Both looked up at his approach. Naomi's face flashed surprise, then shame, before settling into careful blankness. Meghan rose as he drew closer.

"Thanks for coming so quickly."

"What happened?" Aaron directed the question to both of them.

Before either could answer, Principal Watkins opened the office door. "Mr. Grant, thanks for coming. Please, let's talk inside. Ms. Townsend, would you stay with Naomi for a few more minutes?"

Aaron hesitated, glancing at his niece, who refused to meet his gaze.

"It's okay," Meghan assured him, those distinctive dimples appearing with her reassuring smile. "We'll be right here."

Inside the office, Principal Watkins gestured to a chair. "During lunch, there was a physical altercation between Naomi and another student, Vanessa Miller. A teacher intervened before things escalated."

Aaron's stomach clenched. "A physical altercation? That doesn't sound like Naomi."

"I agree, which is why I wanted to understand the full context before making any disciplinary decisions." Principal Watkins adjusted his silver-rimmed glasses. "Several witnesses, including Ms. Townsend, reported that Vanessa was bullying another student.

She was making fun of her clothes, her weight, and her family situation. When the girl began crying, Naomi stepped in."

Aaron tried to picture his reserved niece stepping into a confrontation.

"According to accounts, Vanessa then turned to Naomi, making comments about..." Principal Watkins paused, seeming to choose his words carefully. "About her family loss and living situation. Naomi pushed Vanessa away from the other girl. Vanessa stumbled backward into a lunch table."

"She was defending someone," Aaron stated, relief mixing with unexpected pride.

"Yes, which is why I'm inclined toward leniency. However, physical contact, regardless of motivation, requires a response. I'm assigning both girls to attend after-school conflict resolution sessions next week."

Aaron nodded. "I understand. I'll make sure she's there."

When they returned to the hallway, Aaron found Meghan and Naomi in conversation. His niece looked up as they approached, uncertainty in her expression.

"Naomi," Principal Watkins said. "I've explained the situation to your uncle. You'll attend conflict resolution sessions next Tuesday and Wednesday after school. Until then, you're free to return to classes."

Naomi nodded, eyes flicking to Aaron and then away.

"Go ahead," he said. "We'll talk more at home."

As Naomi disappeared down the hallway toward her next class, Aaron turned to Meghan and Principal Watkins. "Thank you both for handling this with care."

"Ms. Townsend deserves the credit," Principal Watkins noted. "She witnessed the situation and intervened before it got worse."

Meghan shook her head. "Naomi showed remarkable character. Many students would have walked away when they saw someone being bullied."

Principal Watkins excused himself to attend to other matters, leaving Aaron and Meghan standing in the quiet hallway.

"What really happened?" Aaron asked once they were alone.

Meghan sighed, tucking a loose strand of hair behind her ear. The gesture drew his attention to the graceful curve of her neck, a momentary distraction he hadn't foreseen.

"Vanessa Miller has a reputation for targeting vulnerable students," she explained. "Today, it was a student named Lisbeth Rhodes, whose family lost their apartment in a fire. They're living in a shelter during the rebuilding." She paused. "Naomi must have seen something in Lisbeth's situation. When Vanessa started mocking Lisbeth about wearing the same clothes multiple days in a row, Naomi stepped between them."

"And then Vanessa turned on her."

Meghan nodded. "She said Naomi was another charity case whose family didn't want her. That's when Naomi pushed her."

Aaron winced, understanding how those words would cut into Naomi's existing wounds. The cruel remark had sliced through his niece's defenses, hitting the raw fear her discovered in her journal.

Nobody stays anyway.

"For what it's worth, I think Naomi showed tremendous growth. Six weeks ago, she barely spoke to anyone, and today she stood up for someone else who needed help." Meghan's warm brown eyes held his with unexpected directness.

She was right. Despite the circumstances, Naomi had shown empathy for another child facing loss, suggesting emotional progress he hadn't dared hope for.

"I appreciate you being here and supporting Naomi." He glanced at his watch. "I should get back to work. The construction crew is waiting for me."

"Of course. I need to return to my classroom as well. My planning period ends in ten minutes."

They walked together toward the main hallway. At the corridor intersection where their paths would diverge, Aaron was reluctant to end their interaction.

"Ms. Townsend... Meghan," he corrected himself, appreciating her slight smile at the informality. "I appreciate everything you've done for Naomi. The cooking program, today's situation... you've gone above and beyond."

"It's my pleasure. Naomi's a remarkable young woman."

Aaron took a breath, his decision crystallizing. "I know this may be out of line, but I'd like to thank you properly. Let me take you out for dinner."

Meghan blinked, her expression shifting to surprise, followed by a flush that darkened her cheeks beneath her warm brown skin.

"I mean—" Aaron backpedaled, suddenly aware of potential misinterpretation. "As colleagues. I want to show my appreciation for everything you've done for Naomi."

Meghan tilted her head, her expression unreadable. "That would be nice," she said finally. "When were you thinking?"

Relief and unexpected excitement coursed through him. "How about tonight? If that's not too soon. The Village Eatery, about seven?"

"Tonight works." She adjusted the stack of papers in her arms. "I'll see you at seven."

Aaron watched her walk down the hallway toward her classroom, heart pounding harder than it should have. Only after she disappeared around the corner did he realize he hadn't clarified whether this was simply professional gratitude or something more personal.

Because truthfully, he wasn't entirely sure himself.

Chapter 11

The Village Eatery occupied a converted Victorian house near the center of town. Edison bulbs strung across its courtyard, casting warm light over wrought-iron tables. Inside, pressed tin ceilings and dark wood paneling created an atmosphere that was intimate and casual.

Aaron arrived early, choosing a corner table near the windows. He had gone home to shower and change, swapping work boots and construction dust, for dark jeans and a navy button-down shirt. It had been years since he shared a meal with anyone outside family or work, and never quite like this.

He reminded himself that this was dinner and a thank you. Nothing more.

"Aaron?"

He looked up to find Meghan standing beside the table, and his careful distinctions blurred. She had changed into a simple but elegant dress in deep emerald that complemented her complexion. Her natural curls framed her face, catching the ambient light.

"You look nice." Aaron stood to greet her and pulled out her chair.

"Thank you. You clean up pretty well yourself." She settled across from him, setting her small purse aside. "So, how did things go with Naomi when you got home?"

Her directness pleased him. "Better than I expected. She explained her side without the usual one-word answers. She knows she shouldn't have pushed Vanessa, but she doesn't regret standing up for Lisbeth."

"That's progress. She's learning to stand up for what's right, even when it's difficult."

Their conversation flowed through appetizers and entrées, touching on Naomi's adjustment, the cooking program, and life in a small town like Brookside. Meghan's eyes lit up when she discussed history and how preserving stories preserved dignity, especially for communities too often erased or sanitized in textbooks.

"I'm sorry," she said, catching herself mid-explanation about the town's founding. "I tend to turn everything into a history lecture. It's an occupational hazard."

"Don't apologize. It's refreshing. Most people talk about their jobs like they're a burden. You talk like it's a calling."

Meghan smiled. "What about you? Have you always wanted to be in construction?"

Aaron considered the question as their server cleared their plates. "Not exactly. After high school, I started summer work with a construction company in Bristol Heights. It was temporary while I figured out college." He traced the rim of his water glass. "Then my father got sick. Construction paid the bills, so I stayed. By the time he recovered, I'd advanced to crew supervisor, and college seemed less practical."

"You never went back to school?"

Aaron shook his head. "Construction made sense to me. I knew when something was built right. When Frank Donovan approached me about opening the Brookside branch, it seemed like a good opportunity. I never expected my mother's illness would lead to relocating and becoming Naomi's guardian."

"Nothing prepares you for parenting a teenager."

He smiled ruefully. "That's the truth. With construction, I know when the foundation is solid. But with Naomi, I'm always guessing."

As the evening progressed, Aaron found himself sharing details he rarely discussed. He spoke about his estrangement from his brother Ryan after their father's illness, and his gradual drift from the church that once anchored his family.

"My mom never stopped attending, even after Dad recovered and quit going," he explained. "She tried keeping us connected, but work always seemed more important."

"And now?" Meghan asked.

Aaron met her gaze, surprised by his own honesty. "I told myself I'd eventually go back. My mom's faith sustained her through everything... her cancer treatments, my dad leaving... even her final illness. I want that for Naomi, but how can I guide her toward something I walked away from?"

"Maybe she doesn't need you to have all the answers. Maybe she just needs to know you're still searching," Meghan replied. "Faith journeys rarely follow straight lines. Sometimes the detours teach us more than the direct paths."

Her vulnerability encouraged him to ask more. "Have you always been steady in your faith?"

Meghan folded her napkin. "After my dad's accident, my faith was solid. It held me together. But when my mom died..." She paused. "I unraveled. I felt betrayed and angry... as if God had abandoned me."

"What changed?"

"Carol. She was my mom's best friend, and she let me rage and doubt without judgment." Meghan's voice softened. "She didn't try to fix me. She stayed close, prayed, and reminded me that God wasn't afraid of my anger. Then one day, I opened my dad's old journal. It had recipes, memories, and scriptures. Cooking his food brought him back to me."

Aaron paused. "So, the program isn't just about teaching people how to cook."

She shook her head. "No... it somehow became my ministry without my realizing it. It's become a way to honor my dad's memory and my mom's compassion for people who are hurting."

Aaron understood. His career plans had been shaped by guardianship, but he was discovering a new purpose in what once seemed like an obligation.

"I'm not where I used to be with faith," he said. "But I want Naomi to see something solid. And I want to believe there's more to life than grief and guilt."

"There is," Meghan said. "But it takes time. Grace is slow work."

Their conversation turned lighter as they shared dessert and laughed over the failed cornbread attempts during the cooking class. Aaron was drawn not only to her words, but to the way she listened, and how she left space for silence.

Later, as they stepped outside, the evening air carried the scent of approaching rain. Dark clouds obscured stars that had been visible earlier.

"I should have brought an umbrella," Meghan noted, glancing skyward.

"I'll walk you to your car before it starts," Aaron offered.

They crossed the courtyard just as the first heavy drops began falling, quickening their pace as the rain increased. When they reached Meghan's car, the light drizzle had become a steady rainfall.

They paused under a nearby awning. Water droplets clung to Meghan's dark curls, catching light from streetlamps. One drop traced a path down her temple.

Without thinking, Aaron reached toward her face, instinct pulling his hand forward to brush away the raindrop. He caught himself at the last moment, fingers hovering inches from her skin.

Meghan remained motionless. Their eyes met. Rain created a curtain separating them from the world beyond.

He opened his mouth to speak, but his phone rang. The was moment shattered.

Frank Donovan flashed on the screen.

"I'm sorry, I should take this. It's my boss," Aaron explained, frustration battling with duty.

Meghan gave an understanding smile. "Of course. Thank you for dinner."

"Meghan—" But she had already unlocked her car, slipping inside with a final wave before pulling away.

Aaron answered the call, stepping further under the awning as the rain continued.

"Aaron! Glad I caught you." Frank's booming voice carried through the speaker. "We just secured the Bristol Heights municipal complex project. It's a thirty-million-dollar contract!"

"Congratulations," Aaron replied automatically, watching Meghan's taillights disappear.

"The board wants you to head up the project. It will be six months, minimum, on-site in Bristol Heights, starting next month."

The words registered slowly. Bristol Heights, his hometown, and the place where his mother had lived and died. The location he had deliberately left behind.

"Aaron? You still there?"

"Yes. That's... big news."

"Big? It's career-making! This puts you on the regional management track. You could have your own division within three years."

Frank's enthusiasm contrasted sharply with Aaron's uncertainty. "I need your confirmation by Monday. We'll discuss details then."

The call ended with Aaron standing in the rain. This professional opportunity clashed with his new family's personal growth. Six months in Bristol Heights meant Naomi would have to relocate again, abandoning Brookside just as she was building connections. It meant leaving the cooking program and stepping away from the community that had begun welcoming them.

It would mean leaving Meghan Townsend, whose conversation and compassion stirred something he had thought was long dead.

Rain soaked his shirt as he stared at the empty road where her car had vanished. The evening had changed his perspective in ways he couldn't express, revealing choices he hadn't considered when he issued that simple dinner invitation.

Now Frank's offer demanded a decision that would shape the next phase of his life. But for once, he wouldn't rush it. Some choices couldn't be measured like foundations or drawn like blueprints.

As Aaron jogged toward his truck, one question weighed heavier than any construction plans he had ever carried: *What path was he meant to follow?*

Chapter 12

Meghan adjusted a stack of veterinary journals on the coffee table in Olivia's cottage. She stepped back, squinting at the setup, trying to strike the right balance between tidy and lived-in, the sweet spot adoption agencies always looked for.

"It looks too perfect and too staged." Meghan deliberately misaligned one book. "Remember what the adoption preparation guide said. They want to see a real home, not a showroom."

Olivia walked in from the kitchen carrying two mugs of tea, her ponytail frizzy from humidity and nerves. She offered one to Meghan with a sheepish look.

"I've scrubbed the bathroom three times this morning," she confessed, passing a mug to Meghan. "There's that water stain on the ceiling. Should I point out that the leak's been fixed, or—"

"Breathe, Olivia." Meghan's voice was gentle but firm. "This place has been a refuge for healing. Remember how you set up the guest room for Sam while she was recovering after her apartment building caught fire? You had everything she needed to get well, and you made it feel like home."

Olivia's shoulders eased. "That was different. Sam needed medical care, and I knew how to handle that."

"And a child needs love, stability, and someone who won't give up on them. You've got all of that." Meghan gestured toward the photographs on the mantel, including one of Olivia and Samantha taken before Samantha's wedding to Daniel. "You've created safe spaces your whole life. It's why Sam recovered so well here. It's why every stray animal at the clinic calms down the second they see you. And it's why I show up on your doorstep whenever I need some sense knocked into me."

"Or when you're trying to avoid talking about a certain construction foreman," Olivia countered with a knowing smile. The reminder of her natural caregiving abilities had relaxed her. She sank onto the sofa, hands steadier around her mug. "I suppose I've had some practice at the nurturing thing."

"Not practice. It's who you are." Meghan sat beside her friend, their shoulders touching. "That's what the agency saw in your application, and what the social worker will see tomorrow. The same compassion that kept you at Sam's bedside is what will make you an amazing mom."

Olivia nodded, soaking in the reassurance. For years, she prayed about adoption, researched agencies, attended seminars, and saved every penny. Her home had proven itself a haven of healing during Samantha's months of recovery. It stood as a testament to her nurturing spirit that extended beyond her professional veterinary skills.

"Sometimes I wonder if I'm crazy for doing this on my own," Olivia whispered. "Most women wait for marriage before considering children."

"And some follow the path God puts in front of them, even if it's not what everyone expects." Meghan squeezed her friend's hand, feeling the tremor beneath her fingers.

"You know exactly what I need to hear," Olivia said, tension melting from her shoulders. She took a sip of tea and gave Meghan a sidelong glance, mischief back in her eyes. "Speaking of paths that don't look traditional, are we going to talk about your dinner date with the handsome construction guy?"

Warmth rose to Meghan's cheeks. She could picture the way Aaron looked at her across the candlelit table when he spoke about his mother's faith, and the glint of rain in his lashes when they stood beneath the awning. Her chest tightened at the memory.

"There's not much to say." Meghan hoped her tone sounded convincing. "It wasn't a date. It was a thank-you dinner for helping with Naomi, that's all."

"Mmm-hmm." Olivia's skeptical tone matched her raised eyebrow. "That explains why you've mentioned his name seventeen times since you got here."

"I have not," Meghan protested.

"Fifteen in the first hour, and two more while you were organizing my bookshelf." Olivia's expression grew serious, the teasing giving way to genuine concern. "Be careful, Meghan. You've been down this road before."

Meghan got up and walked over to the mantel, adjusting a few family photos. The frames felt cool beneath her fingertips, solid reminders of permanence in contrast to the unsettled emotions swirling within her. "I know. But Aaron isn't Finn."

"No, but there are similarities," Olivia replied softly. "Both of them carry a lot emotionally. And neither one shares your faith the way you need."

That landed like a quiet punch to the gut. Meghan had poured years into her relationship with Finn Lockwood, believing their relationship would lead to marriage. She even accepted that his polite tolerance of her faith would never transform into a genuine spiritual partnership.

"Aaron's situation is different." She adjusted a silver frame with more care than necessary. "He has a faith background. He's just struggling right now."

"And you think you're meant to help bring him back?" Olivia's gentle question held no judgment, only concern. "You remember what they taught us in bible study? You can't missionary-date someone into the kingdom."

Meghan turned, arms crossed. Rationally, she knew Olivia was right. But that didn't stop her from remembering the look in Aaron's eyes when he spoke about wanting to guide Naomi, even while battling with his own uncertainties. That moment had held a depth she couldn't dismiss.

"We're not dating," she insisted, though the words sounded flimsy even to her own ears. "He's Naomi's guardian, and I'm her teacher. What we're doing is creating a support system for a traumatized teenager."

"A support system that includes intimate dinners where you talk about scripture and faith?" Olivia's voice was gentle but unyielding.

Meghan sighed, returning to the sofa. "He told me he's been struggling with his faith since his mom died. But he wants to help Naomi find her own faith. That matters."

"It does. And I know your heart is in the right place. I don't want to see it broken again."

"I appreciate that." Meghan acknowledged her friend's wisdom while an inner voice whispered that some risks were worth taking. She thought of Samantha's pregnancy announcement and that flicker of longing she felt. She was thirty-seven. Some dreams required courage, more than caution.

"I'm being careful," she promised, though her words held more hope than certainty. "I know where the boundaries are."

"Good." Olivia gave her hand a gentle squeeze. "Now help me decide if fresh flowers in the bathroom would seem too calculated or—"

The doorbell rang, cutting through their conversation. Olivia froze, tea mug halfway to her lips.

"Are you expecting someone?" Meghan asked.

"No." Olivia set down her mug and headed toward the door, smoothing her hair. "Maybe it's the social worker wanting to do a surprise check? Oh no, what if she sees I've been stress-cleaning?"

Meghan followed, watching as Olivia peered through the peephole. Her friend's entire posture changed.

"It's Mrs. Davis," Olivia whispered, unlocking the door. "She brings her elderly cocker spaniel to the clinic."

An older woman with silver hair stood on the porch, holding a small gift bag. "Hello, dear. I hope I'm not interrupting."

"Not at all, Mrs. Davis. Please, come in." Olivia stepped aside, gesturing her inside. "This is my friend Meghan Townsend."

"Nice to meet you, dear." Mrs. Davis smiled warmly, then turned to Olivia. "I hope you don't mind me stopping by unannounced. I heard from Dr. Lewis that you're going through the adoption process."

Olivia's cheeks flushed. "Yes, I am. My final home study is coming up soon."

"That's wonderful news. And it's also the reason I'm here." Mrs. Davis's eyes twinkled. "You see, my daughter works for the state adoption services. She mentioned they're always looking for character references from people who've witnessed prospective parents in action."

Olivia blinked. "I'm sorry, I don't understand."

"Honey, do you remember when Tucker needed that emergency surgery last spring? When I couldn't afford the full payment upfront?" Mrs. Davis's voice grew tender. "You not only set up a payment plan, but you organized that donation jar in the waiting room. You sat with me while Tucker was in surgery, brought me tea, and called me every day during his recovery."

Olivia's eyes began to fill. "Mrs. Davis, that was nothing special—"

"It was everything to me and Tucker. You showed more kindness to a lonely old woman and her dog than I've experienced in years." She reached into her purse and pulled out an envelope. "I've already written a character reference for you. All you need to do is give them my contact information."

Olivia stared at the envelope, tears spilling over. "Mrs. Davis, I... I don't know what to say."

"Say you'll accept help when it's offered. And say you'll let that baby know they've got a whole community rooting for them... starting with one grateful woman whose dog is alive because of your compassion."

As Olivia opened the envelope and read the letter, more tears flowed. "This is beautiful. Thank you."

Mrs. Davis patted Olivia's shoulder. "Sometimes God uses the most ordinary moments to show us who someone really is. I'm honored to be part of your journey."

After Mrs. Davis left, Olivia sank onto her sofa, clutching the letter. "I completely forgot about the donation jar."

"That's exactly what makes you perfect for this," Meghan said. "You don't even realize how extraordinary your kindness is."

Olivia wiped her eyes, then looked at Meghan with renewed determination. "You know what? You're right about taking risks when the timing is right. And about having courage."

"What do you mean?"

"I mean, maybe we're both standing at the edge of something new. Maybe it's time to stop being so afraid of what could go wrong, and start believing in what could go right."

Chapter 13

THE HOME ECONOMICS CLASSROOM buzzed with activity as students and volunteers clustered around the cooking stations. Steam curled from bubbling pots, and the warm scents of sautéed onions, melted butter, and rising bread transformed the sterile room into a place that felt like home.

Meghan moved from station to station, checking progress, offering guidance, and making sure no one was burning anything or anyone.

"Don't forget to write down the stories behind your recipes. The history matters as much as the ingredients."

Her gaze drifted repeatedly to the green station where Aaron stood with Naomi. His hands moved through the motions of measuring and stirring, but his attention was elsewhere. His jaw was tight, his brow furrowed. When Naomi asked a question, it took him a beat too long to respond.

Something had changed since their dinner last Friday. The ease they found over candlelight had been replaced with measured distance. Meghan first noticed it on Tuesday in the school parking lot. He greeted her politely, but stepped back, as if he had redrawn a boundary neither of them had discussed.

Approaching their station, Meghan adopted her teacher persona. "How's the cornbread coming along?"

Naomi looked up from her mixing bowl, pride lighting her expression. "I'm trying my grandma's trick. She used to warm the buttermilk before adding it to the dry ingredients."

Meghan was pleased by Naomi's participation. "That's a great technique. So much cooking wisdom gets passed down that way. It sounds like your grandmother knew what she was doing."

The scent of butter melting in their cast-iron skillet wrapped around them, comforting and familiar. Meghan glanced at Aaron, who had tuned back in. "You never mentioned that detail about the buttermilk before," he said.

"You never asked." Naomi's voice was casual, but not sharp. "Sometimes, she let me help cook on Sundays after church. She said I had the right touch for cornbread."

The mention of 'church' created a flicker across Aaron's face. His expression hinted at both nostalgia and regret. He caught Meghan watching him and straightened, clearing his throat.

"When you get a moment, I'd like to talk with you after class." His formal tone was businesslike. "It's about next week."

Despite the leap in her pulse, Meghan kept her professional mask firmly in place. "Of course. I'll be free after we clean up."

She moved on, but kept him in her peripheral vision. Across the room, Daniel was dramatically reenacting his grandmother's biscuit technique, insisting the dough could *"feel"* fear. Meghan corrected his rolling method while keeping half an eye on Aaron, whose attention had drifted back out the window. Naomi had noticed too. Her shoulders were stiffer, her smile fading as she worked beside him.

When presentations began, each group shared the backstory of their dishes. Aaron stepped forward with his niece.

"Naomi and I made cornbread using her grandmother's recipe." He rested a hand on her shoulder. "But before we serve it, I should mention that I'll be traveling for work next week."

The words dropped like a stone. Meghan saw the change in Naomi immediately. Her back slumped, and her face went blank. Hurt flashed through her eyes before she turned them to the floor.

"I'll be going to Bristol Heights to work on a municipal complex project," Aaron continued. "It's about two hours away. I'll be gone Monday through Friday, but I'll come back on the weekends."

An uncomfortable silence fell over the classroom. Students exchanged glances, sensing the tension, but uncertain how to respond. Daniel cleared his throat and looked down at his hands. Someone's chair creaked. The cheerful cooking atmosphere had suddenly shifted into something awkward and heavy.

Meghan kept her expression steady, though her heart sank. Naomi had been making real progress, but now, with one announcement, she was retreating.

"That's..." Naomi's voice cracked in the silence, every word audible to the entire class. "That's fine. Whatever."

A few students shifted uncomfortably. Lisbeth, who had been sitting near Naomi, shot a worried look toward Meghan.

Aaron's hand tightened on her shoulder. "Naomi—"

"Can we just finish this?" She turned back to their cornbread, her movements sharp and disconnected, pointedly ignoring the roomful of people watching.

Meghan quickly stepped in to redirect attention. "The cornbread looks wonderful. Who'd like to tell us about the next dish?"

The rest of the class passed by in a haze of stories, cleanup, and noise that pushed at her thoughts. Once most of the students had gone, Aaron approached the counter where Meghan was logging notes.

"Thanks for waiting," he said, hands buried in his pockets. Without the distraction of cooking, he looked unsure of where to put them.

"Of course. With your new tasking in Bristol Heights, I can imagine things will be a little hectic for you and Naomi." Meghan set her pen aside and gave him her full attention. "How can I help?"

Aaron glanced toward the door where Naomi had left with another student. "I've arranged for Naomi to stay with Darius Washington and his family during the week. He's a foreman from my site."

Meghan nodded, recalling the straightforward man with the warm smile who participated in last month's session with his wife.

"I think I know him. He and his wife Elena came to one of the early sessions. They have three daughters, right?"

"Yes, that's the family. They've been great about everything." Gratitude was woven through his tone. "Naomi isn't thrilled. She knows them, but not well. Darius's oldest daughter is around her age. The problem is that even with this setup, Naomi will have several hours alone after school before the family gets home."

Meghan understood his concern. "You're worried about her isolating herself."

Relief crossed his features at her quick comprehension. "Yes. She's doing better, but everything with her is still fragile. I mentioned you were taking the culinary club to the farmers market this Saturday."

"Yes. We're sourcing ingredients for next week's community meal project."

"Could Naomi join you? And maybe she could participate in some other activities while I'm gone?" His voice was careful, but the weight behind it wasn't. "I know it's a lot to ask. But she connects with you in ways she doesn't with other adults."

Meghan's heart tugged in two directions. She cared deeply about Naomi and wanted to help, but the lines between teacher and guardian were blurring. And it wasn't about Naomi anymore.

"The farmers' market trip would be fine," she said thoughtfully. "It's a school activity with multiple chaperones. As for other events..." She hesitated, weighing her response. "I need to be careful about the boundaries."

Uncertainty shadowed Aaron's gaze, and perhaps disappointment. But he nodded. "Right. I shouldn't have—"

"I didn't say no," Meghan clarified. "How about Naomi joining my Sunday morning volunteer group at Cottonwood Faith Community Center's food pantry? Several students participate, and we always welcome additional hands."

The tension in Aaron's shoulders eased. "That would be perfect. Thank you."

An awkward silence fell, heavy with unspoken undercurrents. Meghan busied herself organizing recipe cards while Aaron shifted his weight from one foot to the other.

"About last Friday—" he began, his voice lowering.

"It was a lovely dinner," Meghan interrupted, trying to stay ahead of her own heartbeat. "Thank you for inviting me."

"I enjoyed it too." His voice dropped further. "More than I expected to."

She looked down, pretending to organize her papers, willing herself not to read too much into the moment.

"Your Bristol Heights project." Meghan shifted the topic as she fought to keep her tone steady. "Isn't that your hometown?"

Aaron nodded, shadows crossing his features. "Yeah. It's where I grew up and where my mom lived until..."

The puzzle clicked into place. Now she could see the reason behind his distance and his mood. Going back would mean reopening a wound that hadn't healed.

"That can't be easy," she offered.

"It's complicated," he admitted. "I haven't been back since my mom died."

Her hands twitched with the urge to reach across the counter, but she kept them firm on the clipboard. "I'll make sure Naomi has the support she needs while you're gone."

"Thank you." Aaron stepped back, preparing to leave. "I should find Naomi. She's waiting in the library."

Once he left, Meghan sat on the nearest stool, letting her teacher's mask fall away.

Every interaction pulled her deeper into their lives. The dinner had crossed an invisible line, turning their relationship into something that was neither purely professional nor clearly defined. What was she doing?

Olivia's warning echoed in her mind: *Be careful.*

Gathering her belongings, Meghan locked the classroom and walked to her car. Evening shadows lengthened across the parking lot as she drove away from the school grounds, her thoughts circling.

The route home took her past Providence Park, its wrought-iron gates glowing in the fading light. On impulse, Meghan slowed near the entrance.

As she paused at a red light, movement across the street caught her attention. A man with silver hair strolled along the sidewalk, leaning on a polished wooden cane. Something about his manner arrested her attention. He maintained his measured pace and dignified posture despite his obvious age.

Meghan hesitated when the light turned green, watching the man pause near a park bench. Even from a distance, something in his posture suggested he was smiling. He lifted his free hand in a deliberate gesture of acknowledgment, though there was no way he could possibly see her through the car window in the deepening twilight.

A car horn sounded behind her. She drove through the intersection, immediately checking her rearview mirror to glimpse the man.

But the bench stood empty. The sidewalk was deserted in both directions. Where had he gone in those few seconds? Meghan slowed her car, craning her neck to search the surrounding area, but found no trace of him.

A sense of peace settled over her. The questions about boundaries and feelings hadn't been sorted out, but they felt less overwhelming now, as if it wasn't all hers to figure out.

As she drove the remaining distance home, she considered her role in Naomi's life, and her connection to Aaron. She wasn't sure if this was friendship, mentorship, something more, or none of the above.

Her father's words echoed: *Sometimes God sends messengers to remind us He hasn't forgotten our deepest prayers.*

At the time, she had thought it a comforting metaphor.

But now, with the image of the silver-haired man's serene presence still vivid in her mind, she wondered if her father's wisdom might hold a more literal truth than she ever thought possible.

Before she could pursue that thought further, her phone buzzed with a text from Naomi: *Thank you for letting me come with you on Saturday. I promise I won't be any trouble.*

Meghan pulled into her driveway and quickly typed back: *You're never trouble. Looking forward to it.*

The response came immediately: *Uncle Aaron says Bristol Heights is where he grew up. Do you think going back there is hard for him?*

Meghan stared at the message, touched by Naomi's perceptiveness despite her own hurt. Here was a fourteen-year-old worried about the very person who just announced he was leaving her for a week.

Meghan typed her reply: *Sometimes places hold a lot of memories. Some of them good, and some more difficult.*

Naomi's response came quickly: *Yeah. I get that.*

Three dots appeared, then disappeared, then appeared again. Finally, another message came through: *Sometimes I think adults try to protect us from stuff, but it just makes us worry more.*

Meghan smiled despite everything. Naomi was wise beyond her years. She typed back:

You're probably right about that.

Naomi: *See you Saturday, Ms. Townsend.*

Meghan: *See you Saturday, Naomi.*

As Meghan turned off her phone, she realized the mysterious stranger hadn't been the only messenger tonight. Sometimes wisdom came through the observations of a grieving teenager who understood more about loss and fear better than some adults were willing to admit.

Chapter 14

Aaron stood in his mother's kitchen, fingertips brushing the worn countertop. Morning light filtered through the faded yellow curtains, casting the same sunbeam patterns he used to trace with his fingers as a boy. Two days into the Bristol Heights municipal project, and he finally found the courage to return to the house where he grew up.

The renovation crew was due tomorrow. Once they started, it would stop being her home and become just another property to prepare for sale. He understood the logic, but logic didn't make this feel any less like a violation. Standing here, surrounded by echoes of his past, Aaron felt like a trespasser in his own memories.

He opened a cabinet. Spice jars were lined up like soldiers, each one neatly labeled in her handwriting. Cinnamon, nutmeg, and paprika. He reached for the cinnamon, twisted off the cap, and closed his eyes. The scent took him straight back to Sunday mornings, when she would stir coffee cake batter to the sound of gospel music playing softly on the radio.

"I'm sorry I wasn't here more," he whispered to the empty kitchen. The renovation blueprints spread across the table looked like intruders—lines and numbers trying to quantify a place that had been sacred.

His phone vibrated in his pocket. Frank Donovan's name flashed on the screen for the third time this morning. Aaron ignored it. Whatever construction emergency was happening could wait another hour.

He walked through the house slowly, letting the memories wash over him, room by room. There was the living room, where she insisted on handmade ornaments for the tree every Christmas. The tiny study, where she tracked bills in careful ledgers. And the back porch, where she taught him how to shell peas, her hands guiding his smaller ones.

Near her bedroom, Aaron hesitated before the closed door. This would be the hardest space to enter. It was where she spent her last days, slowly fading while he prayed for a miracle that never came. His hand trembled as he opened the door.

The room appeared surprisingly undisturbed. Although the hospice bed had been removed, the space still held her personal touches. An antique dresser displayed family photographs. A reading chair was angled to capture the morning light. And a delicate crocheted blanket was folded neatly at the foot of her bed.

Aaron sank onto the edge of the mattress, the weight of her presence pressing through every carefully chosen detail.

The nightstand drawer hung slightly ajar. Inside lay her Bible, its leather binding worn smooth from years of prayer and study, the pages marked with a rainbow of colored tabs. He lifted it carefully, as reverently as if handling a sacred artifact.

The Bible opened to a section marked with purple tabs, her designation for scriptures about faith during hard times. Several passages were highlighted in yellow, with handwritten notes in the margins.

His eyes fell on Isaiah 41:10: *So do not fear, for I am with you; do not be dismayed, for I am your God. I will strengthen you and help you; I will uphold you with my righteous right hand.*

Beside the verse, in his mother's neat script: *For Aaron, when the load feels too heavy.*

The date noted was three weeks before she died.

Aaron's vision blurred. She thought of him even then, marking scriptures to carry him after she was gone. Grief, guilt, and regret surged all at once. The grief he buried, guilt for not being there more, and regret that he hadn't asked for help when the weight became too much.

His phone vibrated again. This time, Naomi's name lit the screen. Aaron composed himself before answering.

"Hey, kiddo. How's everything going?"

"Fine." Just one word, flat as always. Their daily calls had grown shorter each day.

"How was school?" Aaron forced cheer into his voice.

"It was school." A pause. "We had a substitute in history. Ms. Townsend's at some sort of teacher's workshop."

Aaron felt a wave of sadness wash over him at the disappointment in her voice. Meghan's absence would undeniably affect Naomi, who had started to form a special bond with the kind-hearted teacher.

"Did you make it to the conflict resolution session yesterday?" Aaron asked, recalling Principal Watkins' disciplinary decision after the cafeteria incident.

"Yeah." Another pause. "It was whatever."

Aaron exhaled through his nose, rubbing his temple. The program was supposed to help students process emotions and deal with conflict, but Naomi clearly hadn't bought in.

"How are things with the Washingtons?" he asked.

"They're okay. Mrs. Washington makes her rice different from how Grandma did, but it's still good." This small observation represented more information than Naomi had volunteered all week. "Their youngest keeps trying to braid my hair."

Aaron smiled despite his heavy heart. "Is that a problem?"

"I guess not." Her tone mellowed somewhat. "We're going to the farmers' market with Ms. Townsend's group this weekend. She said we could pick out ingredients for a special recipe."

"That sounds great." The mention of Meghan prompted a complicated tangle of emotions. Gratitude for her continued support of Naomi mingled with an unexpected pinch of jealousy that she was collecting moments that he wasn't a part of.

"Yeah, it's kind of cool. Ms. Townsend knows all the vendors. She says we can learn where food really comes from, not just how to cook it." Enthusiasm brightened her voice in a way he hadn't heard during their previous calls. "She said farmers are like historians, keeping traditional growing methods alive."

"She's right about that." Aaron pictured Meghan guiding students through market stalls, her natural ability to transform ordinary experiences into meaningful lessons evident even in Naomi's brief description.

"Anyway, I should go. Mrs. Washington's taking us to get ice cream."

"Alright. Have fun. I'll call tomorrow, okay?"

"Okay. Bye, Uncle Aaron."

After the call ended, Aaron sat still, his mom's Bible resting in his lap. Naomi had opened up more to Meghan in five minutes than she had to him in a week. That stung.

Aaron placed the Bible in a box designated for the personal items he would keep rather than sell with the house. Selling the house still made sense on paper. But the thought of moving Naomi back to Bristol Heights, to a life he didn't even want anymore, weighed heavier now, despite the career boost Frank kept pushing.

His phone buzzed yet again. Frank's persistence said everything. This time, Aaron answered.

"Look, I understand this is tough," Frank said after hearing Aaron's refusal to extend his stay beyond the agreed-upon week. "But this project represents a turning point for your career. Managing it personally would put you in the position of regional director within three years."

"I appreciate the opportunity." Aaron walked into the kitchen where renovation plans awaited his final approval. "But my niece needs me home right now. I'll oversee remotely, and after this week, someone local will need to handle the on-site management."

Frank's exasperation crackled through the connection. "This is exactly what I warned you about when you took guardianship. Personal obligations have a way of limiting professional growth."

The comment lit a fire in Aaron's chest. "Those *personal obligations'* are a fourteen-year-old girl who's lost everyone she depended on. My mom would say her well-being isn't negotiable."

Silence stretched before Frank relented. "I get it, Aaron. I do. Just consider a compromise. Maybe you can do two weeks here instead of one, then alternate weeks until the foundation work is done."

"I'll think about it," Aaron conceded, knowing this was the best he could expect from his ambitious boss.

After reviewing the construction plans and taking notes for the team meeting tomorrow, Aaron locked up the house and drove toward downtown Bristol Heights. As he navigated the familiar streets, he felt a strange mix of nostalgia and discomfort. This place was both a reminder of home and a symbol of the pain he had been avoiding.

Hunger gnawed at his stomach, and on impulse, he pulled into the parking lot of The Country Kitchen, a local diner his family had frequented for years. The retro neon sign flickered with the same uneven rhythm he remembered from decades earlier. Some things in small towns remained stubbornly unchanged.

Inside, it smelled like strong coffee and warm pie. Aaron slid into a corner booth, oddly comforted by the vinyl seats patched with silver duct tape, another feature that had persisted through the years. He ordered without looking at the menu, knowing the day's special was meatloaf with mashed potatoes and green beans.

As he waited for his food, the bell above the entrance chimed. He glanced up, then froze at seeing a face he hadn't seen in nearly three years.

Ryan Grant stood in the doorway, his tall frame lean to the point of gauntness. Despite Ryan's ragged appearance, the brothers' resemblance was unmistakable. They had the same deep brown eyes, identical jawlines, and similar broad shoulders, though Ryan's now hunched slightly as if bearing an invisible weight.

Aaron tensed, uncertain whether to acknowledge his estranged brother or pretend he hadn't noticed him. The decision was made when Ryan's gaze swept the diner and locked with his. Surprise flashed across his brother's face, followed by hesitation, then resolve as he approached the booth.

"Aaron." Ryan's voice sounded rougher than he remembered, weary in a way that suggested more than physical exhaustion. "I heard you were in town working on the municipal complex project."

"News travels fast." Aaron nodded to the seat across from him.

Ryan slid into the booth, fidgeting with a napkin. "Small towns, you know how it is. Dad mentioned seeing you at the old house."

The reference to their father sent a jolt through Aaron. Martin Grant had left their mother during her first battle with cancer, eventually remarrying and starting a second family across town.

Contact had been minimal for years, limited to obligatory holiday cards and awkward encounters.

"I didn't realize Dad was keeping tabs on me." Aaron was unable to keep the bitterness from seeping into his tone.

"He's not." Ryan met his gaze for the first time. "I asked him to let me know if he saw you."

This admission hung as the waitress delivered Aaron's meal. Ryan ordered coffee, nothing more, confirming Aaron's suspicion that his brother's thin frame reflected more than natural metabolism.

"How's Naomi?" Ryan asked after the waitress left.

The question lit a fuse in Aaron's chest. "Why do you ask? You haven't checked on her in over three years."

Ryan's shoulders sagged. "I deserve that."

He cut into his meatloaf with unnecessary force. "She lost her grandmother, *our mother*, and you couldn't even show up for the funeral."

"I couldn't face it." Ryan stared into his coffee cup, shoulders slumping further. "Couldn't face her... or you... knowing I had disappeared when you all needed me."

"You checked out long before Mom got sick again."

Ryan's voice dropped so low that Aaron had to lean forward to hear him. "I know. The pills started after my back injury at the plant. By the time I realized I had a problem, I was too ashamed to ask for help."

Aaron examined his brother, noting details he initially missed. There was a slight tremor in his hands, shadows under his eyes hinting at insomnia, and gaunt hollows beneath the high cheekbones that once charmed the local girls.

"Are you clean now?" Aaron asked bluntly.

Ryan nodded. "Eight months. I'm in an outpatient program in Macon, and I go to weekly meetings." He hesitated before speaking. "Part of recovery is making amends. I wanted to reach out about Naomi sooner, but didn't think I had the right."

The broken man before him seemed impossible to reconcile with the brother who taught him to ride a bike, throw a curveball, and stand up to schoolyard bullies. Anger and compassion warred within him, neither gaining a clear advantage.

"She's adjusting," he said finally. "It hasn't been easy for either of us."

"You always were the responsible one." A ghost of a smile touched Ryan's lips. "Even as kids, you were always building things while I was breaking them."

"She asks about you sometimes," Aaron admitted reluctantly. "She wants to know why her uncle never visits."

Pain flashed across Ryan's features. "What do you tell her?"

"I told her that people handle grief differently. Some run to family, while others run away."

Ryan accepted this assessment with a nod. "That's fair." He sipped his coffee before continuing. "I'd like to see her sometime. Whenever you think she's ready, and when you're ready to let me."

The request put Aaron in an unexpected dilemma. Ryan was yet another adult who could potentially let Naomi down. But he also represented a link to her past, and the grandmother whose absence devastated her.

"I'll think about it," Aaron said, the same noncommittal response he had given Frank earlier. "She's in a fragile place right now."

"I understand." Ryan reached into his pocket, extracting a card. "Here's my number, in case you change your mind. Or if you ever need anything." He placed it on the table. "I'm staying in Macon now. Ironically enough, I'm working in construction."

Aaron pocketed the card without comment. When he paid the bill, some of the initial tension had eased, though the deeper fractures remained unhealed.

Outside the diner, dusk painted the sky in muted purples and oranges. Ryan extended his hand awkwardly.

"It was good seeing you, Aaron. Really."

After a pause, Aaron clasped his brother's hand. "Take care of yourself, Ryan."

Driving to his hotel, Aaron's thoughts churned from the day's emotional impact. He kept circling back to finding his mother's Bible, her notes written just for him, and the unexpected encounter with Ryan. His past had risen in a single, overwhelming wave, demanding resolutions he wasn't sure he could deliver.

In his hotel room, he discovered his phone had died hours earlier. Plugging it in, he was greeted by a barrage of notifications. There were five missed calls from Mrs. Patterson at New Hope Baptist Church, three from Darius Washington, and a text from Principal Watkins that read: *Please call regarding Naomi ASAP.*

Dread washed through him as he dialed Mrs. Patterson.

"Aaron, thank goodness! We've been trying to reach you all afternoon!"

"What's happened?" His voice sounded strange to his own ears, tight with fear he couldn't control.

"It's Naomi." Mrs. Patterson's normally efficient tone carried unmistakable concern. "Darius called when he couldn't reach you. Principal Watkins said Naomi hasn't been to school for two days. The Washingtons thought she was staying with a friend with your permission."

Aaron's knees buckled, forcing him to sit on the edge of the bed. "But I just talked to her. She said she was at school. She talked about the farmers' market."

"I'm sorry, but no one knows where she is. Principal Watkins is organizing search parties. Pastor Morrison has church members checking the local areas. And Meghan Townsend is coordinating with students who might know where Naomi might go."

Meghan.

If anyone could guess Naomi's whereabouts, it would be her.

"I'm leaving now." Aaron was already gathering his keys and wallet. "Tell them I'll be there in about two hours."

He prayed as he ran to his truck, the first genuine petition he had offered in years. "Please, keep her safe," he whispered into the gathering darkness. "Show me where to find her."

The Bible verses his mother marked awakened in his mind as he sped toward Brookside. *Do not fear, for I am with you; do not be dismayed, for I am your God.*

He could only hope those words held a truth that overrode his doubts, carrying a promise that extended to the niece who needed, him now more than ever.

Chapter 15

Meghan's hands trembled as she dialed Aaron's number for the fourth time in an hour. The call went straight to voicemail again. Night had fallen hours ago, and still no word from Naomi. The living room clock ticked loudly in the silence, each second twisting tighter around her chest. She prayed while pacing the length of her living room.

Please, Lord. Please keep her safe.

Outside, rain tapped against the window in a steady rhythm. The storm rolled in not long after Principal Watkins called. Naomi hadn't been at school today or yesterday. The Washingtons assumed she was with a friend, but no one followed up until it was too late. Meghan should have noticed sooner.

She replayed their last conversation, remembering how Naomi had grown quiet when Aaron mentioned his trip. Meghan had missed the signs. The wounds of abandonment often stayed hidden until someone disappeared.

The doorbell broke through her spiraling thoughts. She opened it to find Daniel and Samantha on the porch, rain glistening on their coats. Samantha's baby bump showed beneath her unbuttoned jacket, but worry marked both their faces.

"Any news?" Daniel asked as they stepped inside.

Meghan shook her head, closing the door against the chill. "Nothing. Aaron's phone keeps going straight to voicemail. The police won't treat her as missing for another few hours."

"So, she hasn't been at school," Samantha said, her nursing training showing in her methodical approach. "What about her usual spots? Has anyone checked her friends' houses?"

"Stanley's got the football team canvassing the neighborhoods." Meghan led them to her kitchen, where she had a map of Brookside spread on the counter. "Pastor Morrison has church members checking the library, community center, and the shopping plaza."

Daniel studied the map where Meghan circled potential locations. "What about the places you've taken her? Has anyone gone to the farmers' market?"

Frustration seeped into Meghan's voice. "Yes, we checked. I've been to every place I can think of."

Samantha laid a hand on her shoulder. "Stop blaming yourself."

"I should have seen this coming." Meghan's voice cracked. "When Aaron said he was going to Bristol Heights to work, I saw how she shut down. She's lost so many people, and she's scared and confused. I think she's afraid her uncle won't come back for her."

"This isn't your fault," Daniel insisted.

The doorbell rang again. Stanley entered, tracking in rain and energy. "The team's covered most of southwest Brookside," he reported, removing his wet hat. "No sign of her yet. Audrey's group is checking the north side business district."

"Thank you." Meghan's gratitude cut through her anxiety. Brookside's rallying proved what she had always believed about this town. When a crisis hit, people showed up.

Her phone rang, and she lunged for it. "It's Principal Watkins," she announced before answering.

"Meghan, I've spoken with the officers again. Now that we've confirmed she's missed school two days in a row, they're taking it more seriously. Do you know any places she might go? Somewhere she feels safe?"

Meghan froze, a memory of a conversation from a few weeks ago surfacing. She remembered the day she ran into Aaron and Naomi at Providence Park.

"Wait!" She interrupted whatever Principal Watkins was about to say. "The butterfly garden. She told Aaron it reminded her of her grandmother's garden. I should have thought of it sooner."

"Providence Park closes at dusk," Principal Watkins warned.

"Which means it's the perfect place she'd go to be alone." Meghan was already reaching for her coat. "I'm heading there now. Can you alert the search teams?"

By the time she hung up, the others were ready to move.

"I'll drive," Daniel offered, keys in hand. "Stanley, can you let Pastor Morrison's group know where we're going?"

Fifteen minutes later, they pulled into Providence Park's deserted parking lot. Rain fell in relentless sheets, making the darkness nearly impenetrable. More cars pulled in behind them, including Pastor Morrison, Audrey, and Principal Watkins.

Meghan opened her trunk and handed out flashlights. "The butterfly garden's on the eastern side, near the duck pond. It's tucked away. You won't be able to see it from the main path."

They split into groups of two or three, calling for Naomi as they navigated the slick pathways. Meghan led Daniel and Samantha, using her familiarity with the park to guide them through shortcuts between flowering shrubs and ornamental trees.

"The garden should be beyond these hedges," she said as they rounded a bend in the path. Rain plastered her hair to her forehead, but she barely noticed. All that mattered was finding Naomi before the cold made things worse.

The butterfly garden lay wrapped in darkness, its daytime charm transformed into shadowy figures and whispering plants. Meghan's flashlight cut through the darkness, illuminating rain-drenched flowers and empty benches.

"Naomi?" Her voice competed with the steady drumbeat of rainfall. "Naomi, it's Ms. Townsend! We're worried about you!"

Silence met them, broken only by rain, and distant calls from other search parties. Disappointment threatened Meghan's determination. Doubt crept in. Had she been wrong? Had Naomi gone somewhere else entirely?

But then, there was movement, a flicker under the weeping willow in the center of the garden.

Meghan stepped forward, flashlight beam narrowing on the tree's canopy.

"Naomi?" she called again, softer now, hope rising.

A stifled sob came from behind the thick trunk. Meghan signaled for Daniel and Samantha to stay back as she pushed through the willow's hanging branches.

Naomi sat huddled against the trunk, knees pulled tightly to her chest. Her braided hair was a damp mess, and her hoodie was soaked through. When the flashlight beam found her face, Meghan's heart clenched at the mixture of defiance and vulnerability in the girl's expression.

"Go away," Naomi mumbled, turning her face from the light.

Meghan crouched beside her and pulled off her own raincoat, wrapping it around the girl's shoulders.

"We've been worried sick. Everyone's out here looking for you." Meghan kept her voice calm, even as relief flooded through her.

"Why?" The question held layers of bitterness and hurt. "Nobody stays anyway."

Meghan's heart broke. Those weren't empty words. They were a wound, raw and bleeding. She settled beside Naomi, ignoring the dampness seeping through her clothes.

"Your uncle's been trying to reach you since he found out you were missing. He's on his way from Bristol Heights right now."

Naomi pulled her shoulders inward. "He's moving us there anyway. I might as well get used to being alone again."

Understanding dawned with painful clarity. "Is that what you think? That he's planning to relocate there?"

Naomi didn't respond, simply pulled the coat tighter.

Meghan chose her words carefully, aware that misunderstanding had driven this crisis. "Naomi, has he actually told you that you're moving? Or are you assuming that's what will happen?"

The girl's head lifted slightly, suspicion warring with uncertainty in her expression. "I heard him on the phone talking about career advancement and opportunities."

"Listening to half a conversation doesn't give you the whole story," Meghan said gently. "Adults discuss possibilities all the time without having made final decisions. Your uncle is trying to figure out what's best for both of you."

"But what if he decides Bristol Heights is better for his career?" Naomi's voice trembled. "What if I don't get a say?"

"From what I've seen of your uncle, he cares deeply about what you need," Meghan replied. "Have you talked to him about how you feel? About wanting to stay here?"

Naomi shook her head, looking down.

"Sometimes the people who love us can't read our minds," Meghan continued softly. "They need us to be brave enough to tell them the truth, even when we're scared of the answer."

There was a beat of silence. Then Daniel called out. "Meghan? Is everything okay?"

"We're here," she called back. "Naomi's here. She's safe."

The news spread among the search parties as flashlight beams converged on the willow, and relief transformed tension into celebration. Samantha pushed through the branches, her medical training prompting an immediate assessment.

"You're freezing." She touched Naomi's hand. "How long have you been out here?"

Naomi shrugged. "Since yesterday afternoon, I guess. I went back to the Washingtons' last night to get my backpack and some food when everyone was asleep."

"We need to get her somewhere warm," Samantha said to Meghan. "She's in danger of getting hypothermia."

They helped Naomi to her feet. Her legs wobbled from hours of sitting in the same position. Meghan and Samantha supported her as they walked from under the willow tree. Nearly a dozen people waited for them, including teachers, church members, and students who joined the search.

Pastor Morrison stepped forward, relief written across his face. "Thank God you're safe, child." He removed his coat to provide extra warmth. "You've got a lot of people who care about you."

Naomi looked around, eyes wide. "All these people came for me?"

"And more," Principal Watkins confirmed, already on his phone relaying the good news to other search parties.

Headlights swept over the parking lot. A white pickup truck skidded to a stop, its driver's door flying open before the engine fully quieted.

Aaron. His face was twisted with fear and desperate hope. He scanned the group until his gaze locked on Naomi. Then he was running, feet pounding the wet pavement. He dropped to his knees when he was in front of her.

He pulled Naomi into an embrace so tight it lifted her from her feet. His body curved around her as if to shield her from the entire world, his face buried against her shoulder.

His normally controlled voice broke with raw emotion. "I thought—"

He didn't finish, but he didn't need to. Every person present understood his unspoken fear of losing someone else he loved. Naomi was rigid at first, but then she gradually wrapped her arms around his neck.

"I'm so sorry," she whispered.

He pulled back to cup her face in his hands. "Don't ever disappear like that again. Do you understand? Never."

Naomi nodded, tears mixing with the raindrops.

The crowd began to thin. Pastor Morrison clapped Aaron on the shoulder. "Take her home, son. We'll bring dry clothes, food, and whatever else you need."

Aaron nodded, guiding Naomi toward his truck with an arm wrapped protectively around her shoulders. Meghan hung back, watching this reunion with a mix of relief and something deeper she wasn't ready to name.

Daniel came up beside her. "You ready to head back?"

"I should make sure they're settled first." She convinced herself it was a matter of professional responsibility. But they both knew it was more than that.

Daniel exchanged a look with Samantha. "We'll take you to Aaron's apartment."

An hour later, Aaron's apartment had transformed from a quiet bachelor-and-niece living space to an impromptu community gathering. Elena Washington arrived with dry clothes for Naomi, while her husband, Darius, brought containers of homemade soup. Pastor Morrison's wife brought fresh bread and a fruit tray, and Stanley arranged for Naomi's school absence the next day to allow her to recover.

Throughout the activity, Meghan watched Aaron move through his apartment as if waking from a nightmare. Relief made his movements dreamlike. He kept checking on his niece as if he still couldn't believe she was really safe.

Principal Watkins finally suggested that everyone give the family some space. Meghan had lingered longer than most, ensuring Naomi had everything she needed. With the crisis resolved, it was time to leave them to their privacy.

"I should go too." She grabbed her purse from the kitchen counter.

Aaron appeared beside her. "Could you stay a minute? I want to talk to you."

He led her out to the balcony. Naomi's container garden thrived in the mist. Aaron closed the door behind them. The air was fresh with the scent of wet earth and growing things.

"How did you know she liked the butterfly garden?" Aaron asked quietly.

"She said it reminded her of her grandmother," Meghan replied, voice soft. "It was on that day we ran into each other at the park."

Aaron nodded, absorbing this information. "Thank you for thinking of it when no one else did... and for finding her."

"Anyone would have—"

"No," he interrupted gently but firmly. "Not anyone. You saw what no one else did."

Meghan looked down, focusing on the basil plant instead of the intensity in his eyes.

"I should have seen it coming." She voiced the guilt that had haunted her since Naomi's disappearance. "I noticed her withdrawal after you said you were taking on the Bristol Heights project. She seemed so distant. I just... I didn't act fast enough."

"We both missed it. I've been so focused on this job. I didn't think about how my absence would affect her."

A long silence followed, filled only with the dripping of water from the balcony edge.

"I don't know what I would have done if..." He stopped, unable to complete the thought. "I prayed, Meghan. For the first time since Mom died, I prayed. Begged, really. I promised I would do anything if she would be safe."

The confession was nakedly honest. He didn't pull away. His fingers wrapped around hers.

"In that moment, I realized nothing else mattered. Not the project. Not the promotion. Just her. And just..." His gaze held hers. "Just the people who have become part of our lives."

Meghan felt her heart stop. The moment stretched, filled with unspoken possibility. His free hand moved closer to her face, like that rainy night outside the restaurant, but this time he made his intentions clear.

"Meghan," he murmured, inching nearer.

But then—

"Uncle Aaron? Are you out there?"

Aaron stepped back, releasing Meghan's hand with visible reluctance.

"We should go inside," she said, regaining her composure.

Aaron nodded and opened the door. Before she stepped inside, he touched her arm. "Thank you. For everything."

Meghan gently squeezed his hand on her arm. She quietly gathered her belongings and left the apartment without another word.

As she drove home, the streets were empty and quiet. But her mind wasn't. She had seen something change tonight in Naomi and in Aaron. And in herself. Some walls had cracked, and some facades had fallen.

Healing started in those moments when everything broke open.

She parked in her driveway and sat for a long time, thinking and praying. *Lord, whatever this is, help me walk it right.*

She wasn't sure where this path was leading. But she was already on it. And she knew it was real.

Chapter 16

Aaron pulled into the New Hope Baptist Church parking lot and cut the engine. What was he doing here? He hadn't planned to come today. He hadn't even told Naomi, who was off at a study group. But somehow, here he sat, watching families stream into the red brick building.

Two weeks had passed since that night at Providence Park. It had been two weeks since he discovered Naomi, prayed for the first time in years, and stood on a balcony with Meghan, teetering on the edge of a boundary that both excited and terrified him. The memory of her hand in his lingered, a warm and solid presence, anchoring him in the moment.

The sudden silence after shutting off the engine amplified the pounding in his chest.

He hadn't attended church consistently since his father walked out during his mother's first cancer diagnosis. What once came naturally, now sat strangely on him, like stepping into a language he hadn't spoken in years.

A tap on his window startled him. Daniel Forrester stood outside, his familiar face breaking into a smile.

"I thought that was you," Daniel said as Aaron opened his door. "Good to see you here."

Aaron stepped out, brushing off his slacks. "Honestly? I'm not sure why I came."

Daniel clapped his shoulder. "Sometimes your feet know where to go before your head catches up. Come on, Sam saved us a seat."

The sanctuary welcomed him with the familiar scents of wood polish, old hymnals, a hint of perfume, and aftershave. For a moment, he was ten years old again, squished between his mother and a fidgety Ryan, swinging his legs above the floor.

Samantha gave him a warm smile as he and Daniel slid in next to her. She rested one hand protectively over the curve of new life. The sight stirred something in Aaron, a bittersweet longing for family, for continuity, for things he told himself he didn't need.

"We're glad you came," she whispered. "No pressure. Just be present."

Her words eased the tightness in his chest. Aaron settled into the pew, trying to ignore the curious looks from congregation members who clearly recognized him as a newcomer. His niece's disappearance had been the talk of the town for several days.

The music faded, and Pastor Morrison stepped to the pulpit. The minister's presence commanded attention without demanding it. His voice carried quiet authority, tempered with compassion.

"Today, we explore the meaning of restoration." His gaze swept over the congregation before settling, briefly, but unmistakably, on Aaron. "Not the superficial kind that covers brokenness with fresh paint, but the restoration that transforms what was damaged, into something stronger than before."

Aaron sat motionless as the words hit home. Pastor Morrison opened his Bible, the pages rustling in the hushed sanctuary.

"Zechariah 9:12 tells us, *'Return to your fortress, you prisoners of hope; even now I announce that I will restore twice as much to you.'* " The pastor's voice deepened with conviction. "Prisoners of hope. What a powerful image. These were people caught between what was, and what could be, chained not by despair, but by the possibility of restoration."

Aaron stared at the open Bible in the pastor's hands. That was him, caught between the weight of everything he had lost, and the hope he was afraid to believe in.

"Restoration isn't erasure. God doesn't erase our scars. He doesn't pretend the damage never happened. He uses it. Redeems it. A properly set broken bone often heals stronger at the fracture point than it was before the injury."

Aaron thought of Naomi, her thriving plants, and the journal that used to hold pages of pain, but now contained recipes and gardening notes. He thought of how she hugged him that night in the park, and how she had started emerging from her shell.

Pastor Morrison continued, his words seemingly aimed at his situation. "In construction, a crack in the foundation might look like failure at first. But handled properly, with the right materials and attention? That repair can become the strongest part of the entire structure."

Aaron knew that firsthand. He had overseen dozens of foundation repairs. The reinforced area frequently became the most solid part of the structure.

"The master builder doesn't give up when damage occurs." The reverend's voice carried throughout the sanctuary. "He promises us in Haggai 2:9, *'The glory of this present house will be greater than the glory of the former house. And in this place I will grant peace.'*"

Aaron remained engaged for the rest of the service. Something was shifting inside him, like a door quietly unlocking. He didn't know what it meant, but he knew something was different.

When the final prayer ended and people began moving toward the fellowship hall, he remained seated, needing a moment to process everything.

Daniel waited beside him without saying a word.

"That was..." Aaron searched for words.

"Exactly what you needed?" Daniel suggested.

Aaron nodded, his throat tight.

"Pastor Morrison has a way of doing that. After my late wife Teresa died, I was convinced he preached sermons just for me. Turns out, half the congregation thought the same thing."

They made their way to the back of the sanctuary. Pastor Morrison stood greeting members, his handshake firm as he clasped Aaron's hand.

"Good to see you with us today, Aaron." His dark eyes were warm. "I hope you found something worthwhile in our service."

"I did," Aaron admitted. "Your foundation metaphor hit home."

The pastor chuckled. "It wasn't by accident. Daniel mentioned your line of work, and the Holy Spirit takes it from there." He glanced at his watch. "Will you be able to join us for lunch in the fellowship hall? The men's ministry would love to meet you."

"I appreciate the invite, but I need to get home." Aaron was surprised by his reluctance to decline. "Naomi will be back from her study group soon."

Pastor Morrison nodded. "Understandable. You're welcome anytime. Our men's group meets for fellowship and study on Sunday and Wednesday evenings."

As they crossed into the fellowship hall, Daniel insisted on introducing Aaron to several members. The tables were brimming with potluck dishes, including macaroni and cheese, sweet potato casserole, and banana pudding. These were the kinds of foods that you simply couldn't refuse without risking the disapproval of someone's grandmother.

"Aaron Grant, as I live and breathe!"

Aaron turned to see Darius heading his way, his broad face creased in a welcoming grin. He was dressed in a crisp suit with a vibrant blue tie.

"Darius," Aaron greeted him with genuine pleasure. "I didn't know you went to New Hope."

"Fifteen years strong." He gave Aaron a quick, brotherly hug. "Elena and I started coming when we first got married. Best decision we ever made."

"You two know each other?" Daniel asked, looking between them with interest.

"Darius is my right-hand man at the job site," Aaron explained. "Best foreman I've ever worked with."

Darius waved off the compliment, though pleasure showed in his face. "A man builds things right, or he doesn't build at all. Simple as that."

Their conversation flowed to the community center project and plans for next month's grand opening. Aaron relaxed into the easy rapport, appreciating how effortlessly Darius wove his faith into every aspect of his life, his work ethic, family commitments, and decision-making.

"Wait... I can't believe this," Daniel interjected as their conversation turned to hometowns. "You're both from Bristol Heights?"

Aaron's eyebrows rose in surprise. "Are you from Bristol Heights too?"

"Born and raised," Daniel confirmed. "My parents still live off Maple Avenue, near the old library."

"Small world." Darius laughed. "My cousin lives on that street! Remember that diner on the corner of Main and Powell? The Country Kitchen?"

"With the duct-tape-patched booth seats!" Aaron nodded, memories flooding back. "My family ate there every Thursday. Best meatloaf in three counties."

"And those apple pies," Daniel added with nostalgia. "My dad took me there for my first root beer float."

The three men swapped memories about the community pool where they all learned to swim, the maple trees that set autumn on fire, and the sledding hill behind the elementary school. The conversation opened up a sense of rediscovery, as though he were reconnecting with brothers he hadn't known he had lost.

When Elena came to collect Darius, Aaron took that as his cue to head out. As much as he wanted to stay in this newfound camaraderie, his promise to be home for Naomi came first.

"Same time next Sunday?" Daniel asked as he walked Aaron to the parking lot.

Aaron paused, hand on his truck door. "I'll try."

And for the first time in a long time, he meant it.

Chapter 17

THE DRIVE HOME FELT lighter, as if Aaron carried some of the sanctuary's peace with him. He turned off the usual sports radio in favor of silence, letting Pastor Morrison's words continue resonating.

When he walked into the apartment, sunlight filled the space Naomi had insisted on cleaning the day before. Small changes had transformed their home over the past few weeks. Throw pillows were arranged on the couch, family photos were displayed on shelves, and Naomi's artwork was taped to the refrigerator. The cold, impersonal place they had moved into months ago was becoming home.

On the balcony, Naomi's container garden flourished. He checked the soil moisture in several pots, noticing how each plant bore a label in his niece's neat handwriting: *Basil. Rosemary. Lavender. Mint.* The herbs created a fragrant haven.

Back inside, Aaron spotted Naomi's journal on the coffee table. Unlike months ago, when he accidentally discovered its dark contents, she now left it out without concern. Curiosity prompted him to open it, no longer fearing what he might find. Pages once filled with hopelessness and anger, now contained carefully copied recipes, each annotated with personal notes:

Grandma's cornbread—needs extra butter.

Ms. Townsend's apple crisp—try more cinnamon?

Mr. Forrester's wife's chicken soup—good for cold days.

Aaron felt a tightness in his throat as he turned each page. Every recipe captured her feeling of connection and belonging. These weren't just dishes. They were memories that revealed how she was putting down roots.

The apartment door opened. Naomi walked in, dropping her backpack by the couch. When she saw him, her face lit up, a reaction that never failed to move him.

"You're home early. I thought you had that supplier meeting for work." She headed to the kitchen for a glass of water.

"It was rescheduled for tomorrow." Aaron closed the journal, setting it back in place. "How was the study group?"

"Okay. Lisbeth's hopeless at algebra, but she's helping me with my English essay."

He smiled. The casual rhythm of her words, so different from the guarded quiet of her first weeks here, felt like a victory.

"Have you eaten lunch?"

"Lisbeth's mom made us sandwiches." She flopped on the couch, curling her legs beneath her. "Where were you this morning? Your truck was gone when I left."

"I went to church... New Hope Baptist, where the Forresters go."

Naomi's eyes widened. "Seriously? Why?"

Aaron sat across from her in the armchair.

"I'm not entirely sure," he admitted. "Since that night we found you at Providence Park... when I prayed for you to be safe? It felt like I needed to go back."

Naomi studied him with a gaze that made her seem older than fourteen. "Grandma would be happy. She used to say you'd eventually find your way back."

Warmth expanded through Aaron. "She believed in me more than I believed in myself." He leaned forward, elbows on knees. "I saw the Washingtons there. Turns out they've been going for years."

Naomi traced the pattern on a throw pillow. "I know. They invited me to their youth group once. I haven't gone yet."

"Would you want to?"

She shrugged, but the gesture lacked its usual dismissiveness. "Maybe. Their oldest, Anne, says they do cool service projects and have decent snacks."

Aaron nodded, hearing the tentative interest beneath her casual response. "No pressure. It's just something to think about."

A comfortable silence settled, the kind that had once seemed impossible. Then Naomi asked the question that hit straight to his heart.

"Are we staying in Brookside? Like... for good?"

The way she asked, soft but serious, told him she had been holding that worry for a while. He knew what it cost her to ask. Hope was a risk, especially after everything she had lost.

"What would you like to do?" he countered gently.

Naomi drew her knees up and wrapped her arms around them, holding them close. "I really like it here. School is okay, and the cooking class is a lot of fun. My plants are doing well." She glanced toward the balcony, her expression turning serious. "I don't want to start over again."

Aaron nodded. "I should have told you sooner, but I turned down the Bristol Heights promotion."

"Really?"

"I talked to Mr. Donovan, and we worked out a compromise. I'll manage the project remotely, and only travel if absolutely necessary."

Naomi lifted her head. "So... we're staying?"

"We're staying." The words grew more solid each time he said them. "We're not moving anytime soon. Brookside is home now."

Naomi unfolded from her guarded posture, her shoulders relaxing. "Good."

That one word held more than approval. It carried trust.

They drifted into lighter topics of movies she wanted to see, an event at the community center, and dinner plans. They weren't getting through the days anymore. They were building a life.

Later that evening, with Naomi tucked away in her room, Aaron stood alone on the balcony, surrounded by the scents of her herb garden. The lights of Brookside shimmered across the horizon, quiet and steady.

Somewhere out there was Meghan's house. Maybe she was grading papers. Maybe she was getting ready for the week. He wondered if she ever thought of him the way he kept thinking of her.

He closed his eyes, allowing the recollection of that night on the balcony to rise to the surface. The sensation of her hand in his, the spark in her eyes. It was a moment of connection that was both unresolved and undeniable.

As he gazed at the cluster of lights that might contain her home, Aaron let himself imagine what it could be like to share evenings like this with her. He pictured her sitting in one of the balcony chairs while he watered the plants. Naomi would be inside, laughter echoing from the kitchen. He envisioned a home filled with warmth and possibility.

The longing these images stirred surprised him. When had this woman woven herself into his vision of what could be? When had her presence become so natural in his thoughts that imagining her here felt like a memory rather than a dream?

Whenever it started, it had grown quietly. And now, he couldn't stop picturing her in his world.

Sleep came easier that night than it had in months. Aaron dreamed of unfinished houses with expansive windows and open kitchens. Meghan's distinctive scent, cinnamon and vanilla, drifted through rooms not yet built.

He woke before sunrise, the dream still vivid.

He rose and dressed while the apartment remained quiet. Naomi was still sleeping. On the balcony, he watched the sun break over the eastern horizon, painting the sky in shades of promise.

Peace settled over him, not because life had become easy, but because he finally understood his direction.

He took a deep breath. Something had broken open during Pastor Morrison's sermon, like soil thawing after winter's frost. The faith his mother nurtured in him as a child wasn't lost after all. It had been buried, waiting for the right season to emerge again.

Maybe this was that season, a season not for renewed faith alone, but for a heart beginning to open again.

He thought of Meghan's smile and the dimples that appeared when she laughed. She carried quiet strength and had an uncanny ability to see what others missed. She wasn't just a part of Naomi's journey. She was becoming part of his.

He looked toward the sky, light growing brighter with each moment.

The glory of this present house will be greater than the glory of the former.

Aaron meditated on that verse as the first rays of sunlight touched Naomi's herbs. Each leaf stood out in vivid detail.

Maybe that promise didn't apply only to buildings.

Maybe it applied to hearts, too.

Chapter 18

Greater Pines High School faculty members filled the seats at their monthly staff meeting, flipping open notebooks and sipping lukewarm coffee. Meghan adjusted her notepad, only half-listening as Stanley discussed the upcoming basketball tryouts. Her mind was already on Thursday's cooking program. The apple spice cake recipe needed tweaking, with perhaps less sugar and more cinnamon to better bring out the local orchard's harvest.

Principal Watkins cleared his throat, pulling her attention back to the room. "Next item on our agenda is program highlights. I want to take a moment to recognize Ms. Townsend's culinary initiative."

Meghan straightened in her chair as Principal Watkins projected a graph onto the whiteboard showing red and blue lines rising in parallel arcs.

He adjusted his silver-rimmed glasses and continued. "As you can see, students enrolled in the cooking program show a ten percent increase in attendance, along with improved performance across multiple subjects."

Audrey, her blue-streaked bun barely containing her enthusiasm, leaned forward. "My art students are applying those presentation skills in their portfolios. The visual components are really clicking with them."

Daniel nodded in agreement. "Their writing has changed as well. There's more depth and cultural understanding. Essays about family traditions have gained a richness since they've started connecting what they're learning to their own heritage."

Meghan's heart warmed at her colleagues' observations. What started as a homage to her father had evolved into something much larger.

Principal Watkins continued. "In light of these results, the administration has approved Ms. Townsend's proposal to expand the program next semester." He turned toward Meghan. "With the community center opening soon, we see a natural partnership forming. Ms. Townsend, perhaps you could explain further."

Meghan gathered her thoughts, aware of all eyes turning toward her. "The new community center will include a commercial-grade kitchen designed for public workshops. I've spoken with the project manager about hosting classes that connect students and the community through food and cultural traditions."

She didn't mention that the *"project manager"* was Aaron, or how their conversations drifted past logistics into more personal territory.

"Excellent," Principal Watkins said. "This is exactly the kind of community integration the board wants."

The meeting rolled on, but Meghan's thoughts wandered to the center's upcoming grand opening scheduled for next month. She pictured students demonstrating cooking techniques in the gleaming new kitchen, elderly members sharing traditional recipes, and families gathering around shared tables.

And in every version of that vision, Aaron appeared, guiding the space, grounding her with his steady presence.

The meeting finally ended, and teachers began gathering their things. Audrey approached, her perception too keen to miss Meghan's distraction. "Earth to Meghan," she teased, gathering her colorful sketch portfolio. "You checked out somewhere around budget item seven."

Meghan smiled, collecting her notes. "I was mentally reviewing the details for Thursday."

"Mmm-hmm." Audrey's expression suggested she wasn't convinced. "And do these details include a certain foreman who suddenly has strong opinions about where the ovens should go?"

Heat rose to Meghan's cheeks. "Our meetings are strictly professional."

"Sure they are," Audrey replied with exaggerated innocence. "Just like Stanley and I are *strictly professional*, going out to dinner this Saturday."

Before Meghan could respond, Daniel joined the conversation. "Dinner plans? Sam's been wanting to try that new Italian place. We should double-date."

"We're not dating," Meghan asserted quickly. "Audrey was—"

"Just teasing Meghan about her interest in Aaron Grant," Audrey finished, completely unrepentant.

Daniel raised an eyebrow. "Speaking of Aaron, he's made some major changes. He's been coming to church regularly and even joined the men's Bible study."

This information caught Meghan off guard. She knew he attended a few services, but not that he had stepped this far into his commitment. Warmth unfurled inside her, a reaction she masked behind her professional calm.

"That's good for Naomi." She kept her tone deliberately neutral. "Consistency is important for her."

"True." Daniel's perceptive gaze seemed to see more than Meghan wanted to reveal. "He shared some powerful insights last week. That man's rebuilding more than community centers these days."

As the conversation drifted to weekend plans, they headed toward the parking lot. Meghan was still turning over Daniel's words when she spotted a white pickup parked beside her sedan. It took her a moment to register the tall figure leaning against the hood, arms crossed over his chest. Even from a distance, the stillness of his stance told her exactly who it was.

"Well, well." Audrey elbowed Meghan. "Looks like your *strictly professional* foreman awaits."

Daniel chuckled. "We'll let you two get back to those kitchen specifications."

They left with knowing smiles. Meghan walked toward the truck, suddenly self-conscious of her plain cardigan and flats, an outfit she had selected that morning without anticipating this unexpected encounter.

Aaron straightened as she approached, sunlight catching the bronze highlights in his hair. He wore dark jeans and a charcoal button-down, sleeves rolled up to reveal forearms marked by years of hard labor. His usual serious demeanor softened when their eyes met.

"Hey," he greeted, his deep voice warm. "I hope I'm not interrupting anything."

"No, you're fine. The faculty meeting just wrapped up." She repositioned her shoulder bag to conceal a momentary flutter of nerves. "What brings you by?"

"I was doing a final walk-through at the community center." He paused, seeming to weigh his words. "But really, I wanted to thank you... for everything you've done for Naomi."

Meghan picked up on the subtle shift in his tone, wishing his gratitude encompassed more than Naomi.

"Really, there's no need for thanks. She's the one putting in the hard work."

"That's why I came." A breeze ruffled Aaron's shirt as he glanced in the direction of Providence Park. "I was hoping we could talk about Naomi. And about... some other things. If you have time."

The vague *other things* hung between them. Meghan hesitated, but only for a breath.

"I'd like that."

They made their way across the crosswalk. Meghan and Aaron walked side by side, deliberately avoiding any physical contact. She was highly conscious of Aaron's proximity, his tall stature, the faint aroma of cedar and soap, and the way he adjusted his pace to keep in sync with hers.

Providence Park welcomed them with bright trees and scattered leaves. Fallen leaves crunched beneath their feet as they strolled past the duck pond. The sounds of families and joggers created a peaceful backdrop.

"Naomi updated her garden growth chart this morning," Aaron said as they walked. "She's tracking pH levels now. She's remarkably detailed for someone who claimed to have no interest in plants a few months ago."

Meghan smiled, thinking of how the hesitant teenager was opening up. "Plants don't lie. You nurture them, and they grow. They reflect the care poured into them."

Aaron's pace slowed. "She's different since that night at the park. She's starting conversations now instead of responding when there's no other choice."

Meghan nodded. "Her participation in class has improved too. She raised her hand three times during yesterday's discussion about the Great Migration."

Aaron's expression reflected quiet pride. "She told me that at dinner last night... said the discussion was about how family recipes traveled north during that period."

"Right! We talked about how food preserves culture during geographical transitions."

They paused near the pond, watching the ducks glide across the water.

"I've made some decisions lately." His gaze was fixed on the distant shoreline. "Regarding myself, Naomi, and our future."

Meghan turned toward him, noting the creases around his eyes that spoke of the responsibilities he shouldered alone. "What kind of decisions?"

"I told you I turned down the Bristol Heights promotion." He stated it plainly, but the gravity of his choice was apparent. "Naomi needs stability more than I need to climb the career ladder. We're going to stay in Brookside."

"I know that couldn't have been easy. How did your company respond?"

"My boss wasn't thrilled," Aaron admitted with a half-smile. "But we reached a compromise we can both live with."

They resumed walking, following the path as it curved around ancient oak trees whose branches created natural archways overhead. Meghan sensed Aaron had more to say, so she ventured carefully.

"Can I ask how you reached that decision? Beyond Naomi's needs, I mean."

Aaron slowed until they were nearly at a standstill under a colorful maple tree. His voice dropped lower. "Everything changed that night we searched for Naomi. I realized I'd been chasing success while neglecting what truly matters... my family and the relationships I've formed." His eyes met hers before returning to the path ahead. "Some connections, I didn't know I needed until they began changing me."

Meghan's pulse quickened. The moment pulsed with unspoken meaning.

"What does Naomi think about staying?" she asked, redirecting toward safer ground.

His expression gentled with affection. "She's relieved. She told me she likes it here and wants to stay."

"It sounds like she's putting down roots. Literally and figuratively."

Aaron nodded, but then a cold raindrop hit the path. Then another. Within seconds, the sky opened.

"There's a gazebo near the butterfly garden." Meghan moved faster along the path. "We can wait it out there."

They dashed through the downpour, reaching the white wooden structure as the shower became truly drenching. The gazebo wrapped around them like a sanctuary, rain cascading off its roof in silvery sheets.

"That came out of nowhere." Aaron ran a hand through his dampened hair.

Meghan smoothed her skirt, grateful they reached shelter before becoming completely soaked. Her heart raced, but not from the sprint alone.

"I've been thinking about what you said on the balcony," Aaron said after a moment, his voice barely audible above the rain's percussion on the wooden roof. "About prayer."

Meghan turned toward him, surprised by this spiritual direction. "What about it?"

"It wasn't panic that night. A change had already begun. Ever since meeting you, watching how you live your faith daily... it's moved me."

Meghan blinked at the personal comment. While she always tried to live her faith authentically, she rarely received such direct acknowledgment of its impact.

"It's not separate from me. My faith is part of who I am."

Aaron nodded. "I've started going to New Hope Baptist regularly. I've been attending men's Bible study on Thursdays too. They're patient with all my questions." A self-deprecating smile touched his lips.

"Daniel mentioned you'd been going. I'm glad."

Aaron stepped closer, the gazebo's limited space bringing them within inches of each other. "It's more than that. I've built things my entire adult life. But I've been building on the wrong foundation."

Raindrops glistened in his hair. One slid down his temple. Meghan reached up without thinking, brushing it away. The simple touch drew them into stillness.

Aaron's eyes, usually so controlled, darkened with unmistakable emotion. "Meghan." The way he said her name questioned everything that lingered unspoken.

The moment stretched, and the rest of the world was held at bay, as if the park itself was waiting.

Movement at the pond's edge disrupted her focus. She glanced past Aaron's shoulder. A distinctive figure stood in the rain without apparent concern for the heavy shower.

A man with silver hair leaned on a polished wooden cane, watching the gazebo with calm intensity. Even at this distance, Meghan recognized him as the same mysterious stranger she had glimpsed near Providence Park after the cooking class.

Seeing him again stirred an inexplicable certainty that his presence carried a significance beyond coincidence.

"Meghan? What is it?" Aaron's voice drew her attention back to him.

She shook her head quickly. "I thought I saw..." She turned back toward the pond, but the silver-haired man had vanished. The shoreline stood empty, offering nowhere he could have disappeared to so quickly.

"Saw what?" Aaron turned to follow her gaze, scanning the landscape.

"Nothing," Meghan said, unsettled. "It must have been a trick of the light."

Thunder rumbled in the distance as Aaron searched her face, but he decided against probing further.

"The community center's grand opening is next month," he said, his voice steady. "I'd like you to come with me. Not as the cooking program leader, but as my guest."

This wasn't just a simple invitation. It marked a significant shift in their relationship from colleagues to something more.

Meghan's heart responded with quiet joy.

"I'd like that."

Relief and warmth transformed his features. They stood together as rain continued to fall, each lost in thought about this meaningful turn in their connection.

Behind them, unseen by either, a silver feather drifted onto the gazebo bench, glinting in the faint light. It served as a reminder of a presence that had physically departed but perhaps lingered in spirit.

The rain gradually transitioned into a fine mist, and park visitors emerged from their makeshift shelters, resuming activities disrupted by the unpredictable whims of the season.

"I really ought to get you back to your car." His tone revealed a hint of reluctance at bringing their time together to an end.

As they strolled back toward the parking area, the walkways glimmering from the rain, Meghan took one final look at the pond. She still wasn't entirely sure about what, or who, she had seen. But one truth settled in her spirit with certainty. The path she and Aaron were walking was no simple coincidence. It had been crafted by hands much more powerful than their own.

Chapter 19

Aaron adjusted his hard hat and surveyed the community center's main atrium with a critical eye. The building's transformation from skeletal framework to a nearly finished structure was complete. Every time he stepped into a finished space, he was reminded why he loved this work of turning a vision into structure, and possibilities into places.

"Looking good, boss." Darius's experienced gaze swept across the exposed beams and polished floors. "The electricians wrapped up the pendant light installations this morning. Inspection's set for Thursday."

Pride swelled in Aaron as he admired the soaring ceilings. "The way the light diffuses is perfect. It's exactly as we envisioned."

"It's better than perfect." Darius pointed toward the corner windows where the afternoon sun created patterns across the hardwood floors. "Those extra skylights were worth every penny of the budget adjustment."

The space felt alive now, built for conversations and celebrations. He could picture neighbors gathered here, sharing meals, stories, and laughter.

"The kitchen's the real showstopper." Darius swung open the double doors. "Top-of-the-line equipment with that warm, home-kitchen vibe Meghan wanted. You nailed it."

Her name sparked the same tightness that had been settling in Aaron over the past few weeks. He let his palm glide over the cool stainless steel, seeing her in his mind as she moved through the kitchen, outlining how each workstation would serve the people who came here.

"She'll love it," Aaron said, his voice low.

Darius gave him a look, but mercifully didn't say anything. They discussed final paint schedules, delivery timelines for the remaining furnishings, and the landscaping beginning next week.

Aaron's phone vibrated in his pocket. Frank Donovan's name flashed across the screen, triggering tension. He excused himself, ducking into the future administrative office for privacy.

"Frank," he answered, keeping his tone professional despite the implications of this fourth call in three days.

"Aaron." Frank's booming voice filled the line without preamble. "Bristol Heights Municipal Council wants confirmation about the project's leadership. After reviewing your work on the Brookside Center, they want you. I'll need your decision by Friday."

Aaron pinched the bridge of his nose in frustration at the continued pressure. "We've been over this. I've made arrangements for remote oversight."

"Remote oversight isn't the same as your physical presence, and you know it." Frank's voice carried the edge of a man unaccustomed to compromise. "This is the career advancement we talked about when you joined the company. Regional director track, Aaron. You could have your own division within three years."

It was a prestigious and lucrative offer that his old self would have jumped at. But he thought of Naomi, laughing and building friendships now. Then he considered Meghan. The thought of uprooting that now felt wrong.

"I appreciate the offer, but my family situation—"

"—is precisely why you should consider it," Frank interrupted. "A higher position means better compensation. It would mean better schools for your niece and better opportunities all around."

"Better doesn't always mean more. Naomi's thriving here, and that's not something I'm willing to sacrifice. I've made my priorities clear." Aaron surprised himself with the conviction in his voice.

Silence stretched across the connection before Frank sighed, resignation coloring his tone. "Friday, Aaron. I'll need your final decision, in writing, by the end of the day on Friday."

After the call ended, Aaron remained motionless, staring at nothing. Four months ago, this decision would have been an easy yes. Career advancement represented security and a path forward. But now, everything had changed.

His phone chimed with a reminder that the cooking class started in thirty minutes. He glanced at his dusty jeans and work shirt. There was no time to go to his apartment and change, so he headed straight to school.

When Aaron arrived, the home economics room hummed with activity. Students moved between workstations. Meghan moved through it all with grace, firm and encouraging, her presence anchoring the chaos. He paused in the doorway, scanning the room until he spotted Naomi.

Gone was the withdrawn, silent girl who arrived in Brookside. In her place stood a young woman demonstrating knife techniques to a pair of elementary students. Her voice carried certainty as she explained proper finger positioning.

"Safety first. Keep your fingers curled under, like a claw, so the knife can't reach them." She guided the small hands into the correct formation.

His throat tightened. This confidence, this light in her, was a gift he hadn't dared to hope for when she first arrived.

"She's a natural teacher." Meghan appeared beside him, her proximity sending a wave of awareness through him.

She wore a burgundy dress that hugged her curves, and her hair was styled in a neat twist, revealing the graceful arch of her neck.

"It's astonishing to think she's the same girl who wouldn't speak or make eye contact just a few months back." He breathed in her vanilla-cinnamon scent.

Meghan nodded. "She's healing because she feels safe. You gave her that."

"We *both* gave her that," Aaron corrected, meeting Meghan's gaze. His fingers itched to brush the loose curl resting against her cheek.

Their eyes held for a beat, a silent connection shimmering between them, needing no words.

A timer chimed.

"Everyone, gather around!" Her professional demeanor returned as she moved toward the demonstration counter.

Aaron watched her lead the group into a circle. She outlined plans for their special grand opening, excitement lighting her features.

"I have thrilling news! We're cooking at the new community center kitchen when it opens. We'll prepare recipes and dishes from the many cultures represented in Brookside. Principal Watkins has approved transportation. When you go home, ask your parents if they'd like to volunteer as chaperones."

Murmurs of excitement rippled through the group. Naomi glanced toward Aaron, a question in her eyes that he interpreted. Would he participate?

Aaron stepped forward without hesitation. "As the project manager for the community center, I'd be happy to give everyone a tour of the facility before the cooking begins. I can show you how the spaces were designed to bring people together."

The words emerged without forethought, driven by a raw sincerity that bypassed professional courtesy. Meghan's delight at his offer sent warmth cascading through him.

Her smile deepened, her dimples making a brief appearance. "That would be perfect."

The remainder of the class whizzed by in a blur. Aaron caught sight of Naomi shooting him brief smiles, indicating the mending connection that was gradually forming between them.

Once the clean-up was done, his niece came over.

"I'm going to the library with Lisbeth to research sweet potato recipes." She casually threw her backpack over one shoulder, embodying teenage nonchalance. "Her mom said she can drop me off at home before dinner."

Aaron nodded. "Send me a text when you're on your way."

Once she left, only he and Meghan remained. She was sorting recipe cards at her desk. Aaron walked toward her, his heartbeat accelerating with each step.

"Need help carrying anything to your car?"

Meghan looked up, her warm brown eyes crinkling at the corners as she smiled. "Just this folder and my purse today. But having your company for the walk would be nice."

They strolled side by side through the deserted hallways, their shoulders occasionally brushing. In the parking lot, the sun was beginning to set, stretching shadows across the asphalt as they reached Meghan's vehicle.

"Naomi and I were talking about Thanksgiving plans last night."

Meghan tilted her head, listening attentively. "Will you be heading to Bristol Heights for the holiday?"

Aaron shifted his weight, conscious of his dusty work boots and the construction debris likely clinging to his clothes. "No… we're staying in Brookside. We've decided to make some new traditions."

Meghan's smile deepened. "It's wonderful that you two are making new memories with each other."

"It is," Aaron agreed. "We hoped you would join us for Thanksgiving dinner at our place."

Meghan stood perfectly still, her expression unreadable. Then joy transformed her features with a radiance that caught his breath.

"I'd love to. I was dreading another holiday alone. I was going to spend it with my mom's friend Carol, but she's visiting her daughter in Michigan this year."

Gratitude flooded through him. "Naomi will be thrilled. She's planning enough food to feed a small army."

Meghan laughed, the sound melodic in the quiet parking lot. "I'm happy to contribute a dish or two. My father's sweet potato pie is something of a tradition."

"Perfect." Aaron was conscious of his reluctance to end their conversation despite accomplishing his objective. "I should let you go. I'm sure you have grading to finish."

"And you have a community center to complete." Meghan unlocked her car but made no immediate move to enter it. Her fingers brushed his arm in a touch that sent sparks through him. "Thank you for inviting me. It means more than you know."

"Thank you for saying yes," he replied quietly.

Her vulnerable honesty stirred emotions Aaron had kept locked in for months.

"Drive safely." He knew the time wasn't right for anything deeper.

As her car slipped out of sight, a lightness settled over him, brighter than anything he had carried in months.

Driving home, Aaron took an impulsive detour. The truck pulled him into Providence Park's empty parking lot just as the setting sun painted the western sky in vibrant oranges and purples.

The park paths lay quiet in early evening transition. It was too late for families with young children, but too early for couples seeking romantic twilight strolls. Aaron walked toward the white gazebo where he and Meghan had sheltered from the sudden rain.

As the structure came into view, he slowed his pace. The gazebo wasn't empty. A man sat on the inner bench. His silver hair caught the fading light, and a polished wooden cane rested across his knees. His patient and expectant posture suggested he might be waiting for someone.

Aaron approached respectfully, not wanting to intrude on a private moment. "Good evening," he offered as he reached the gazebo steps. "Mind if I join you?"

The man looked up, his weathered face creasing with a smile. His deep-set eyes held surprising warmth. "I've been expecting you, son. This seat's been waiting."

Under different circumstances, the odd greeting might have put Aaron on edge. But the man's presence carried an inexplicable sense of familiarity, though they had never met. He sat beside him, the wooden bench warm from the sun.

"This is a beautiful spot." The silver-haired man gestured toward the pond with his cane. "Perfect place for important conversations, wouldn't you say?"

Aaron nodded, remembering his rain-soaked time with Meghan. "It seems to inspire honesty."

"Honesty," the man repeated thoughtfully. "That's a good word. You know something about building structures that last, I expect."

"Yes. I'm in construction." The man's perceptiveness piqued Aaron's curiosity.

"But lately, you've been building more than walls and beams, haven't you?" the elderly man queried.

Aaron was surprised by this stranger's accurate assessment. "Do we know each other?"

The man chuckled. "I've known you longer than you might think." He tapped his cane against the gazebo floor. "Foundation is important in any worthwhile project, wouldn't you agree?"

"Always," Aaron replied, applying his professional knowledge to the unexpected philosophical turn. "Without a proper beginning, nothing else stands securely."

"Well, son, it's the same when it comes to matters of the heart. Relationships built on shifting sand tend to collapse when storms come. But those anchored to bedrock... well, those endure the test of time."

The biblical reference wasn't lost on Aaron. It paralleled Pastor Morrison's recent sermon series on establishing Christian homes.

A quiet unease threaded through him. This stranger possessed insights into his life. His slow return to faith. The painstaking effort he was undertaking to restore trust with Naomi. And the developing connection between him and Meghan.

"How do you know when the time is right for the next phase?" Aaron inquired.

The man's penetrating gaze seemed to tap into wisdom beyond ordinary experience. "The Master Builder always knows. Trust the blueprint and trust the timing." He tapped his cane again, this time against the bench.

They sat quietly as the sun disappeared behind the trees.

The man sighed and reached for his cane to lift himself from the bench.

"I should be on my way." He stood with surprising steadiness for someone who appeared so frail. "Mind helping an old man down these steps?"

Aaron rose, reaching out his arm for support. The moment their hands met, electric and sacred energy surged between them. In that brief instant, Aaron felt a sensation of being seen and understood, surpassing any ordinary human connection.

"Thank you, son." He patted Aaron's hand with gnarled fingers that carried surprising strength. "Remember what I said about timing. Trust the blueprint even when you can't see the finished design."

Aaron watched him walk away. When he turned back to the bench, a silver feather rested where the man had sat. It gleamed unlike any bird plumage he had ever encountered. The object seemed to glow faintly, even in the fading light.

He lifted it carefully. No rational explanation presented itself for the object's presence or unusual properties. Yet, holding it instilled peace, as if the strange encounter had been meant to happen as it did.

Tucking the feather into his shirt pocket, he returned to his truck. He didn't need answers. Not yet.

His phone buzzed with a text from Naomi: *On my way home. Can we order pizza tonight? I'm too tired to cook.*

Aaron smiled, typing back: *Pizza sounds perfect. I'll order when I get home.*

Another text appeared before he could put the phone away. This one from Meghan: *Thank you again for tonight. I can't wait for Thanksgiving. Sweet dreams.*

His fingers hovered over the keyboard. There were so many things he wanted to say, but he settled on: *Sweet dreams to you too.*

Whatever came next, he wasn't walking alone.

Chapter 20

Meghan guided her cart down the baking aisle of Grocery Haven Super Market. Her handwritten list, copied from her father's recipe journal, crinkled between her fingers. The store bustled with pre-holiday shoppers, all on similar missions to prepare for the day's celebrations.

She paused at the stacked cans of pumpkin, debating whether to add them to her cart's growing lineup of ingredients. Sweet potatoes, eggs, and vanilla were accounted for. Aaron said dinner would be simple, just the three of them. Still, she wanted to contribute something meaningful. Her father's sweet potato pie offered that, a quiet legacy folded into a flaky crust and memory.

"Fresh nutmeg makes all the difference." Meghan selected a small container of whole nutmeg and a grater. There would be no pre-ground spice for this recipe. Her father had been adamant about that detail.

Her phone rang as she reached for brown sugar. Olivia's name flashed across the screen, prompting an immediate smile as Meghan answered.

"Please tell me you're not scrubbing baseboards again," Meghan teased by way of greeting.

Instead of Olivia's expected laugh, a shaky breath came through the line.

"Olivia? What's wrong?" Concern flooded through Meghan as she steered her cart to a quieter corner near the organic foods section.

"It's happening, Meghan." Olivia's voice trembled. "The agency called. My application has been approved. I'm going to be a mother."

The words landed like sunlight breaking through clouds.

"Oh, Olivia!" Joy erupted from Meghan, drawing glances from nearby shoppers. "That's incredible! When did you find out? What did they say?"

"About twenty minutes ago. My caseworker called personally." Olivia's voice steadied. "There's paperwork, and I have to wait through a final review, but they've matched me with a little girl. She's four years old, Meghan. Her name is Lillian, but everyone calls her Lily."

"Lily," Meghan repeated the name, and it settled like a warm blessing. "It's perfect. When will you meet her?"

"The first supervised visit is next week. But Meghan—" Olivia's voice caught. "What if I'm not ready? What if I mess this up? What if she doesn't like me?"

Olivia's vulnerable tone took Meghan aback. Her confident friend rarely showed such uncertainty.

"What if she does like you?" Meghan countered gently. "What if everything goes perfectly?"

"That's what scares me most," Olivia admitted. "If it goes well, then it's real. Then I'm responsible for another person's happiness and healing. What if I can't handle being a single mom?"

Meghan paused to collect her thoughts. "Remember what you told me about taking risks when the timing is right? About having courage?"

A pause, then a shaky laugh. "I hate it when you use my own words against me."

"That's what friends are for."

They talked as Meghan continued shopping, her list forgotten. Olivia described the transformation of the guest bedroom into Lily's space. It was now a cozy nook filled with books, soft lights, and a star-patterned comforter. Before they ended the call, Meghan had everything she needed for her father's pie, and one extra item she hadn't planned for. She selected a small stuffed elephant, soft and gray with stitched ears... something for Lily.

The cashier scanned each item at checkout. "Are you planning a big Thanksgiving dinner?"

Meghan smiled. "I'm helping out with one. I'm making my dad's sweet potato pie."

The cashier responded with a nod and a smile. "Those lucky folks are in for a treat!" The woman placed the items into grocery bags. "My grandmother used to say that homemade pies carry love in every bite."

The words stayed with Meghan as she loaded the groceries into her car. Her father's recipes had infused her life with love over the years, serving as reminders of comfort and care, helping to keep his memory alive, even in his absence.

Meghan sat at her desk sorting papers. The final day before Thanksgiving break brought a relaxed atmosphere to the building. Students had mentally departed for their five-day weekend, and teachers were wrapping up necessary tasks before the brief reprieve.

A light tap on her open door signaled Audrey, who entered with her usual dramatic flair and a fresh streak of copper in her hair that glinted like autumn leaves.

"Plans for the holiday?" She perched on the edge of a student's desk.

"Just a small dinner with friends." Meghan was deliberately vague, though her mind was buzzing with thoughts about the upcoming meal with Aaron and Naomi.

Audrey's raised eyebrows indicated that she wasn't convinced.

Heat touched Meghan's cheeks. "Okay, okay... you got me. Aaron invited me to Thanksgiving dinner. It's not a big deal. It will be just the three of us."

"Not a big deal," Audrey echoed with a knowing smile. "Just sharing one of the most family-centered holidays of the year... totally low-key."

Meghan busied herself straightening the already-neat stacks of paper. "Naomi shouldn't be alone with just her uncle on Thanksgiving. This will be her first holiday without her grandmother."

Audrey's skepticism could power a small appliance. "Mmm-hmm. And that's the only reason you're going?"

Meghan didn't answer. She didn't have to.

Audrey's expression softened. "You know, I saw them at church on Sunday. Aaron had his arm around Naomi's shoulders during the closing hymn. She leaned into him like she knew she was safe. It was sweet."

The image created an ache in Meghan, not sadness, but tenderness. "They've come a long way."

"They have." Audrey leaned forward conspiratorially. "I also heard something interesting from Stanley. He said Aaron's been talking to Pastor Morrison about baptism... for himself."

Meghan's breath caught. "Really?"

"Stanley might have been eavesdropping, but he sounded sure." Audrey studied Meghan's face. "You look like someone just told you Christmas came early."

Meghan ducked her head to hide her smile, but her heart was racing. That Aaron was contemplating baptism wasn't a minor detail. It was like a spiritual doorway cracking open into new and exciting depths.

"I remember how you used to lecture me about keeping professional boundaries with my students and their parents," Audrey continued. "Funny how those rules have gotten... flexible."

"This is different," Meghan protested, then paused. "It feels destined somehow. Like I was meant to be in their lives."

"And they in yours?"

Before Meghan could respond, the first-period bell rang, saving her from having to answer a question she wasn't ready to voice.

As Audrey left, she called over her shoulder. "Enjoy your *'small dinner with friends.'* And Meghan? Stop overthinking it."

Alone in her classroom, Meghan pressed a hand to her fluttering stomach. Tomorrow wasn't just dinner, it was a step forward into something she had been afraid to name.

Her phone buzzed with a text from Aaron: *Naomi wants to know if you prefer cranberry sauce from scratch or the canned kind. She's determined to get everything perfect.*

Meghan smiled as she typed back: *Tell her from scratch is wonderful, but I'll love whatever she makes. See you tomorrow.*

His response came quickly: *Looking forward to it. More than I probably should admit.*

Her fingers hovered over the keyboard. There were so many things she wanted to say, but she settled on: *Me too.*

She tucked her phone away, but the flutter in her stomach remained. Tomorrow would bring more than turkey and gratitude. It would bring the chance to discover what this growing connection between them might become.

Chapter 21

Thanksgiving morning dawned clear and bright. Meghan woke up early, excited to devote the time and attention her father's beloved sweet potato pie recipe deserved.

His treasured recipe journal lay open on the countertop, its recognizable handwriting guiding her through the steps she knew so well. With each motion of peeling sweet potatoes, measuring spices, and preparing the crust, memories surfaced like waves.

She heard her father's voice in her mind: *Always warm the milk before adding. Cold ingredients make for a tough pie.*

In the kitchen, his presence hovered close as she worked. One memory rose above the rest, a quiet November morning nearly twenty-five years ago. Her father's hands had guided her small ones as she mashed sweet potatoes and mixed cinnamon with sugar.

Cooking is science with soul, Meggie-girl. Know the chemistry, but don't forget the love.

The kitchen smelled of vanilla, cinnamon, and nutmeg. Meghan closed her eyes, letting the scents wrap around her like a hug from the past. She recalled Thanksgiving mornings in her childhood, her father bustling about while her mother set the table with their best dishes. The memory ached sweetly, like pressing on a healing bruise. Years eased grief's sharp edges, turning her pain into cherished remembrances.

When the pie was in the oven, she got ready. She chose a deep burgundy dress that was festive, but not flashy, and she took extra time to shape her curls.

Staring at her reflection, she swallowed hard. This wasn't an ordinary dinner. The way her pulse leaped when she thought of Aaron's steady hands, or that smile that softened his whole face, pushed the evening into unmistakably deeper territory.

Lord, guide my heart. If this isn't right, close the door. But if it is...

The timer beeped, saving her from finishing that thought.

She removed the pie, golden and fragrant. After letting it cool, she packed it in its carrier and gathered two small gifts. A gardening journal for Naomi with detailed illustrations of herbs and flowering plants, and for Aaron, a book about faith perspectives in construction throughout history. It highlighted how cathedrals and sacred spaces had been built for worship through craftsmanship. She hoped it struck the right balance, personal but not overdone.

Her palms were damp on the steering wheel as she pulled into Aaron's complex. She parked and took a breath before making her way to their third-floor unit.

Aaron opened the door before she could knock, as if he had been watching for her arrival. He looked relaxed in dark jeans and a fitted sweater, his smile genuine and... nervous?

"Happy Thanksgiving. You have perfect timing. The turkey just came out of the oven."

As he took the pie carrier from her hands, their fingers brushed, the contact brief but electric.

Entering the apartment, Meghan marveled at its transformation. The once-sparse living space now glowed with fall décor. Miniature pumpkins arrayed on side tables, a fall wreath hung on the wall, and sprays of wheat and dried berries filled simple vases. The bland neutrality had evolved into thoughtful personalization.

More surprising was the aroma. Savory roast turkey mingled with sage and rosemary, accompanied by the distinctive scent of homemade rolls. The tiny kitchen appeared to have been maximized for the occasion, and the countertops were covered with serving dishes awaiting distribution to the dining table.

"This is incredible." Meghan took it all in. "I had no idea you could cook like this."

Aaron smiled sheepishly. "YouTube tutorials deserve most of the credit. Naomi handled the rolls."

Naomi emerged from her bedroom, wearing a navy dress that fit the moment perfectly. Her braids were styled in a crown with a few tendrils framing her face. "Don't let him fool you. He's been practicing recipes all month. The trash can is full from his test batches."

Meghan laughed. The easy teasing between them was a far cry from the tense silence that once filled this home.

"Want a tour before dinner?" Naomi asked, clearly proud of the space. "The apartment's completely different since the last time you were here."

Meghan accepted the invitation.

Naomi led her through the modest apartment, pointing out all the changes. What had once been empty corners now featured bookshelves filled with novels and history texts. The walls held photos of Naomi's grandmother alongside more recent snapshots of Naomi and Aaron from school events.

"And this is my favorite part." Naomi slid open the balcony door.

The container garden had burst into life, with herbs overflowing from their pots in fragrant waves. Lush rows of basil, mint, lavender, and rosemary stood proudly, highlighted by decorative containers and a newly built wooden shelf system.

"These are amazing. You've developed quite a green thumb."

Naomi beamed. "The basil keeps trying to take over everything. Uncle Aaron built the shelves. He stayed up half the night getting the angles right."

Meghan ran her fingers over the smooth wood. It was solid, well-crafted, and thoughtful, just like the man who made it.

"Dinner's ready whenever you are," Aaron called, prompting them to return inside.

The sight of the table took Meghan's breath away. New dishes and cloth napkins transformed the space. A centerpiece of pinecones and candles made it feel intimate and intentional.

Once seated, Aaron reached for her hand. "Would it be okay if we prayed together?"

Meghan nodded. They bowed their heads and joined hands.

Aaron's voice took on a depth she hadn't heard before. "Heavenly Father, thank You for bringing light into our lives, for healing in Naomi, and for Meghan's friendship. Please bless this food and the hands that prepared it. Amen."

His thumb moved almost imperceptibly across Meghan's knuckles.

"Amen," Meghan and Naomi echoed.

The meal unfolded in laughter and stories. Naomi recounted Lisbeth's disastrous attempt at pumpkin bread, and Aaron shared tales of construction catastrophes. When Meghan served her pie, Aaron took one bite and stilled.

"This tastes exactly like my grandmother's," he said with amazement. "She made this every Thanksgiving."

"Really?" Meghan was touched by the connection.

He nodded. "After my grandmother died, my mom tried to recreate it, but she never quite got it right."

"It's my dad's recipe. He was insistent about using fresh nutmeg, warming the milk first, and using real vanilla beans instead of extract."

Aaron's expression turned reverent. "You brought my grandmother back to me. Thank you."

Before the moment could deepen further, Naomi's phone chimed with an incoming message.

"Lisbeth wants to video chat. Can I?"

"Go ahead," Aaron replied, the interruption breaking the spell.

After she left for her room, Meghan gathered the empty dessert plates and carried them to the kitchen.

"Let me help with the dishes. You did all the cooking."

Aaron joined her at the sink, their shoulders brushing in the kitchen's limited space. "You don't have to. You're our guest."

She filled the sink with warm, soapy water. "I want to."

He acquiesced and reached for a dish towel. They fell into a rhythm of washing, rinsing, and drying. With both of them in the kitchen, the space felt smaller, and the air was thick with unspoken words.

"I've been meaning to thank you. Those verses you've shared with me have helped more than you know."

Meghan was pleased by his openness about spiritual matters. "I'm glad. Sometimes the right scripture comes at exactly the right time."

"It did," he admitted, shelving the dried platter. "I've started reading my devotional again. Song of Solomon 2:10-13 hit me hard last week."

She knew the verses well. Her heart raced. "It's about seasons changing, right?"

"It also speaks about recognizing when the right time has arrived," Aaron clarified, his voice dropping lower. "And when it does, you can't stay in mourning forever."

Their hands met beneath the soapy water. Neither pulled away, fingers intertwining before separating.

"You remember I told you that Naomi and I are staying in Brookside," Aaron said after a moment.

Though she already knew, hearing him say it again released a tension she hadn't realized she was holding. Relief surged through her so intensely that her knees weakened. She couldn't suppress how much she had worried about him leaving.

He turned, leaning against the counter so close she could see the gold flecks in his eyes. "Some things are more important than my career."

Her mouth went dry. He was going to kiss her. She could see it in the way his eyes dropped to her lips, the way he leaned in...

"Uncle Aaron?" Naomi called from the hallway. "Is it okay if Lisbeth comes over tomorrow? Her parents said she could if it's all right with you."

The interruption diffused the moment's intensity. Aaron took a step back, putting space between them.

"We can talk about it when you're off the phone," he called in response.

The moment passed, but the charge remained. An authentic spark moved between them, unburdened by pretense.

Later, as Meghan gathered her things to leave, Aaron walked her to the door.

"Thank you for today. Having you here made it feel like Thanksgiving again."

"Thank you for including me," Meghan replied with equal sincerity. "I had a wonderful time."

He stepped forward and opened his arms in silent invitation. She moved into his embrace, as though the moment had been rehearsed in her heart long before it happened.

As she settled against him, she closed her eyes, reveling in the warmth of his chest and the steady heartbeat beneath her cheek. His cedar aftershave wrapped around her, earthy and grounding.

When she finally pulled back, Aaron's hands stayed on her shoulders, his eyes locking with hers, and stealing her breath.

"Drive safely." His voice held a quiet promise, protective and tender.

Walking to her car, she sensed his eyes on her. Once she slid behind the wheel, she whispered a verse that followed the one Aaron mentioned:

My beloved is mine and I am his.

It wasn't a declaration. Not yet. But undeniably, it was the beginning of something true.

Chapter 22

Even in Georgia's mild December, the town square looked like something out of a Christmas card. Evergreen garlands curled around lamp posts, and twinkle lights shimmered in every storefront. Aaron stood at his apartment window, watching workers mount an enormous wreath on the community center's entrance across the park. The grand opening was scheduled strategically between Christmas and New Year's to maximize community participation.

Behind him, half-unpacked boxes labeled *Christmas* cluttered the living room. His mother's ornaments were carefully wrapped in tissue and egg cartons. He and Naomi picked out a tree from the church youth group's lot yesterday, another milestone in their growing relationship.

His phone buzzed on the kitchen counter. Frank Donovan again. This was the fourth call this week. Aaron considered letting it go to voicemail, but duty won out.

"Morning, Frank." He walked toward his bedroom for privacy.

"Hope I'm not interrupting your Saturday," Frank began, his tone deceptively casual. "I was checking on those community center completion reports. The board meets on Monday morning."

Aaron glanced at his laptop. The documents waited for his final review. "They'll be in your inbox by the end of the day. I'm going over the invoices now."

"Good, good." Frank paused, the silence weighted with an unspoken agenda. "Listen, the Bristol Heights project manager is transferring to our Charlotte office. The position opens January fifteenth."

The implied offer hung in the air. Aaron closed his eyes, drawing a deep breath before responding. "I appreciate your confidence, but my decision hasn't changed. Brookside is my home now."

"Can't blame a man for trying." Disappointment crept through Frank's light delivery. "The board wanted me to remind you that the door's always open."

After the call, Aaron leaned against the hallway wall, tension gradually leaving his shoulders. Six months ago, turning down such an opportunity would have been unthinkable. Now, staying felt like laying the final stone in a foundation he intended to keep.

Christmas music floated from Naomi's room. , but the soft, traditional hymns his mother used to play. This was another small miracle in their journey toward healing.

Aaron checked his watch. There was just enough time to unpack another box before heading to New Hope for the men's breakfast.

"Uncle Aaron?" Naomi appeared in the hallway, already dressed despite the early hour. Her dark braids were neatly arranged, and she wore an emerald sweater that was as bright as holly. "Can we put up the tree tonight? After your church thing and my study group?"

Warmth spread through his chest at her initiative. "Absolutely. And I thought we could order pizza and make it an event."

"Can we invite Ms. Townsend? She said her Christmas decorations are still in storage because she's been swamped with grading."

The suggestion caught him off guard, though it shouldn't have. Naomi saw more than she let on.

"That's thoughtful of you." He tried to sound casual, but his voice came out rougher than intended.

Naomi tilted her head. "You don't mind?"

"Not at all," Aaron replied, too quickly. "Ms. Townsend's been good to both of us. She's welcome anytime."

A knowing look crossed Naomi's face, but she simply nodded. "I'll text her. She gave me her number for the cooking program group chat."

Naomi slipped back into her room. Aaron stood there for a long moment, his heart thumping. Meghan would be here in his home, helping them decorate their tree. That was an entirely different kind of evening.

Shaking himself from his thoughts, he grabbed his keys. The men's breakfast wouldn't wait, and Pastor Morrison didn't believe in tardiness.

New Hope Baptist's fellowship hall buzzed with energy. Thirty men ranging from teenagers to retirees gathered around tables laden with breakfast casseroles, bacon, and scrambled eggs. The air smelled like coffee, aftershave, and cinnamon rolls.

Aaron sat beside Daniel, who passed a platter of biscuits his way. "I saved you from Stanley's health food table." Daniel pointed toward an assortment of yogurt and granola. "The man thinks we're all training for the NBA."

"Much appreciated." Aaron slathered his biscuit with butter. "How's Sam feeling? Is she still fighting morning sickness?"

Daniel's face softened with the tender concern of an expectant father. "It's starting to ease up. The doctor says she should have more energy in the second trimester."

Pastor Morrison approached the podium, his commanding presence quieting the room without a formal call to order. The minister's silver-streaked hair caught the morning light streaming through the stained-glass windows.

"Brothers, as we approach the celebration of our Savior's birth, I'm reminded of Joseph's role in the nativity story. It's often overshadowed, but it was vital to God's plan for redemption."

Aaron leaned forward, not wanting to miss a word.

Pastor Morrison continued. "Scripture gives us few of Joseph's words, but his actions speak volumes. When faced with the news of Mary's pregnancy, he initially planned to quietly break their engagement to spare her public disgrace... an act of compassion when cultural norms demanded harsh judgment."

The room remained silent, thirty men considering this ancient example with fresh eyes.

"Then, after the angel's visit, Joseph embraced a calling that would upend every expectation for his life. He accepted responsibility for a child not biologically his own. He prioritized his family's safety and fled to Egypt when Herod threatened the child's life."

Aaron's throat tightened as the parallel to his journey with Naomi resonated. Hadn't he faced an unexpected guardianship? Hadn't he struggled to balance his ambitions with his family's needs?

"Our culture measures success through accolades and promotions." Pastor Morrison's gaze swept the room, connecting with individuals rather than addressing the collective. "But God measures success differently. In Matthew 25:21, the master doesn't say 'Well done, good and successful servant,' but rather, *Well done, good and faithful servant.*"

Beside Aaron, Daniel nodded in silent agreement. His journey from grieving widower to expectant father echoed the transformation Pastor Morrison described.

The message settled into Aaron's mind like mortar between foundation stones, connecting aspects of his life he had kept separate. After breakfast, when discussion groups formed, he shared more than he had in weeks.

"Six months ago, my identity was tied to construction," Aaron admitted to the small circle including Daniel, Darius, and two other men. "When my mom died, and Naomi became my responsibility, I saw it as—" He paused, searching for honesty instead of polish. "I felt it was a burden."

Darius nodded in understanding. "I used to think providing for my family meant being gone for jobs that paid more money. I almost lost my marriage chasing that lie."

Julian Dawson, a retired firefighter whose quiet wisdom commanded respect, leaned in. "What changed for you, Aaron?"

Aaron didn't hesitate. "The night Naomi disappeared. I didn't know where she was or if she was hurt. Nothing else mattered. Not my job or the next promotion. All that mattered was that she was safe. That's when everything shifted."

"That's the heart of fatherhood," Julian said, his weathered face kind. "Commitment beats biology every time."

The conversation continued, men sharing struggles and victories with rare vulnerability. Two hours later, when the gathering wrapped up, a lightness settled over Aaron, as if he finally set down a burden he hadn't realized he had been carrying.

Outside, Daniel fell into step beside him. "Do you have any plans for the rest of the day?"

Aaron began, an idea forming as he spoke. "I could use some advice. I'm trying to figure out a Christmas gift for someone special."

Daniel's eyes gleamed with mischief. "Would this *someone special*' happen to teach history and bake apple crisps on Thursdays?"

Heat crept up Aaron's neck. "Am I that obvious?"

"Only to anyone paying attention." Daniel laughed and clapped his shoulder.

They reached their vehicles, but neither moved to leave. Aaron leaned against his truck, suddenly serious. "I haven't had feelings like this since... well, never, if I'm honest. This is all new territory. Naomi's still healing, and Meghan's her teacher. The timing's—"

"Complicated?" Daniel finished.

"Right."

"Healing doesn't only happen when everything's perfect," Daniel said. "New beginnings often blend with other life changes." He fished his keys from his pocket. "Come on. The mall opens at ten. We should look for something there. I can grab something for Sam's stocking while we're at it."

They wandered through the town's modest shopping center for nearly an hour. Aaron's uncertainty grew with each store they passed. Nothing seemed adequate to express his feelings toward Meghan.

"What about jewelry?" Daniel suggested as they passed a display of glittering necklaces.

Aaron shook his head. "Too intimate for whatever this is."

"Fair point. Books? She's always quoting literary references in faculty meetings."

"Possibly," Aaron considered, yet it felt lacking in warmth given their connection.

They continued walking, discussing options. Aaron nearly suggested giving up when a small specialty shop caught his eye, showcasing handcrafted wooden utensils, leather-bound journals, and artisanal pottery.

"Wait." He changed direction mid-stride. "This might be it."

Inside, Aaron gravitated toward a display of cherry wood utensils. He traced the smooth contours of a serving spoon, appreciating the craftsmanship. Each curve followed the grain, naturally guided. It reminded him of his developing relationship with Meghan—slow, thoughtful, genuine.

"These are nice." Daniel picked up a matching set of salad servers. "Practical but personal, especially given that she loves cooking."

Aaron nodded as an idea crystallized. "These are well-crafted, but I could make something like this." He turned the spoon over, studying the technique. "I have a small woodworking setup at the apartment. My grandfather taught me to carve when I was growing up."

"Even better. A handmade gift would show her you put real thought into it."

With the decision made, Aaron dropped Daniel off at his car, then stopped at his favorite specialty lumber supplier and selected a piece of maple with striking grain patterns. With its strength veiled by beauty, this wood reminded him of Meghan.

Returning home, he found a note from Naomi. She had gone to her study group at the library and would return by five. It was the perfect time to begin his project.

He laid out his tools in the small workshop he created in the apartment's storage closet. The process of measuring, cutting, and shaping centered him. He allowed his mind to reflect on the morning's insights.

For years, he defined himself through career success. But did that matter? Was what he built for others more important than what he built with Naomi? With Meghan?

Hours passed as he shaped the maple into an elegant serving spoon that would fit comfortably in her hand. As he began sanding and smoothing the rough edges to a silken finish, he contemplated what message to add.

A verse Meghan quoted during a challenging cooking class, when a student's failed recipe prompted tears, came to his mind:

Weeping may stay for the night, but rejoicing comes in the morning.

With painstaking care, he burned the words slowly into the handle. The scent of scorched maple rose around him as the scripture emerged in permanent testimony.

The apartment door opening and closing announced Naomi's return, but he remained focused, completing the final letter before setting the tool aside. Satisfaction warmed him at the result—simple yet elegant, practical yet meaningful.

"Uncle Aaron?" Naomi's voice called from the hallway.

"In here." He quickly covered the spoon with a cloth before she appeared in the doorway.

She peeked in, her backpack still slung over one shoulder. "Ms. Townsend said she can come by around seven to help decorate."

Aaron hoped his expression remained calm despite his pulse quickening. "Great. You still want pepperoni and mushrooms on the pizza?"

"Yes, please." Naomi hesitated, shifting her weight as if gathering courage for her next words. "Can I ask you something? It might be weird."

Aaron set aside his tools and gave her his full attention. "You can ask me anything, weird or otherwise."

"Are you and Ms. Townsend, like—" She paused, discomfort evident in her posture. "Are you two dating or something?"

Heat rushed to his face as he fumbled for an appropriate response.

"It's complicated, Naomi." He rubbed the back of his neck. "Ms. Townsend has been incredibly supportive of both of us. I respect her tremendously."

"That's not an answer," Naomi remarked, her grandmother's characteristic bluntness creeping into her voice.

Aaron sighed, recognizing that her question called for honesty instead of avoidance. "You're right, it's not. The truth is, I care about her deeply. But there's her being your teacher, and... I don't know what to tell you, Naomi. The timing feels off."

Naomi touched her finger to her chin. "I think she likes you too. She gets this look when she hears your name."

"What kind of look?"

"Kind of like the one you have right now."

Aaron laughed at being read so easily by a fourteen-year-old. "When did you get so wise?"

"Grandma always said I noticed things other people missed." This time, when Naomi mentioned her grandmother, there wasn't the usual hint of pain in her voice, another small indication that she was healing. "For what it's worth, I wouldn't mind if you two dated."

His chest tightened with tenderness for his niece. "Thank you."

Apparently, having received whatever confirmation she sought, Naomi headed toward the living room. "I'll clean up before she gets here."

As his niece prepared for their guest, Aaron returned to his makeshift workshop, uncovered the wooden spoon, and stared at it for a long moment.

The carved scripture caught the light. He traced the words with his finger, and suddenly the full weight of what he was doing hit him. This wasn't just a gift. This was a declaration. He was carving his feelings into wood, making them permanent and undeniable.

What if Meghan didn't feel the same way? What if she saw this as too much, too soon? What if he was reading more into their moments together than was there?

Aaron set the spoon down. In a few hours, Meghan would be here in his home, helping them decorate their tree, being part of their family traditions. His heart hammered against his ribs. He had faced down construction deadlines, financial pressures, and the challenge of raising a grieving teenager. But the thought of revealing his heart to Meghan Townsend terrified him more than any of that.

Because losing her would break something in him that he wasn't sure could be repaired.

Chapter 23

T HE PIZZA WAS GONE, and the Christmas tree was decorated. Meghan left not long ago with a plate of leftovers and a sprig of mistletoe that Naomi had playfully pressed into her hand.

Aaron lay awake, staring at the ceiling, as memories of the evening replayed in his mind. His earlier worries turned out to be unfounded. He could still hear Meghan's laughter while they worked together to untangle the Christmas lights, how seamlessly she blended into their family traditions, and the warmth in her eyes when Naomi asked her to place the star atop the tree. His anxiety about revealing too much, too soon, seemed foolish now.

But in the quiet darkness, new concerns surfaced. The wooden spoon sat wrapped and waiting in his closet, the scripture he carved into its handle feeling more significant with each passing hour. He even decided to add a wooden bowl with her name etched on the bottom as an additional gift. Christmas was only days away. Soon, he would hand her these gifts, and there would be no taking back what they represented.

The evening marked a pivotal point in their relationship. The way she looked at him when she said goodnight, coupled with the lingering touch of her hand on his arm as she thanked him for including her, spoke volumes. There was no mistaking the shift that was taking place. This had evolved beyond mere friendship or casual attraction. It had become something more profound and disconcerting.

A soft whimper from Naomi's room pulled him from his thoughts. The words were too quiet to make out, but full of pain. Aaron sat up, pulling on a T-shirt as he went to her door.

"Naomi?" he called gently, giving a soft knock. No answer, just more muffled distress. He opened the door.

Moonlight spilled through her blinds. Naomi thrashed under the covers, face contorted with the unmistakable anguish of a nightmare. Tears traced down her cheek.

"Grandma," she sobbed. "Don't go. Please don't go."

Aaron crossed the room and sat on the edge of her bed. "Naomi. Hey, wake up, kiddo. It's just a dream." He touched her shoulder.

Her eyes flew open, dazed at first, then embarrassed. She sat up, quickly wiping tears from her face. "Sorry. Did I wake you?"

Aaron brushed damp strands from her forehead. "You don't have to apologize. Do you want to talk about it?"

She shook her head, pulling her knees to her chest. Then, after a pause, she nodded. "It was Christmas morning at Grandma's house. The tree was lit, and cinnamon rolls were baking. Everything felt perfect. But then she started to fade... like she was turning into a ghost. I tried to hold on to her, but I couldn't. She just disappeared."

Fresh tears welled as she described the dream. Aaron placed an arm around her shoulders, grateful she didn't pull away.

"I miss her so much," Naomi whispered against his shirt. "Especially now, with Christmas coming. She loved Christmas."

"I know." His voice cracked. "I miss her too."

The admission opened a door. They shared their pain, giving it a voice instead of carrying it alone. They stayed like that for a long time, holding space for grief instead of hiding from it. Then the memories started coming, quietly at first, then all at once.

"She made those ridiculous reindeer pancakes." He smiled despite the ache. "The ones with chocolate chip eyes and bacon antlers."

Naomi sniffled and gave a watery laugh. "And she sang off-key to every carol, but nobody was allowed to mention it."

"She used to wrap empty boxes to make the tree look full." The memory was vivid despite years of missed holidays during her final Christmas season. "She said a Christmas tree needed accessories like any good outfit."

They kept trading stories until the tears slowed and the ache dulled. Somewhere in the middle of all that remembering, Aaron realized something. Remembering didn't have to hurt. Honoring her meant sharing her, not avoiding her.

"You know what Grandma used to tell me?" Naomi said after a while, her voice stronger. "She said people never really leave as long as we keep remembering them. She said remembering is a way of keeping their love with us."

The wisdom hit Aaron in the chest. His mother was speaking through Naomi, offering guidance even in her absence.

"She was right. And she'd want us to keep finding joy and build lives she would be proud of."

Naomi nodded, exhaustion finally winning as she slumped against the pillows. Her breathing slowed as she drifted toward sleep.

That's when Aaron noticed the feather in her hand. It was long, silver, and familiar. It looked like the same feather he found in the gazebo weeks ago.

He didn't remember giving it to her.

"Where did you get that?" He touched the feather lightly.

"Found it on my windowsill last week," Naomi murmured, already half-asleep. "It reminds me of the man."

"What man?" Aaron asked, but Naomi had already surrendered to slumber, her breathing deep and calm.

He tucked the blanket around her shoulders and stayed a while, eyes drawn to the mysterious feather still clutched in her fingers. It glowed faintly in the moonlight, not reflecting light, but as if the glow came from within.

Feathers didn't glow. But then again, not much seemed to follow the rules of logic lately. Not the silver-haired man who appeared so unexpectedly. Not the peace that kept slipping into Aaron's life when he least expected it. And certainly not the way Meghan Townsend walked into their world and changed everything.

Rising carefully to avoid disturbing Naomi, Aaron walked back to his room. He went to the window and looked out. The sky sprawled out above him, a tapestry speckled with stars. The constellations looked exactly as they had months ago, when he stood in this very spot, wrestling with doubts about his future, his purpose, and his capability to care for his niece.

Tonight felt different. Not because life had suddenly become easy, but because he wasn't walking blind anymore. There was direction now, purpose beyond mere survival. Their little family, formed from broken pieces, was becoming something whole.

And Meghan was part of that. Tonight had been a beginning. But what if he wasn't ready for what came next? What if loving her meant risking everything they had built?

His phone buzzed on the nightstand. A text from Meghan: *Thank you for tonight. I loved being part of your traditions. Sweet dreams.*

Aaron stared at the message, his heart hammering. Whatever came next with the community center opening and the questions about their future, he wouldn't face it alone. Not anymore.

He typed back: *Thanks for making it so special. Sleep well.*

As he set the phone down, Aaron caught sight of his reflection in the dark window. For the first time in months, the man looking back at him didn't seem lost.

Chapter 24

MEGHAN SURVEYED BROOKSIDE'S COMMUNITY center kitchen, admiring the polished stainless steel countertops that reflected overhead lights. Rustic wooden bowls overflowed with colorful bell peppers, fresh herbs, and locally grown vegetables, ready for the first cooking demonstration.

She adjusted a sprig of rosemary that had fallen out of place. Everything looked exactly as she had imagined. Better, even.

Behind her, voices grew louder as people filtered into the main atrium. The grand opening ceremony would start in thirty minutes, the culmination of months of planning. Through the kitchen's tall windows, Meghan spotted Aaron weaving through the crowd, greeting community leaders with an ease she never would have expected when they first met.

"I can't get over the transformation." Audrey appeared at her side, her copper highlights glinting in a sophisticated updo. "Do you remember that first parent-teacher conference? He could hardly string two sentences together. And now, here he is, charming Mayor Thompson."

Meghan's lips curved as Aaron shook hands with the mayor. His charcoal suit jacket stretched across broad shoulders, a striking departure from his construction clothes but natural on his tall frame.

"People grow when they're given space to." Meghan accepted the recipe cards from Audrey. "He and Naomi both."

Speaking of, Naomi entered the atrium with Miranda Bolton and her husband, Noah. Daniel's sister and brother-in-law were here in support of the community. Naomi walked between them, and when Miranda, or Mandy, as she preferred, said something that made her laugh, the girl who once hunched, as if she wanted to disappear, now stood tall in a purple dress. She caught Meghan's eye and waved.

"I should finish setting up before the kids arrive," Meghan said, turning back to the demonstration station. "The middle school cooking club goes first, then the senior citizens' heritage recipe presentation."

"I'll help." Audrey tied an apron over her dress. "Stanley's busy with the basketball team's refreshment booth." A smile played across her lips as she mentioned the coach's name, a development that hadn't escaped Meghan's notice these past few weeks.

What had begun as planning for the fall festival, blossomed into coffee dates and shy glances. Just yesterday, Meghan spotted them walking hand in hand through the school parking lot. Stanley's tough exterior melted when he was around Audrey's artistic spirit.

Together, they arranged the remaining ingredients and reviewed the schedule of events. Meghan paused to admire the hand-carved wooden spoons on display. Each was made by a different person, representing the diverse traditions and skills that would now have a home in this space.

Her gaze traveled back to the atrium, where Aaron now conversed with Pastor Morrison near the entrance. A silver Christmas star suspended above them caught the morning light, sparkling with promise.

"Meghan, do you have a minute?" Olivia's voice floated in from the doorway.

Meghan turned to find her friend looking radiant in a forest green dress, her smile bright with the quiet joy that settled over her in recent weeks.

"Always for you." Meghan wiped her hands on a kitchen towel. "Is everything okay with the adoption paperwork?"

"Everything's going smoothly. But that's not why I wanted to talk." Olivia glanced meaningfully at Audrey, who immediately raised her hands in surrender.

"I'll go check on the student displays in the east wing." Audrey removed her apron. "I'll be back in fifteen minutes."

When they were alone, Olivia crossed the kitchen with that familiar mix of gentleness and honesty Meghan had come to love.

"So, are we going to talk about what's happening between you and Aaron?" Olivia moved deeper into the kitchen.

Heat rose to Meghan's cheeks despite her attempt at composure. "I don't know what you—"

"Meghan," Olivia interrupted with friendly exasperation. "I've known you since Pastor introduced us after your breakup with Finn. I know the signs."

The memory of that introduction brought unexpected warmth. Olivia's pastor wisely connected them, as he had also introduced Olivia to Samantha during her painful separation from her ex-boyfriend, Paul Winston.

Years earlier, Olivia's own personal heartbreak shaped her into a compassionate guide for women navigating broken relationships. Her strength helped Meghan and Samantha through their darkest moments, creating a deep friendship among the three women.

Meghan picked up a spoon and rearranged the utensils, mostly to avoid Olivia's knowing eyes. "We've built a good partnership, for Naomi's sake and the cooking program. That's all."

"That's all?" Olivia's skeptical tone made clear she wasn't convinced. "Then why has his name come up in every conversation for the past month? And don't get me started on the forty-five-minute recap of Thanksgiving dinner with him and Naomi."

Meghan sighed, leaning against the counter. "It's complicated."

"Most worthwhile things are," Olivia countered, her voice softening. "But complicated doesn't mean it's not worth exploring."

Meghan considered her response. "There is something between us. But I wasn't expecting it, and I'm still Naomi's teacher."

"For one more semester. And even now, it's mostly after school with the cooking program."

That was true. But Meghan's worries ran deeper than logistics. "It's not only that. Remember Finn?"

Olivia's expression reflected immediate understanding. The name alone conjured painful memories of Meghan's three-year relationship with a man whose courteous tolerance of her faith had never moved into a true spiritual partnership.

"Aaron isn't Finn, Meghan. And from what you've told me, he's actively reconnecting with his faith."

"He is," Meghan conceded. "But what if my involvement complicates that? What if he's only interested in..." She hesitated.

"What if he's only what?" Olivia prompted.

"What if his spiritual interest is about getting closer to me, and not about God?" The question revealed Meghan's deepest fear of history repeating itself.

Olivia considered this with the thoughtfulness that made her such a valued friend. "That's fair. But Meghan, not everyone follows Finn's pattern."

Through the window, they saw Aaron kneel beside a woman in a wheelchair, listening as she pointed out something above them. The care and patience in his body language spoke to the man's character.

Olivia studied her friend's face with concern. "Okay, I hear you. Promise me you'll guard your heart until you're sure of his motives."

Before Meghan could respond, the kitchen door opened, and Principal Watkins peeked in.

"There you are." Relief was clear in his voice. "Mayor Thompson wants to mention the education partnership in her remarks. She's asking for you."

Meghan smoothed her dress. "I'll be right there."

Once Principal Watkins left, Olivia squeezed Meghan's hand. "We'll talk later. For what it's worth, I'm praying for both of you."

The simple words anchored her as she stepped into the crowd. She paused in a quiet alcove to gather herself, the sound of mingling voices swelling around her. Her car was still full of final exams that needed grading. A reminder that life didn't pause when your heart was full.

She stood and admired the center's massive Christmas tree. Handmade ornaments, tiny rolling pins, and painted cookie cutters decorated the branches, a perfect blend of tradition and new beginnings.

"Ms. Townsend." Aaron's voice rolled over her like a slow wave. She turned, and there he was, close enough that his scent of cedar and clean snow wrapped around her.

"Mr. Grant," she responded, her formal address a half-hearted attempt to reestablish her composure. "The center is magnificent. You should be proud."

"*We* should be proud," he corrected, his gaze holding hers. "This kitchen wouldn't exist without your vision for the cooking program."

The way he said, *'we'*, sent a fragile anticipation through her chest.

"I wanted to introduce you to someone." Aaron gestured to a distinguished man approaching from the main atrium. "This is Frank Donovan, my boss and owner of Donovan Building Contractors."

The man extending his hand exuded authority. He sported silver-streaked dark hair, a tailored suit, and the self-assured air of someone accustomed to commanding respect. "Ah, so you're the renowned Ms. Townsend. Aaron speaks highly of your program."

"The pleasure is mine." Meghan was delighted despite being caught off guard by the introduction. "Your company has created something truly special for Brookside."

Frank nodded. "Aaron's leadership made it happen. Speaking of leadership, I've had a chance to review your proposal. It's innovative and ambitious, but sound. I like it."

Confusion stirred in Meghan. "My proposal?"

Frank's eyebrows rose. "Have I spoken out of turn? Aaron submitted it with your name—"

Before she could press further, Mayor Camille Thompson's amplified voice filled the atrium, announcing the ceremony's commencement. Frank excused himself to join other the dignitaries near the podium, leaving Meghan with questions.

"What proposal is he talking about?" she asked once Frank moved out of earshot.

Aaron looked sheepish. "I planned on telling you about it after the opening. It's a proposal to expand your cooking program. It would include construction training for at-risk youth. We're hoping to connect cooking and building. The vision is to instill healing through creating, like you did with Naomi."

The idea captivated her right away. It encompassed all her beliefs.

"I've been thinking about it since watching Naomi in class," he admitted. "I see how it helped her deal with grief. I thought, why not offer the same to other kids?"

Warmth unfurled in Meghan's chest. He hadn't only understood her vision. He had built on it.

"It sounds wonderful. I'd love to hear more about it when there's time."

"There's one more thing—" he began, but Naomi appeared beside them, interrupting the moment.

"They want both of you by the stage." Her earlier reserve was absent as she looked between them. "They told me to tell you it's something about an educational partnership."

The moment for private conversation dissolved as duty called. Following Naomi to the stage, Meghan wondered what else Aaron planned to say. What other surprise might follow their partnership proposal?

The ceremony opened with speeches about collaboration and restoration. Meghan stood with Principal Watkins and spoke about the school's role. From the stage, she spotted students, elders, and families alike, each one part of the vision she had prayed over for months.

Near the back, partially obscured by a support beam, stood a figure that caught Meghan's attention.

The man with silver hair leaned lightly on a polished wooden cane as he observed the proceedings. This was the same mysterious stranger she noticed near Providence Park, and again during her rain-sheltered conversation with Aaron in the gazebo.

His appearance carried unmistakable intention. When Pastor Morrison stepped forward to offer the dedication blessing, the silver-haired man inclined his head, as though affirming something only he understood.

The pastor's resonant voice filled the atrium. "As we dedicate this community center, we recognize it as more than mere walls and windows. This structure represents restoration. Restoration of community, intergenerational connections, and faith expressed through service."

Murmurs of agreement rippled through the crowd as the reverend continued. "Speaking of restoration, I invite you all to our special Christmas Eve service at New Hope Baptist. Several community members will share testimonies of God's restorative work in their lives this past year, celebrating how the Light of the World illuminates even our darkest seasons."

As Pastor Morrison extended this invitation, Meghan noticed a change in Aaron's expression. A fleeting vulnerability crossed his face before his usual countenance returned. The pastor's words had struck something deep.

When the ceremony ended, activities filled the halls. Meghan paused to watch Naomi teach the younger kids how to hold a knife. Her confidence was unshakeable, her patience a gift. Meghan's throat tightened with pride. This was what healing looked like.

Hours passed in productive chaos, the grand opening achieving everything its planners had hoped. By late afternoon, the thinning crowds signaled the event's natural conclusion.

Outside, the season's first snowflakes drifted lazily from a pewter sky, dusting the parking lot with patterns that enhanced the building's Christmas decorations.

Meghan stood beneath the community center's covered entrance, watching the snowfall transform the landscape. Its beauty captured her attention so completely that she didn't hear Aaron approach until he spoke.

"Perfect ending to a perfect day. The snow on opening day feels like a blessing."

Meghan nodded, appreciating his perception. "It does. A fresh beginning."

They stood close, the snow drifting around them. She turned, heart thudding.

"Aaron, what was the other thing you wanted to tell me? Before we were interrupted earlier?"

He looked at her, snowflakes catching in his dark hair like stars against the night sky. For a heartbeat, she thought he might speak a truth that would tip the scales between them. Instead, he stepped back.

"It can wait for another time. You said you needed to finish grading tonight."

She nodded. His restraint felt like a gift, an acknowledgment of her responsibilities and her boundaries.

"Thank you for today. For everything." She meant it more than he could know.

"Drive safe," he replied. "The snow's beautiful, but it makes for slippery roads."

Meghan drove through the increasingly snow-dusted streets. Her mind spun from the day's events, fixating on the proposal, the silver-haired stranger, and Aaron's thoughtful expression during Pastor Morrison's invitation to share restoration stories.

Pulling into her driveway, she remained in her car, watching the snow. The simple beauty prompted her to pray.

Lord, if this is Your plan, show me. And if it's not, give me the strength to let it go.

No immediate answer presented itself. There was no voice from heaven, no supernatural sign. Only the certainty that some questions required patience.

As she gathered her grading materials and stepped into the swirling snow, she remained unaware that across town, Aaron Grant stood at his apartment window.

In his palm, he held a silver feather, contemplating proposals far more personal than community programming. But what Aaron couldn't see was the figure standing in the shadows of the parking lot below his building.

Ryan Grant leaned against his car, staring up at his brother's lit window, his face etched with conflict. He pulled out his phone and stared at an unsent text message that simply read: *I need to tell you something.*

After a long moment, he deleted it and drove away, leaving only tire tracks in the fresh snow.

Chapter 25

Aaron sat in the corporate office, his shoulders tense from a morning jam-packed with paperwork. The contract spread out before him represented more than just another sheet of paper. It symbolized permanence. It was a choice made freely by him and not dictated by external forces.

Frank Donovan's voice from their phone call at dawn resonated in his memory: *Regional manager, Aaron. You've earned this. The Bristol Heights expansion will proceed under Darius's supervision, but you'll oversee all southeastern operations from Brookside.*

The offer surpassed anything Aaron envisioned when he first joined Donovan Building Contractors two years ago. It was more than a promotion. It proclaimed that his life was now anchored here, in this Georgia town that had become home for him and Naomi.

Thank You, Lord.

Prayer no longer felt foreign on his lips. He signed with steady hands, confirming what his heart had known for months.

The office door swung open. Frank stepped inside, his presence filling the room. The tailored suit and salt-and-pepper hair projected authority, but the Christmas tie decorated with miniature construction tools revealed a personality beneath the professionalism.

"All set?" Frank's gaze dropped to the signed contract.

Aaron slid the document across his desk. "Signed and sealed. Thanks for making this position work around me staying in Brookside."

Frank tucked the papers into his portfolio. "Don't thank me for good business sense. Your connections to this community are invaluable. That community center has brought in three new contracts since the grand opening." He paused, studying Aaron with sharp eyes. "Though I suspect your reasons for staying have less to do with business than I initially thought."

Aaron experienced a sudden warmth in his neck. Frank had seen him with Meghan during the ceremony, and the subtle raise of his eyebrow communicated as much.

"Family comes first," Aaron remarked, even though it felt like only a fraction of what was correct.

Frank nodded, accepting his explanation without pressing for more details. "The board meeting is scheduled for January fifth. They'll make everything official then, although at this point, it's merely a formality."

After Frank departed, Aaron turned to the window. Brookside glowed under the fresh snow, and the sidewalks bustled with holiday shoppers clutching steaming cups. A year ago, he had been struggling to survive from day to day. Now, he was rooted here.

His phone vibrated against the desk. Ryan's name still startled him after years of silence.

"Hey."

"I got your message about the land purchase going through. Congratulations."

"Thanks. It's a good property. Two acres, mature trees, just outside town limits." Their conversations moved with cautious care, trust rebuilding one exchange at a time.

"Mom used to say you'd build your dream house someday." Ryan's mention of their mother created a momentary silence. Their shared loss had become a bridge rather than a chasm. "She kept that sketch you drew in high school. I found it in her bedside table."

Aaron felt a tightening in his throat. "I didn't know that."

"Yeah, well..." Ryan cleared his throat. "Do you remember Dad driving us past those fancy houses on Oakwood Drive? You said you'd build something even more spectacular."

The memory surfaced unbidden. He and his brother would race their bikes down the steep streets, stopping for popsicles at Marvin's Corner Store during hot summer days, and their usually reserved father would point out architectural details with rare enthusiasm.

"I remember. Those Sunday drives were the only times Dad seemed interested in what I wanted to do."

"He talks about your community center now. He showed me the newspaper article when I visited last week. I never thought I'd see the day he would brag about either of us."

The words settled into Aaron's chest with unexpected weight. His father, absent through so much, was proud now. Grace operated beyond logic sometimes.

"Listen, I've been thinking about what you said... about the Christmas Eve service."

The invitation had been impulsive. Ryan lived in Macon, less than an hour from Brookside. Church wasn't his preference, but Aaron still extended the invitation.

"You're welcome anytime. Naomi would love to see you."

A pause stretched between them, heavy with unspoken history. "I'll think about it. Still figuring some things out. But... thanks."

They concluded with small talk, but something had shifted. The distance between them was shrinking incrementally.

Aaron checked the clock. The afternoon had vanished. Gathering his coat and keys, he locked the office and nodded farewell to the receptionist, who was decorating her desk with a miniature Christmas tree.

Driving home, he absorbed Brookside's holiday transformation. Garlands adorned lampposts. The square featured a nativity scene. Lights twinkled in every window. The town radiated hope alongside festivity.

Meghan's car sat in the parking lot of his apartment complex. She wasn't expected for another hour.

Laughter drifted from the kitchen as he paused in the entryway, savoring the unexpected domestic warmth.

Naomi stood at the counter, measuring flour. Beside her, Meghan worked dough with a rolling pin. Her curls were secured with a red scarf, and flour dusted her emerald sweater.

"The secret is maintaining even pressure across the rolling pin. My dad said baking's half science, half intuition."

"Like construction," Aaron announced his presence, setting his keys on the entry table.

Both turned toward him. Meghan's smile illuminated the room.

"Uncle Aaron! You're early!" Naomi wiped her flour-covered hands on a dishcloth. "We started Christmas cookies. Ms. Townsend's teaching me her dad's special gingerbread recipe."

"I hope that's okay," Meghan added. "Naomi texted that she finished with her study group early, so I came after the faculty meeting."

Aaron hung his coat before entering the kitchen, absorbing the warmth of the scene. "It's more than okay. Do you need another pair of hands?"

"Definitely," Naomi's enthusiasm bubbled over. "We need four dozen cookies for the community center's Christmas boxes."

For the next hour, the kitchen hummed with activity and laughter. Aaron discovered he had a knack for icing, while Naomi brought her artistic flair to life with intricate snowflake designs.

"Where did you learn to do that?" Aaron asked as Naomi completed another symmetrical design.

She shrugged, pleasure coloring her expression. "In art class. Ms. Sinclair taught us geometric designs."

"They're beautiful," Meghan said with genuine admiration.

Naomi accepted the compliment gracefully. "Grandma used to let me help with Christmas cookies. She had these special metal cutters shaped like stars. She always said every cookie needed a little sparkle to be perfect."

Aaron met Meghan's eyes over Naomi's head. The memory flowed effortlessly, filled with warmth yet free of tears.

"Speaking of special touches, the land purchase was finalized today."

"For the house?" Meghan's hand stilled on the rolling pin.

"Two acres, with excellent southern exposure and rich soil."

Her eyes brightened. "That's wonderful, Aaron. When will you start construction?"

"Spring, most likely. I'll need to prepare the site this winter."

"Can I see the plans?" Naomi asked, pausing in her decorating.

Aaron blinked in surprise. She had shown minimal interest in his construction projects before. "Sure. They're in my office. We can review them after we finish here."

They kept working together. Once the final tray cooled, Naomi announced her need for a shower.

"I need to wash all this flour out of my hair." She disappeared toward the hallway.

With Naomi gone, Aaron became acutely aware of Meghan's presence. Vanilla and jasmine emanated from her as she moved with fluid grace, transforming mundane cleanup into choreography. Their arms brushed as they sorted cookies, creating currents of unspoken tension.

"Would you like to see those house plans while Naomi showers?" His voice emerged rougher than he intended.

"I'd love to."

Aaron led her to his converted home office. The space reflected his methodical nature with a drafting table positioned for optimal light, books neatly organized by subject, and walls adorned with framed blueprints of past projects. He retrieved a portfolio from beside his desk, extracting a collection of architectural drawings.

"This is the main structure." He unrolled the first sheet across the drafting table.

Meghan leaned closer, her proximity igniting a spark of awareness within him. Lamplight accentuated the elegant curve of her neck as she studied the plans. He could feel the warmth emanating from her, so near that it intertwined with his own.

"The kitchen is enormous." Her eyes glided across the page.

"It's designed for someone who loves to cook." Aaron's voice dropped to a lower register. "It has double ovens, expanded countertops, and stone floors for heat retention."

He watched her study the designs, her lashes fluttering as she absorbed every detail. Her lips parted in concentration, and he could almost see the unspoken questions taking shape. Her fingers followed the lines with an almost instinctive understanding.

Having her in his space settled something inside him, like a piece finally clicking where it belonged.

"And this wraparound porch..."

"Is perfect for container gardening. These windows provide optimal light for year-round herbs."

When Meghan looked up, their faces were closer than either realized. Aaron counted the gold flecks in her brown eyes, memorizing the lashes framing them. Understanding dawned in her expression, and her lips parted with the realization.

"Aaron, these features..."

"Happen to match everything you've mentioned loving." His voice roughened with emotion he no longer attempted to hide. "I was listening."

Color deepened in her cheeks, rich against her warm brown skin. His hand covered hers where it rested on the blueprint, the touch both tender and electric. Her fingers felt smooth against his work-roughened palm.

"It's beautiful." He focused on the pulse beating visibly at her throat's base. "Whoever lives there will be blessed."

Aaron's gaze dropped to her lips, then returned to her eyes in silent question. The space contracted, the world beyond fading into irrelevance. He leaned forward, the magnetic pull nearly irresistible.

"Uncle Aaron?" Naomi's voice interrupted from the hallway. "Is Ms. Townsend still here? I want to show her my container garden."

The moment was broken, but Aaron's hand lingered on Meghan's for one heartbeat longer. When he withdrew, emptiness replaced where their fingers had intertwined.

"We should join her." Meghan stepped back from the drafting table.

After admiring Naomi's herbs and discussing optimal winter care, they gathered in the living room where Naomi arranged Christmas decorations with artistic flair.

When the time came for Meghan's departure, Aaron walked her to the door.

"I wanted to ask you something before you leave." He faced her directly. "There's a Christmas Eve service at New Hope Baptist. Naomi and I were hoping you'd join us."

Surprise, pleasure, then reluctance flickered across her expression. "That's sweet of you to ask. But I usually go to the Cottonwood Faith Community Center's service with Olivia. It's been our tradition since my mom died."

The refusal contained no rejection, only honest acknowledgment of her prior commitments.

"Of course," he replied, nodding in understanding despite the deep sense of disappointment he felt. "Traditions matter, especially during holidays."

"They do, but so do new ones." She hesitated, weighing her words. "Let me talk to Olivia. Maybe we can find a way to attend both services, or alternate years."

The possibility that she might consider sharing future Christmases with him sparked hope.

"No pressure. The invitation remains open, whatever you decide."

Meghan halted at the door, her container of cookies precariously held in one arm. "Thank you for tonight... and for making me feel so welcome in your home."

"You're always welcome here." The truth behind those words held a depth that went far beyond their surface meaning.

After she left, Aaron stood at the window watching the snow drift in lazy spirals. Naomi came to join him.

"You should have told her," she said with the straightforwardness typical of youth.

Aaron glanced at his niece. "Told her what?"

Naomi rolled her eyes with classic teenage exasperation. "It's obvious that you're building that house for her. You're in love with her."

The blunt statements startled a laugh from Aaron. "Since when did you become a relationship guru?"

"I'm fourteen, not four. You both do that weird staring thing when you think no one's watching."

Aaron considered denying it, then abandoned the pretense. "I told you before, it's complicated."

"Adults always say that. But it doesn't look complicated to me. You like her, she likes you." She turned back toward the falling snow.

"Moving too fast can cause unnecessary pain," he said finally.

"Christmas is coming," she pointed out. "It seems like a perfect time for miracles."

After she retreated to her room, Aaron remained at the window. His gaze fell on the blueprints still scattered across his desk. The house was designed with Meghan in mind, built around a future he dared imagine. A future founded on restored hope and trust.

Whether that future included Meghan remained uncertain. Yet as Aaron rolled the blueprints and returned them to their portfolio, he chose hope over doubt, trust over fear.

Outside, snow fell in quiet curtains. Brookside shimmered with more than holiday lights. It shimmered with possibility, and Aaron allowed himself to believe his heart had finally found its way home.

Chapter 26

MEGHAN RUBBED HER TEMPLES, trying to ease the persistent throb behind her eyes. Five hours of grading mid-year exams had extracted their toll. Her dining room table lay buried beneath history essays, each one awaiting her red pen's assessment. She completed two classes, but the remaining stack sat like a challenge, mocking her earlier hopes of finishing before the faculty Christmas party.

Winter sun stretched long shadows across her frost-covered lawn as she glanced through the window. A lone festive wreath adorned her front door, the only seasonal decoration in her home. Between grading, planning, and cooking classes, holiday preparations had dropped to the bottom of her priorities.

Then there was Aaron's invitation, casual in delivery, but lingering like a melody from a favorite song.

There's a Christmas Eve service at New Hope Baptist. Naomi and I were hoping you'd join us.

She hadn't responded yet. How could she? Every year, she commemorated the service at Cottonwood Faith Community Center with Olivia's family. Altering that tradition wasn't just a logistical issue. It would signify a profound change within the depths of her heart.

Thanksgiving memories replayed in vivid detail. She could hear Aaron's voice softening as he prayed over their meal, recall the brush of their hands as they passed dishes, and picture the easy harmony they shared at the sink, washing and drying dishes together, as if they performed that dance a thousand times before.

He's Naomi's guardian. A parent figure for a student under your care.

There was no denying it anymore. Her affection for Aaron had grown into a clear, undeniable attraction, and the veneer of professional distance was thinning by the day.

Meghan stretched, wincing as her shoulders protested after hours spent bent over her student's work. The clock showed 4:30 p.m., giving her just enough time to shower and change before heading to Principal Watkins' home for the faculty gathering. With a resigned sigh, she capped her pen and stepped away from the table, vowing to tackle the rest in the morning.

Under the hot water, her thoughts returned to Aaron and how profoundly he had changed over the past few months. The grief-hardened man she met in spring had opened gradually, revealing gentleness, thoughtfulness, and quiet strength. She had witnessed his deep care for Naomi, his careful rebuilding of what life had torn apart, and his earnest journey back toward faith.

"I need to try to keep things professional," she said aloud, the words sounding hollow as they echoed off the shower tiles.

But her professional interest didn't quite explain the way her heart raced each time his name lit up her phone. Nor did it account for the dreams that featured his hands, work-roughened, but tender in unexpected ways. And it certainly didn't clarify why his laughter had become one of her favorite sounds.

Dressed in winter-white slacks and a forest green blouse, Meghan styled her curls loosely and kept her makeup minimal. She looked composed, like the teacher everyone knew. Inside, however, the lines she had once drawn with such clarity were beginning to blur.

Principal Watkins' home radiated warmth and festivity. Twinkling lights adorned the banister, and elegant garlands framed each doorway. Stanley held court in one corner, entertaining new teachers with coaching stories. Audrey floated between rooms, her maroon-streaked hair pinned with tiny snowflakes that sparkled under the lights.

"Meghan!" Daniel's cheerful greeting drew her attention. He handed her a glass of sparkling cider. "We were starting to worry that grading had taken you hostage."

"It nearly did." She accepted the beverage gratefully. "I still have two more classes of essays to finish tomorrow."

"The joys of teaching." Daniel chuckled, his expression relaxed in a way that spoke of contentment since marrying Samantha. "How's the cooking program expansion progressing? Sam told me the community center kitchen has been booked solid through March."

"The response has exceeded all of my expectations." Pride warmed her voice. "We've added three new instructors, and Aaron's been invaluable with the design engineering."

Daniel's eyebrow arched at her nonchalant mention of Aaron. "Speaking of Aaron, he's made quite an impact at men's Bible study. Last week, he led our discussion of Nehemiah, and the process of rebuilding both physical and spiritual walls. His perspective on connecting construction concepts to faith was truly eye-opening."

Meghan blinked. She knew Aaron attended services, but leading a study? Cautious hope bubbled up, tempered by memories of Finn's early enthusiasm, which slowly faded into mere tolerance.

"He's not just showing up," Daniel continued, clearly picking up on her interest. "He's committed. He and Pastor Morrison meet weekly for discipleship discussions."

Before Meghan could respond, Samantha appeared beside Daniel, her growing baby bump visible under a red sweater.

"There you are. I've been looking for you." Her observant gaze took in Meghan's expression. "Is my husband gossiping about men's ministry again?"

Daniel raised his hands in playful mock-surrender. "I'm simply sharing ministry updates with a colleague," he remarked with a laugh.

Samantha looped her arm through Meghan's. "Of course you are," she said with a warm smile. "Why don't you come help me with the dessert table? Those cookies won't arrange themselves."

Gratefully, Meghan followed her into the kitchen. Their friendship had deepened since Samantha's marriage to Daniel, built on shared experiences of navigating faith through difficult seasons. Samantha's pregnancy and approaching motherhood added another dimension to their bond.

"Daniel means well, but he sometimes forgets that not everyone moves at the same pace." Samantha rearranged Christmas cookies on a silver platter.

"There's nothing to move forward with," Meghan protested weakly. "Aaron and I work together on the cooking program. That's all."

Samantha's gentle laugh held no judgment. "If you say so. But for what it's worth, Daniel says Aaron mentions you in nearly every conversation." She placed a comforting hand on Meghan's arm. "Sometimes God brings people into our lives when we least expect it. Daniel appeared just when I'd given up hope that I'd ever find someone."

"Aaron's only beginning to reconnect with his faith." Meghan voiced the concern that troubled her most. "After what happened with Finn, I promised myself I wouldn't compromise. I need someone who shares my walk, not someone who merely tolerates it."

"And that's wise," Samantha agreed. "I had the same concerns after my breakup with my ex-boyfriend. But there's a difference between someone tolerating your faith and someone seeking truth for themselves. From what I've seen, and from what Daniel shares, Aaron's genuinely growing."

Meghan didn't immediately respond. She wanted to believe that. Desperately.

She smiled and turned to chat with her other colleagues. But Samantha's words lingered. By eight o'clock, exhaustion had taken its toll. Meghan slipped on her coat and headed for the door, waving goodbye to the group. Outside, the air was crisp, and the sky was dotted with soft, clouded stars.

Instead of turning toward home, she drove downtown. Without conscious thought, she pulled into Heavenly Delights Diner's parking lot.

The bell chimed as she entered, and the scent of fresh coffee and cinnamon enveloped her. Willow Barnes, the owner of the cozy café, looked up from behind the counter, her skin glowing under the warm lighting. Her welcoming presence made Heavenly Delights the heart of Brookside's community.

"Meghan. You're just in time for the last slice of sweet potato pie." Willow wiped her hands on her apron.

"You know I can never resist your pie," Meghan replied, returning the warm greeting. "I'm surprised you're open this late."

Willow's laugh carried a warmth that comforted countless residents through difficult seasons. "Business has been booming since the community center opened. I had to extend the hours. I couldn't keep turning people away at two o'clock anymore." She gestured toward the back, where two new servers arranged desserts.

"I hired extra help to manage the dinner crowd, but Anna's still here for breakfast and lunch."

Meghan smiled, pleased by Willow's success. Her gaze swept the half-empty diner, pausing when she spotted a familiar figure in a corner booth.

"Is that Olivia?"

Willow nodded, pouring steaming coffee into a mug. "She's been nursing that cup of tea for almost an hour. Looks like she could use some company."

Meghan walked across the diner and slid into the booth across from Olivia. Her light brown hair was pulled into a messy bun, several strands escaping to frame her tired face.

"Of all the diners in all the towns," Meghan said with a smile, drawing Olivia's attention from the papers spread before her.

"Meghan... what are you doing here? I thought you had the faculty Christmas party tonight."

Willow approached with coffee and pie. "I left early. Something told me I needed to stop here before heading home. A divine nudge, perhaps?"

"Or your addiction to Willow's baking," Olivia teased, some of her usual spark returning. She pushed aside her papers, creating space on the table. "These forms are driving me crazy. There's so many questions to answer."

"You're going to do fine," Meghan assured her, taking a bite of perfectly spiced pie. "Any child would be blessed to have you as their mother."

"From your lips to God's ears." Olivia sighed, sipping her tea. "But enough about my problems. Why are you really here? What's going on?"

Meghan traced the rim of her coffee mug, gathering courage to voice what she had barely admitted to herself.

"Aaron invited me to Christmas Eve service with him and Naomi at New Hope Baptist." The words rushed out like water through a broken dam.

Olivia blinked. "And that's causing this crisis because..."

"Because accepting means not going with you and your family at Cottonwood," Meghan explained. "Because it feels like I'm crossing a line... because I'm afraid I'm falling for him."

There. The truth lay exposed on the diner table, as visible as Olivia's adoption paperwork.

"And that scares you."

"It terrifies me. After everything that happened with Finn..." She hesitated, struggling to articulate her deepest fear. "What if his faith is temporary? What if he drifts away like Finn did? I can't go through that again."

The old wound throbbed beneath her words. She had spent three years with Finn Lockwood, hoping his initial enthusiasm for church would evolve into a genuine spiritual partnership. Instead, it eroded to reluctant tolerance and resentment of her *religious restrictions.* The breaking point came when he dismissed her faith as *"comfortable crutch"* instead of her spiritual foundation.

Olivia reached across the table, covering Meghan's hand with her own. "But every relationship involves risk, even the good ones."

"I know, but—"

"But nothing. I've watched you keep everyone at arm's length since your heart got broken. I get it, but if you keep shielding yourself from the chance of pain, you'll also miss out on experiencing joy. And I don't want that for you."

Olivia was right. She had built walls around her heart and relied on her work as a form of emotional armor.

"Do you think God might be doing something new in my life?"

Olivia answered thoughtfully. "I think the Meghan Townsend I know would pray for discernment instead of letting fear guide her choices. You'll figure out what to do."

They chatted more until Meghan's pie was gone and Olivia's tea had cooled. In the parking lot, they shared a tight hug goodbye.

The drive home gave Meghan time to process their conversation about fear-based decisions. Had she been using professionalism as a shield? The question followed her into her driveway, where she cut the engine and sat in the darkness.

Gathering her purse, she made her way up the walkway, the motion-sensor light illuminating a package on her doorstep. She approached cautiously. There was no label, just a small card atop the wrapped box.

Once inside, she set her keys on the entry table and carried the package to her kitchen. She opened the card.

For the woman who nourishes others through food and wisdom. Thank you for sharing both with Naomi and me. – Aaron

Inside the box was a hand-carved wooden bowl, smooth and rich, with the lustrous sheen of maple. Turning it over, she gasped.

Her name was etched on the bottom, the handwriting unmistakable.

She ran her hand along the grain. This wasn't a gift pulled from a store shelf. Aaron made this. He chose the wood, shaped the curves, and burned the inscription.

It wasn't just thoughtful. It was intimate.

Through the kitchen window, she spotted movement. Outside, across the street where the neighborhood park began, a figure stood beneath a streetlamp. Despite the distance, she distinguished silver hair and the distinctive shape of a wooden cane. The man stood perfectly still.

She tried to make sense of his presence. The silver-haired stranger lifted his hand in greeting, sending an inexplicable wave of certainty through her. Without thinking, she reached for her phone and dialed Aaron's number.

He answered on the second ring, his deep voice sending warmth through the connection. "Meghan? Is everything okay?"

"Yes. I... I wanted to thank you for the bowl. It's breathtaking." Her gaze returned to the window, only to find the silver-haired man had vanished.

"I'm glad you like it. I wasn't sure about leaving it without saying anything, but Naomi thought it would be more special that way."

Meghan ran her fingers along the smooth wooden rim. "She was right. Did you make this yourself?"

"My grandfather taught me woodworking. It's been a while since I've created anything, but I wanted to do this for you."

The vulnerability in his tone unraveled her defenses. Before she had a chance to second-guess herself, the words spilled out.

"About Christmas Eve." Her voice was steadier than expected. "I'd love to go with you and Naomi to the service at New Hope."

When Aaron spoke again, the quiet happiness in his voice confirmed to her that she had made the right decision.

"We'll swing by and pick you up at six."

As they said goodnight, she returned to the window, searching for any sign of the silver-haired man. Finding none, she cradled the wooden bowl in her hands. It represented faith, effort, and quiet intention.

She felt herself stepping beyond safe boundaries, ready to walk forward with her heart open and her fears surrendered. She would no longer allow past wounds to dictate her future.

Chapter 27

The community center kitchen buzzed with the scent of slow-roasted meats, vegetables, and spices. Aaron adjusted the flame under his pan. Savory aromas curled upward and cut through the winter chill tapping at the windows. Outside, long shadows stretched across the parking lot as dusk arrived earlier each day, Christmas drawing closer.

The expanded cooking program hummed with energy. What once fit inside a high school home economics room now sprawled across the entire kitchen. Today's session brought familiar faces and new volunteers, all working together to prepare holiday meals for Brookside's homebound residents.

Aaron's gaze landed on Naomi, who was on the other side of the kitchen. She stood beside an elderly woman, patiently guiding her through the steps of kneading dough. The way she modified her actions to align with the woman's pace filled him with tenderness. This wasn't the same withdrawn, sorrowful girl who clung to silence when they first arrived in Brookside. She had blossomed into someone who reached out to others, embracing connection.

"Look at her." Darius paused beside Aaron with a tray of chopped vegetables. "It's hard to believe that's the same girl you brought to the job site months ago."

Aaron couldn't hide his smile. "God's been doing good work in her."

"Amen to that." Darius clapped Aaron's shoulder before heading back to his station.

Across the kitchen, Elena, Darius's wife, took center stage as she explained the traditional Puerto Rican dish they would prepare.

"*Pasteles* are special." Elena's melodic accent flowed through the kitchen as she unwrapped a banana leaf to reveal the treasures within. "Back home in Puerto Rico, we make these for Christmas and celebrations. They take time and patience, but the result..." She closed her eyes dramatically, pressing her fingers to her lips in a chef's kiss. "Worth every second."

Aaron watched Elena slice the moist bundle, revealing a golden interior with tender pork, olives, and colorful vegetables. Aromatic steam drew appreciative murmurs from participants.

"The dough, what we call masa, is made from green plantains, *yautía*, and sometimes pumpkin." Elena passed out small samples to eager hands. "We season the filling with *sofrito* and achiote oil. The banana leaf wrapping gives it flavor you cannot get any other way."

Aaron took a bite, savoring the layers of flavor blooming across his palate. It was earthy and savory, with hints of garlic and whispers of sweetness. It tasted like a story passed down from one generation to another, too rich to be rushed.

As the lesson got underway, his eyes found Meghan moving between stations. She wore a soft, asymmetric sweater that hugged her curves without trying. Her curls were pulled into a loose knot, with tendrils falling free. Calm and focused, she answered questions without missing a beat, unbothered by the organized chaos around her.

Their eyes met across the room, and warmth spread through him at that glance. The dynamic between them had shifted ever since she agreed to join him for the Christmas Eve service. The distance that once existed between them was slowly diminishing. They hadn't put a name to it yet, but that connection was unmistakably there.

"Uncle Aaron, can you help me?"

He turned his attention to his niece. She stood before a mountain of green plantains with a peeler in her hand. "Elena says we need twenty more for the next batch, but my arm's about to fall off."

Aaron chuckled and reached for the peeler. "Let's trade. You can start mixing the masa, and I'll handle this."

They worked side by side, the hum of the kitchen surrounding them. Naomi watched his hands make quick work of the plantains. "You make that look easy. Where did you learn to peel vegetables so fast?"

"At construction sites." He smiled at the memory. "Long projects meant long days, and everyone pitched in for lunch. Early in my career, I didn't have money to spare, so I offered to help cook instead. I got good at prepping food for meals."

Naomi nodded. "Ms. Townsend says cooking helps with math and problem solving."

The mention of Meghan drew Aaron's attention to her station, where she instructed a teenager on folding banana leaf wrappers. Her movements combined grace and efficiency, with nothing wasted.

"She's coming to Christmas Eve service with us, right?" Naomi's voice dropped conspiratorially.

Aaron nodded, becoming intensely interested in the plantain in his hand. "Yeah, she is."

Naomi smiled like she knew more than she let on. "Good. She should be with us for the holidays."

Before he could respond, Elena swept back to check on their progress. "Perfect timing. Naomi, come help with the next demonstration? Your masa looks excellent."

Naomi's face lit up at the praise. With a quick glance at Aaron for permission, she followed Elena with extra bounce in her step.

Aaron kept peeling, letting the noise and movement fill his senses. This was what healing looked like. Not the absence of grief, but the presence of something new and steady growing in its place.

"We're running low on achiote oil and bay leaves." Meghan stood close. The proximity jolted him, a magnetic pull he had been trying to resist since Thanksgiving. "I've got more in my car, but I'll need help carrying everything."

"I'm your guy. Where are you parked?" He wiped his hands on a towel.

"East lot, near the garden beds. We should hurry. The snow's started picking up."

Outside, quiet snowfall had transformed the world. Thick flakes drifted from the sky, blanketing the parking lot. Their boots crunched softly over the powder, their breath rising in clouds.

"It's beautiful." Her face tilted upward as snowflakes danced around them. "I never tire of the first real snow of the season."

Aaron studied her profile, captivated by the contours of her face. The arc of her jawline drew his gaze to the fullness of her lips. He noticed these details before but never appreciated them until now.

"Did you have snow growing up?" His voice emerged deeper than he intended.

"Rarely in this part of Georgia." She led him toward her vehicle. "When it snowed, my dad would drag me outside before it melted. He called it *'God's frosting on creation's cake.'*"

The image made Aaron hungry for more. He didn't just want to hear these pieces of her past. He wanted to be part of what came next.

Meghan unlocked her car, opening the passenger door to reveal several grocery bags. "I brought extra supplies just in case. Elena mentioned she might need ingredients that can be hard to find."

As she reached for the heaviest bag, Aaron moved to help. Their hands brushed around the paper sack, her fingers warm despite the chill. Neither moved, the contact sending electricity through his veins.

When Meghan looked up, snowflakes caught in her eyelashes and dusted her curls, framing her face like winter's magic. The vulnerability in her expression cracked something hardened deep within Aaron. Desire surged through him with unexpected intensity, not just physical attraction, but yearning to connect with her beyond words.

He whispered her name. "Meghan."

Her lips parted, but no words came. In her eyes, Aaron recognized permission and a lowering of walls that had separated them for months.

He leaned forward, narrowing the gap. Their lips touched cautiously at first, but then, her warmth pulled him in, and her mouth yielded to him. The intensity of her response awakened Aaron's long-dormant heart to a previously unremembered capacity for such tenderness.

His thumb skimmed her cheek, and Meghan relaxed into his caress, swaying closer. The grocery bag was forgotten as her hand rested against his chest. Even through his coat, the warmth of her palm pressed over the frantic rhythm beneath.

The kiss wasn't rushed. It was sure, an opening to something both quietly longed for. When they separated, he leaned his forehead against hers. Her eyes stayed closed, her breath mingling with his.

"I've wanted to do that since Thanksgiving," he admitted, his voice low and intimate. "Ever since the night we found Naomi at Providence Park."

Her eyes opened. The look in them, raw and honest, struck an emotional core deep within him. "I've wanted you to. Even when I acted like I didn't." Her confession ignited a rush in his veins.

Aaron traced her lower lip, still marveling at how right this all was. "You're beautiful." The words barely touched the truth pulsing inside him.

"So are you." She lifted her hand to touch his face, brushing his jaw with a gentleness that made his breath catch.

For seconds more, they stayed like that. Wrapped in falling snow and surrounded by an atmosphere that felt both sacred and serene. "We should probably get these supplies inside before Elena sends a search party," Meghan suggested, yet she made no effort to pull away from his touch.

Aaron nodded, reluctantly lowering his hand from her face. He let his fingers trail down her arm before breaking contact. A glint on her dashboard caught his eye as they gathered the groceries. Partially hidden beneath a stack of paper lay a silver feather. It was identical to the one he found in the gazebo at Providence Park. He still kept it in his pocket.

"Where did you get that?" He couldn't keep the surprise from his voice.

Meghan followed his gaze, frowning. "The feather? I'm not sure. I found it on my dashboard after the community center opened. It was..." She paused, confusion in her expression. "It was after I saw a man with silver hair. He was watching from across the street, and when I looked back later, he was gone."

Aaron's pulse quickened. "Was he using a wooden cane? Did he have deep-set eyes and a weathered face?"

Meghan's expression shifted to surprise. "Yes. You've seen him too?"

Before Aaron could explain his own encounter with the mysterious stranger, a voice called.

"Meghan! Aaron!" Audrey waved frantically, her vibrant hair visible even through the falling snow. "Elena needs those ingredients now! The final demonstration starts in five minutes!"

"We're coming," Meghan shouted back, gathering the remaining bags. She turned to Aaron. "We should talk about this later... about everything."

Aaron agreed, taking several bags from her arms. "You can count on it."

As they hurried through the snow, Aaron marveled at how much had changed. Months ago, he had been a man merely surviving. Now, he was awakening again to love, to faith, to a purpose bigger than pain.

The matching silver feathers couldn't be a coincidence. They had to be signs of something greater.

Inside, the kitchen welcomed them with warmth and noise. Elena rushed to meet them, grabbing ingredients as the next round of cooking resumed.

Aaron caught Meghan's eye across the kitchen. She smiled, and that smile stirred every cell in him. He was alive again. And he wasn't alone.

He glanced toward Naomi, who was laughing with the younger children as they cleaned up. Her smile radiated a level of happiness he hadn't witnessed in years. This was the essence of true restoration from God. It wasn't about just fixing the broken pieces, but about sowing new seeds in their place that could blossom into something beautiful.

Chapter 28

Meghan sat in her kitchen, balancing the phone between her shoulder and ear as she arranged cranberry-orange muffins on a ceramic platter. This would be her contribution to the church fellowship meal later that evening.

"I still can't believe you're not coming with us to Cotton-wood this year. This will be the first Christmas Eve service without you since your mother passed away." Carol's melodic voice flowed through the line, filled with maternal concern and gentle empathy.

Meghan adjusted the burgundy napkin beneath the muffins. "I know. It feels strange to break with tradition, but..."

"But this Aaron Grant has become special to you," Carol finished, years of life experience woven into her words.

"He's definitely different from what I expected." With the distance between them, the words came more easily, especially since Carol was still visiting her daughter in Michigan. "When we first met, he was all edges. His mom had just died, and suddenly, he was caring for his teenage niece."

"That's a heavy load for anyone to shoulder alone."

"It was nearly crushing him." Memories of those early days flooded back. "But he's changed so much. It's not just that he's going to church... but he's seeking. And he's incredibly patient with Naomi. He's different from when we first met."

"Sounds like he's putting in the effort." Approval colored Carol's tone. "Unlike a certain someone whose name we won't mention."

Meghan fiddled with a loose thread on her sweater. The not-so-subtle reference to her previous relationship still stung, though the pain no longer cut like it used to.

She shut her eyes. "What if I'm seeing what I want to see? What if—"

"What if the sky falls and chickens start speaking French?" Carol quipped. "Meghan Elise, you've spent so many years preparing for heartbreak, you've forgotten what real joy feels like."

The loving reprimand hit home. "That's not fair," she protested weakly.

"It *is* fair," Carol countered, her tone softening. "Sweetheart, I watched your mother shrink away from life after your father's accident. She thought that opening her heart would only lead to more pain. By the time she realized what that fear had cost her, it was too late."

The comparison sent a chill through Meghan. Her mother's gradual withdrawal following her father's death led to her physical decline, which was attributed to heart disease. But friends knew it was actually caused by her prolonged grief.

"Do you think I'm doing the same thing?" Meghan questioned.

"I think your heart was made to love. Whether that's Aaron, or someone else, that part of you deserves a chance to be heard."

The line went quiet. Meghan stared at the muffins, each one meticulously arranged, each a representation of care and effort.

She didn't have a chance to respond. Just then, her doorbell chimed, indicating the arrival of the floral delivery for Aaron's apartment. It was a simple evergreen arrangement for Christmas dinner the next day.

"I have to go," Meghan murmured, but Carol stopped her before she could hang up.

"Honey, give him a chance. And give yourself that chance as well."

After saying goodbye, Meghan signed for the flowers and stored them in her refrigerator. The delicate arrangement of white roses and evergreen sprigs mirrored her own life. It was lovely, but required careful attention, able to thrive or wither with the proper care.

The morning blurred by as she wrapped Naomi's gift of a professional-grade container gardening set and laid out her dress. Through each task, Carol's words resonated in her mind, threading themselves into every quiet moment.

While brewing a second cup of tea, movement on her kitchen counter caught Meghan's eye. At first, she thought it was the sunlight playing tricks. But as she stepped closer, her heart skipped.

The silver feather now lay beside her purse. She moved it to her desk drawer weeks ago. It emitted a subtle luminescence that defied explanation. More startling than its relocation was the faint glow pulsing from its surface.

"That's not possible." Meghan reached toward it with hesitant fingers.

The feather warmed her palm, weightless in a way that defied explanation. As she held it, she remembered the silver-haired man watching from across the pond at Providence Park, his mysterious appearance at the community center opening, and his presence outside her home the night she called Aaron about Christmas Eve services.

Uneasy, but strangely comforted, Meghan tucked the feather into her purse and tried to shake the chill over her skin.

By five-thirty, she stood before the mirror. Her dress was black and gold with a modest neckline and an A-line skirt that fell just below the knee. Her curls framed her face, pinned back with her mother's tortoise-shell combs. She inhaled deeply, steadying her nerves.

Aaron's text arrived right on time: *We're here whenever you're ready. No rush.*

Meghan stepped into the crisp twilight, carrying the platter of muffins, Naomi's gift, and her purse. Aaron's white truck idled in her driveway, exhaust puffing into the cool air. As soon as he spotted her, he climbed out and jogged over to help.

"Merry Christmas Eve," he greeted, his smile warm enough to chase away the cold. The burgundy tie at his collar highlighted the russet strands in his beard, and Meghan's heart fluttered hard against her ribs.

Naomi waved from inside before scooting to the middle seat as Aaron opened the door.

"You look so pretty!" Naomi admired Meghan's dress with teenage enthusiasm. "I wasn't sure what to wear. Does this look okay?"

She wore a deep purple dress with a modest neckline. The silver pendant around her neck caught the light. It was a delicate silver feather suspended on a chain, similar to the one in Meghan's purse.

"You look beautiful," Meghan assured her, her curiosity rising about the necklace's origin. "That pendant is lovely."

"Uncle Aaron gave it to me this morning." Naomi touched it lightly. "It matches the one he's wearing."

Only then did Meghan spot the small silver pin adorning Aaron's lapel, another feather, identical to Naomi's pendant and the one in Meghan's purse. The coincidence sent a shiver along her spine that had nothing to do with the winter evening.

"They're beautiful," Meghan murmured, meeting Aaron's gaze across Naomi with unspoken questions.

"I'll explain later," he promised quietly as he started the engine.

On the drive to New Hope Baptist, Naomi described the decorations at the Washingtons' home while Aaron shared holiday memories about his mother. The ease between the three of them soothed Meghan's nerves.

The church parking lot overflowed. Inside, the sanctuary shone with light from hundreds of candles interspersed among evergreen garlands. Traditional crimson poinsettias lined the altar, and white cloths adorned the communion table.

"Daniel and Sam are here." Aaron guided them toward a pew near the middle where the Forresters had saved space. Daniel stood to welcome them, his warm smile encompassing all three as they settled beside them.

Samantha's pregnancy had blossomed in recent weeks, her baby bump unmistakable beneath her dress. She squeezed Meghan's hand in a silent greeting.

"Mandy and Noah are seated near the front with Pastor Morrison's wife," Daniel noted, pointing out his sister and brother-in-law. "They've been helping with the children's program."

Aaron nodded, but his attention was drawn to movement by the sanctuary doors. Meghan followed his stare. She saw a tall, slender man awkwardly entering the church. Though she had never met him, his features were distinctly reminiscent of Aaron's, making his identity obvious.

"Ryan," Aaron whispered.

Meghan watched emotions flit across Aaron's face. Surprise. Cautious happiness. Hesitation. And ultimately, determination. He half-stood before stopping himself, clearly conflicted between remaining with them and going to his brother.

"Go," Meghan urged softly, understanding the significance of this moment. "We'll be right here."

Aaron's face lit up with gratitude as he grasped her hand before heading to the entrance. Meghan witnessed the reunion between the brothers. It started off hesitantly, but quickly became warmer as Aaron rested a hand on Ryan's shoulder, guiding him to a vacant spot on their pew.

The brothers settled into place just as Pastor Morrison stepped into the pulpit, his presence capturing everyone's attention, his voice filling the sanctuary.

"Tonight, we celebrate the greatest restoration story ever told. It's the moment when divine love stepped into human brokenness, and made a way for healing for all creation."

The service unfolded with traditional readings, familiar carols, and soft-spoken prayers. During a particularly moving rendition of *What Child Is This,* Aaron reached for Meghan's hand. She took it immediately, warmth rising at the simple yet powerful gesture.

Following communion, Pastor Morrison returned to the pulpit.

"This year, I've invited several members to share their experiences of restoration. Scripture tells us in Psalm 107:2, *'Let the redeemed of the Lord tell their story.'* These testimonies will serve as powerful reminders that the Christmas story is alive and flourishing in our lives today."

Three people shared brief, yet impactful accounts of healing. One spoke about a physical recovery from illness, another discussed reconciliation in a broken marriage, and the last narrated their path to freedom from addiction. Each story demonstrated divine intervention in ordinary human situations.

"Our final testimony comes from someone who recently joined our congregation." Pastor Morrison directed his attention toward their pew. "Aaron Grant, would you be willing to share your journey with us?"

Without hesitation, Aaron stood and walked confidently to the front of the sanctuary.

He cleared his throat and locked eyes with Meghan before addressing the congregation.

"Six months ago, I came to Brookside filled with anger and resentment towards God. I had just lost my mom, and unexpectedly found myself taking care of my fourteen-year-old niece. I felt I'd been abandoned... and I placed the blame squarely on God."

A deep hush enveloped the sanctuary as Aaron explained how looking after Naomi had pushed him far beyond his limits of self-sufficiency.

"I realized I couldn't fix my niece's pain," he admitted. "For the first time in my adult life, I was confronted with a challenge that I couldn't tackle on my own."

He spoke candidly, expressing his grief and confusion without reservation. He revealed how Naomi's suffering humbled him and described the way the community rallied around them. And then...

"But everything changed when an unforeseen angel invited us to a cooking class at the school."

Meghan's cheeks warmed as Aaron recounted their first encounter. He described her compassion toward Naomi, how she seamlessly integrated her faith into everyday moments, and how patiently she honored his spiritual journey without judgment or pressure.

Tears welled in her eyes as Aaron talked about his slow return to faith. He mentioned his weekly conversations with Pastor Morrison, his morning Bible study sessions with Naomi, and the camaraderie and support from the men's fellowship, which he had believed was gone forever.

"I came to Brookside with a hardened heart. But God refused to allow it to stay that way. Tonight, I'm grateful for the pain, because it brought me here. The pain led me to faith, family, and love."

He returned to the pew, slipping his hand into Meghan's once more. This time, she gripped tightly, as if making a vow.

The service ended with the traditional candlelight ceremony, hundreds of small flames illuminating the faces throughout the sanctuary as *Silent Night* filled the space with its reverent melody. Meghan stood between Aaron and Naomi, their three flames forming a quiet triangle of hope.

Afterward, the congregation moved to the fellowship hall for a celebration meal. Conversation and music created a joyful atmosphere as people filled plates with holiday favorites. As they mingled, Aaron introduced Meghan to members of the congregation.

The evening's emotional intensity had overwhelmed Meghan. Excusing herself, she slipped into the church's meditation garden. The winter night enveloped her in stillness, with stars visible despite nearby town lights. Her breath formed clouds in the frosty air as she gathered her thoughts.

"Beautiful night," a gentle voice observed from nearby.

She turned, startled to find the mysterious man seated on a stone bench a few feet away. How she had missed him upon entering the garden defied explanation. His silver hair caught the starlight, luminescent against the darkness. The polished wooden cane resting across his knees gleamed.

"You're the man I've been seeing!"

He smiled, and deep lines crinkled around eyes that held unexpected brilliance. "My name is Liam. And you're Meghan Townsend, history teacher and cooking program coordinator."

His knowledge of her identity should have frightened her, yet his presence radiated peace rather than threat. She moved closer.

"Who are you? Why do you keep appearing?"

Liam's smile deepened, amusement dancing in eyes that appeared ancient and youthful. "I'm just a traveler who occasionally delivers messages."

"Messages?" Her hand unconsciously moved to her purse, where the silver feather rested.

"Reminders, perhaps," he amended, his gaze following her movement. "Reminders that timing isn't accidental. That some connections are established long before we recognize them."

"The feather." She retrieved it from her purse. "It was you who left it in my car. What does it mean?"

"That's for you to discover." Liam rose from the bench with surprising grace for one who appeared so frail. "But Scripture offers a clue in Ecclesiastes 3:1. *There is a time for everything, and a season for every activity under the heavens.*"

The well-known verse echoed Carol's earlier counsel to trust in God's timing instead of holding onto fear-driven control. Just before Meghan could reply, the garden door swung open, flooding the area with golden light.

"Meghan?" Aaron's voice carried concern as he stepped outside. "Is everything all right?"

She turned toward him, about to introduce Liam, when she realized he had vanished again. The stone bench stood empty, and no footprints marked the frost-covered path. Disoriented, Meghan blinked, scanning the small garden for any sign of his departure.

"I was just getting some air, and speaking with..." She tucked the feather back into her purse with trembling fingers and hesitated, uncertain how to explain the inexplicable.

Aaron moved closer as he studied her face. "You met Liam," he stated rather than asked, certainty in his tone.

Surprise rippled through her. "You know him?"

His voice lowered to blend in with the garden's tranquil ambiance. "I've met him before, just once. We had a conversation one day while I was at the gazebo in Providence Park. He gave me a lot to think about."

Meghan pieced together the clues. Aaron's silver feather pin and Naomi's matching pendant. "The feathers?"

He nodded, his expression both bewildered and reverent. "Yeah. I've never figured out where it originated from or why it seems to glow."

Goosebumps prickled across Meghan's arms despite her warm coat. "Who do you think he is?"

Aaron's gaze lifted to the star-filled sky above them, a look of awe on his face. "The scriptures tell us to show kindness to strangers, for some have entertained angels without knowing it."

While they searched for an explanation that might quench their curiosity, they both acknowledged the divine orchestration behind their converging paths.

"We ought to head back inside. Naomi saved dessert for us. Are you ready?" Aaron extended his arm.

Meghan answered, her heart full. "Yes. I'm ready."

Chapter 29

AARON STOOD IN HIS kitchen, whisking eggs in a ceramic bowl. Christmas carols played from the speaker on the counter, filling the quiet apartment with festive ambiance. The scent of cinnamon and butter perfumed the air, taking him back to his mom's holiday breakfasts in Bristol Heights.

It was 7:15 AM. Naomi would sleep for another hour, giving him time to perfect the sweet potato pancakes he wanted to make. The batter sizzled as it hit the hot griddle, pulling him into the rhythm of cooking, though his mind lingered on last night's candlelight service.

He could still feel the microphone in his hand when Pastor Morrison asked for testimonies. His legs carried him to the front before his brain even registered what he was doing.

He remembered Naomi's wide eyes, Daniel and Samantha's encouraging nods, and Meghan, sitting beside his niece, watching with quiet support. That memory anchored him even now.

Six months ago, I came to Brookside filled with anger and resentment towards God. I had just lost my mom, and unexpectedly found myself taking care of my fourteen-year-old niece. I felt I'd been abandoned... and I placed the blame squarely on God.

Aaron felt lingering peace from his public declaration. The burden of hiding his faith had lifted, replaced by the freedom of authenticity. More surprising was the response afterward. Men from the congregation shared similar stories, handshakes turned to embraces, and new connections formed where isolation had reigned.

He flipped the golden pancakes and arranged them on a serving platter, adding sliced strawberries and a light dusting of powdered sugar. Fresh coffee brewed, its rich aroma complementing the breakfast scents.

A creak sounded in the hallway. Naomi shuffled into the kitchen, rubbing sleep from her eyes. Her braids were wrapped in the satin scarf Meghan had recommended. Despite her groggy expression, excitement sparked across her face as she caught the scent of breakfast.

"You made Grandma's pancakes!"

Aaron nodded. "Sweet potato pancakes with cinnamon butter. I found her recipe card in that box from her house when I went to Bristol Heights."

Naomi crossed to the counter and poked at the stack. "They look good," she decided, a smile tugging at her lips. "Hers were a little darker, though."

"She added more brown sugar." Aaron set the plates on the table. "These are a bit healthier."

"It's Christmas." Naomi pulled orange juice from the refrigerator. "Healthy food is illegal today."

Aaron laughed. "Fair enough. Next year, I'll follow her recipe exactly."

The casual reference to future holidays together didn't escape either of them. Naomi's smile bloomed fully as she slid into her chair.

"Merry Christmas, Uncle Aaron."

"Merry Christmas, Naomi."

They ate together, Naomi talking about her favorite parts of the service and Aaron sharing memories from his own childhood Christmases. The grief was still there, but it didn't feel as sharp. Somehow, talking about the ones they had lost made their presence feel closer.

"Can we open some of the presents before Meghan gets here?" Naomi asked as she carried her empty plate to the sink.

Aaron checked the time. "Sure. She's not coming until eleven."

They moved to the living room where their tree sparkled with white lights and a collection of ornaments. Some were new, others were transported from his mother's collection.

"You first." Naomi placed a small package in his hands.

Aaron unwrapped the paper. Inside lay a leather keychain with his initials burned into the surface.

"I made it in shop class," Naomi explained, a hint of shyness coloring her words. "Mr. Taylor helped with the leather stamping."

Aaron ran his thumb across the smooth surface, emotion tightening his throat.

"It's perfect." His voice roughened with feeling. "Thank you."

Naomi ducked her head, looking pleased by his reaction. "Meghan says you might need something since you keep misplacing your keys."

The casual reference to Ms. Townsend as *"Meghan"* was another understated suggestion of the changing dynamics of their relationship.

"Your turn." Aaron passed her a rectangular package.

Naomi tore into his present. It was a waterproof garden journal with her name embossed in gold. As she flipped through it, her fingers skimmed the delicate paper.

"It's for the balcony garden. Now, you can record everything you grow."

"Thank you," Naomi murmured, flipping through the blank pages awaiting her notations.

They continued exchanging gifts, blending practical items like clothes and school supplies with more personal selections reflecting their growing understanding of each other's preferences. Aaron's last gift, a professional gardening toolkit with her name engraved on each handle, delighted her.

After the wrapping paper was cleared away, Naomi headed to her room to call her friends. Aaron carried Meghan's gifts to the tree and sank into his chair, his mother's Bible in his lap.

The leather binding warmed in his hands. He opened to where a silk bookmark held his place, the pages falling naturally to Isaiah

61. The words that once seemed distant now resonated with personal significance.

The Spirit of the Sovereign LORD is on me, because the LORD has anointed me to proclaim good news to the poor. He has sent me to bind up the brokenhearted, to proclaim freedom for the captives and release from darkness for the prisoners...

Aaron traced the words with his finger, the prophetic language of restoration speaking directly to his experience. The Scripture continued: *They will rebuild the ancient ruins and restore the places long devastated; they will renew the ruined cities that have been devastated for generations.*

Rebuilding. Restoration. Renewal. The terminology associated with construction in the sacred text suddenly clicked into place. His expertise revealed striking metaphors for spiritual insight. Proper preparation was vital for foundations, regular maintenance was essential for structures, and sometimes, damage presented opportunities for improved design.

His mother had underlined verse four in red, her neat handwriting filling the margin:

For Aaron. The Lord rebuilds through human hands guided by divine purpose.

The note, penned during her final illness, carried a prophetic significance he hadn't fully comprehended until now.

He sat lost in thought when a knock sounded at the door. He checked the clock. She was right on time.

Meghan stood in the corridor, snowflakes melting in her curls. She wore an emerald dress and a cream-colored cardigan. Several wrapped packages were balanced in her arms, and a tote bag hung from her shoulder.

"Merry Christmas," she greeted him.

"Merry Christmas." He stepped aside, his breath catching as she passed. Her presence warmed the apartment more than the heater ever could.

He reached for her packages, their fingers brushing. Even that brief contact sent a current coursing up his arm.

"You're right on time." His voice was deeper than he had intended.

"Teachers are never late." Meghan's laugh was melodic.

As she removed her coat, Aaron noticed how the emerald dress complemented her skin tone. The sight of her, relaxed and festive, in his home by choice, filled him with something beyond physical attraction. She brought wholeness wherever she went.

"Something smells wonderful." She loosened a knitted scarf from her neck, revealing the elegant curve of her throat.

"Sweet potato pancakes. It was my mom's recipe. I saved some for you." Aaron set her packages beneath the tree while trying to maintain his composure.

Meghan's expression warmed. "Your mother's recipe? That's special, Aaron."

This woman looked beyond superficial gestures to the deeper meaning, a perception that made her even more attractive.

Naomi emerged from her room at Meghan's arrival, her earlier excitement returning in full force. "Meghan! Merry Christmas!"

"Merry Christmas, Naomi." Meghan embraced the teenager with genuine affection.

They settled in the living room, and Aaron served coffee and the promised pancakes. Meghan took her first bite, and her reaction was telling.

"Oh, this is heaven." She momentarily closed her eyes in delight.

Watching her relish that mouthful filled him with pleasure. She didn't just consume her food. She fully immersed herself in the experience.

He committed it all to memory. He cherished the way the sunlight highlighted the golden flecks in her brown eyes, how her fingers curled around her coffee mug, and the subtle changes in her expression whenever something moved her. Each detail reinforced the certainty that this woman was destined to be a permanent part of his life. She was essential to his sense of fulfillment.

When it came time to exchange gifts, Naomi took charge. As Meghan unwrapped the personalized herb markers Naomi had made, her voice quivered.

"How did you know rosemary was my favorite?" she asked.

"You always touch the rosemary first when you come into the classroom." Naomi said it as if it were obvious. "And you said it reminds you of your dad."

The emotion visible on Meghan's face was breathtaking. She squeezed Naomi's hand in wordless gratitude.

Last but not least, was Aaron's gift, carefully positioned beneath the lowest branches of the tree. When Naomi placed it in Meghan's hands, he held his breath.

Meghan unwrapped the package and lifted the lid from the wooden box.

The serving spoon rested on a rich burgundy velvet cloth. Its maple wood gleamed, the grain patterns accentuated through meticulous sanding and finishing. Aaron poured his heart into its creation, each curve designed to fit perfectly in Meghan's hand. The verse from Psalm 30:5 was exquisitely rendered in precise lettering.

She lifted the utensil from its case and traced the carved scripture.

"This is... extraordinary. You made this?"

He inclined his head.

Meghan rotated the spoon to inspect it from every angle. Her eyes lifted to meet his, emotion making them luminous. "Thank you. It's the most beautiful gift anyone has ever given to me."

The moment lingered, and Naomi quietly slipped away to her room, leaving them alone.

"Your testimony last night... it resonated with so many people. Pastor Morrison said that three men talked to him afterward, expressing interest in joining the men's ministry."

Aaron massaged his neck, feeling slightly uncomfortable. "I didn't plan to say half of what came out. Most of it came out on its own."

"Maybe that's why it reached so many," she said, reflecting. "People aren't looking to see perfection. They're yearning to see what's real and authentic."

Aaron watched her, awed by her knack for cutting straight to the heart of the matter.

"I have something for you." Meghan retrieved a package from beside her chair.

Aaron opened it to find a leather-bound journal, its cover embossed with his initials in gold.

"It's waterproof construction paper." A smile played at the corners of her mouth. "They're special pages that won't tear when they get wet. And it has grid lines for when you need to make measurements. The engineering department at Greater Pines uses it to take their field notes when it rains."

The thoughtfulness behind the gift moved Aaron. She understood his work needs and appreciated both functionality and quality.

"This is perfect. How did you know I needed this?"

"You mentioned you ruined three sets of notes during a rainstorm one week," Meghan reminded him. "I listen when you talk, Aaron."

They had both been listening and observing each other. They had been learning from each other in a thousand small ways, like how she took her coffee, which Bible verses comforted him, and why rosemary made her pause by the classroom windows.

With Naomi in her room, the space on the couch felt charged. Aaron shifted closer, drawn by an invisible force he no longer wished to resist. Meghan's eyes widened at his proximity, but she didn't move away.

"There's something I've wanted to tell you." His voice dropped to an intimate register. He t

ook her hand, marveling at how it fit his own. Delicate yet strong, soft yet capable, her smooth skin against his calloused palm ignited awareness within him.

"You've become important to me. Not because of the cooking program or Naomi. You matter to me."

Color deepened in Meghan's cheeks, and her fingers tightened around his.

"Aaron." His name carried layers of meaning on her lips.

Before she could finish, Naomi's bedroom door opened, and her footsteps padded toward the living room. Aaron reluctantly let go of Meghan's hand.

"I'm still here," he whispered, the promise extending beyond the interrupted conversation to something much larger.

Meghan nodded as Naomi entered, blissfully unaware of the moment she interrupted.

They spent the next hour chatting and laughing, but the air had changed. Every look, and every accidental touch, hummed with unspoken anticipation.

As the afternoon softened toward evening, Naomi became engrossed in the new novel Meghan had given her. Aaron turned to Meghan, ready to pick up where they had left off. The time was right.

But before he could begin, Meghan picked up her coffee cup from the side table. Her fingers tightened around the ceramic as if anchoring herself to something solid.

"I have something I want to share with you. Yesterday, I received an unexpected opportunity." Her formal tone made Aaron uneasy.

He nodded, encouraging her to continue while tamping down the apprehension her tone triggered.

"The State Education Department has selected me for their winter teaching workshop in Macon," Meghan explained. "It's a prestigious program. Only twenty educators are chosen statewide. It's six weeks of training that starts on January fifth."

The words hit like a wrecking ball. Six weeks apart, immediately after New Year's. They would be separated right when they had started to acknowledge the deeper currents flowing between them.

"That's a fantastic opportunity. Congratulations." He forced enthusiasm into his voice while his heart constricted.

"Thanks," Meghan replied, though her smile wavered. "This network could open doors I've only dreamed about."

Aaron struggled to maintain his composure, refusing to let the rising devastation become visible. His mind raced with calculations. It would be six weeks of her absence, when every day in her presence had become essential to him. The timing cut with deliberate cruelty.

"Macon isn't far," he heard himself say, even as disappointment carved a hollow ache beneath his ribs. "It's less than a two-hour drive."

Her expression suggested she had already considered this. "That's true, but the schedule will be intense. It'll be twelve-hour days, plus project work on most evenings."

Aaron's heart sank even lower. He had begun to envision a future with her woven into his daily life. And now, just when they were on the brink of something substantial, she would be leaving.

"You should definitely go for it," he insisted, despite the protest screaming through every fiber of his being. His hands ached with the effort of remaining still, not reaching for her, not asking her to stay.

An emotion flickered across her face. Had she secretly hoped he would ask her to decline? The thought occurred too late for him to explore, as the momentum of their conversation carried them forward.

"I've already accepted," she admitted quietly. "The deadline for me to respond was yesterday."

Her final statement crushed his immediate hopes. Aaron struggled to organize his thoughts and express his feelings, as every part of him urged him to object, to claim her time, and seek a priority he had no right to ask for. The self-discipline he developed through years of handling construction crises enabled him to maintain a composed façade despite his inner chaos.

"We'll figure it out. I know we will." The words emerged with more confidence than he felt.

The conversation shifted, yet the quiet ache remained. Had their moment of possibility passed before materializing? Was this separation a test, or unfortunate timing?

As the sun dipped lower and the day drew to a close, Aaron wondered if God's perfect timing ever included interruptions. Ones that tested faith, stirred longing, and stretched hearts.

Aaron watched Meghan, unsure if this marked the beginning of an intimate bond or a pause they would first need to endure. Hope flickered, but it was tempered by uncertainty. Whatever came next, he would hold on, because a connection this real and sacred was worth waiting for.

Chapter 30

F ROST CLUNG TO THE Heavenly Delights' windows when Meghan pushed through the door three days after Christmas. The scent of fresh pastries wrapped around her, but her coffee remained untouched, steam curling upward. Across the booth, Olivia studied her with the patient perception born from years of friendship.

"Okay, spill it. You've been staring at that mug for five minutes." Her ponytail bounced as she tilted her head. "The coffee won't improve with age, you know."

Memories of the past few days flooded back. Aaron's heartfelt testimony at New Hope Baptist, the mysterious encounter with Liam in the garden, and the tender moment they shared during the candlelight service when Aaron's fingers intertwined with hers.

"It was..." Meghan searched for words to describe it all. "It was extraordinary."

Olivia leaned forward, chin propped on her palm. "Tell me everything."

Meghan recounted the events, including Aaron's reunion with his estranged brother Ryan. She hesitated when describing the silver-haired stranger, uncertain how to explain an encounter that defied logic.

"So, this mysterious Liam has appeared to both of you? And he's left identical silver feathers?" Olivia's expression was thoughtful rather than skeptical.

"Aaron believes he might be..." She paused, embarrassed to voice the possibility aloud.

"An angel?" Olivia finished, her voice dropping to match Meghan's hushed tone. "Hebrews 13 says that some have entertained angels without knowing it."

Meghan exhaled. If Olivia, with her grounded faith and sharp intuition, could believe it, then maybe she could too.

"What bothers me most isn't Liam. It's this opportunity in Macon. Aaron seemed supportive when I told him about it, but I could see his disappointment."

Meghan explained that the Carter Institute winter leadership workshop in Macon was six weeks of intensive training, networking with top educators, and curriculum development opportunities that could transform Greater Pines' history department.

"Any other time, I wouldn't hesitate about accepting. But now, with Aaron and Naomi, and everything changing between us, the timing feels wrong." She wrung her hands.

"Or maybe the timing's exactly right," Olivia suggested. "Six weeks apart might help you see what you both want from each other."

"What if the distance shows our connection's not strong enough? What if Aaron decides a relationship with his niece's teacher is too complicated?"

A smile curved Olivia's lips. "And what if you're building walls again because opening your heart still scares you?"

Before Meghan could respond, Willow appeared at their table with fresh pastries, her warmth lifting Meghan's spirits.

"Cranberry scones, still warm from the oven. They're perfect for solving life's bigger questions."

"How do you know when we're having a crisis?" Olivia accepted the plate.

Willow laughed. "It comes from years of working in this diner. Besides, Meghan only stirs her coffee counterclockwise when something heavy is on her mind." She patted Meghan's shoulder before returning to the counter.

Meghan broke a scone in half, the tart sweetness bursting across her tongue. "Okay, enough about me," she said, changing the subject. "How did your home inspection go?"

Olivia's expression brightened. "It went better than I hoped. The social worker complimented my *child-centered living environment.* Those were her exact words."

They chatted about adoption updates and Olivia's nesting preparations for the next half hour. For a while, Meghan let herself drift away from the ache in her chest.

As they prepared to leave, bundling into winter coats against the December chill, Olivia clasped Meghan's hands between hers.

"Meghan, don't forget what God told Joshua. *'Be strong and courageous. Do not be afraid; do not be discouraged, for the Lord your God will be with you wherever you go.'"*

The scripture settled into Meghan's heart, its promise carrying renewed relevance.

"Even in Macon?"

"Even in Macon." Olivia hugged her.

The words followed Meghan home, echoing through the still-decorated living room. She knelt beside her bed and prayed.

Lord, I'm scared. Please show me the way.

Peace didn't arrive dramatically. There were no heavenly voices and no sudden clarity. Instead, her phone chirped from the nightstand with Principal Watkins' name flashing on the screen. Taking a breath, Meghan answered.

"I've spoken with the Carter Institute," he began without preamble. "They're willing to modify your schedule to help with your traveling back and forth."

"A modified schedule?" Meghan repeated, hope flickering.

"The core programming would require you to be there Monday through Thursday. Fridays can be done through virtual participation. This would allow you to come back to Brookside for the weekends. It's unprecedented, but your exceptional application persuaded them to compromise."

Gratitude flooded through Meghan as she absorbed this unexpected solution. "That would be perfect. Thank you so much for advocating on my behalf."

After the call, she sat for a moment. This wasn't a coincidence. It was grace.

Without waiting, Meghan gathered her coat and car keys. Aaron's construction office closed at five. If she hurried, she might catch him before he left for the day.

Winter twilight draped the town as she pulled into the lot of Donovan Building Contractors. Through the half-open window, she saw Aaron bent over blueprints, his shirt sleeves rolled to reveal strong forearms, and his tie loosened at his throat. Graphite smudged one hand as he made notes. Meghan remained in her car, gathering her courage.

"Be strong and courageous," she whispered, bolstering her resolve.

Inside, the reception area stood empty, most of the staff having departed hours ago. She moved toward the lighted office.

"Can I interrupt?" Meghan asked.

Aaron looked up, pleasure transforming his face. "Meghan! This is an unexpected surprise."

She stepped into his office. "I hope I'm not intruding."

"Never," he assured her, moving around the drafting table.

Up close, she detected the cedar notes of his aftershave, a scent that had become familiar from their Thanksgiving dinner. The memory of that intimate meal in his apartment, exchanging gifts and stories until late into the evening, warmed her.

"I wanted to talk to you about the Macon workshop." Determination steadied her voice.

Aaron's expression remained open. "I know Principal Watkins is pleased. He told Daniel it's one of the most prestigious education programs in the state."

Surprise flickered through Meghan.

A smile graced his lips. "When something is important to someone I care for, I take it upon myself to find out as much as possible about it. Principal Watkins shared some of the details with me when I spoke to him yesterday."

"You spoke with him?" Meghan asked, appreciating his investment in her work.

"I wanted to understand exactly what this opportunity meant for your career."

Warmth swept within Meghan at this revelation of his thoughtfulness that surpassed anything she had experienced in previous relationships.

"He was able to work out a compromise for me. I'll be in Macon Monday through Thursday, but I'll be able to come back on Fridays and spend the weekends here in Brookside."

"That sounds perfect. With that arrangement, six weeks will fly by."

"You believe that?" Meghan searched his face for any sign of reservation.

Instead of answering, Aaron's gaze held hers, the afternoon glow from the window highlighting flecks of amber in his deep brown eyes.

"Meghan, can I show you something?"

Curiosity piqued, she nodded. Aaron stood, retrieving a portfolio from his drafting table. He opened it, extracting several sketches that he placed on the small table.

Meghan leaned forward, examining detailed renderings of the land surrounding the house they had discussed while baking cookies at his apartment. These new sketches revealed areas she hadn't seen previously. There were walking trails connecting different garden zones. There was a sheltered gazebo overlooking what appeared to be a small pond. And most importantly, there was an expanded kitchen garden with plenty of space for preparing meals.

"This garden area connects to the kitchen through French doors. I've designed built-in seating for informal get-togethers." He paused, meeting her gaze. "The main kitchen opens to a family dining space large enough for holiday gatherings and meals."

Meghan absorbed the implications. These were visions made visible, and a future embracing their passions. It was a home designed for a shared life, not solitude.

"You've created space for a family," she said.

"I couldn't help myself." He smiled. "Architects are dreamers at heart. We design spaces for the lives we hope to live."

Tears stung her eyes. "Macon isn't so far. It's about a ninety-minute drive. And we'll have the weekends..." She hesitated, uncertain how to categorize what existed between them.

"To continue building," Aaron supplied, his eyes never leaving hers. "Not just houses, but trust and a connection. Meghan, these past months have awakened something I thought died long ago. I never thought I'd have the capacity to imagine a future of joy."

He reached across the table, his hand covering hers. The professional atmosphere of the office gave way to an intimate truth too powerful to conceal.

"I've fallen in love with you. Slowly, deeply, and completely. I didn't plan to say it now, but I can't hold it in any longer."

The declaration hung between them. Meghan's heart thundered, each beat urging her to respond as Aaron's fingers tightened around hers, his thumb sweeping slow circles over her knuckles.

"You don't have to say anything. I just... wanted you to know."

She had imagined this moment countless times, had rehearsed every possible response. But when faced with Aaron's unfiltered sincerity, her caution dissolved like morning mist under sunlight.

Her whisper was barely a breath. "I fought it, convincing myself it was inappropriate while Naomi was my student and your reclaiming of faith was too new, but Aaron... I love you, too."

Joy bloomed across his handsome features. He stood, pulling her up with their intertwined hands. They were inches apart. Meghan took in every detail of his face, noting the line of his angular features, the faint crinkles beside his eyes deepening when he smiled, and the fullness of his lower lip that stirred a flutter within her.

"May I?" His voice dropped to a husky timbre that sent shivers down her spine.

At her nod, Aaron closed the distance. His kiss was warm and certain, an answer to questions that had haunted them both. Her hand rested on his chest, feeling the steady rhythm of his heart. His touch was reverent, tender, and full of the passion they had both kept contained for too long.

Unlike their snow-covered kiss at the community center, this one was slow and lingering, as if making up for the time they had held back.

When they broke apart, Aaron pressed his forehead to hers. He kept her close, his forehead resting against hers as they shared breath.

"Every time you smile, I think about kissing you, especially when those dimples show. I get distracted by thoughts that are not exactly appropriate..."

Meghan laughed, breathless. "And I've been wondering if I was imagining the way you look at me."

"Believe me, you're not imagining it." Aaron's hand rose to cradle her cheek. His thumb traced the curve of her lower lip, the tender exploration lighting a fire that cascaded through her veins.

They remained entwined, savoring a connection too precious for a hasty conclusion. Eventually, the world returned to them through the darkened windows and the ticking clock.

"I should go," she said, though she made no move to step away. "You have work to finish."

"Nothing that can't wait." Aaron's hands settled at her waist. "Though Naomi's expecting me home for dinner."

The mention of his niece brought practical matters back into focus. "Have you told her? About us?"

His expression softened with affection. "She told me weeks ago that my feelings were obvious to everyone, except possibly you."

Heat rushed to Meghan's cheeks at her student's perception. "Teenagers see everything!"

"She'll be thrilled." Aaron brushed a loose curl from Meghan's forehead. "You've become important to her, and not only as her teacher."

Aaron took Meghan's hand as they gathered coats, his expression turning serious. "Don't worry about Macon. Six weeks will pass, and we'll have our weekends."

Meghan was grateful for his support. "You're sure?"

He helped her into her coat with gentle attentiveness. "I'm sure. Your dreams matter to me. I want to support you as you've supported me."

Outside, Aaron walked Meghan to her car. He paused and bent to kiss her once more before opening her car door.

"Text me when you're home."

"I will," Meghan promised.

As she drove home, Christmas lights twinkled across porches, and carols filled the radio. The silver feather pulsed within her purse. Meghan smiled. She didn't have all the answers. But she knew one thing for sure. She wasn't walking this road alone.

Chapter 31

FROST ETCHED CRYSTALLINE PATTERNS across Aaron's truck windshield as he sat in the parking lot of Brookside's Greyhound station. The early January sky sagged gray and heavy, mirroring the hollow ache beneath his ribs. Across the pavement, Meghan checked her luggage with the attendant, her orange coat a vivid flare against the muted wintry palette.

Six weeks. The timeframe stretched before him like a sentence he hadn't agreed to serve. Six weeks without her smile or the familiar fragrance that always announced her arrival. Six weeks that seemed to widen in front of him with every passing second.

Meghan turned toward the truck, a carry-on clutched in her gloved hands. Aaron stepped into the biting cold, crossing the distance with deliberate strides. Salt-crusted concrete crunched underfoot, the only sound in the stillness.

"You didn't have to wait." Her breath formed small clouds. Those captivating dark eyes held a mixture of gratitude and regret that mirrored his own.

"I wanted to." Aaron reached for her bag, their gloved fingers brushing. Even through the wool, the contact sparked warmth. "Did everything check through okay?"

Meghan nodded, curls escaping her knitted cap. One spiral brushed her cheek, prompting him to push it back. His gloved fingers lingered, tracing her cheek. A flush bloomed beneath her warm complexion.

"The workshop coordinator arranged for my bigger suitcase to be delivered to the dormitory. This is just for the trip." She leaned into his touch.

They stood facing each other, neither quite ready to name what loomed ahead. Around them, travelers hurried past, hunched against the cold. But in their little bubble, he felt only the magnetic pull of Meghan.

"I never thanked you for supporting my decision to go." Meghan's voice dropped low, sending heat through him despite the freezing temperature.

He swallowed the selfish protest crowding his throat. *Don't go. Stay with me.* Instead, he pushed it down and gave her what she needed.

"Your passion for teaching is part of what makes you who you are. I'd never stand in the way of that."

Her smile broke through, dimpled and tender. "I'll miss you. More than the teacher protocol allows."

That was all it took. He stepped forward, cupping her waist with one hand, her cheek with the other. She tilted up toward him, eyes warm and wide. When their lips met, it wasn't rushed. It was reverent. It was a kiss that held promise and deep-rooted feelings.

She gripped his coat, as if anchoring herself. He let everything he couldn't say pour into that kiss—respect, tenderness, desire, and hope. She tasted of the cinnamon that lingered from morning tea, sweet and uniquely her.

He pulled her close, molding her against him like an answered prayer. Even through coats and scarves, she fit him. She was made for him.

Her soft gasp undid him, and when he deepened the kiss, she welcomed him. Her fingers traced the back of his neck, threading through his hair, sending fire down his spine. He etched every detail into memory. The flavor of her, the sensation of her, and the way her lips moved with his, like she had been waiting her entire life for this moment.

When they separated, her eyes stayed closed a second longer, lashes dark against flushed cheeks.

"That should last us until your first weekend home." His voice was rough with a longing he could only partly express in this public setting.

Meghan's eyes opened, revealing depths of emotion that mirrored his own. "If that was meant to make leaving easier, it's having the opposite effect." Her fingers lingered against his profile in a touch that branded him more effectively than any physical mark could have.

He pressed his forehead to hers, breathing her in. "I'll be here waiting for when you get back."

Meghan's eyes met his. "Six weeks isn't forever."

"And we have weekends. Four days apart, then three together. I like those odds." Aaron was reluctant to release her even as the bus attendant called for final boarding.

He kissed her once more, leaving them both breathless.

"Go be brilliant. I'll be waiting."

Meghan stepped back, her eyes never leaving his. "I'll call when I get there."

Aaron felt the physical ache of her absence, though she stood only feet away.

She boarded with one final glance over her shoulder. Their eyes met through the window. She pressed her hand to the glass. He lifted his in return, holding her gaze until the bus disappeared around the corner.

And then she was gone.

The drive to the construction site blurred by. Aaron's mind replayed their kiss on a continuous loop. He could still feel the tenderness of her lips, the gentle pressure of her body against his, and the faint sound she made as he pulled her closer. This memory only intensified the longing he felt from their separation. His body missed what his heart had begun to embrace.

He shook his head and forced himself to focus, reminding himself that work provided the structure he needed when his personal life threatened to spiral into chaos.

The land he purchased hummed with activity despite the early hour. Darius had organized the crew with his typical efficiency. Foundation trenches were marked with stakes, and the heavy equipment was in place. Aaron parked near the site trailer, surveying what would eventually become his home. *Their* home, if all went as hoped.

"There he is." Darius strode purposely across the frozen ground, clipboard in hand. His breath formed white puffs in the chilly air, but enthusiasm brightened his voice. "I thought you might have forgotten about us, especially after all those goodbye kisses I pretended not to see at the bus station."

Heat crawled up Aaron's neck. "I have no idea what you're talking about," he muttered, taking the clipboard to review the day's objectives.

Darius laughed, clapping him on the shoulder with brotherly affection. "Man, I saw that goodbye kiss. Don't worry. Your secret's safe with me... and the twenty other people pretending not to watch you two recreate a Hallmark moment."

Aaron shook his head, a reluctant smile creeping onto his lips despite his embarrassment. "It's complicated."

"The best things usually are. So, have you accounted for a certain teacher's book collection in this house you're building?"

Aaron hesitated, but Darius's expression showed only sincere curiosity. "The library will have built-in shelves from floor to ceiling," he responded. "And the kitchen's getting double ovens since a certain someone enjoys experimenting."

Darius nodded. "That's what I figured. You're not just building for today, you're building for the long haul. Speaking of which, your design modifications came in yesterday. Did you intend to extend the garden beds on the south side?" He arched his eyebrow in inquiry.

"Yeah... I'm looking for better light for herbs and vegetables. It's practical." Aaron chose to overlook the implication behind the question.

"Uh-huh." Darius's doubt was unmistakable. "And the reading nook with the bay window that overlooks those garden beds? Is that because it's also practical?"

Aaron gave up the pretense. "Fine. Yes, I'm designing this with Meghan and Naomi in mind. It's a home for both of them."

"Both of them," Darius repeated with approval. "I like that. She's good for you, brother. She's worth waiting for."

Aaron agreed, feeling the truth of that statement settle into his bones.

The workday progressed. Aaron monitored the foundation work, consulted with subcontractors about electrical layouts, and revised timelines to accommodate delays. The physical labor provided a welcome diversion from the emptiness that had crept in since watching Meghan's bus depart.

His phone vibrated in his pocket. Ryan's name lit up the screen, still enough of a surprise to catch him off guard despite their gradually mending relationship.

"Hey, Ryan. Is everything okay?" Aaron wiped dirt from his hands as he stepped away from the excavation noise.

"It's better than okay... I got the apartment! The one in Brookside I told you about? I'm moving in next week."

Aaron leaned against his truck. When Ryan first mentioned the possibility of relocating closer to Brookside, Aaron had tempered his expectations. His brother's recovery from addiction remained delicate, his eight months of sobriety a foundation still being tested.

"That's great news." Aaron was glad, though he still harbored reservations. "Do you need help with the move?"

"I was hoping you'd offer. I don't have much. There's what I've gotten since rehab. But having you there would mean a lot."

The request, typical between brothers, represented another step toward mending their strained relationship. Aaron felt warmth in his chest as another piece of family reconciliation fell into place.

"Tell me when. Naomi and I can both help."

Ryan's voice carried vulnerability when he responded. "You'll bring Naomi? You trust me around her?"

Aaron didn't hesitate. "You're her uncle, Ryan. You're family. And you're putting in the hard work. That's what matters."

Silence stretched, filled with unspoken history.

"Thanks, Aaron. That means more than you know." Ryan's voice was rough.

Once the call ended, Aaron looked out at the crew finishing for the day. Restoration was happening all around him—on land, in relationships, and in the slow but steady healing of his own heart.

That evening, after dropping Naomi at Lisbeth's for a study session, Aaron drove to Providence Park. The winter landscape stretched bare and silent, the trees reduced to skeletal silhouettes in a charcoal sketch. His boots crunched on the frozen gravel as he followed the path toward the gazebo.

The wooden structure stood empty, its white columns stark against the winter twilight. He climbed the steps, remembering the rainy afternoon he and Meghan had sheltered here. He sat on the bench, pulling his coat tighter against the evening chill.

"Lord," he whispered. "I don't understand Your timing. When everything seemed to be falling into place..."

"Waiting has a purpose."

Aaron turned to find Liam at the gazebo entrance, his silver hair luminous in the darkness. He leaned on his polished wooden cane. This time, he wasn't surprised by the mysterious stranger's appearance.

"You have a talent for finding me when I need help."

A smile transformed Liam's features, deep lines crinkling around eyes that sparkled with brilliance. "Perhaps it's *you* who finds *me* when you're ready to listen."

He joined Aaron on the bench, his movements reflecting a fluidity that seemed at odds with his apparent age. For a while, they said nothing, watching the stars appear.

"Meghan, the woman I'm seeing, is going away for six weeks." The words were gravel in Aaron's throat.

Liam nodded, seemingly unfazed by this revelation. "Six weeks feels like forever when it's measured by a heart's longing."

"It shouldn't bother me this much. It's a great opportunity for her, and she deserves it. I should be focusing on supporting her, not feeling sorry for myself." Frustration tinged Aaron's tone.

"Both can be simultaneously true." Liam spoke with a wisdom that seemed beyond the ordinary. "You can cheer her on, while also acknowledging your own sadness. The heart doesn't compartmentalize as neatly as we might wish."

A question emerged from his deepest uncertainty. "Why now? Why is this happening when everything was beginning to make sense?"

Liam's weathered hands rested on the carved handle of his cane. "Have you considered that foundations require time to set properly? If you rush the process, the entire structure becomes compromised."

The construction metaphor struck Aaron. "So, you're saying this separation might strengthen what we're trying to build together?"

Liam's voice was reverent. "Sometimes waiting isn't solely about postponing the journey. It can also be about preparing us for it."

Aaron's hand reached into his coat pocket, his fingers finding the silver feather he had carried since their initial encounter. It felt warm despite the freezing temperature.

"The feathers... Meghan has one, and so does Naomi. What do they signify?" He pulled out the intriguing object.

Liam's smile widened, his eyes reflecting the starlight with unusual brilliance. "What do *you* think they signify, Aaron Grant?"

The question beckoned a deeper understanding. Aaron studied the silver feather, its shiny surface catching the light from the nearby path.

"Maybe... wings, like those of an eagle, soaring above life's circumstances, instead of being overwhelmed by them."

Liam's expression was warm, with what might have been pride. "That's very insightful. Often, changing your perspective can alter everything. From the ground, separation can feel like a loss. But from high above, the eagle perceives the larger picture unfolding... the complex connections weaving together toward a divine purpose."

Aaron's phone vibrated with an incoming call. Meghan's name appeared on the screen, sending his pulse racing. He swiftly glanced at Liam, who nodded at him with encouragement.

"Go ahead." Liam rose from the bench with ease. "Some conversations shouldn't wait."

Aaron answered the call, Meghan's voice coming through with unusual urgency. "Aaron? I'm really sorry to bother you so late."

"You're never a bother. What's wrong?" Concern sharpened his awareness.

"I've made it to Macon, but there's been an emergency at the dormitory." He could detect the strain in her voice. "A pipe burst on the third floor, and the entire building is flooded. They've evacuated everyone. The workshop coordinator is trying to secure other accommodations, but with twenty educators displaced..."

Worry knotted in Aaron's chest at the thought of Meghan stranded without a safe place to stay. He pictured her in an impersonal waiting area, luggage at her feet, uncertainty clouding the expressive eyes he missed so much.

"Where are you now?" He quickly calculated the distance between Brookside and Macon, mapping the fastest route.

"I'm at a coffee shop near campus. They've been kind enough to let us wait here while arrangements are made. But with the state basketball championship in town this weekend, all the hotels are booked."

The thought of her being stuck in an uncomfortable predicament, or potentially missing the eagerly awaited workshop, pained him. Helplessness washed over him, but a strong sense of determination surged within. He couldn't change the situation, but he could propose a solution.

"I'm on my way." The decision was formed and solidified instantly.

Silence stretched across the connection. "Aaron, it's a two-hour drive, and it's past eight."

"It doesn't matter. I can have Naomi stay overnight at Lisbeth's. I'm sure her mom won't mind. I'll be there by ten-thirty." He mentally ran through the arrangements he needed to make for Naomi. The late hour and treacherous winter roads should have given him pause, but he could only focus on reaching Meghan.

"I can't ask you to do that," Meghan objected.

"I'm not waiting to be asked. Text me the coffee shop address. I'll be there as soon as I can. We'll find you a place to stay before the night is over." His heart thundered, driven by an instinct to protect and provide for her.

After ending the call, Aaron turned to express his gratitude to Liam, only to find the gazebo empty. The man had vanished without a sound, leaving no trace on the frost-covered boards. Only a silver feather remained on the bench, identical to the one he held in his hand.

He retrieved it and stepped down from the gazebo. Isaiah 40:31 whispered through his spirit. Renewed strength. Rising above challenges. Wings like eagles. This metaphor aligned with everything that lay ahead. Not only the miles he needed to cover to reach Meghan, but also the road they might walk together.

He hurried toward his truck, mind racing with the logistics. He needed to call Lisbeth's mother about Naomi staying overnight, contact Darius about possibly starting late tomorrow if the drive back took longer than expected, and ensure his truck had enough gas for the trip.

Yet, despite these hurdles, relief enveloped him. While it was inconvenient and his plans had been thrown off course, he would see Meghan tonight, a week sooner than expected. This realization ignited excitement within him, even as he chided himself for finding a silver lining in her unfortunate situation.

As he jogged to his truck, he felt a profound trust in God's timing, however puzzling it might be. Tonight, he would drive, and tomorrow, they would start learning to soar.

Chapter 32

MEGHAN SQUEEZED HER EYES shut and counted to ten while gripping her phone. "Another crisis with housing? This is unbelievable."

Frustration laced her voice, breaking through her attempts to remain calm.

"I understand your frustration, Ms. Townsend," replied Marcus Wheeler from the Institute Housing Services. "An electrical fire in the maintenance area has affected the entire east wing. Safety protocols necessitate immediate evacuation until the building can pass inspection."

Just three weeks into the Macon workshop, and her housing situation felt like a bad joke. First, there was the burst pipe that forced her to leave the dormitory upon her arrival, and now, an electrical fire threatened the temporary apartment she had finally managed to settle into.

"This is the second emergency in three weeks." Meghan pinched the bridge of her nose. "I came here to concentrate on developing a curriculum, not play musical chairs with housing."

"I sincerely apologize for the inconvenience," Marcus said. "We're doing our best to locate alternate housing, but with the regional education conference happening, every nearby hotel is booked. Our options are..." He paused. "Well, they're pretty limited."

Meghan's gaze wandered to her desk where her presentation materials lay carefully arranged for that afternoon's session. The thought of packing everything up again made her stomach sink.

"What other options do I have?" She forced professionalism back into her voice despite the turmoil churning in her chest.

"We found rooms at local hotels for most participants. Unfortunately, the availability is..." Marcus cleared his throat. "Virtually nonexistent. The conference has filled accommodations within a twenty-mile radius."

Meghan collapsed onto the edge of her bed, trying to figure out how a distant hotel would impact her grueling fourteen-hour days. The Institute's strict schedule left little room for sleep, and even less for lengthy commutes.

"However," Marcus continued, and she noticed the uncertainty in his tone. "A member of our local board has offered their guest apartment. A Mr. Finn Lockwood? He said you two were acquainted."

The name hit like a punch to the stomach. Finn Lockwood. Five years ago, their relationship crashed and burned when what she thought was respectful acceptance of her faith, revealed itself to be condescension. He had called her *"closed-off"* when she refused to compromise her beliefs.

"Ms. Townsend? Are you still there?"

Meghan took a deep breath. "I'm here. Yes, I know Mr. Lockwood."

"He mentioned you worked together on some cultural preservation initiatives?" Marcus was clearly reading from notes, spouting Finn's sanitized version of their history. "His property includes a separate guest apartment above the garage. He says it's completely private, with its own entrance. Given the circumstances, it might be your best option."

When Meghan didn't immediately respond, Marcus pressed on. "I get that this is less than ideal. If you'd prefer to stay in a hotel farther from campus, we can sort out transportation, but just know that would significantly increase your travel time."

Meghan swallowed her reluctance. She doubted Finn knew how deeply those final conversations wounded her, and she had no desire to revisit that pain. But her presentation was scheduled for today, and she wasn't up for a long commute from a hotel twenty miles away. Aaron would undoubtedly be concerned, but his supportive nature had always been dependable throughout their relationship.

"I appreciate the offer." Her choice became clear despite her lack of enthusiasm. "Please convey my thanks to Mr. Lockwood."

Marcus arranged access for her to retrieve her necessary materials before the smoke damage escalated. Meghan ended the call and stared at the ceiling. This was another disruption and another complication in what should have been a straightforward step in her professional journey.

She picked up the Greyhound ticket from her nightstand, the same round-trip pass she purchased every weekend since the program began. Those three days with Aaron and Naomi had turned into her lifeline, providing the only real escape from the exhausting fourteen-hour days with unfamiliar faces.

She texted Aaron with the update, trying to sound neutral, even as her insides trembled. His reply came almost instantly.

You amaze me. Focus on your presentation today. The rest will fall into place. Call tonight if you can. I love you.

Those few words melted some of her tension. His steady presence, even from miles away, had become something solid to lean on.

She texted back, adding a heart emoji that would have seemed childish months ago but now felt necessary.

I love you too. Can't wait for Friday.

Drawing a deep breath, she stood and turned toward her notes. She wouldn't let a fire or Finn Lockwood derail the work she had poured herself into.

The Institute's great hall hummed with energy as educators presented innovative frameworks for historical education. Meghan stood at the lectern, outlining her curriculum approach that integrated primary-source analysis with community-based learning.

She gestured toward her presentation slides. "When students can see the local impact of national movements, history stops being abstract. The Harlem Renaissance isn't just an artistic movement in textbooks. It's the root of the music, language, and traditions still alive in their own communities."

Department heads and education specialists nodded, several making notes as she continued. For three weeks, Meghan had worked toward this moment. Now the message was landing.

As she concluded to appreciative applause, Dr. Thaddeus Holloway, the Institute's director, approached with a rare smile.

"Exceptional framework, Ms. Townsend." His academic formality was softened by genuine enthusiasm. "You've struck the perfect balance between academic rigor and practical application. That's what effective education requires."

Meghan's chest swelled with pride. They didn't hand out compliments here, especially not to first-time participants. Her framework had resonated as intended, garnering attention from educational leaders capable of implementing these approaches statewide.

During the working lunch, department heads clustered around her with questions about assessments, adaptations for rural schools, and technology integration. When her phone vibrated in her pocket, she ignored it, focusing on a question about assessment methodology.

Only when it vibrated persistently did concern flicker through her. Excusing herself, she stepped into the corridor to check her screen. Naomi's name and three missed calls stared back at her.

Her stomach dropped. Naomi never called during school hours, and especially not three times. She dialed back immediately.

"Meghan? I've been trying to reach you!"

"What's wrong? What happened?" Dread coiled in her stomach at the uncharacteristic urgent tone of the teenager.

"It's Uncle Aaron." Naomi's voice cracked. "They said he fell from some scaffolding at the construction site. They took him to Lakeside Hospital. Mr. Forrester's driving me there now."

The world tilted. Every bit of oxygen seemed to vanish from the hallway. Construction accidents. Falls from scaffolding. The statistics Aaron casually mentioned during dinner conversations about job site injuries rushed through her mind.

"How serious is it?" Her voice came out strangled, almost unrecognizable. "Is he conscious? Please... tell me exactly what happened?"

"I'm not sure," Naomi answered. "Someone called from Uncle Aaron's phone. They said something about one of the supports collapsing. Mr. Washington's with him at the hospital."

Meghan pressed her palm against the wall, her body suddenly weak. Images assaulted her imagination. Aaron's strong body broken on concrete. Blood pooling beneath him. Paramedics rushing to stabilize injuries she couldn't bear to envision. Her chest constricted with panic.

"I'm on my way. I'm leaving right now," she whispered, more to herself than to Naomi.

"But your presentations—"

"They don't matter," Meghan interrupted, her fierce conviction slicing through the shock. "Nothing's more important than this. Text me any updates. I'll be there as soon as I can."

She hung up and hurried back to the conference room. Her hands trembled so violently that she nearly dropped her presentation materials. Dr. Holloway looked up as she neared.

"I have a family emergency," Meghan explained, her professional façade intact despite the anxiety coursing through her. "There's been an accident back home. My partner, Aaron... he's in the hospital."

Dr. Holloway nodded empathetically. "Go. Mr. Jenkins can cover your afternoon session. Is there anything we can do to help?"

"No, but thank you. I need to leave right away." Meghan's throat constricted with each word.

The next hour passed in frantic activity as she packed what she could from her apartment, which would soon be evacuated. Relief flooded through her that she wouldn't have to depend on her ex-boyfriend for lodging. She called a taxi to the car rental agency and stood gripping the counter while an excruciatingly slow clerk processed her paperwork.

"Is there any way to expedite this?" Desperation edged her normally composed voice. "It's a medical emergency."

The clerk glanced up, finally seeing the distress in Meghan's expression. "Let me see what I can do."

Each passing minute felt like an eternity as her mind spiraled through a whirlwind of worst-case scenarios. Construction accidents were perilous, often resulting in spinal damage, traumatic brain injuries, and internal hemorrhaging. The statistical knowledge that usually benefited her as an educator now tormented her with the grim potential outcomes.

When the clerk finally handed over the keys to the compact sedan, Meghan snatched them up and took off.

Rain poured as she navigated Macon's unfamiliar streets, her windshield wipers struggling to cope with the relentless downpour. The highway loomed before her as the weather deteriorated.

Lord, please keep him stable. Let me reach him in time. Please don't take him from me.

Memories flooded through her mind. The fateful phone call about her father's accident. The endless hospital hallway seen through the bewildered eyes of a thirteen-year-old. The chilling news communicated in a stark consultation room. Years later, the same scenario was replayed when her mother suffered a heart attack. Another urgent summons, a frantic race against time, and an arrival too late for final farewells.

At one point, she had to pull over, sobbing so hard that she couldn't see.

Not Aaron. Please, Lord... not again.

The storm intensified, slowing traffic to a crawl, as accidents reduced the lanes to a standstill. Each delay twisted her panic, her imagination conjuring images of worsening conditions, as critical moments passed while she sat trapped in the rain-soaked gridlock.

The usual ninety-minute drive turned into an agonizing three-hour ordeal, plagued by accidents and poor visibility. When Brookside's familiar exit appeared, her shoulders were tense and aching. Her lower lip throbbed from biting it during the more nerve-wracking stretches of highway.

The emergency entrance of Lakeside Community Hospital shone like a beacon. She parked, almost forgetting her purse as she dashed across the parking lot, her shoes splashing through puddles without a thought about them getting soaked.

The emergency department's automatic doors whooshed open, exposing the hectic urgency of the medical scene. Harsh fluorescent lights illuminated the nurses' stations, the curtained examination bays, and the families waiting, their faces expressing everything from boredom to utter fear.

Feeling disoriented, Meghan scanned the sea of people, searching for a familiar face. Her gaze landed on Samantha, clad in royal blue scrubs at the end of the corridor, engrossed in conversation with another nurse at the central station.

"Sam!" she called out.

Daniel's wife looked up, recognition flooding her features. She hurried over, her pregnant belly more pronounced beneath her scrubs.

"Meghan, thank God you made it safely!" Samantha embraced her before leading her toward a quieter corridor. "Daniel texted that you were driving from Macon. We've been worried sick about you on these roads."

"Aaron..." That single word contained all her questions, all her fears, all her desperate need for information.

"He's stable and alert. He's on the fourth floor, room 412. They admitted him for observation and to manage his pain."

"How bad is it?" Meghan followed as Samantha guided her toward the elevator.

"He has two broken ribs, a fractured ankle, and a dislocated shoulder, plus a mild concussion," Samantha answered, her clinical tone somehow providing comfort through its straightforwardness. "A scaffold support gave way, but fortunately, he wasn't at full height. They said he was about twelve feet up instead of thirty."

As the elevator ascended, Samantha continued providing more medical context. "He'll be uncomfortable for several weeks, but with proper care, his injuries should heal completely."

Relief weakened Meghan's knees as the elevator doors opened.

"He could have died." Emotion threatened to engulf her now that the immediate fear began to subside.

"But he didn't. Naomi's with him, and I know she'll be relieved to see you." They approached room 412.

Meghan paused at the threshold, taking a moment to regain her composure before entering. Inhaling deeply, she pushed the door open and walked inside.

The sight that greeted her was one she would never forget. Aaron lay against the pillows, his once-vibrant complexion now ashen against the pristine white hospital linens. A large bruise extended from his temple down to his cheekbone, darkening to almost black beneath his eye. A jagged gash near his hairline had been stitched closed, the surrounding skin swollen and inflamed.

His left arm was secured in a sling, immobilizing his shoulder. Bandages wrapped around his torso showed where the hospital gown gaped. Monitors beeped beside him, tracking his vitals and dispensing medication through an IV in his right hand.

What broke Meghan's heart was witnessing the effort it took for him to turn his head toward the door. She could see the grimace of pain he tried to suppress, and how he controlled his breathing to minimize the discomfort from his broken ribs. This man, who epitomized strength and tenacity, was now confined to painful immobility.

Despite his injuries, Aaron's expression changed dramatically when he saw her. His face brightened with gladness. Naomi, who was sitting next to the bed, turned to face the doorway, relief spreading across her face at Meghan's arrival.

"You didn't have to come," Aaron rasped as she approached the bedside.

"I had to... nothing else mattered." Tears welled in her eyes as she reached for his uninjured hand, entwining their fingers in that familiar connection that sustained her during their time apart.

His skin emitted warmth, and the steady pulse beneath her fingertips crumbled her composure. It reassured her of his life, reminded her of his presence, and testified to the miracle of his survival.

Naomi rose to embrace Meghan. "I told her she didn't need to rush back, but she wouldn't hear of it."

She returned the teenager's hug, aware of the underlying fear behind her half-hearted attempt at humor.

"Nothing could have kept me away." Her throat constricted around words that seemed inadequate for the tidal wave of emotion crashing through her.

As Naomi stepped away, Meghan refocused on Aaron, taking note of the details she had overlooked in her initial shock. She took in the lines of worry etched around his eyes, the deliberate way he held himself, and the fear lurking behind his forced smile, which made her heart ache with a strong desire to alleviate his pain.

"I should fall off scaffolding more often if it brings you home early," Aaron joked weakly.

"Don't you dare," Meghan shot back, laughter and tears mingling as she leaned over the bedrail.

The kiss she placed on his lips was soft. She was mindful of his injuries, Naomi nearby, and the sterile smells of the hospital all around them. She tasted her tears and sensed his emotional vulnerability. Amid the hospital's odors, a whiff of his cedar aftershave reminded her of who he was. Aaron was still, fundamentally and miraculously, here.

Drawing back, she explored his face, cataloging his injuries while silently giving thanks for what could have been a catastrophic situation, yet wasn't.

"You scared years off my life, Aaron Grant."

His good hand lifted to caress her cheek, thumb brushing away the moisture with a tender reverence that sent warmth cascading through her.

"I'm sorry for scaring you," he murmured. "But having you here makes even broken ribs seem worthwhile."

"Gross," Naomi chimed with her typical teenage candor, though her relieved smile contradicted the protest. "I'm off to find the vending machines while you two get mushy. Want anything?"

Her casual question, so ordinary amid the recent calamity, eased a tension Meghan hadn't known she was holding. As Naomi departed, Meghan perched on the edge of the bed, Aaron's uninjured hand clasping hers.

"I've never been so frightened. When Naomi called, all I could think was, *not again.'* Not another phone call, another hospital, another..." She couldn't finish the sentence.

Understanding softened his gaze. "But I'm not lost... just temporarily damaged. Repairs are all that's required."

The construction metaphor, a staple of his life philosophy, elicited a gentle laugh from her. "Still the builder, I see. Even from a hospital bed." She gently squeezed his hand.

"Structure is my language," Aaron replied sleepily, struggling to stifle a yawn. "Besides, damage offers a chance to refine the design. That's the core of restoration."

As Aaron's eyelids drifted closed, Meghan remained, watching his features relax into tranquil slumber. The monitors provided their rhythmic assurance of his well-being. Outside, the storm

raged on, rain lashing against the windows as the afternoon transitioned into evening.

But the foundation held strong.

Chapter 33

Aaron shifted against the pillows, wincing as a sharp pain shot through his ankle. The white cast encased his leg from his toes to midway up his calf, and after three days of bed rest, the confines of his bedroom felt increasingly stifling. Even the ceiling had turned into an object of annoyance, serving as a blank slate for his restless thoughts.

He reached for the glass of water on his nightstand, but the movement triggered a wave of lightheadedness. The concussion, though invisible, proved to be just as exasperating as his fractured ankle. Every twist and turn demanded careful forethought.

"Do you need anything?" Naomi stood in the doorway. The dark circles shadowing her eyes hinted at the sleepless nights she spent checking in on him.

Aaron tried to muster a smile. "I'm fine, kiddo. Don't you have a science test to study for?"

"It can wait. Meghan will be here soon."

He couldn't help but notice once again how easily she referred to *'Meghan'* instead of Ms. Townsend, marking one of many signs of the shifts in their relationship. The routine of care they established touched and frustrated him in equal measure. He hated being the one who needed help instead of providing it.

"You're scowling again," Naomi said playfully. "The doctor said you're supposed to stay positive."

"I'm pretty sure that's not scientifically validated," Aaron countered, though he consciously relaxed his expression.

"Proverbs 17:22 says otherwise," Naomi beamed. "*'A cheerful heart is good medicine, but a crushed spirit dries up the bones.'* Meghan and I looked it up yesterday."

Aaron's chest tightened with pride. This girl, who once kept everyone at arm's length, was quoting scripture at him. God was doing something extraordinary in her life.

The doorbell chimed, and Naomi brightened. "That's Meghan. She said she might come early."

She vanished down the hallway, and Aaron tried to smooth his shirt and sit up straighter. He despised this helplessness, being stuck instead of being the man he always strived to be. Meghan seeing him like this only made it worse.

Moments later, her voice filled the living room. He heard laughter, hers and Naomi's, and it lifted his spirits despite everything.

"Knock, knock." Meghan stood in the doorway, a grocery bag in one hand and papers in the other.

Despite his discomfort, Aaron's heart raced at her presence. He took in every detail—the graceful line of her neck, the curve of her hips beneath her fitted slacks. Most striking was the spark in her eyes when they connected with his.

"You're early." He couldn't hide his delight.

"Principal Watkins rescheduled this afternoon's meetings. I brought soup from Willow's diner and those history articles you asked about."

She crossed to his bedside and kissed his forehead. Her lips lingered, her warm breath displacing the sterile smell of ointments and antiseptic wipes.

"You're a sight for sore eyes." He reached for her hand.

"And you could definitely use a shave. How about I help with that after lunch?" Her fingers trailed along his jaw where stubble had accumulated.

The offer shattered his illusion of being self-sufficient. Sudden frustration washed over him.

"I can handle it," he snapped, more harshly than he intended, withdrawing from her touch.

She stilled but didn't pull away. Instead, she cupped his face and looked him square in the eye.

"Listen closely, Aaron Grant." Her voice was low and intense. "Your worth isn't tied to what you can do. Allowing yourself to be vulnerable doesn't lessen your worth in my eyes. It simply makes you human. Let me help you... not because you're incapable, but because love lightens the load."

Her words penetrated, and the knot in his chest slowly unraveled. "I'm not used to feeling weak. Especially not in front of you."

"Then let me show you that it's okay. All of it."

Aaron's hand lifted to the back of her neck while his other arm circled her waist, drawing her closer until she perched on the edge of his bed. The urge to draw strength from her presence overtook his previous resistance.

"What did I do to deserve you?" he murmured.

"Nothing. That's what makes it grace."

Their kiss began slowly, then deepened. He tilted her head to give himself better access. Meghan responded, her mouth opening in invitation. The flavor of coffee, cinnamon, and something uniquely Meghan overshadowed the discomfort of his injuries.

A throat cleared at the door.

"Should I come back later?" The teenager's tone carried more amusement than embarrassment.

"No need." Meghan quickly stood and gave Aaron's hand a reassuring squeeze before she headed toward the kitchen. "I was just about to heat some soup for lunch."

Aaron chuckled, watching Meghan disappear toward the kitchen.

"It's Monday," Naomi commented, lingering in the doorway. "Isn't Meghan supposed to go back to Macon today?"

The question emphasized the unusual circumstance. According to the schedule Meghan had set up with Dr. Holloway, she was supposed to be in Macon from Monday to Thursday, and back in Brookside from Friday to Sunday. She should have been back at the workshop today.

"Principal Watkins granted her emergency leave. She'll head back tomorrow to finish out the rest of the week," he clarified.

Aaron shifted uncomfortably, guilt nagging at him for disrupting her professional obligations. Though he was grateful for her immediate response to his injury, he hated knowing her presence here was preventing her from seizing a vital career opportunity.

Naomi assisted him to the living room, where he settled into the recliner, elevating his leg on the footrest. Sweat beaded along his hairline from the exertion.

Lunch came and went with enjoyable conversation. Meghan caught him up on her workshop, while Naomi talked about school. Aaron listened, half-distracted by the recollection of their interrupted kiss.

After Naomi left for her study group, Meghan cleaned up the lunch dishes and returned to the living room. She sat on the couch next to his recliner.

"You're quiet. Is the pain worse today?"

A rueful smile touched his lips. "Stanley says I'm the most impatient man he's ever met."

"No surprise there." Meghan's eyes sparkled with affection.

The mention of Stanley brought back memories of their chat during yesterday's physical therapy session. "Did you know he and Audrey are getting serious now?"

Meghan nodded. "It seems fast, but they both seem sure about it."

Aaron studied her face as he voiced the question that had consumed his thoughts during his sleepless nights. "What do you think? Do you believe a few months is enough time to truly know someone?"

Meghan didn't look away. "Sometimes, it's not about how long you've spent together... it's about the depth of the connection. Some people date for years and never genuinely understand each other... and others click instantly."

Aaron extended his hand, and she joined him, kneeling beside the recliner. Her fingers slipped into his.

"I never saw this coming." His voice was rough with emotions he could no longer hold back. "When I came to Brookside, I was just trying to survive. I wanted to build the business and take care of Naomi. But then you showed up, and suddenly, everything felt like it was within reach again. Every plan I make, now includes you."

"God's full of surprises."

"I've been thinking about our future and what we might build together, once I recover and your workshop wraps up."

Before he could continue, his phone buzzed with Ryan's name lighting up the screen. This was his brother's third check-in of the day. A frustrated sigh escaped before Aaron could rein it in.

"I should take this. He's been on edge ever since the accident." The words scraped out of him, heavy and unwelcome when every part of him yearned to stay locked in this moment with her.

"I'll get your medication while you talk." Meghan brushed her lips over his cheek.

"Hey Ryan, is everything okay?" Aaron attempted to refocus his thoughts.

"Just checking in. How's the pain today?"

Aaron observed Meghan heading towards the kitchen. "It's tolerable. The doctor says I'm healing well, though not as quickly as I'd like."

"It's never going to be fast enough for you," Ryan replied, teasingly, evoking memories of their relationship before the estrangement. "Listen, I was wondering if I could swing by tonight? There's something I wanted to run by you."

The request surprised Aaron. Though their relationship had recently improved, Ryan seldom took the initiative to visit without an important reason. "Sure. Is everything alright?"

Aaron could hear Ryan taking a deep breath on the other end of the line. "I've been offered a permanent position at the supply company, complete with benefits. I was hoping to come by and tell you more about it in person."

Pride surged through Aaron. After eight months of sobriety, steady employment, and rekindled connections, his brother's recovery exceeded all his hopes. "That's great news, Ryan! Come over. Meghan is here, but she won't mind. Why don't you come by around eight?"

After ending the call, Aaron watched as Meghan returned with his medication and a glass of fresh water. "Ryan's coming over tonight. He has some news he wants to share."

"That's wonderful," Meghan said warmly. "His visits mean so much to you both."

Meghan welcomed not only him and Naomi, but also Ryan. Her ability to accept and see beyond past mistakes drew Aaron's heart toward hers in ways that continued to surprise him.

The remainder of the afternoon passed peacefully. That evening, after dinner, Meghan mentioned her plans to return to Macon.

"I should leave early tomorrow morning," she said as she arranged his medications on the nightstand. "The forecast calls for ice, and I'd rather drive in the daylight."

Though she had spent the weekend in the spare room of his apartment, the knowledge that tomorrow would begin another separation settled heavily in Aaron.

"I wish you didn't have to go back at all."

"Three more weeks." Her fingers entwined with his. "Then the workshop ends, and we won't have this separation anymore."

"That's still too long." Aaron drew her closer until she sat on the edge of his bed.

"But it's worth it." Meghan's free hand moved to rest directly over his heart.

His hand cradled her face and traced her lower lip with his thumb. "I love you, Meghan Townsend."

They kissed again, slower this time, but no less meaningful. When they parted, her fingers lingered on his chest.

"I should go. You need to rest," she whispered.

"Stay a little longer," Aaron requested, reluctant to let her go. But she slipped away, and he counted the minutes until his brother arrived.

Ryan arrived promptly at eight, looking better than he had in years. After sharing a greeting with Meghan, he joined Aaron in the living room, settling into the chair across from his recliner.

"My apartment's really coming together," Ryan remarked about his new place, which had become much cozier and more welcoming since Aaron and Naomi lent a hand during his move two weeks ago. "I can't thank you enough for all the help with the move."

"We were glad to pitch in." Aaron was relieved to see how well his brother was adjusting to life in Brookside. "Naomi loved organizing your bookshelves. She said you have excellent taste in books."

Ryan laughed in a way Aaron hadn't heard in years. He leaned in, resting his elbows on his knees.

"That's what I wanted to talk to you about. Not books, but about my new job. I told you that the supply company offered me the assistant manager position. But there's more."

Aaron nodded, encouraging his brother to continue.

"I've been going to a recovery support group at New Hope Baptist. It meets on Tuesday nights, and Pastor Morrison is one of the facilitators."

Aaron was aware his brother had been attending meetings, but hadn't realized he had found spiritual support at the same church where he had rekindled his own faith.

"Why didn't you say anything about it before?"

Ryan shrugged. "I wanted to make sure it stuck before telling you. Being clean for eight months is the longest I've managed since the injury."

Aaron leaned forward to meet his brother's gaze. It takes strength and commitment to accomplish all you have. I'm proud of you."

Surprise flickered across Ryan's features, reminding Aaron of their childhood and of the brother he had once known before pain and addiction had created chasms between them.

"I appreciate you saying that. Like they say in the program... I'm taking it one day at a time."

Aaron nodded, then spoke after a few moments of silence.

"Now it's my turn. There's something I'd like your opinion on. I've been waiting for the right moment." He pulled out a small velvet box from under a magazine on the side table, opening it to reveal a simple yet elegant diamond ring.

Ryan's eyes widened, his face transforming with a smile. "I had a feeling you were heading this way. I've seen how you look at her and how she looks at you."

"Do you think it's too soon?"

Ryan shook his head. "Some things you know, and when it's right, it's right. One thing recovery teaches is recognizing the difference between impulse and certainty. What I see between you and Meghan is certainty."

Aaron felt comforted by the validation from his brother, who had once been his closest confidant before addiction caused a rift. They spent the next hour discussing his plans, with Ryan suggesting ideas that uncovered an unexpected romanticism beneath his practical facade.

The brothers embraced as Ryan left, marking another milestone in their relationship. The conversation reinforced Aaron's conviction about turning possibilities into intent. The only remaining variable was timing, now dependent on Meghan's workshop schedule and his recovery.

Later that night, after Meghan had retired to the guest room and Naomi had gone to her bedroom, Aaron was unable to sleep despite his physical exhaustion. His conversation with Ryan had been more productive than he had expected, and his brother's support for his plans was both unexpected and affirming.

A faint noise from the balcony captured his attention. Bracing himself, he stood up carefully, grabbed his crutches, and made his slow, painful trek down the hallway. Through the glass doors, he spotted Naomi sitting on the small bench, surrounded by her plants, a blanket draped around her shoulders against the night chill.

The cold air rushed in as he opened the door.

"Can't sleep?" he asked, maneuvering onto the balcony.

Naomi glanced up, shook her head, then shifted to create space on the bench.

Aaron sat, his leg extended awkwardly in front. Above, stars shone through the winter darkness with striking clarity, their light undiminished by the city's glow in the cloudless night.

"Want to talk about it?"

Naomi plucked a leaf from the rosemary plant and rolled it between her fingers, releasing its aromatic oils.

"When I heard about your accident, I thought it was happening again. First my parents, then Grandma, and..." She trailed off.

Understanding dawned as he recognized the fear concealed in her words. "You were afraid that you might lose me, too."

She nodded, her face obscured, but the slight shake of her shoulders indicated unspoken emotions. "It's stupid, I know."

He softened his voice, aiming to say the right things. "It's not stupid at all. Given everything you've been through, it's completely normal."

"Nothing about our situation is normal," she said, a touch of her characteristic directness returning.

"You're right. But I need you to hear me out." He waited until she faced him, moonlight reflecting the tears flowing silently down her cheeks. "I'm not going anywhere. Not by choice, and definitely not because of anything I can control."

"But you can't guarantee that!" The brutal honesty of her adolescence cut through his adult reassurances.

"You're right. But while I can't predict what life has in store for us, I can promise you that Brookside is our home now. This is where I've chosen for us to live, and where I intend to raise you while building our future together."

She leaned her head on his shoulder. "Thank you, Uncle Aaron."

They watched the stars trace patterns in the winter sky. A notification from his phone disrupted the peaceful moment. It was a message from Dr. Holloway, the director of the Carter Institute, addressed to all workshop participants and their emergency contacts.

He quickly skimmed the text, excitement growing inside him. "It's about Meghan's workshop. They're shutting down for unforeseen repairs due to burst pipes and electrical issues. They've decided not to continue with the program. They concluded everything the day after Meghan left."

Joy surged through him as he showed the message to his niece, who instantly brightened. "So, she's staying for good? No more back and forth?"

"Yes, she's staying for good," he confirmed. Meghan would stay in Brookside, continuing to be part of their daily lives.

As they stepped inside, the burden of his injury eased, and his impatience began to dissipate. Each step felt like a divine choreography, far superior to any human blueprint. This journey marked their transition from hesitant guardianship to a profound, abiding love... from fractured ties to restored relationships.

Now that they would no longer be apart, he would soon pose the question that had resided in his heart for so long. Their story was on the brink of a new chapter, filled with pages they would create together in the life and home God was building.

Chapter 34

Meghan gathered the last of her things from Aaron's apartment. After weeks of supporting his recovery, the idea of going back to her own place brought a tug of bittersweet emotion. The overnight bag she packed in a rush the night of his accident had expanded into a corner of the guest room as the days extended into weeks.

"Are you sure you don't need me another day?" She watched Aaron move around the kitchen, still cautious but more confident, even with the walking boot on his ankle.

"I'm sure." He filled two mugs with coffee. "You've given up enough already. Besides, the physical therapist says I'm cleared for solo showers now."

Heat rose to Meghan's cheeks at Aaron's teasing. "You're impossible! That was Daniel and Ryan helping you with your showers, and you know it!"

These weeks had rewritten their relationship in quiet, intimate ways. She had sat beside him during grueling therapy sessions, helped him shift positions at night when the pain medication wore off, and even washed his hair in the sink when the cast made bathing too complicated.

"You've made incredible progress. The doctor was impressed yesterday." Meghan accepted the steaming mug he offered.

Aaron's fingers brushed against hers as he passed the coffee. The heat in his gaze sent a familiar spark through her.

"Only because I had the best nurse."

"I think Naomi deserves most of that credit," Meghan protested, though his praise thrilled her.

"She had a remarkable role model." He set his coffee down and stepped closer, one hand cupping her cheek.

Dr. Holloway's notification of the cancellation of the rest of the Carter Institute workshop had become an unforeseen blessing. What initially felt like a professional setback turned into relief as she stayed in Brookside, balancing her time between supporting Aaron's recovery and continuing her work remotely.

Meghan tilted her head as Aaron kissed her. What started as a gentle hug deepened. Her hands slid behind his neck, her body pressing into his. She luxuriated in his taste—coffee, mint, and something distinctly Aaron.

The moment was broken by the sound of the front door opening.

"I'm back! Did Meghan leave yet?"

"Still here." Meghan stepped reluctantly from Aaron's arms as Naomi appeared in the kitchen doorway, her school backpack slung over one shoulder.

"Great! Ms. Sinclair let us out early. She asked me to let you know there's a faculty meeting tomorrow at nine."

"Thanks for the heads-up. I'll see you both tonight for dinner." Meghan picked up her overnight bag and purse, conscious of Aaron's gaze tracking her movements.

Naomi's smile turned playful and a bit mysterious. "Definitely. Oh, and make sure you wear something nice... maybe that burgundy dress Uncle Aaron likes."

Meghan raised an eyebrow, her curiosity piqued by the unusual request. "Any particular reason?"

"Nope... just because," Naomi replied, her eyes shimmering with mischief.

Meghan looked between Naomi and Aaron. Something was definitely going on. "Alright then... the burgundy dress it is," she conceded, playing along with whatever surprise they were planning.

Aaron accompanied her to the door. In the privacy of the entryway, he pulled her close once more, kissing her again. His hands framed her face as his mouth claimed hers with an unhurried exploration that left her breathless.

"Until tonight," he murmured.

Meghan's drive home passed in a haze. Her house looked the same, but after three weeks away, it felt different—quiet, almost lonely. Dust had accumulated on bookshelves, mail had piled beneath the slot in her front door, and the houseplants drooped from neglect.

She touched a wilting fern by her kitchen window. "I know. I abandoned you for a man with a broken ankle. Let me make it up to you."

After watering the plants and sorting the mail, she sat at her desk to work on the curriculum frameworks requested by Principal Watkins. Although the workshop ended earlier than planned, its influence on her career remained significant.

Department heads across the state requested her integration model for their districts. The Georgia Education Board invited her to present at their summer conference. Even Dr. Holloway suggested she consider publishing her approach in academic journals.

Meghan dedicated her afternoon to accomplishing various tasks, only briefly interrupted when Olivia confirmed their coffee date, and Samantha sent over ultrasound images of her growing baby.

Around three o'clock, her doorbell rang. A delivery courier stood on her porch, holding an enormous arrangement of dark purple and creamy white tulips.

"Delivery for Meghan Townsend." He presented the flowers and a small envelope before leaving.

Once Meghan placed the arrangement on her coffee table, she opened the envelope. The small card revealed Aaron's distinctive handwriting:

Meghan, having you in our home for three weeks has spoiled me completely. The apartment feels empty without you. Would you meet me at the gazebo in Providence Park at sunset? The spot where rain once sheltered us now holds new possibilities. With love, Aaron.

Warmth spread through her. Even though they had been together daily during his recovery, something about his note felt special.

She had several hours until sunset, enough time to prepare for whatever Aaron had planned. After finishing her work, she enjoyed a relaxing bath with lavender-scented bubbles. As she donned the burgundy dress Naomi specifically requested, she reflected on how her life had changed since August.

The woman who meticulously organized her classroom and enforced firm boundaries would hardly recognize the Meghan staring back at her in the mirror. This new Meghan's eyes sparkled with excitement at the thought of seeing a man she had known for less than eight months.

The drive to Providence Park was quiet, her thoughts too crowded for even the radio. Bare trees lined the road as she parked at the main entrance. She tightened her coat, shielding against the cold and the nervousness fluttering within her.

The first silver feather caught her attention immediately. It was propped against a rock at the beginning of the path. Unlike the mysterious ones that had appeared before, this feather had been placed there deliberately, with a small piece of parchment tied to its stem with a burgundy ribbon.

The Lord makes firm the steps of the one who delights in him. Psalm 37:23.

Meghan lifted the feather. The scripture spoke to their journey, steps guided by divine purpose, not chance. Tucking the feather and note into her pocket, she continued along the path, eyes alert for what awaited.

The second feather appeared twenty paces later, propped against a massive oak tree, bearing scripture and attached with an identical burgundy ribbon.

Your word is a lamp for my feet, a light on my path. Psalm 119:105.

Her heart raced as she pressed on, eyes scanning for the next marker. Four more feathers guided her deeper into the park, each bearing an inscription that emphasized loyalty, divine direction, and love's transformative nature. When the gazebo appeared, the rays of the setting sun bathed its white columns in golden light.

The structure was dramatically different from its usual simplicity. White lights adorned the railings and ceiling, creating a starry canopy in the early evening. Greenery intertwined with the railings. In the center stood Aaron.

His tall frame was unmistakable. He wore a charcoal-gray suit that emphasized his broad shoulders and a burgundy tie that matched her dress.

"You found me." His deep voice carried through the evening stillness.

Meghan held up the feathers. "I followed your breadcrumbs. Though I'm pretty sure there's a fairy tale warning about that."

Aaron's laugh, rich and unguarded, warmed the space. "It's a good thing I'm not a witch with a candy house."

"No, just a builder with a gazebo." Meghan climbed the steps, aware of each heartbeat, each breath, each movement bringing her closer to this man who had become essential to her existence.

Upon closer inspection, the signs of Aaron's injury were apparent in the faint shadows under his eyes and the careful way he favored his booted ankle. However, his face radiated joy, making his physical discomfort almost easy to overlook.

"The scriptures... they speak of pathways, journeys, and divine direction." She exhaled in the evening chill.

Aaron took her hand, his warm fingers intertwining with hers. "Nothing about our journey has been by chance, Meghan. Not even that first collision in the school hallway."

She leaned into his touch. "When I first met you and Naomi, I saw the obstacles. She was a student needing support, and you were her guardian needing help."

"And I saw a teacher who unashamedly stepped beyond the traditional boundaries. You gave me strength when I didn't have it to hold myself up," Aaron confessed.

Meghan's heart filled, and tears brimmed in her eyes at his candidness. He reached into his pocket and withdrew a small velvet box.

"This isn't how I planned this moment, but..." He gestured ruefully at his walking boot. With careful movements, he eased himself to one knee. As he opened the velvet box, a princess-cut diamond sparkled between two smaller gems, glinting under the gazebo's illumination.

"Meghan Elise Townsend," he began, his gaze unwavering. "You've helped me regain my faith. You taught Naomi that family can extend beyond blood connections. And you made me understand that love is a choice and a gift, renewed each morning, just like God's mercies."

He presented the ring. "I want to wake up to those new mercies with you every morning, and build a home filled with faith and love. Meghan... will you marry me?"

Meghan's heart overflowed.

"Yes," she whispered, the single syllable encapsulating all her certainty. Then, with joy breaking free from her emotions, she exclaimed, "Yes, Aaron! Yes, to building a life together! Yes, to new mercies each morning! Yes, to everything!"

Aaron's smile radiated pure happiness. He lifted the ring from its velvet nest and slipped it onto her finger. It fit beautifully, as if affirming a divine orchestration.

Standing, he enveloped Meghan in a warm embrace. Their lips met, and the kiss combined longing with tenderness, perfectly harmonious as he moved his mouth against hers.

When they finally separated, both gasping for breath, Aaron rested his forehead against hers. His eyes made promises he would fulfill once they exchanged their marital vows.

"I love you," he murmured.

"And I love you... even more than I ever thought was possible."

As twilight descended, Meghan caught a glimpse of movement in her peripheral vision. Turning within the circle of Aaron's arms, she spotted a familiar figure seated on a distant bench. A man with silver hair and a wooden cane silently observed their celebration.

"Aaron," she whispered, nodding toward the bench. "It's him... it's Liam."

Aaron turned his head, wrapping his arm around her waist. They watched as Liam raised his cane in quiet acknowledgment, a wordless smile creasing his weathered face.

"Should we go over and speak to him?" She was curious about the enigmatic man who seemed to appear at the pivotal moments in their lives.

Aaron began to speak, but when they looked back, Liam had disappeared. No sounds revealed his departure, and the frosty path showed no signs of his presence. Only a solitary silver feather glimmered on the bench where he had been seated.

Aaron's expression was contemplative but untroubled. "Psalm 91:11 tells us, *'For he will command his angels concerning you to guard you in all your ways.'* I guess some things aren't meant to be explained."

Meghan nestled against Aaron's shoulder.

"Shall we go share our news with Naomi?" Aaron's voice was soothing as it brushed against her hair.

"Did she know?"

"Who do you think helped me with all those feathers?" His smile reflected pride in witnessing his niece's healing.

Meghan turned to kiss him again, sealing the promise of their future—passion, partnership, and family. Her fingers grazed his jaw, memorizing the sensation of his skin and the soft tickle of his evening stubble. Aaron matched her fervor, drawing her closer. When they parted, his eyes glowed with yearning and reverence.

"We should go before I forget we're in a public park." His voice was thick with longing.

They descended the gazebo steps into the darkening evening, grounded in grace and guided by love.

Chapter 35

Aaron stood on the newly finished porch of their future home. He ran his fingers along the cedar railing, admiring the work his team had poured heart and soul into over the past few weeks. The oversized kitchen windows faced east, perfect for Meghan's herb garden. Naomi's container garden would fit along the wraparound porch. Every corner of this place had been planned with love.

Darius headed up the graveled driveway, kicking up small puffs of Georgia clay with every step. His easy grin matched the confident rhythm of his stride.

"The electricians finished the second-floor wiring this morning. We're ahead of schedule for the first time since breaking ground."

Aaron let out a breath. "Right on time for the wedding. Meghan's already arranging where all the furniture will go."

Darius chuckled. "Elena's the same way. We've been married for fifteen years, and she still moves our living room around every spring. She says it keeps things interesting."

"Meghan's got this whole plan for merging our book collections. Apparently, it's a three-day process, and there's a particular method to it that I'm not qualified to handle."

Darius clapped him on the shoulder. "Welcome to married life, my friend."

This spring, he and Meghan would stand before God and everyone they loved, committing to forever. He hadn't seen that coming, but he was grateful every day that it had.

"Speaking of weddings, Elena asked me to confirm the headcount for the reception. She's coordinating with Willow on the catering." Darius handed over the clipboard with inspection reports.

"Right now, we're at one hundred and twelve. It might be more if Frank talks his wife into coming."

The mention of his boss sparked gratitude and disbelief. What began as a straightforward working relationship had developed into a full partnership.

"Regional partner," g mused, as if reading his mind. "Not bad for the guy who showed up in Brookside less than a year ago, scowling at anyone who dared speak to him."

"I wasn't that bad," Aaron protested.

"Man, you growled when I suggested adding those garden beds behind the community center." Darius shook his head, his expression holding no judgment, only acknowledgment of the transformation he witnessed in Aaron. "Now look at you. You're building a house with a reading nook because the woman you love likes spending afternoons with a book."

Before Aaron could respond, his phone vibrated. It was a reminder about their premarital counseling session with Pastor Morrison. He scribbled his name on the report before handing the clipboard back.

"Our premarital counseling's in thirty minutes. It's time to get some spiritual wisdom."

During his drive to New Hope Baptist, Aaron reflected on all the changes since he arrived last summer. It wasn't the buildings or the new businesses. It was the way people folded him into their lives until Brookside stopped feeling like a stopover, and started feeling like home.

Pastor Morrison stood as Aaron entered his office. They shook hands, but the formality faded, their handshake evolving into a brief hug that would have felt foreign months earlier.

"You're right on time." Pastor Morrison motioned toward the two chairs. "Meghan texted that she might be a few minutes late. She said her faculty meeting ran long."

A knock announced Meghan's arrival. Aaron's heart performed its now-familiar acceleration at the sight of her. She looked beautiful in a green dress, and her ring sparkled as she waved hello. She slid into the seat beside Aaron, and the scent of jasmine and vanilla wrapped around him. Her fingers found his, and he exhaled.

Pastor Morrison began by opening the well-worn pages of his Bible. "Ephesians 5 serves as the foundation for today's discussion as we focus on enriching your spiritual partnership. *'Submit to one another out of reverence for Christ.'* Before addressing the roles of husbands and wives, Paul introduces mutual submission as the essential framework for what is to come."

The following hour moved like a long-anticipated dialogue. They talked about shared values and what it meant to center their marriage around faith. Aaron kept getting sidetracked whenever Meghan's fingers traced circles on his palm or her knee brushed against his.

"You mentioned wanting to include Naomi in your family devotions," Pastor Morrison noted as their session neared its conclusion. "Have you three talked about what that might look like?"

"We've already started reading scriptures together. She's opened up more than I thought she would," Aaron replied.

"She appreciates honesty," Meghan added, her voice warming with fondness for the teenager who would soon become her stepdaughter. "She's not looking for perfection. She says she wants to have a genuine relationship with God."

"I've seen a difference in her," Pastor Morrison commented, looking pleased. "Mandy Bolton said Naomi volunteered to assist with the children's summer program."

A tight swell of gratitude and pride moved through Aaron. Naomi had made significant progress since that first difficult spring, much like the dogwood trees, blooming vibrantly after a quiet winter.

After prayers and schedule confirmations, Aaron and Meghan walked hand in hand through the courtyard. Flowers scented the air, and sunshine lit the path.

"I have meetings all afternoon," Meghan said as they approached her car, regret coloring her voice. "And I need to get started on planning for next year's integrated history program."

"And I should get back to the site," Aaron replied, though he didn't feel ready to part ways. "But I was thinking of driving to Bristol Heights after. To visit Mom."

Meghan's expression softened. "Want company?"

He thought about it, weighing the comfort of her presence with the need to go alone.

"Not this time. But thanks."

She nodded without a hint of disappointment or pressure. "Text me when you're headed back. Naomi and I are making lasagna for dinner. Your brother asked about my garlic bread."

Aaron pulled her close. One hand cupped her face, thumb brushing her cheek. "Have I told you today how much I love you?"

"Not since your text this morning." Her smile created those distinctive dimples that never failed to captivate him.

Aaron lowered his mouth to hers in a kiss that began tenderly, mindful of their public location. When they finally parted, both breathless, Meghan's eyes held promises that sent heat through him.

"Two more months," she whispered, her voice carrying meaning beyond its simple syllables.

"Two months, twenty-one days, three hours, and thirty-six minutes," Aaron specified, his precision drawing laughter from Meghan's lips. "But who's counting?"

A few hours later, Aaron stood among the quiet headstones in Bristol Heights Memorial Gardens. Dogwood trees scattered blossoms across manicured lawns, their petals drifting on the breeze. He carried a small bouquet of his mother's favorite daffodils, their sunny faces bright against the gray granite.

His mother's headstone stood beneath a maple tree, its simple design reflecting her practical nature. *Dorothy Marie Grant, Beloved Mother, Faithful Servant.* The engraving was followed by dates that chronicled seventy-two years of determined living despite circumstances that might have crushed weaker spirits.

Aaron knelt beside the marker, laying flowers against the cool stone. He traced her name with his fingertips.

"Hi, Mom," he began, his voice rough with feelings too profound for easy expression. "I know. I should have come sooner."

Birds sang in nearby trees, their melodies providing a soundtrack to his overdue conversation. He sat beside the headstone as if in an adjacent pew during the church services they once shared.

"Naomi's doing better than I could have imagined," he continued, finding ease in speaking his thoughts aloud. "She's developing your gift for nurturing. Our balcony garden has been taken over by her herbs, flowers, and vegetables."

Sharing became easier as he described the home under construction, the thriving community center, and his growing partnership with Frank Donovan. With each success he recounted, he felt a burden lift, as if he was gaining his mother's approval in return.

"But the biggest news is Meghan." His voice softened with reverence. "Mom, she's amazing. She's a history teacher. And she leads a cooking program that's changing the community. She shows patience with Naomi in ways I never could. And her faith? It's the real thing. I didn't think I'd ever find someone like her."

Wind rustled the leaves, and Aaron described Meghan in detail. He told his mother about her compassion and tender care during his recovery from the construction accident.

"We're getting married. I wish..." His voice faltered, her absence striking fresh. "I wish you could be there. You said God had a plan. I didn't believe you then... not really. I used to think that was something you said to survive hard days. But I do now, Mom. You were right. I see it now."

As sunset bathed the cemetery in gold, Aaron shared more about his rediscovered faith, his growing bond with Ryan, and his hopes for a family that would go beyond his mother's legacy of love. The one-sided conversation provided a catharsis he hadn't realized he needed.

"I think you would approve of it all. Maybe you're seeing it, from heaven."

As Aaron was leaving, he saw a solitary silver feather lying at the base of the headstone. It resembled those that marked key moments in his relationship with Meghan and Naomi.

"Liam?" Aaron called out as he scanned the cemetery for the man with silver hair. The serene grounds revealed no signs of life, yet the presence of the feather hinted at answered prayers, and a heavenly influence that seemed to hold more weight than mere coincidence.

Peace filled him as he tucked the feather into his pocket alongside the matching one he carried daily. The guilt of missed visits and unspoken words to his mother lifted like mist under strengthening sunshine. Forgiveness, both given and received, enveloped him.

"I'll be back soon. Next time, with Meghan and Naomi... maybe even Ryan, if he's ready." He brushed grass from his knees as he stood.

On the drive back to Brookside, Aaron was too preoccupied to even turn on the radio. By the time he parked at the apartment complex, the windows were glowing against the dark sky.

Inside, the scent of garlic and tomato sauce surrounded him. Laughter wafted from the kitchen. Naomi's youthful chatter blended with Ryan's deeper voice and Meghan's harmonious notes. The essence of family, belonging, and rejuvenation exceeded what he had longed for months before.

Meghan appeared in the entryway, flour dusting one cheek, and happiness in her eyes.

"You're just in time." She moved to welcome him with a sweet kiss. "Ryan's teaching Naomi how to make homemade pasta. It's a bit of a mess, but in the best way possible."

Aaron buried his face against her neck, inhaling the scent that had become synonymous with home. Her arms encircled him as if offering strength through her presence.

"How was it?" she asked softly, her fingers tracing soothing patterns against his back.

"Healing," Aaron replied, the single word encapsulating a complicated emotional journey. "Guess what? I found a silver feather there, just like ours."

Meghan drew back, her eyes widening. "Liam?"

"There was no sign of him, but it felt like he'd been there. It was like he was trying to tell us that we're exactly where we're meant to be."

Before Meghan could respond, Aaron's phone sounded. Olivia's name flashed across the screen. Startled, he glanced at Meghan and picked up, activating the speakerphone.

"Aaron? Is Meghan with you?" Olivia's voice vibrated with excitement.

"She's right here. Is everything okay?"

The delight in Olivia's controlled tone bounced through the connection. "Yes! The adoption agency called! My application's moving forward! Lily will be coming home soon!"

The room exploded with joy. Meghan clapped her hands over her mouth. Aaron let out a whoop. Naomi and Ryan joined in, and for a few minutes, the world was full of celebration and laughter, imbued with sacred joy.

After dinner, as Ryan left and Naomi worked on her homework, Aaron stood with Meghan on the balcony. Stars pierced the velvet darkness, reflecting the peace within Aaron's heart.

His arms tightened around her, anchoring her to him, and the messy life God was crafting, more stunning than he could have imagined. The feather stayed in his pocket. And so did hope.

Chapter 36

MEGHAN STACKED THE LAST pile of exam papers, her movements automatic after years of teaching. As she reached for her planner, sunlight caught the diamond on her ring finger, sending rainbow prisms dancing across the pages.

She paused, her breath catching. That ring represented more than jewelry. It was a promise of a future built on faith, unexpected timing, and divine orchestration.

"Ms. Townsend?"

Lisbeth Carter stood in the doorway, transformed from the timid girl Naomi defended last semester. Her shoulders were squared now, her voice steadier, though her smile still carried traces of shyness.

"I brought my extra credit essay." Lisbeth stepped inside, clutching papers against her chest. Her gaze dropped to Meghan's hand. "Oh wow! Your ring! It's even more beautiful up close. I love how it catches the light."

Meghan's face warmed at the compliment. "Thank you, Lisbeth. Sometimes I still can't believe it's real."

Lisbeth placed her papers on the designated tray but lingered. "My mom wanted me to thank you again for suggesting the cooking classes. She's been going to the ones at the community center, and she says they're helping her feel..." Lisbeth searched for the right word. "Connected again. After everything with the fire, it's been tough."

That quiet confession touched Meghan. This was exactly what she hoped for when she created the program years ago, after her father's death.

"I tried her peach cobbler last Thursday, and it was amazing. Recipes carry more than ingredients, you know. They hold memories and love in every step."

Lisbeth responded with enthusiasm. "Naomi says the same thing about her grandmother's recipes." Her expression brightened. "She's thrilled about you and Mr. Grant. She says it was *divine orchestration.'* Those are her words, not mine."

Meghan's chest warmed at hearing that. "I suspected she had a role in that *'orchestration'* herself."

The teenager laughed softly, nodding in agreement. "She showed us pictures of how she helped set up the gazebo for Mr. Grant's proposal. She said the silver feathers were her idea."

A group of students appeared in the doorway, their chatter echoing off the walls. Lisbeth stepped back with a quick wave. "See you tomorrow, Ms. Townsend!"

The next half-hour flew by in a flurry of last-minute questions, overdue assignments, and—much to Meghan's astonishment—a constant stream of congratulations regarding her engagement. Once the final students trickled out, Audrey appeared in the doorway. Her black hair was now enhanced with bright fuchsia streaks, and the silver bangles on her wrists jingled as she moved.

"Ready to report to wedding central command?" she asked, enthusiasm bubbling in every syllable. "The girls have commandeered Heavenly Delights with enough coffee and magazines to fuel a small army."

Meghan laughed, grabbing her tote. "You make it sound like a military operation."

Audrey's perfectly arched eyebrow shot up. "Oh, honey, you're getting married. *Simple'* sailed out the window the moment you said yes."

Excitement mixed with a touch of nervousness in Meghan's stomach as she thought about her ever-growing to-do list. Still, she couldn't suppress her smile. They had picked the perfect date, late spring, right after the school year ended, but before the summer heat set in. The community garden would be in full bloom, making the entire day feel like a celebration of fresh beginnings.

"It won't be that complicated. Just a simple ceremony, a reception, and then our honeymoon in Savannah. Everything else is just details," Meghan mused, locking her classroom door behind her.

Audrey linked arms with her as they walked outside. "Famous last words! But don't worry... that's what we're here for. Thank goodness you have us to back you up."

Heavenly Delights buzzed with its usual afternoon energy. Willow greeted them from behind the counter.

"The wedding crew claimed the corner booth. And yes, I saved you some of those lemon squares you love." She was already preparing Meghan's favorite tea.

In the back, Samantha and Olivia had taken over the largest booth, its surface buried under notebooks, fabric swatches, and bridal magazines. Samantha's baby bump was impossible to miss beneath her flowing maternity dress. Beside her, Olivia radiated energy, practically glowing since receiving approval for her adoption.

"There she is!" Samantha stood to hug her, studying Meghan with the keen eye of a healthcare professional. "You look wiped out. Is grading season taking its toll?"

Meghan nodded. "I have loads of exams, projects, and meetings," she admitted, sliding into the booth. "But I'm managing it."

"You're running on fumes. You need some sugar before you hit a wall." Olivia nudged a plate of lemon squares toward her.

After taking a bite, Meghan let out a contented sigh. What began as professional relationships had blossomed into true sisterhood. These women had become her family, steadfast pillars in her life.

"I come bearing news!" Audrey declared, claiming the fourth seat with theatrical flair. "The florist confirmed she can get those tulips you wanted. And Stanley talked to Pastor Morrison... the worship team is officially on board for the ceremony."

Olivia opened a leather-bound planner filled with neat lists and color-coded sections. "That's another item checked off. We still need to finalize the menu if Willow's handling the catering."

"Speaking of food..." Samantha rubbed her rounded belly. "We had our ultrasound yesterday. Baby boy Forrester is healthy and right on schedule."

"A boy!" Meghan's face lit up. "Daniel must be over the moon!"

Samantha rolled her eyes fondly. "He's already planning little league and fishing trips. I had to remind him that this baby won't be throwing baseballs for quite a while."

Meghan turned to Olivia. "What about your adoption paper-work?"

Olivia's face transformed with barely contained excitement. "The final home study happened yesterday. Now I'm just waiting for Lily to come home. It could be weeks or months, but..." Her voice caught. "I'm officially going to be a mom."

Meghan reached across the table and squeezed her hand, tears pricking her eyes. After years of waiting, Olivia's dream was finally within reach.

Audrey's eyes sparkled mischievously. "And in less dramatic n ews... Stanley finally asked me to date him exclusively. It took him long enough! The man can devise complex basketball strategies, but he needed months to realize that I wasn't just being friendly."

Their laughter drew glances from other tables, but none of them cared. This moment captured everything they cherished.

Answered prayers, promises fulfilled, and families formed not only by blood, but by faith, love, and unbreakable friendships.

"So, when do we get to meet Lily?" Audrey asked, turning back to Olivia.

"Soon, I hope. The caseworker said—"

"Wait." Samantha held up a hand, interrupting. "Did anyone else hear that? About Stanley asking you to be exclusive?"

Audrey's cheeks flushed. "What about it?"

"Nothing. It's just..." Samantha grinned. "You've been complaining about his cluelessness for months. Now that he's finally caught on, are you sure you want him?"

"Samantha!" Olivia laughed, playfully swatting at her friend.

"What? I'm just saying... sometimes the thrill of the chase is more exciting than the actual catch."

Meghan watched their banter with amusement.

Audrey spoke with feigned seriousness. "For your information, Stanley is absolutely worth the wait. Even if he *does* over-analyze everything."

"Like what?" Meghan found her curiosity was piqued.

"Last week, he spent twenty minutes debating whether holding hands at the movies qualified as *'appropriate progression'* in our relationship. Twenty whole minutes! I finally just grabbed his hand myself."

More laughter rippled through the group.

"That sounds like Aaron," Meghan admitted. "He said he researched engagement rings for months before buying mine."

"That's an entirely different ballgame," Olivia countered. "Engagement rings are a big deal. Stanley was worried about holding hands."

"Hey, some people just need time to process everything," Samantha said, defending Stanley. "Daniel and I dated for over a year before he proposed, but even then, he still spent two weeks planning the perfect way to ask."

"Two weeks is nothing," Audrey leaned forward. "Try two months of Stanley *evaluating our compatibility.* I half-expected him to whip out a spreadsheet."

"Who knows... maybe he did," Meghan suggested, laughing.

"Don't give him any ideas," Audrey groaned, rolling her eyes.

As their laughter faded, Willow appeared with a fresh pot of tea and more lemon squares.

"You ladies seem to be having way too much fun over here... mind if I join in?"

"We're just planning the wedding," Olivia explained. "And delving into our analysis of relationships."

Willow nodded. "Those are two of the most dangerous topics known to womankind. Do you need something stronger than tea?"

Samantha arched an eyebrow. "We might, especially if Audrey keeps us in the loop about Stanley's courting tactics."

"Very funny," Audrey muttered, but she was smiling.

A wave of contentment washed over Meghan. This was real friendship. Messy, imperfect, and full of the kind of teasing that came from true affection. As she watched her friends banter, she realized that while her life was changing dramatically, some things would remain constant.

As their laughter subsided, Meghan received a text from Aaron: *Can't wait to see you this evening. I have something special planned. Love you.*

She smiled as she typed back: *Looking forward to it. Almost done here.*

"Is that Aaron?" Olivia asked, noticing her expression.

"He's just checking in about our dinner plans for tonight. He's been a little mysterious about it."

"That man is always up to something," Samantha commented. "Daniel says that Aaron's been sketching designs non-stop lately."

"Well, we *are* in the process of building a home together," Meghan acknowledged, then she paused for a moment. The idea still felt surreal at times. Here she was, planning a life with someone, and creating a space that would belong to them both.

Audrey started gathering the scattered magazines. "Speaking of which, we should probably let you get going, seeing as you've got a mysterious evening ahead."

Meghan glanced at her watch, surprised to see how much time had flown by. "You're right. I don't want Aaron to worry about me taking too long."

As they picked up their things, Olivia took Meghan's hand. "I'm so happy for you. Truly. After everything you've been through..."

"Thanks, Olivia. That really means a lot to me."

The friends exchanged hugs and made promises to catch up again soon. Meghan walked to her car. She was grateful for the afternoon spent with her friends. It provided the normalcy, support, and laughter she needed, reminding her how blessed she was.

Whatever Aaron had in store for tonight, she was ready for it.

Chapter 37

After hugs and goodbyes at the diner, Meghan headed home, her thoughts already on the evening ahead. Aaron's text hinted at a surprise waiting for her at the house.

Their house, she reminded herself with a smile. It wasn't just a construction site anymore, but a future they were building together.

The property came into view, nestled between old oaks. The siding glowed in the afternoon light, and the land offered privacy without feeling isolated.

Pulling into the gravel driveway, Meghan slowed. Something was different. Just days ago, the yard had been a mess of equipment and half-finished landscaping. Now, neat garden beds framed the porch, young plants stretching toward the sun and bordered by fresh mulch.

Aaron's pickup truck was parked by the garage. She grabbed her purse and headed toward the front door. After Sunday's church service, Aaron had given her the key, an act that nearly made her cry right there in the pew.

The interior welcomed her with the scent of fresh paint mixed with something delicious wafting from the kitchen. Drawn by the enticing aroma, Meghan found Naomi busy at the kitchen island, her dark braids cascading forward as she arranged a variety of items onto a serving platter.

"Meghan!" The teenager looked up, beaming. "You're early. Uncle Aaron said you'd be stuck planning until at least six."

Meghan set her bags on the built-in bench near the mudroom entrance. "We finished early. What's all this? And what happened to the front yard?"

Naomi's smile turned secretive. "That's the surprise. Uncle Aaron's out back."

Curious, Meghan wandered through the expansive great room. Every corner held reminders of their planning sessions where they merged her love of natural light, Aaron's desire for open space, and Naomi's aspiration to have cozy reading nooks by the windows. All of these dreams were now a reality, captured in the wood, stone, and sunlight streaming in.

As she stepped out to the covered porch, gauzy curtains billowed in the spring breeze. She spotted Aaron crouched next to a raised garden bed, absorbed in his work.

"I hear there's a surprise waiting for me," she called, stepping onto the porch.

He turned, and his face lit up when he saw her, as if she were the only thing in the world worth noticing.

"You're early." He rose with the fluid grace that returned since his ankle healed. In a few strides, he closed the distance, wrapping her in an embrace that dissolved the last tension from her body.

She looked up for a kiss, and he didn't disappoint.

When he pulled back, his hand remained at her waist. "Come see what we've been working on. It's why I asked you to meet us here instead of the apartment."

He guided her to the back of the property, where the yard sloped toward the pond. What had been bare earth days earlier now featured a series of garden beds arranged in a pattern that became increasingly familiar with each step closer.

"Wait..." she began, her breath hitching. "Aaron... this is the layout from my dad's garden."

Emotion closed her throat as she took in the details. In the center was a circular herb garden, bordered by rectangular beds that resembled spokes on a bicycle wheel. This design had been captured in photographs from her childhood home, where her father had taken immense pride in its practicality and aesthetic appeal.

"Carol found some old photos of your dad's garden in your mother's albums. Naomi and I thought... maybe this could be our special gift to you."

Tears blurred her vision as she recalled Aaron's puzzling Saturday disappearances, his clothes often caked in mud from those *"final landscaping touches,"* and Naomi's odd questions about plant zones that were far different from her current interests in container gardening.

"We planted all of your dad's favorite plants." Naomi had joined them, her excitement bubbling over. "The herbs are in the center, veggies are around the edges, and flowers line the borders. Carol said he always told you food gardens need beauty just as much as they need nutrients."

Meghan laughed through the tears. *Beauty and nourishment belong together, Meggie-girl. Don't ever let anyone tell you that you have to choose one over the other.*

Aaron's arm slid around her waist as he led her toward a wrought-iron bench that overlooked the garden.

"There's something else we want to show you... take a look at the cornerstone of the center bed."

Meghan blinked away tears. Embedded in the stone was a small bronze plaque featuring engraved text:

Kendrick Townsend's Legacy Garden
A garden to feed both body and soul
Planted with love

Her hand flew to her mouth, voice lost in the moment. She traced her father's name on the inscription, now eternally commemorated in this place that would sustain their family for many years to come.

Aaron's voice was rough with emotion. "Every time we harvest from this garden, we'll remember the man who shaped who you are. You carry his legacy within you every day... this garden simply gives it deeper roots."

His words broke through Meghan's sorrow, transforming it into overwhelming gratitude that brought fresh tears to her eyes. Her father would never be able to walk her down the aisle, witness the wonderment of his grandchildren, or share in the laughter at Sunday dinners. Still, his presence was threaded into every facet of the life she was building with Aaron and Naomi.

"This is absolutely incredible..." She hugged them both, these individuals who had begun as professional obligations, but had evolved into her indispensable family. "I can't believe you did all of this."

"It was mostly Uncle Aaron," Naomi admitted with characteristic honesty. "I helped with the design and planting, but he did all the heavy lifting."

"And it was worth every minute," Aaron said, pulling Meghan closer to him with his arm around her waist.

As twilight approached, they settled on the porch swing Aaron installed last weekend. The oversized swing accommodated all three of them as they watched fireflies dance above the newly planted beds.

"Actually, there's another surprise," Aaron said. "Though this one wasn't planned."

Meghan raised an eyebrow. "More surprises? You're setting quite a standard, Mr. Grant."

His laughter warmed the gathering darkness, and he pressed his lips briefly against her temple. "This surprise arrived at the school after you left. Principal Watkins came over and brought it by. Naomi, would you do the honors?"

The teenager rushed inside and returned with a hefty envelope bearing the Georgia Department of Education seal. Meghan's hands shook as she opened it. She immediately recognized the letterhead from the course she had applied to before Aaron's accident shifted her priorities.

She read aloud: *Dear Ms. Townsend. We are thrilled to inform you of your acceptance into the Educational Leadership Certification Program commencing this September. Due to your exceptional application and the innovative curriculum frameworks developed during your time at the Carter Institute, we are pleased to offer you a place in our hybrid learning cohort. Rather than requiring a full-time residency, this format will only necessitate your attendance at monthly weekend intensives at our Atlanta campus.*

As the meaning of the words registered, they began to blur together. This opportunity offered a path to professional advancement without isolation, a way to advance her career without sacrificing family connections, and a means to bring her aspirations to life without stepping back from everything she had worked to achieve.

"They've never offered a hybrid format before," Meghan said, still processing what all this could signify. "This program usually demands a full-year residency in Atlanta."

Aaron looked ready to burst with pride. "When he came over to drop this off, Principal Watkins said that this is a pilot program for exceptional candidates. I guess you made quite an impression."

Meghan stared at the letter, feeling a clear path forward beginning to unfold before her.

"This is perfect! I can keep teaching at Greater Pines while I complete the certification. One weekend a month in Atlanta is totally doable."

Aaron's fingers caressed her shoulder. "It doesn't start until September, so we have all summer to adjust to married life before you take on these new responsibilities."

The consideration in his voice struck her anew. Unlike her previous relationship, Aaron consistently supported her career aspirations.

She leaned closer to him. "God's timing never ceases to amaze me. Each door opens at precisely the right moment."

Her phone chimed from her purse, capturing her attention. The caller ID displayed a number she didn't recognize. Curious, she reached for her cell.

"Unknown caller. It's probably about the wedding." She showed the screen to Aaron before answering. "Hello, this is Meghan Townsend."

A male voice she hadn't heard in over five years sent a jolt rippling through her. "Meghan? It's Finn. Finn Lockwood."

The voice of her ex-boyfriend, once familiar but now strangely distant, left Meghan momentarily at a loss for words. Aaron went still, placing his hand over hers in silent reassurance.

"Finn. This is... unexpected," she managed, maintaining a steady tone.

"I know. I'm sorry to call out of the blue," he replied. "I just wanted to see how you were doing after you left Macon so suddenly. I hope everything worked out okay with your emergency."

Memories surged back of the dread surrounding her abrupt departure after Aaron's accident—the panic when Naomi called, the frantic drive back to Brookside.

"It did, thank you." Meghan's professional training helped her retain her composure despite the surprise contact. "And I never got a chance to say this, but I appreciate your offer of accommodations while I was there."

"I'm glad I could help." Finn paused. "Listen... I was hoping to talk to you about something. Do you have a minute? It's about a professional matter."

Aaron's hand pressed slightly around hers, and she reciprocated the gesture of comfort.

"I'm here with my fiancé and his niece, but yes, feel free to continue." She felt it was important to clarify the context of her circumstances right away.

A short pause followed her statement. "Fiancé. Congratulations," Finn responded, though his tone was difficult to decipher. "Well, I was reaching out because I've recently accepted a position with the Georgia Sports Hall of Fame, and your cooking program has piqued our interest for a potential exhibition partnership. I had intended to reach you through official channels, but I thought a direct call might be quicker."

Relief blended with interest as Meghan absorbed his explanation. The Georgia Sports Hall of Fame didn't appear to have any obvious connection to her cooking program.

"I'd be happy to talk about it," she replied. "Could you email the details to my school account?"

"The exhibition director would prefer a face-to-face meeting," Finn replied. "We're developing a major initiative that associates community health, cultural foodways, and athletic performance. The integration of your program's model could provide the foundation we're hoping to create."

Aaron stayed steady beside her, exuding an air of trust.

"When did you have in mind?" Meghan asked, despite feeling uneasy about the unexpected request.

"How does next Tuesday sound? We could meet for lunch at The Village Eatery. I'll bring Laura Hartwell, our exhibition director, and we can go over the specifics. This could significantly fund your program, potentially allowing for statewide expansion."

Meghan weighed the conceivable advantages for her students against her discomfort with the unforeseen request. Five years since their relationship ended seemed like ample time to set established professional boundaries.

"One o'clock at The Village Eatery sounds fine," she decided.

"Perfect. I'll send over the preliminary documents for you to look at beforehand. And Meghan?" His voice shifted slightly. "It's good to hear your voice again. I'm glad things are going well for you."

After the call, Meghan sat reflecting on the unexpected intersection of her past and present. Aaron waited silently as she gathered her thoughts.

"That was Finn Lockwood." She was fully aware that Aaron already recognized the name. "He wanted to follow up after I was supposed to stay at his guest apartment during the Macon workshop. We didn't have a chance to talk before I came home when you had your accident."

Aaron nodded, his expression revealing no signs of judgment or insecurity. "And there's something about a partnership with your cooking program?"

"Yes... apparently, the Georgia Sports Hall of Fame is planning an exhibition on cultural foodways and athletic performance," Meghan clarified, still processing the startling proposal. "He wants to meet next Tuesday to discuss a possible collaboration."

"Interesting timing," Aaron observed. "Do you think he knew about our engagement?"

The question, posed with genuine curiosity rather than insecurity, reinforced the solid groundwork of their relationship. "If he didn't know before, he certainly does now. The past is behind us. Finn represents a closed chapter in my life. Whatever opportunity he's presenting doesn't change that."

Aaron drew her closer, their lips meeting in a kiss that was both tender and fervent.

"I love you. And I trust you completely," he stated.

"I love you too. Whatever lies ahead, we'll face it together," she murmured.

As darkness enveloped their future home, Meghan contemplated the upcoming meeting. There was something about the way Finn spoke that felt a bit off. It didn't seem entirely like the straightforward professional connection he claimed it to be.

But that was a concern for another day. Tonight, surrounded by the garden that honored her father's memory and the man who had helped cultivate it, she felt she had everything she needed.

349

Chapter 38

Aaron tapped the steering wheel, his jaw tight as he drove toward The Village Eatery. Pain shot through his ankle from the site work the day before, but that wasn't what had him so tense. It was the meeting. This morning, Finn messaged Meghan informing her that Laura Hartwell, the exhibition director, would be absent due to a family emergency. That meant their *"professional meeting"* would now consist of just him, Meghan, and Finn.

"You sure you're okay with this?" he asked for the third time since they had left the apartment.

Meghan reached over, stilling his hand with hers. "I'm glad you're coming with me. I'd rather have you there than face him alone."

Her words triggered complex emotions. He felt satisfaction in her wanting his presence, but unease at her wavering confidence. Did she sense something troubling in Finn's message?

"Did he say something that made you uncomfortable?" Aaron kept his tone level, but the heat behind it crept in.

"No, not really." Meghan's voice carried uncertainty. "But since the director's not coming, I feel better if you're with me during the meeting."

The admission fueled Aaron's resolve. No matter what professional opportunity Finn offered, Aaron wouldn't let Meghan navigate the complexities of their past relationship alone.

He maneuvered the truck into The Village Eatery's parking lot. Aaron noticed a charcoal sedan with Macon plates parked near the entrance, undoubtedly Finn's car.

"There he is," Meghan whispered as they entered, nodding toward a corner table where a man in a crisp navy suit sat consulting his phone.

Aaron took a breath as he studied Finn Lockwood. The man exuded sophistication and professionalism, with the assured demeanor of someone accustomed to getting what he wants.

Aaron's fierce pride swelled as he placed his hand on the small of Meghan's back. The diamond ring on her finger sparkled, affirming that this extraordinary woman had chosen him as her future husband.

"Remember, this is just a meeting, nothing more," Meghan murmured, her fingers intertwining soothingly with his grip.

Finn looked up when he spotted Meghan. The smile that brightened his face sent an unwelcome surge of emotion through Aaron.

"Meghan!" Finn rose, extending his hand in greeting. His gaze lingered on her face before moving to Aaron. "And you must be her fiancé. I'm Finn Lockwood, the Development Director for the Georgia Sports Hall of Fame."

Aaron's handshake might have contained perhaps more pressure than necessary, but he couldn't help it. "Aaron Grant," he replied, "I work with Donovan Building Contractors."

Meghan's shoulder pressed against him as they sat, providing quiet reassurance. A server came over to take their drink orders, unaware of the emotional current brewing beneath the table.

Orders were placed, and Aaron forced himself to focus as Finn withdrew a portfolio from his briefcase. The initial small talk about Brookside's growth and Macon's recent developments faded as Finn opened to a detailed exhibition proposal.

"The Georgia Sports Hall of Fame is launching a major initiative. We're calling it, *Roots to Results: Cultural Foodways and Athletic Excellence.* The concept explores how traditional cooking methods across diverse communities provide nutritional foundations for athletic achievement."

Aaron forced himself to listen objectively. The concept was clever, and the mockups were impressive. The interactive displays paired traditional family recipes with various athlete profiles.

Aaron fidgeted under the table as Finn's gaze kept drifting to Meghan. Each glance ignited waves of annoyance. Logically, he knew this was a business meeting, but his primal instincts were alert. He catalogued each expression and unnecessary touch as Finn passed documents across the table.

"We've been on the lookout for an educational component." Finn leaned closer to Meghan, speaking in a manner that felt overly personal to Aaron. "When I saw how your program incorporates history, culture, and practical nutrition, I knew it was what our exhibition needed."

Aaron resisted the urge to drape his arm around her. Instead, he channeled his tension into memorizing every detail of the proposal, determined to make his presence beneficial to Meghan.

Her expression was thoughtful as she examined the materials. "It's an intriguing concept. But I'm curious about how our program could expand to a statewide museum exhibition."

"That's where the funding comes into play," Finn explained, oblivious to Aaron's internal struggle. "The Hall has secured a grant from the Culinary Heritage Foundation. A total of seventy-five thousand dollars would be allocated to expanding the program. We're looking to partner with Greater Pines as the educational pilot location, utilizing your curriculum as the base."

Aaron's eyebrows shot up at the figure, his admiration for Meghan's work eclipsing his pangs of jealousy. That sum could elevate her program from a local triumph into a model that would be recognized statewide. It was a serendipitous opportunity, exactly the kind of advancement they discussed during their late-night talks concerning her dreams.

As Finn elaborated, Aaron picked up on his repetitive mentions of *"our time in Macon"* and his casual remarks about *"that food festival we went to."* These seemed like carefully calculated reminders of their shared past, intending to invoke nostalgia while subtly pushing Aaron to the sidelines.

"The timeline seems quite ambitious," Aaron noted, studying the proposed schedule while fighting to keep his tone even. "You're looking to launch this before the school year starts in September?"

"Yes. We would need to get started immediately." Finn looked over at Meghan. "This would entail some summer hours to revise the curriculum. I would, of course, be available if you run into any issues."

Aaron tapped his foot against the floor, trying to channel the frustration simmering beneath the surface. The idea of this man alone with Meghan, reminiscing about their past and perhaps trying to rekindle what they once shared, ignited a searing irritation in him that no degree of Christian patience seemed to be able to quell.

"That timeline overlaps with our honeymoon and wedding plans." Meghan's fingers interlaced with his, their connected palms resting on his thigh. "We're getting married after the school year ends."

Finn's smile faltered just enough for Aaron to notice. This glimpse of genuine emotion sparked satisfaction in him, which he attempted to temper with Christian kindness, achieving only partial success.

"Congratulations once again," Finn said, although the words appeared to take effort. "We can certainly make adjustments to accommodate your schedule. This opportunity is too valuable to pass up."

"Thank you. We would appreciate that," Meghan replied. "The potential for expanding this program could impact countless students all over Georgia."

"Not to mention the professional recognition," Finn added, his tone dripping with a warmth that set Aaron's teeth on edge. "You've always deserved a wider platform for your innovative approaches, Meg."

Meg. Aaron had never shortened Meghan's name out of respect for the elegance her parents had chosen. Finn's casual familiarity raised heat under his collar.

He took a sip of water, using the moment to regain his composure. Their server's timely appearance with the check provided a welcome interruption. She smiled, oblivious to the undercurrents at their table.

As Finn reached for the check, Aaron intercepted. "Company expense. Donovan Contractors is happy to support local education."

Aaron knew the assertion wasn't lost on Finn, whose smile tightened at the edges. "That's generous. The Hall of Fame appreciates that."

Outside, sunshine warmed the parking lot. They concluded with handshakes and promises of follow-up communication. Aaron noticed Finn held Meghan's hand for a moment longer than necessary.

"It's been great seeing you again. Regardless of the exhibition outcome, I'm glad you're doing well."

"Thank you, Finn. I'll review these materials with Principal Watkins and get back to you next week." Meghan's voice remained pleasant, giving nothing beyond courtesy.

Aaron's hand rested on her back as they turned, his fingers spread possessively. The touch calmed him. This intimate contact communicated feelings that words couldn't convey. *She belongs to me now.*

The thought instantly triggered a disquieting sensation. Meghan wasn't an object to possess. She was a partner with whom he had immense trust. Still, that primitive response persisted, raw and embarrassingly powerful.

The silence inside his truck felt oppressive as they pulled away from the restaurant.

Before Meghan came into his life, jealousy was an emotion he rarely experienced. What was there to envy when his focus was on work and family? But now, with her, that feeling welled up inside him with troubling intensity.

They waited at the red light, and Aaron fixated on the traffic signal. The enforced pause released the words lodged in his throat.

"He still has feelings for you."

Meghan turned toward him. "What makes you say that?"

His gaze stayed on the light, purposely avoiding her eyes. "Everything. The way he looked at you when he thought I wasn't paying attention... how he still calls you *'Meg'* as if he has any right to do that. And all those hints about your past together." He tightened his grip on the wheel. "He's not just interested in your cooking program, Meghan."

The traffic light turned green. Aaron accelerated, perhaps more aggressively than necessary, his frustration translating from his foot to the pedal.

"Aaron... Finn and I are ancient history. Whatever feelings he might still have doesn't change anything between us."

Aaron exhaled. "I know that in my head, but I hated seeing the way he looked at you, as if he still had some sort of claim on you. It fired up something inside me that I'm not proud of. I know it sounds immature, but I wanted to make it clear that you're with me now. I know... it's embarrassingly caveman-like."

A small smile curved Meghan's lips, catching him off guard. "I noticed."

"Was I that transparent?"

Her hand covered his where it rested on the console. "To Finn... probably not. You managed to keep your cool pretty well for someone who looked like they were about to snap a fork in half."

Her comment brought a reluctant laugh out of him.

"Do you remember what you said on our first real date? About construction being your language?" Her fingers slipped between his, centering him more effectively than any words could.

Aaron nodded, recalling their dinner from months ago.

"Well, I've become fluent in Aaron Grant. I can interpret almost every emotion that crosses your face. I see your protectiveness, your pride in my work, and even your jealousy. It all comes from your love for me... and I trust you."

"I'm sorry," he said. "I should have better control over my jealousy than this. I *do* trust you... completely. Please believe that."

Her grip on his fingers tightened. Her acceptance of his entire self, including the jealous and primal aspects he preferred to deny, allowed him to breathe easier than he had since Finn's call days earlier.

They pulled into the high school parking lot, where Meghan had a faculty meeting waiting for her. Aaron faced her, taking both her hands in his.

"This exhibition is a great opportunity. I don't want my issues to interfere with that."

"We'll decide everything together. That's what partners do," she assured him.

Leaning forward, she pressed her lips to his. Her thumb caressed the stubble that had begun to reemerge despite his morning shave. The sweetness of her dispelled his thoughts of Finn, professional concerns, and everything external to the connection uniting them.

When they separated, the tension he had felt dissolved beneath her tender care.

She gathered her materials for the meeting, her reluctance unmistakable in her movements. "I'll be done by five. Are we still on for dinner?"

"You can count on it."

He watched her stride confidently across the asphalt toward the school entrance. Her occasional waves to colleagues reminded him of the extraordinary woman who chose him, wore his ring, and would soon share his name and home.

As he exited the parking lot, his phone rang through the truck's hands-free system. Frank Donovan's gruff voice filled the cab.

"Grant, we need to talk. Can you swing by the office? There's an urgent issue that needs your attention."

Aaron checked the clock. It was three-thirty. With Meghan occupied until five, he had plenty of time to tackle whatever crisis Frank had uncovered.

"On my way," he replied, already redirecting his truck toward downtown Brookside.

As he drove, he shifted into work mode, his mind racing with thoughts about the challenge awaiting him.

Chapter 39

Having resolved the issue his boss called about, and with time to spare before dinner with Meghan, Aaron drove to their property. He hadn't planned the detour, but the pull was unmistakable. He needed to reconnect with their home and stand where future promises were becoming real.

He parked beside the detached garage and admired the scenery. The siding had been installed earlier that week. The house rested in the landscape as though it had existed there for many years.

As he walked toward the front porch, he saw a figure moving near the foundation. He quickened his pace, concern for site security driving him forward. But as he got closer and recognized the individual, he slowed down. The distinctive silver hair and rhythmic tapping of a wooden cane against the concrete were unmistakable.

"This is exceptional craftsmanship, Aaron. Establishing a proper foundation is crucial, especially when building a home for love."

Liam spoke without turning, his aged hand running along the foundation's edge.

"Liam... I wasn't expecting to find anyone here," Aaron replied.

When he turned toward Aaron, Liam's deep-set eyes exuded a wisdom that transcended ordinary life experience. "Some visits can't be scheduled. They happen when they're most needed, not when they're expected."

There was no small talk. No pretense. Just the intense gaze and quiet certainty that defined their encounters.

"It seems you arrived carrying a heavy burden," Liam observed. "Is there something you're afraid of?"

"I'm just trying to figure out a complicated work situation," Aaron countered, his denial too forceful sound convincing.

"Are you sure about that?" Liam inquired, not from a place of judgment, but with a perception too sharp to dismiss. His eyes seem to contain centuries of wisdom. "Perhaps, you're not afraid of losing her. She's yours as surely as dawn follows the night. But maybe what you fear is whether you're enough. Is your faith strong enough? Is your past unblemished enough? Is your future stable enough?"

Liam's assessment exposed Aaron's hidden insecurities. Finn's polished demeanor, his history with Meghan, and his esteemed position stirred comparisons that Aaron had never considered until now.

Liam's gnarled hand rested on Aaron's shoulder. "Trust isn't founded on guarantees. It's about choosing to have faith when skepticism is much easier. It's about believing that the unseen foundation will endure, even when circumstances suggest otherwise."

Aaron felt the weight of Liam's words resonate with his understanding that concrete requires faith during those vital curing phases, when strength develops unnoticed beneath the surface.

His phone rang with the distinct tone of his supplier, indicating a call he couldn't afford to ignore.

"Excuse me a moment." Aaron stepped away to answer. The exchange with his lumber supplier lasted two minutes—confirmation of delivery schedules and pricing for their master bathroom fixtures.

When Aaron turned around to resume their conversation, he found himself alone. The spot where Liam had been standing was vacant, but Aaron hadn't heard footsteps or a car engine. He looked around in every direction, but found no sign of the mysterious man, despite the clear sightlines that should have made leaving unnoticed impossible.

A solitary silver feather lay on the foundation wall where Liam's hand had rested. Aaron picked it up with reverence, feeling its warmth against his palm. This enigmatic token served as another reminder of things that couldn't be explained, but were no less real.

He finished his inspection of the construction progress with the wise man's words echoing in his mind. Liam was right. Trust wasn't built through guarantees. The doubts, comparisons, and the need to prove himself wouldn't strengthen their future. But faith could.

At the apartment, Naomi stirred a pot of sauce on the stove, her braids piled high on her head.

"You're here early. I thought you and Meghan were having lunch with that guy from the museum," she remarked.

Aaron set his keys on the counter. "We did. The meeting finished, but Meghan had to rush off to a faculty meeting afterward. What's cooking?"

Naomi pointed toward the bubbling pot. "I'm making Grandma's spaghetti sauce. I found the recipe in one of the boxes you brought from Bristol Heights." She hesitated, uncertainty shadowing her features. "Is that okay? Using her stuff?"

Aaron hugged his niece, disregarding her half-hearted protests about tomato stains. "She'd love seeing you cook her dishes."

Naomi's bright smile illuminated the room, reflecting how much they had overcome since those challenging early weeks. As they prepared dinner, Aaron regained his perspective. The contrast between Finn's fleeting presence and the enduring connections in this cozy kitchen clarified for him what truly mattered.

When Meghan arrived thirty minutes later, Aaron greeted her at the door, pulled her into an embrace, and kissed her as if he meant it, because he did.

"Wow," she gasped when they separated, her eyes deepening to rich amber shades. "That's quite a welcome home."

"Just reminding myself how blessed I am," he murmured, giving her a meaningful look. "And maybe reminding you, too."

Meghan's smile showcased those adorable dimples he loved. "No reminders needed. But I appreciated your approach."

Over dinner, conversation shifted to the exhibition.

He passed her the garlic bread Naomi had prepared with impressive skill. "This funding would significantly help your program. Statewide implementation could affect thousands of students beyond Greater Pines."

"Do you think it's worth pursuing, even with Finn involved?"

Aaron nodded. "Absolutely. Sure, this opportunity may have come through him, but the work? The vision? That's all you. It has to be divine intervention."

He reached for her hand across the table, the silver feather in his pocket a reassuring weight as he continued. "I believe in you. And I believe in what we're building together. Foundations don't need to be visible to be strong."

Later that evening, after Naomi retreated to finish her homework, Aaron and Meghan stepped onto the balcony. He moved behind her, sliding his arms around her waist, resting his chin against her temple. She relaxed into him, the perfect fit against his sturdy frame.

"I've been mulling over something Liam said." His voice was low and near her ear.

Meghan turned within his arms. "You saw Liam? When?"

"At the house site this afternoon. He was checking out our foundation." Aaron's hand traced her jawline. "He said that establishing a proper foundation is crucial, especially when building a home for love."

Her eyes searched his, brimming with curiosity.

"He has a way of understanding things, including the fears I didn't want to admit to."

Meghan's hands climbed up his chest to wrap around his neck. "What fears?" she asked, her breath warm against his face.

"Fears that I'm not enough compared to someone like Finn. That I'm not polished enough, not educated enough... not sophisticated enough for a woman of your caliber and grace."

Her expression softened into fierce tenderness, her eyes radiating a certainty that settled into his soul like foundation stones.

"You're my everything," she whispered. "You're everything I prayed for when I'd lost hope in believing such prayers could be answered. You're everything God knew I would need."

Aaron's throat tightened. Her declaration sealed the final cracks doubt had created. Above them, stars blinked awake in the night sky.

The wisdom Liam shared transformed from an abstract concept into a lived reality as Aaron held the woman he would soon call his wife. Their hearts beat in synchronized harmony beneath the vast canopy of stars. Their foundation had been tested, and it held.

Chapter 40

MEGHAN SURVEYED THE COMMUNITY center kitchen, which had transformed over the past year from an empty shell to a sanctuary. Vanilla and cinnamon scented the air from that morning's final cooking session of the semester. Tomorrow, this space would overflow with wedding guests, but today she claimed these precious moments where healing had taken root through food and faith.

"I can't believe we did it."

Olivia burst through the doorway, clipboard clutched against her chest, joy radiating from her face despite the exhaustion etched around her eyes.

"Final headcount is one hundred and thirty-six," she said, breathless with excitement. "And the museum grant paperwork cleared this morning."

Relief flooded through Meghan as she polished the stainless-steel countertops. The funding for the Georgia Sports Hall of Fame's exhibition arrived at the perfect moment, ensuring the program's future. With seventy-five thousand dollars secured, they could expand the cultural foodways education throughout the state.

"God's timing really is flawless," Meghan remarked, putting aside her cloth. "The wedding, the grant, and now your adoption approval..."

Olivia's expression transformed at the mention of her daughter-to-be. "I'm waiting for the final court date now. After all these years of hoping and praying, in a few weeks, I'll finally be someone's mom."

Meghan pulled her friend into a warm hug, holding tight to the woman who had journeyed through valleys to reach this joyful occasion. When they pulled apart, Olivia glanced at her clipboard.

"The decorating team will be here in about thirty minutes. Sam's bringing the flowers from her car now. Can you handle arranging them while I go check on the cake?"

Meghan laughed. "Go... I think I can manage my own wedding flowers just fine."

After Olivia left, Meghan took a moment to breathe. Tomorrow, she would officially become Meghan Elise Grant. A delicious mix of anticipation and joy fluttered in her stomach at the exciting thought.

Just then, Samantha waddled in, her eight-month pregnant belly leading the way, arms full of greenery and white roses.

"I come bearing botanical treasures," she announced. "And strict orders from my husband not to lift anything heavier than baby's breath."

Meghan hurried to take the flowers from her. "Daniel's right. You should be resting, not hauling all of this around."

Samantha sank into a nearby chair, cradling her rounded belly. "Pregnancy isn't an illness. Besides, I wouldn't dream of missing the chance to decorate for my favorite couple. This little one's been kicking all morning. I think he's excited about tomorrow, too."

One by one, volunteers trickled in. There were friends from church, colleagues from school, and Aaron's construction crew. Under Audrey's energetic guidance, they transformed the community center into a breathtaking haven.

"The arch goes there. And those garlands need to hang exactly like the sketch. Stanley, honey, that's not centered." Audrey's purple-streaked hair bounced as she directed Stanley, who adjusted the floral displays with surprising skill. Who would've imagined he would become putty in Audrey's hands?

Hours flew by, and when Meghan stepped back to take in their handiwork, she sighed. Twinkling lights cascaded through flowing garlands, while the delicate tulle draped over chairs created an intimate atmosphere. The vision exceeded her wildest dreams.

Then, a realization struck her like a flash of lightning. This wasn't just a celebration. This marked the beginning of forever.

Feeling overwhelmed, she slipped into the library adjacent to the main hall. Shelves filled with books provided her a much-needed respite from the tumult outside. She needed a chance to sort through the emotions swirling beneath her carefully maintained façade.

"I thought I might find you hiding in here."

Meghan turned toward the doorway where Carol stood, affection written across her face. With her silver hair elegantly arranged in an updo, she emanated the grace of her seventy years, despite the challenges life had handed her.

"I'm not hiding," Meghan protested weakly. "I'm just taking a breath."

Carol smiled. "Your mother did the same thing before her wedding. She disappeared into the church library for twenty minutes while everyone else was in a frenzy."

The comparison to her mother, who had been gone for over fifteen years, choked Meghan up. Carol settled beside her on the small sofa.

"I've been saving this for you." She reached into her handbag and withdrew a small package wrapped in tissue paper. "Your mother would have wanted to give this to you herself."

Meghan's fingers trembled as she unwrapped layers to uncover an exquisite lace handkerchief. Its delicate fabric was slightly yellowed with age, but its beauty was undeniable.

"She carried this when she married your father. It's been passed down through four generations of women in your family, tucked into their bouquets," Carol elaborated.

Tears filled Meghan's eyes as she traced the intricate pattern. "I thought everything was lost after the house was sold."

"I kept what I could. I knew you'd need a piece of them with you... especially today." Carol's hand covered Meghan's with warm comfort.

Despite her attempts to stay composed, a tear slipped down Meghan's cheek. With a tenderness transcending any biological connection, Carol gently wiped it away.

"Your parents would be so proud, not just of tomorrow, but of the incredible woman you've become, and the lives you've touched." She folded the handkerchief into Meghan's hands.

"I miss them so much. Dad should be walking me down the aisle. Mom should be fussing over my dress..."

Carol cupped her face, her gaze unwavering. "They see you, sweetheart. Hebrews says we're surrounded by a great cloud of witnesses. They're part of that cloud, looking down from glory."

The image of her parents cheering her on from heaven brought fresh tears, not the bitterness of grief, but the healing essence of cleansing.

Carol lifted Meghan's chin until their eyes met. "Tomorrow, you'll carry them with you when you walk that aisle. Their love, their values, their faith... all of it lives in you."

They embraced, holding each other close in a hug that delved deep into their souls. Meghan tucked the handkerchief into her purse, ready to face tomorrow with the past close to her heart. As she prepared to walk toward Aaron, she felt assured that her parents would be right there alongside her.

That evening, the garden behind The Village Eatery glowed with string lights as the rehearsal dinner wound to a close. Meghan sat beside Aaron at the head table, surrounded by their dearest friends and family. Naomi and Olivia were on her left, while Ryan and Daniel sat to Aaron's right, forming a lively circle of companionship that radiated outward.

"If I could have everyone's attention, please." Aaron's voice echoed across the intimate gathering. His fingers intertwined with hers beneath the table, their palms together in a silent pledge.

The room quieted, all eyes fixed on the man whose journey from cautious outsider to beloved member of the community had been witnessed by everyone present.

"First, Meghan and I want to express our gratitude to each of you for being part of our story." Aaron's voice resonated with emotion. "You've been with us from the beginning. Your support has challenged us, encouraged us, and laid the groundwork for the future we're building together."

Murmurs of agreement rippled through the attendees as Aaron continued.

"Many of you are aware that Meghan's cooking program started as a tribute to her father. But what she created has gone far beyond just recipes. It has built bridges between generations, cultures, and communities."

His gaze locked with hers before returning to the crowd. "In honor of that legacy, and to help it grow further, I'm proud to announce the establishment of the Kendrick Townsend Memorial

Scholarship Fund, aimed at supporting students pursuing education in the culinary arts."

Gasps of surprise filled the garden as Aaron revealed the details. It was a permanent endowment, financed by profits from his construction business, that would grant annual scholarships to deserving students.

She couldn't speak... she could barely breathe. He had honored her father in a way that would keep his name alive in every meal prepared with love.

His hand tightened around hers, an understanding flowing between them without the need for words.

From the far end of the table, Ryan stood, his face reflecting a peace earned through months of healing and mending relationships.

"I'd like to propose a toast," he stated, his voice steadier than anyone had heard in years. "To my brother and his bride. You've shown me the meaning of true restoration. I'm twelve months sober today, and I wouldn't be standing here without your belief that broken people can be made whole again."

Aaron's eyes glistened as he shared a silent moment with his brother, one that encompassed their shared journey to healing. Naomi leaned across the table to grasp her uncle Ryan's hand, drawing him back into their family circle.

The remainder of the evening passed in celebratory toasts and shared stories, with love made manifest through the presence of their community.

As guests started to depart, Aaron tugged Meghan toward the restaurant's garden. String lights formed a starry canopy above blooming plants and winding stone paths, crafting an atmosphere that felt almost ethereal.

"Come with me?" he asked softly.

Meghan nodded, allowing him to lead her to a stone bench partially concealed by flowering jasmine. The sweet scent enveloped them as they sat. Aaron wrapped his arm around her waist. His warmth against her side brought her comfort, his steady heartbeat a counterpoint to her quickened pulse.

"In just twenty-four hours, you'll be my wife." His lips brushed her ear, making her shiver.

"And you'll be my husband." Meghan turned within the circle of his arms until their faces aligned. "After all this time of waiting, it feels surreal."

Aaron's hand lifted to cradle her face. "Tomorrow we'll exchange vows before God. But there are things I want to say to you privately... just us. No audience."

He took both her hands, his grip firm but tender.

"Meghan Elise Townsend," he began. "I promise to cherish your strength and your tenderness, to support your dreams without hindering them. I vow to create space for your career and our family, never forcing you to choose one over the other."

Tears pricked her eyes as he laid bare his heart. He saw her—all her fears and hopes—so clearly.

"I vow to truly see you every day... not just your beautiful face, which takes my breath even now, but the brilliant, kind soul underneath. I promise to love you more with each passing year, even when we're old and gray."

Tears streamed down Meghan's cheeks as she took in the heartfelt promises. Without a moment's pause, she gazed into his ocean-deep eyes and shared her own vows. "Aaron James Grant. I promise to be your safe place, to build a home alongside you, and to respect your leadership as we journey together in faith."

As if on cue, the garden dissolved around them as Aaron's mouth found hers. This kiss was passionate, possessive, and filled with promises for their shared future. His fingers wove through her hair, and she melted into him, fingers clutching his shirt.

When they finally broke apart, both were breathing heavily. Aaron leaned closer, resting his forehead against hers. "I have something for you," he said quietly.

He withdrew a small package from his jacket pocket, the wrapping embellished with silver accents.

Inside lay a silver frame, exquisite in its simplicity. But what stole Meghan's breath was the arrangement within. Two identical silver feathers were mounted on either side of a polished silver cross, their surfaces gleaming with the same enchanting luminescence that had captivated her months before.

"Our feathers," she whispered in awe.

"With Christ in the center, exactly where He belongs," he replied.

After a moment, Meghan reached into her purse, producing a package she had carried for this special occasion.

"I have something for you as well," she said softly.

Aaron unwrapped it, his expression transforming with wonder as he revealed the leather-bound family Bible. Their names were embossed in gold on the cover. When he opened it, he discovered pages marked with colorful ribbons, each indicating the scriptures that had guided their path together.

"For our home," Meghan spoke gently. "For the family we'll raise together, and for the legacy rooted in the foundation that God has laid."

Aaron's eyes shone with emotion as he drew her in for another kiss, this one softer, yet equally powerful. They both remained unaware of the silver-haired man watching them from the shadows.

Liam's presence went unnoticed as the couple gathered their belongings and strolled hand in hand toward the garden exit. Only after they disappeared did he move from his position, his wooden cane tapping against the stone pathway as he approached the bench they had vacated.

He pulled a third silver feather from his pocket, its surface shimmering with an inner light that defied natural explanation. He released it, allowing the plume to float on invisible currents through the evening air.

The feather drifted gracefully, as if guided by intent, landing on the silver frame Meghan held as she walked alongside her future husband. It nestled against the frame, completing the trio of feathers that symbolized their journey. Past, present, and future, united in faith's embrace.

Liam's voice carried on the night breeze. "Soar now. *Those who hope in the Lord will renew their strength. They will soar on wings like eagles.*"

The ancient promise from Isaiah 40:31 hung in the evening air as Liam gradually faded into the garden shadows, his mission fulfilled. The couple continued toward the future God had in store for them. A future founded on strength and forged from brokenness. Faith had guided them from uncertainty to assurance, and together, they would rise, soaring in the warmth of love's embrace.

Epilogue

One Year Later

Sunlight filtered through the oak leaves in the Grants' backyard as Meghan inhaled deeply, enjoying the smoky scent of hickory mingling with the fragrance of fresh-cut flowers. Laughter danced in the air, surrounding their gathered friends and family. She set down the final dessert plate, her gaze drifting to Aaron, who was leaning casually against the deck he had built with his own two hands.

It had been one year. Three hundred sixty-five sunrises waking up to his sleepy smile, and three hundred sixty-five sunsets of falling asleep in his embrace. The land they once called a construction site was now a home, and her once-guarded heart had opened, embracing the fearlessness born of his love.

"Uncle Aaron!" Naomi's voice reverberated across the yard as she led a small group of neighbors toward Meghan's eastern garden beds. "I'm giving another tour. Are you coming?"

Meghan's heart swelled at the sight of Naomi, her braids adorned with beads, fingers caked with dirt, embodying her spirit in every way that mattered. The withdrawn teenager she once knew had blossomed into a confident young woman filled with purpose.

Aaron lifted his glass in response. "You go ahead. I'll catch the next one."

Naomi beamed and turned back to her audience, enthusiastically gesturing toward the vibrant tomato vines and rows of basil. What began as a small balcony container garden had expanded into a produce-sharing initiative benefiting dozens of families throughout Brookside.

Meghan arranged the last blackberry cobblers, setting one aside for later. She noticed Ryan walking toward Aaron. Seeing the brothers together stirred a tenderness within her, as a newfound bond replaced the emotional gap that had long existed between them.

Ryan's clean-shaven face and self-assured stance spoke of the twenty-four months he had battled for his sobriety, ultimately emerging victorious. The apartment above Brookside Hardware and the new position at Donovan-Grant Construction gave him a sense of purpose beyond mere survival. The brothers stood in companionable silence, and while Meghan couldn't hear their conversation, their relaxed body language told its own story.

Everywhere she turned, she was surrounded by the people she cherished, along with those whom God had woven into their lives. Daniel and Samantha lounged in a shady corner, their baby peacefully cradled in his mother's arms. Elijah's solemn expression mirrored his father's, but the spark of alertness in his eyes was all Samantha.

Audrey and Stanley worked together near the buffet, expertly preparing platters like seasoned professionals. With their wedding set for October, they moved with a synergy that made them seem married already. On the concrete court Aaron had poured himself, teenage boys played basketball. Stanley had his whistle conveniently draped around his neck, just in case.

Further across the yard, beneath a sprawling magnolia tree, Olivia sat with her daughter, Lily, perched on her lap. The adoption, finalized just eight months earlier, transformed their lives with a love that transcended blood connections. Lily's copper curls glinted in the sunlight as she handed flowers to Willow, who graciously accepted each one with exaggerated delight.

So many lives were intertwined, with tales of restoration unfolding alongside their own. Meghan smoothed the fabric of her cream sundress and walked over to Aaron. Pastor Morrison signaled his readiness for the blessing, but she wanted a moment with her husband before calling everyone together.

"There you are." Her smile colored her voice as she reached him. The man who once intimidated her with his intensity now grounded her with his steady presence.

"Pastor Morrison is ready whenever we are." She moved into his space, inhaling the woodsy aroma of his aftershave that had become synonymous with the scent of home.

"I'll gather everyone," Ryan replied with a nod, confidently making his way to round up the crowd, a stark contrast to the uncertainty he had exhibited a year ago.

Aaron's lips brushed against her temple. "Happy anniversary, Mrs. Grant."

Her smile widened as their eyes locked, and she couldn't resist the blend of mischief and tenderness that characterized their private moments. "Happy anniversary, Mr. Grant."

"You look stunning in that dress. It makes me want to reconsider our hosting duties."

"Behave," she whispered, though she couldn't hide the glint of excitement in her eyes, hinting that they might explore that thought later. "We have guests."

"For now." His thumb traced circles on her palm, sending a private message that resonated within her soul.

Their moment faded as everyone gathered. Meghan and Aaron stepped into the center of the yard, where tables formed a large rectangle. Their guests, family by blood and by choice, took their seats, having shared meals countless times before.

Pastor Morrison began, his voice carrying clearly without the need for amplification. "One year ago today, we witnessed the covenant, not just between two individuals, but between their faith and the life that God had prepared for them. Today, we celebrate the blessings that flow from that promise."

Meghan held Aaron's hand during the prayer. Steady and sure, their relationship was built on trust, sacrifice, and divine timing.

As the meal commenced, she moved among their guests, exchanging hugs, laughter, and second helpings. Throughout the afternoon, she sensed Aaron's gaze following her. Each time she looked up, his eyes met hers, overflowing with unspoken affection.

As the sun dipped lower into lavender and rose hues, Aaron nodded toward the gazebo by the pond. This wedding gift had become their personal sanctuary during both intense moments and intimate celebrations.

She nodded back, and fifteen minutes later, they slipped from the festivities. Aaron held her hand as they strolled along the flagstone path he had crafted himself, each stone selected to create the design leading to the white gazebo overlooking the water.

"I can't believe it's been a year," she said, sinking onto the cushioned bench. "It feels like yesterday and forever at the same time."

Aaron sat beside her, his arm sliding around her waist. "It's been the best year of my life."

"Mine too."

For several moments, they sat in silence, watching fireflies begin their evening dance. Then Aaron reached into his pocket.

"I have something for you... a first anniversary gift."

She sat up, eyebrows raised in curious delight. "I thought we agreed to wait until later."

"Some things can't wait," he replied, pulling out a small velvet pouch. "Besides, I saw you sneaking your gift behind the refrigerator this morning."

She burst into laughter. "That was supposed to be a clever hiding spot."

"You married a builder, sweetheart. I notice everything."

With mock indignation, Meghan playfully swatted at his arm. "Fine. You go first, then."

Aaron tipped the velvet pouch into his palm, revealing a delicate silver charm bracelet.

"There's one charm for each milestone of our first year together." His finger touched the tiny silver feather dangling from the bracelet's clasp. "This one represents our wedding day."

As he fastened the bracelet around her wrist, he explained the significance behind each charm. "The house represents our move-in day. The book is for your leadership certification. And the apple signifies Naomi's school award."

Her eyes glistened as she examined each tiny silver token of their experiences. "Aaron, it's wonderful. How did you find silver feather charms that match ours?"

"I had them custom-made." His pleased expression at her pleasure deepened her love for him. "And there's room for many more milestones to come."

Her fingers traced the delicate chain, her heart racing with the news she was on the verge of revealing. Even the most exquisite gift paled in comparison to what grew beneath her heart.

"It's my turn." Meghan's eyes danced with barely contained eagerness. "I have a gift for you, but it's not something I can wrap."

She took his hand and placed it on her abdomen. For a split second, confusion clouded his face, then understanding dawned on his features.

"Meghan? Are you...?" His voice came out hoarse and unsteady.

A smile broke across her face, tears spilling down her cheeks. "I'm eight weeks pregnant. We're due in early January."

The joy that lit up Aaron's face mirrored the wave of emotions Meghan felt when Dr. Langford confirmed her suspicions. A child. *Their* child. A living testament to love, blessings, and promises fulfilled beyond her wildest dreams.

"A baby," he stammered, awe turning the simple words into sacred worship. His hand lingered on her stomach, as if he could envision the miracle developing beneath his palm. *"Our* baby."

Meghan covered his hand with hers, their fingers intertwining above the life they had created together. "I've wanted to wait until today to tell you."

He pulled her into a kiss so tender and fierce that it left her breathless.

"I love you... more than I ever thought possible."

"And I love you," she murmured, tracing the strong contour of his jaw with her finger. "More with each passing day."

As twilight fell, Meghan noticed a small object gliding through the tranquility. They turned in unison to witness a single silver feather descending from above, shining with the same ethereal glow they had seen before.

The feather landed on her lap. No trees stood nearby to have cast it off, and no birds soared overhead in the encroaching darkness. Yet, there it was.

"Look," she breathed, pointing toward the western sky.

A rainbow arched across the horizon, brilliant, striking, and seemingly impossible. No rain had fallen, and the skies had been clear. And still, there it was, stretched across the heavens, radiant and undeniable.

"Genesis 9:16," Aaron recited, his arm drawing her closer. "*'Whenever the rainbow appears in the clouds, I will see it and remember the everlasting covenant between God and all living creatures of every kind on the earth.'*"

The promise wasn't confined to ancient texts. It was unfolding in the present.

"It's Liam's blessing," she whispered, sensing the enigmatic presence of the stranger who seemed to be there in spirit, if not physical form.

"For the baby," Aaron agreed, his hand returning to settle once more against her belly where their child grew beneath her heart.

Their fingers remained entwined above the miracle blossoming within her, the silver feather nestled between their palms. Behind them, the celebration continued its cheerful rhythm. In front of them, the rainbow dimmed into a starlit promise. Between them, their love grew stronger with every heartbeat, breath, and shared moment of their journey.

Their anniversary represented more than a point in time. It signified the journey they shared. They had built a home that welcomed them, fostered a community that uplifted them, and raised a teenager who was flourishing under their care. The silver feather stood as a powerful emblem of divine alignment, transcending any earthly understanding.

As darkness enveloped their gazebo, Aaron and Meghan shared another tender kiss. The warm feather between their hands symbolized the truth revealed through their connection. They would never forget that God's greatest blessings often manifest as glimmers of silver hope entering the lives of those awaiting His miracles.

THE END

I hope you enjoyed Soaring in Faith.
Please consider leaving your review.
Be sure to continue for an EXCERPT from the next book in the
Wings of Faith Series,
Running with Grace.

Excerpt from Running with Grace

THE X-RAY OFFERED NO clarity. Eight-year-old Gabrielle Miller's lungs appeared clear, yet her breathing told a different story. Her chest rose and fell with quiet struggle, each breath a question unanswered. The bloodwork didn't help. It only deepened the mystery. Elevated white cells. No infection. No obvious reasons. Her fever continued to spike, undeterred by the cocktail of medications Dr. Brandon Lawson had ordered.

Brandon stood alone at the lightbox display, arms crossed, the glare reflecting off the film but illuminating nothing useful. Thirteen years in emergency medicine should have given him the tools to solve this. But tonight, it seemed as if all his training had met its match in an eight-year-old girl with eyes too tired for her age.

The ER buzzed behind him. Nurses called out vital signs, and stretchers rolled in with the clatter of a world constantly teetering between disaster and rescue. The rhythm was familiar. Predictable, even. Except for Gabrielle. She didn't fit any pattern he knew.

"Dr. Lawson, we need you in trauma two." Jessica Whitaker's voice cut through his concentration. The auburn-haired nurse appeared beside him, her usually calm expression drawn tight. "Frederick Brooks from the I-185 accident."

Brandon's stomach tightened. The sixty-three-year-old construction worker's pickup truck collided with a semi during the evening thunderstorm. The preliminary report included internal bleeding, blunt-force trauma, and likely head injuries. He had survived the impact, but barely. Brandon suspected he wouldn't survive the night.

"Vitals?" Brandon asked, already moving toward the trauma bay.

"Blood pressure is dropping fast. Dr. Martinez requests a surgical consult, but..." Jessica's statement dwindled to silence.

Frederick Brooks was dying.

The next forty-seven minutes blurred into a frenzy of adrenaline, orders, and increasingly desperate measures. He worked alongside Dr. Allegra Martinez, doing everything their training allowed. The man's body fought, just like his weathered hands had likely fought to build half the bridges in this region. Brandon's own father had been that kind of man—quiet, determined, sacrificial. It was hard not to see him in Frederick's still form.

At 12:34 AM, the monitors flatlined.

Brandon stood motionless as the last tone echoed, long and final. Dr. Martinez placed a hand on his shoulder, her wise brown eyes reflecting the grief they all experienced when medicine reached its limits.

"We did everything we could, Brandon," she said quietly.

Brandon nodded, not trusting his voice, and stripped off his gloves. His movements were mechanical. Detached. Frederick's family waited in the consultation room, expecting some version of hope. He would have to walk in and dismantle it.

Where is God when children suffer? Where was He when Frederick's truck hit that guardrail?

The bitter thought emerged unbidden. He stopped praying the night Dr. Stephanie Whitmore died, her faith intact even as cancer destroyed her body. If God wouldn't heal someone who dedicated her life to serving others, who believed without wavering, then what hope did any of them have?

He had once believed God met him in these moments. Now, he wasn't sure God showed up at all.

Brandon walked toward the break room, and his weariness went beyond physical fatigue. He was surrounded by the hospital's organized disorder. Monitors beeped, staff rushed with purpose, and families waited, praying for outcomes that medicine couldn't guarantee.

"Dr. Lawson?" Hanna Vaughn intercepted him near the nurses' station, her salt-and-pepper hair escaping from its clip after hours of constant motion. The veteran nurse mentored half the staff at Lakeside Hospital. "Frederick's daughter wants to speak with you."

Brandon's hands clenched. These conversations never got easier. "Alright. Give me five minutes."

He entered the break room, wanting some quiet time before seeing Frederick's family. The fluorescent brightness seemed too sterile, too removed from the raw human pain that had defined his evening. He rubbed his face with both hands, trying to catch his breath, something Gabrielle still couldn't do.

He couldn't stop thinking about that little girl. Her brown eyes were too big for her face, and her chest heaved, every breath a battle. Her parents sat in the waiting area, praying, pleading, clinging to hope that slipped through their fingers like smoke.

"Dr. Lawson's been incredible with the tough cases," Jessica's voice drifted from the hallway. "And that new chaplain supervisor? She's been lifting everyone's spirits. She brought cookies last week and sat with the Calloway family the whole time their son was in surgery."

Brandon's shoulders tightened. Another chaplain, full of good intentions, offered hollow comfort and meaningless statements about divine will. He had no patience for people who spoke of God's love while children suffered and good men died on operating tables.

"False hope," he muttered, pushing himself to his feet.

The sole place in the ER where he knew he wouldn't be disturbed was the supply closet. Brandon slipped inside, surrounded by medical equipment and supplies that represented his true faith—science, medicine, and human knowledge fighting against chaos and death. He leaned against the metal shelving, closing his eyes.

Footsteps echoed in the hallway outside, accompanied by the soft murmur of voices. Brandon could identify the rhythm of his colleagues' discussions, the well-known tempo of a hospital that was constantly in operation. Somewhere in the distance, Gabrielle's monitors continued their steady beeping, marking the medical mystery that defied his expertise.

Jesus wept.

The scripture emerged from somewhere deep in his memory, a remnant from his childhood faith that died alongside Dr. Whitmore. John 11:35, the shortest verse in the Bible, once provided comfort. Now it came across as a mockery. If Jesus wept over death and suffering, then why didn't He prevent it?

Brandon's pager buzzed against his hip, but he ignored it. Frederick's family could wait a moment longer. He needed time to pull himself together, time to put his mask back on before telling them their world had just changed forever.

Footsteps passed in the hallway, then faded. The automatic doors at the main entrance hissed open and closed as someone entered the department. A woman's voice, warm and gentle, spoke quietly to the nursing staff, but Brandon paid little attention.

He closed his eyes, steadying his breath. Soon, he would walk into that consultation room and crush whatever hope Frederick's family still had.

The supply closet door remained slightly ajar, a thin line of light marking his refuge. Brandon stayed motionless in the shadows, unaware that someone had noticed the partially open door and was even now moving toward it with quiet, purposeful steps.

Please continue reading Running with Grace: Brandon and Grace's Story

Before the Vows: A Soaring in Faith Wedding Story Novelette

Want More of Aaron & Meghan's Story?

It's the wedding week you didn't get to see. From Aaron's bachelor gathering with the guys to Meghan's bridal shower with her closest friends. From the emotional rehearsal dinner to the moment they finally say, *"I do."* Experience the anticipation, the laughter, the tears, and the romance of Aaron and Meghan's journey from engagement to their wedding day.

Discover:

- Aaron and Naomi's heartfelt father-daughter moment

- Meghan's bridal shower and the women who became family

- The bachelor gathering that strengthens brotherhood

- Behind-the-scenes wedding day preparations

- Private moments before the vows

And so much more...

This exclusive **BONUS Novelette** fills the gap between their engagement and the epilogue.

This Novelette is available exclusively to newsletter subscribers as a FREE thank you gift.

He found redemption.
She found home.
Together, they found forever.

The journey from
'almost' to 'always.'

Also By Barbara Jane Oliver

ALTHOUGH THESE NOVELS ARE part of a series featuring inter-connected characters, the main romance centers on a unique story-line with its own arc and resolution. Each book can be enjoyed as a standalone novel, making it a pleasurable independent reading experience.

WINGS OF FAITH SERIES

- Before the Blessing: A Bristol Heights Novella (Colton & Nicole): Download FREE When You Subscribe to My Newsletter

- Renewing His Hope Book 1: Daniel & Samantha: Available Now

- Soaring in Faith Book 2: Aaron & Meghan: Available Now

- Running with Grace Book 3: Brandon & Grace: Available 25 May 2026

BRISTOL HEIGHTS SANCTUARY SERIES

- Sanctuary in His Arms Book 1: Joshua & Simone: TBA

- Sanctuary of Truth Book 2: TBA

About the Author

Barbara Jane Oliver is a faith and inspirational based author who lives in the beautiful state of Georgia with her loving husband and partner in all non-crimes, Ronald. She has been an avid reader from an early age, often hiding in her parents' closets to finish reading her books. Her love of reading nurtured her creative mind and sparked a passion for writing. She is also a U.S. Army Veteran and has been a registered nurse for over 20 years. Barbara and Ronald have a wonderful, blended family that includes two daughters, three grandsons, and two great-granddaughters.

I hope you enjoyed this novel. If so, please visit my website for a list of my current and upcoming publications.

Author Web Page: https://barbarajaneoliver.com/

Instagram: https://www.instagram.com/barbarajaneoliver-author/

TikTok: https://www.tiktok.com/@bjoliver7

CLICK HERE for **Free Novella** and **SIGNUP** for my Newsletter.

Thank you so very much.
Barbara Jane Oliver

She thought love always left.
Until he chose to stay.

Some things are more beautiful
after they've been restored.

Visit Author Website For Additional Information

Thank You For Your Support